FAREWELL LEICESTER SQUARE

Persephone Book N°14
Published by Persephone Books Ltd 2000
Reprinted 2010
First published by Robert Hale 1941

Endpapers taken from E. Q. Nicholson 'Black Goose' c. 1938,
cotton fabric hand-printed using two lino blocks.
Reproduced by courtesy of Tim Nicholson and
the York City Art Gallery.

Typeset in ITC Baskerville by Keystroke,
Tettenhall, Wolverhampton

Printed and bound in Germany by
GGP Media GmbH, Poessneck

on Munken Premium (FSC approved)

ISBN 978 1 903155 035

Persephone Books Ltd
59 Lamb's Conduit Street
London WC1N 3NB
0207 242 9292

www.persephonebooks.co.uk

FAREWELL LEICESTER SQUARE

by

BETTY MILLER

with a new preface by

JANE MILLER

PERSEPHONE BOOKS
LONDON

CONTENTS

PREFACE

Betty Miller's first novel, *The Mere Living*, was published in 1933, when she was twenty-two. Victor Gollancz was clearly impressed by her precocious gifts and went on to publish her next two novels, *Sunday* and *Portrait of the Bride*, in quick succession during 1934 and 1935. As her publisher, Gollancz must have believed that he had found an ambitious and promising young author; and one of his 'readers', in recommending *Sunday* for publication, wrote of its 'very delicate and exact description . . . whole passages of sustained beauty [and] scenes of considerable dramatic intensity.'

So Betty Miller was understandably devastated when Gollancz rejected the novel she sent him in 1935, which had the provisional title of *Next Year in Jerusalem.* When this eventually came out six years later, in 1941, it was as *Farewell Leicester Square* and it was Robert Hale who published this and the three novels she wrote in the wake of this débâcle. It is an astonishing novel in many ways, complex and moving; and there can be little doubt that its rejection in 1935 was a predictable if upsetting response to its subject matter. Betty Miller was twenty-five when she wrote it and had been married for two years to the psychiatrist Emanuel Miller. She had also given birth to her first child, Jonathan.

This was not the first of her novels to have a man as its central character. She was, as her friend Marghanita Laski once said, good at men: Mark, in *Sunday,* is a cold fish and sensualist, an Englishman marooned in a rich, provincial French family, and an intriguingly exploitative outsider. In *Farewell Leicester Square* Alec Berman is a sophisticated modern hero, intricately understood in his mental and physical life and as an ambitious and successful maker of films. He is also a Jew, and this is stranger than it may seem; for nowhere else in her writing, before this novel or after it, did Betty Miller even touch on Jewish experience, while here she confronted, with unfashionable candour and determination, English anti-semitism and the damage it could inflict.

She was not, by and large, thinking about anti-semitism's more brutish manifestations (though it was only a year or so before Cable Street, and there is evidence in the novel that she knew something of what was going on in Germany). Rather, her focus was on the silky, slippery presence of anti-semitism in England amongst precisely those people who would never have admitted to it. She was also concerned with the self-hatred it could produce, especially in those Jews who had for one reason or another been encouraged to think of themselves as English and to admire and wish to participate in the traditions of tolerance on which the English so prided themselves, then as now.

Betty Miller was born in 1910, the second of the four children of Jewish parents living in Cork. Her father owned several tobacco shops and was active in the cultural and political life of Cork and of its Jewish community. He was also

a JP, responsible for sentencing IRA prisoners; and it became clear by 1920 that the family should leave Ireland. Her mother's family had moved to Sweden from Poland, just as her father had moved to Ireland from Lithuania. Adopted languages and loyalties were an inheritance. In addition, Betty spent nearly a year in a French sanatorium and boarding school in her early teenage years.

So that even by the time the family arrived in London in 1922, after two years with her mother's family in Sweden, her Jewishness may have seemed to her no more than one aspect of an elaborate European identity. She resisted all religion, though never unquestioningly, and there can be no doubt that there was a good deal about her own Jewish upbringing that she hoped to escape in adult life. Her novels deal with varieties of middle-class and mostly English family life, though Irish and French versions may be thought to offer alternative perspectives on this. Yet she certainly drew on her childhood in her early novels and on her marriage in the later ones. In others of her novels and in one or two autobiographical fragments she dealt obliquely with the experience of difference and the effects of seeing oneself and of being seen as an outsider.

Farewell Leicester Square's rejection by Gollancz, a publisher well-known for his Jewish family's long history of comfortable accommodation to English life and ways (indeed, he became a Christian in the later part of his life), can only have confirmed and justified the novel's pessimism for Betty Miller. She had announced to Gollancz that the novel was about 'the social and psychological conflicts of a Jew in the modern world'

and she cheerfully urged a friend to expect to read in just a few months 'one of the best novels Victor Gollancz Ltd have ever published'. It seems likely that he was frightened off in ways that the novel itself could be said to predict.

Just as Betty Miller had bearded St John Ervine, the Irish writer, as a seventeen-year-old determined to become a writer, so Alec in the novel throws himself on the sleekly benevolent Richard Nicolls, maker of films and encourager of young entrants to the business. Even as he welcomes Alec and agrees to give him his first foothold in films, Nicolls is made to contemplate his young supplicant:

> He observed the characteristic blunt head, prominent ears; the black tough hair. It was a commonplace mask, slightly vulgar, with the energetically coiled ambitious nose. The eyes alone had distinction: dark, unusually intense, and hooded, in a fine romantic way, by heavy lids. His voice had about it a trace of racial sibilance: but that, thought Nicolls, seeing how adaptable, how anxious to conform was this young man Berman, he would soon lose. Five, ten years would see him talking, acting like the English public-school Jews whom Nicolls periodically encountered at the board meetings of his companies. Men who always gave him a slightly odd sensation as he conversed with them: who had succeeded in the extraordinary feat of ousting all trace of their origin, not only from their accent and behaviour, but actually from their physique. Despite which complex achievement (for which he was not with-

> out admiration) they struck him always as essentially unreal, hollow men. They existed in a curious limbo between the two races: their reality lost in the rôle they had adopted, and that rôle itself without reality. . . .

This is an extraordinary passage, heavy with warnings. It combines the refinements of anti-semitism with a delicate sense of class and its articulation amongst different groups and generations of Jews in England. It also suggests the attraction such an exotic outsider might have for this bleached and enervated English gentleman, who is still just managing to hold his own in an explosive new industry simultaneously struggling to keep up with but also to distinguish itself from Hollywood as well as Europe. Then 'commonplace' and 'vulgar' are words that Alec appropriates for his own use, as Betty Miller does herself. There are strictures here that Alec shares and that Betty Miller shares. 'Commonplace' is the word Alec uses when he thinks about his own brother and about the man his sister is going to marry, for instance. He is prepared to admit to himself that he is repelled by his best friend, Lew's, appearance, to the point of hatred. Yet it is with this friend and only with him that the contortions of anti-semitism are transformable into the material of mocking fantasy and retaliation. In response to Lew's 'nobody wants us and we've nowhere to go. Short of some particularly classy form of Euthanasia I don't see any way out,' Alec replies,

> 'Oh, they'd never allow that. . . . We're too valuable . . . . We make the best persecutees ever . . . absolute

> *cordon bleu*. And I can quite see the necessity . . . somebody's got to be the whipping boy. Only we've held the post so long, I think it's about time they gave us a Sabbatical holiday. The Aryan world ought to pension us off.'

It is this humorous self-consciousness or (as Alec knows many would call it) paranoia – one reviewer referred to Alec's 'morbid sensitivity' – and his capacity to imagine what others think of him, that are offered as intrinsic ingredients of his vitality and his sensitivity to other people. Alec knows intimately the quality of Nicolls's distaste for his ambition, and when, years later, he meets Nicolls's son Basil, he wonders to himself, 'Does he mind I'm a Jew?' while privately registering contempt for this effete young man, by whose 'elegant will-to-obscurity' he can still feel disparaged.

The film-making world itself, both Englishly genteel and brashly, energetically Jewish (though also Hungarian), even in the 1930s, thrived on a precarious balance between its two wings, as it were, a kind of collaboration or marriage; though there may be those who would see the continual and arbitrary lurching between those extremes as characteristic precisely of what has always been worst about British films: trying to please with a factitious Englishness and patriotism rather than asserting a voice of their own. In her novel's title – itself the title of one of Alec's films – Betty Miller catches exactly the nostalgic, populist jingoism of so many films of the period.

Alec's family is not poor, but his father is relatively uneducated, and a lifetime of emigrations has intensified his

determination to control his family, at least. He combines 'the characteristics of the English Victorian father with those of the Lithuanian-born Jewish patriarch.' It is an unpromising mixture, yet that Jewish/English combination may have the potential for good outcomes as well as bad, Miller seems to suggest. When Alec refuses to work in the family's tobacco shop in Brighton and instead snatches at the chance to be a virtually unpaid tea-boy for a year in a film company, his father throws him out and announces that he expects never to set eyes on him again. Alec takes him at his word, endures a hard year or two as an apprentice in London and emerges into the central action and interest of the novel as already a well-known film director.

In the same letter where she jokingly boasts of what she is about to bestow on the unsuspecting Gollancz, Miller describes her first visit to a film studio and the set of what was, in fact, *The Secret Agent*: 'I had a *most* interesting time, seeing John Gielgud & Peter Lorre do a scene together (despite the fear of being nearly roasted to death by sun-arc lamps, & tripped up & hung by innumerable cables & whatnots)'. Her younger brother, Julian, joined Gaumont-British at the same time, introduced to Michael Balcon by Emanuel Miller and employed for his first assignment as a very junior assistant to Alfred Hitchcock, who was making *The Thirty-Nine Steps*. Betty Miller was clearly intrigued by this world that Alec enters and inhabits with such gusto, and the novel mimics film in some respects, its chapters set out as a kind of script, with title sequences, flashbacks, set pieces for the stars, linking passages, close-ups, tracking shots and even premières.

Alec's sensuous and fastidiously organised nature is convincingly matched to his making of films. Yet even though he becomes quite rich and famous and the lover, serially, of several film stars and of one in particular for a number of years, there is a sense of there being some impediment, of a disappointment or emptiness in his life and his career. His films have become formulaic, constrained, though he is always good at the detail. He is blocked in some way by his own ambivalence, his hopeless love affair with all that rejects him, his inability to love who he is and where he comes from.

Betty Miller wrote well about families and about marriages and what happens to them. In her own life, she was wryly amusing on the subject and entirely alert to the possibility of comic discrepancies in the household of a child psychiatrist like her own. Here, the themes of the novel are worked out through the marriage of Alec with Catherine, the daughter of Richard Nicolls. The marriage is between an older man and a younger woman, as Betty's own was and as her parents' had been. It is a 'mixed' marriage, entered upon by both of them with a consciousness of what is involved and even an enthusiasm for what it may be thought to represent, though neither of them can bring themselves to discuss these matters and they are too proud to acknowledge the threat of difficulties conventionally anticipated in marriages like theirs. For both of them there is an attraction of opposites, the appeal of the unfamiliar.

Alec may have had affairs with film actresses, but he has kept his distance from them. Yet he has a curiously vivid sexual

presence, and his passion for Catherine, this drained and studiedly unglamorous Englishwoman, so coolly trivial in some ways, but so impressively confident about who she is, is made continuous with the dangerous seductiveness to him of everything English that has the potential to undermine him, strip him of strength. An early scene in the novel describes his wanderings in Brighton and his appreciation of the grand terraced houses there that have not yet been turned into boarding houses. The scene and his feelings about it announce the plot of the novel and its hero's dilemma:

> His young impressionable senses devoured this English scene, its tones, its nuances, made it all a part of himself, of his deepest emotions: so that, later on, years later, even if this culture by which he had been seduced should ultimately reject him, he would yet be incapable, like a man fixated upon the charms of the one woman he has loved, of turning elsewhere for spiritual life, or even consolation.

Alec is driven in his work and in his marriage by a terror of exile from all this, of the sudden, nightmarish sequestration of everything he values, by his sense of having no natural rights to the culture and place he loves and relies on. As an artist he knows his own need for the stuff and detail of English life, as the essential material he works with in his films. This need and his fear of losing his subject-matter is replicated by his terror of losing his family and his child in exactly the way that his own father lost him, his son. Alec's life begins both to reverse

and to repeat his father's as he tries and fails, just as his father did, to maintain control of his family life.

The novel does not reflect Betty Miller's own experience in any straightforward way, though she clearly drew on aspects of her Cork childhood for the scenes of Alec's growing up in Brighton. She did not herself marry 'out', though there is every reason to suppose that she hoped for a marriage in which the narrow discipline of her father's régime and the sometimes inward-looking expectations of her own childhood would be replaced by intellectual openness and some confidence in the strength of a hybrid inheritance.

In many ways she must have felt she had achieved this, particularly in the early days. The novels she wrote after her marriage have often been thought to gain from the psychological and psychoanalytic understandings to which Emanuel introduced her. She took pleasure in her role as wife and mother, though she also longed to be freer to write and was inclined to be wittily self-critical about her lack of talent as a homemaker. She made many friends amongst writers and artists and intellectuals. Isaiah Berlin, whom she knew well as a young woman, spoke of her 'moral charm' and wrote of his last meeting with her to Sarah, Betty's daughter (born in 1937):

> She seemed to me to be unchanged: gentle, acutely sensitive, receptive, infinitely truthful and accurate, with a quality difficult to describe, which the Germans call *Innerlichkeit* – inner light which shone through everything she said like remote but steady candlelight.

She was a friend of the writers Rosamond Lehmann, Olivia Manning and Stevie Smith and emancipated in many ways from both her own upbringing and from most contemporary expectations of women. Yet both she and Emanuel seem in their different ways to have been haunted by Jewishness, and even by religion, though Betty never wrote about these aspects of her life again. Emanuel grew more and more to resemble the Jewish patriarch of Betty's novel and it seems likely that she used aspects of his younger self in her portrait of Alec; and Betty herself was drawn in later years to revisit the synagogue in Bayswater where she had gone as a girl and in which she was married. She was diagnosed as having Alzheimer's disease at the age of forty-nine, and she died of it at fifty-five. She appears occasionally to have spoken Hebrew words during her illness.

The six-year gap in her output of novels that followed her rejection by Gollancz suggests that her confidence in herself as a writer had been undermined. She did, however, write three more novels once *Farewell Leicester Square* had finally been published, and an excellent and much admired biography of Robert Browning, which was published in 1952. She also published stories and, especially during the 1950s, a number of original and elegant essays and reviews, which were published in journals like *The Twentieth Century* and *Cornhill*. She had written several chapters of a biography of Kipling when she became ill and abandoned it. The second of her later batch of novels, an unusually fine one about women and war called *On the Side of the Angels*, was published in 1945 and reissued in 1985. Jenny Hartley has written about this novel:

'To write such a subtle study of militarism and aggression was a remarkable feat during the war. Miller's interest in the psychology of warfare – where it comes from, what it does to people – follows [the psychoanalyst Joan] Rivière's pre-war diagnosis of the innate aggression in the human psyche . . . .' It may well have been her most mature novel in terms both of its psychology and its precise and pared-down language.

The last novel she wrote, *The Death of the Nightingale*, which was published in 1948, took her back to the Ireland of her childhood and to a family riven by secrets and treacheries, and by the lasting injuries caused by a denial of the past. But the IRA background at the source of the novel makes a poor substitute in that novel for the particularities, the cadences and smells and sights of the Jewish childhood she starts from at the beginning of *Farewell Leicester Square*.

This is not the place to spell out resolutions and endings in the novel, and besides, Betty Miller, with a true sense of the complexity of the character she has created and the serious implications of the issues she has raised in *Farewell Leicester Square,* offers few, if any. It is clear that this was an immensely important book for her to write. It allowed her to interrogate her own ambivalence about being both Jewish and English, to see this in relation to marriage and family and children, and to set her story within a subtle account of class and prejudice in contemporary England. The fact that this might have struck many readers in 1935 as unguarded, and also, perhaps, exaggerated and offering too many hostages to fortune, is likely to be read as a strength more than sixty years later. It is written boldly and honestly. What St John Ervine called her 'high, if hysterical sense of language' is much less in evidence than in her earlier novels, though there is a little of this in the opening chapters.

We know how one powerful English Jewish publisher reacted to the book. He would not have been alone, I suspect, in wishing the novel had never been written. So it must have been a great relief to its author when Robert Hale eventually published the novel, two years into the Second World War, by which time squeamishness on the subject had become a wholly inadequate response to anti-semitism and its consequences: already an acknowledged and terrible reality in Europe.

The few reviews of the novel that remain are largely admiring, though they also give us inadvertent insight into precisely the world Betty Miller is writing about. There is a sense of the novel's being read as a useful guide to the strange ways of Jews, offering many 'incidental sidelights on the Jewish temperament' and showing what one reviewer outrageously referred to as 'some of the difficulties the average non-race-conscious individual has in dealing with these tragic people.'

At the very end of her working life Betty Miller reviewed the autobiography of Rudolph Hoess (the Commandant of Auschwitz): a book she described as 'strange and terrible' and no less so 'for the misleading normality of the early pages, describing a lonely childhood, a passionate love of nature and of animals.' There are good reasons to regret, I think, that Betty Miller did not write more about 'the social and psychological conflicts of a Jew in the modern world.' Few writers have done it better.

Jane Miller
London, 2000

TO HENRY AND ALBERT

FAREWELL LEICESTER SQUARE

'Moab hath been at ease from his youth, and he hath settled on his lees and hath not been emptied from vessel to vessel, neither hath he gone into captivity; therefore his taste remained in him and his scent is not changed.'

Jeremiah

PART I

CHAPTER ONE

PREMIÈRE

Already the crowds were gathering. Hungry for spectacle, for some event to mar routine and entertain their idleness, they stood shoulder by shoulder, faces strained all in one direction; magnetised by a similar curiosity. Pressed close one against the other, heedless of personal constraint, they waited, persistent, unyielding in their intention. Soon, very soon now, the celebrities would be arriving. It was for this that they stood, that they gathered in their innominate mass: to catch if only a glimpse of those certain individuals who – promiscuously ceding up their privacy to gossip-writer and press-photographer – flood-lit, picked out, seemed, in this strange dimension of publicity, to live, to act out consciously, as it were, and in heightened significant fashion, the obscure suburban pattern of their own lives.

Searchlights wavered slowly, mistily, across the dark sky. Beneath, was the enormous grey façade of the theatre: pulsating with Neon lights; bathed in a startling up-flung radiance. The glass doors were open: scarlet drugget made a path across the pavement. Beyond, the foyer, under its

brilliant chandeliers, was massed for the occasion with motley flowering azaleas, with deep-scented hyacinths and banks of drooping ethereal fern. An attendant stood motionless, full of monstrous dignity: maroon and purple uniform, cap smartly oblique. Two men, the house manager and the publicity manager, in the impersonal dress-clothes that were no less a livery and, therefore, jaded for all their resplendency, surveyed with worried calculating eye the clock, the traffic outside, and the clock again. Obviously it would be impossible, once again, to get the performance started anywhere on time . . . they would arrive at the last moment; and then congregate, as they always did now that these occasions had become a social excuse, in the foyer: parading, laughing, chattering; between smiles glancing furtively for the approach of the press-photographer: resisting all efforts of the attendants, the manager himself, to divert them into the auditorium where, silenced, darkened, they must perforce take second place to the entertainment itself.

And already (for despite these predictions they began at last to arrive, and in their numbers) before they reached the centre of the foyer they were hesitating, pausing; revealing a desire to congregate: in the eye of the manager, sheep-like victims of predestination, behaving precisely as he had anticipated. . . . The famous foyer of the Piccadilly Dome Theatre received them; with its gilded nude statues, its gold mosaic ceiling, its rainbow fish swimming under illuminated fountains, its mirrors, its antique arm-chairs; a foyer unparalleled anywhere else in London for its vastness, its baroque luxury, its splendour that had in the last

instance something leeringly moron about its total lack of restraint.

Outside, one after another, the big saloon cars were gliding to the kerb. They came gently, accurately to a stop, reined in by powerful smooth-working brakes. The hand of the attendant smartly wrenched up the door: shiny patent-leather feet, narrow feminine feet alternatively sought the running board; the attendant offered an impersonally gloved hand: heads ducked forward and out. Quickly, they re-adjusted, they straightened themselves, recapturing dignity: caught already, as they stood upon that privileged carpet, in the glare of the floodlights; the woman gazing with soft preening eyes at the dark mass of the crowd that, multi-faced, pressed forward on either side; during which time the man paused to give instructions to an impassive dove-grey chauffeur. He came back and touched her under the elbow: 'Come, my dear.' A flash of priceless fire in her ears, on her wrist: they mounted together the three shallow steps of the theatre, her skirt of chiffon velvet trailing slightly behind her as they went.

At once they were surrounded, swallowed up. The foyer was already crowded to capacity: it was difficult even to move. Only the press-photographers and the gentleman whose duty it was to assist the latter in picking out celebrities were able to insinuate themselves with surprising ease through the dense mass of people: and every now and then a white blindness dazzled them all as the cameras got busy, first in one corner and then another. 'Take your seats, please: *take-your-seats*!' Repeated cry of the attendants, scarcely heard above the babel of voices. The air, centrally heated, was warm and brittle: fur

wraps parted, revealing the haggard sophisticated bodies; sheathed now, in materials diaphanous and multi-hued; in a perfume – mere aura of the personality – that breathed lightly, dangerously upon the senses. Flowers, naïve and fleshly, were twined among chemically brightened curls: lay as a disguise over meagre infecund breasts. They talked, laughed: and carmined mouths left the stain, betrayal of their falsity, upon cigarette-ends. . . . This man, that woman, trailed even now by a remorseless camera, had features so often reproduced, so well known, as to appear *passé*, second-hand in their very familiarity. Like the professional features of well-known actors, they suffered a subtle deterioration from exposure to the desiccating element of publicity. . . . And the process still went on. The camera, sly sycophant, intercepted their path: magnesium revealingly flared; a camera shutter winked lewdly: and his or her value as an individual, a unique entity, was cheapened once again by yet another popular and marketable reproduction.

Inside the theatre itself, beneath a stage banked up with flowers, an orchestra specially augmented for the occasion was playing softly, glibly, the theme-songs of former British-Alliance pictures. From the great domed ceiling, far above, concealed lamps imparted a roseate twilight, muted: a sheltered, fanciful light like that of a sick-room, and soothing as a child's syrup to nerves weary of reality. The long ranks of plush seats were filling up at last. 'This way, please Sir: this way, Madam.' Girls in yellow satin trousers, with caps provocatively tilted upon an array of curls as formal in their *ensemble* as a barrister's wig, examined the various tickets, the

elaborate invitation cards (Dress Circle, these) and led the way briskly, satin rump shining, to allotted seats. 'B/19? In the centre, Sir.' People stood up, unwillingly averted, to let latecomers file past them. They craned their necks unashamedly to stare up at the Dress Circle, where the press-photographers were still busy among the wealthy and notorious. Then, satisfied, they edged themselves more comfortably into their seats, they loosened their wraps, and sat turning over the glossy pages of the presentation programme, superb in its covers of stiff silver. . . .

From somewhere in the gallery, where nameless and unimportant people had paid for their seats, there came an impatient, persistent clapping.

The lights all over the house began to dim down. Silence settled instantly upon the auditorium; a deep hush of expectation. . . . Abruptly, tall, velvet curtains swept aside with a rustle. An immense screen, pale and flickering, loomed upon the audience and in the same moment there came the sudden harshness of the soundtrack's musical score taking over where the orchestra had finally ceased. A flying Mercury, flattened, futuristic, appeared, holding his wand. And then: –

BRITISH-ALLIANCE PICTURES
PRESENT
A Julius M. Schwab Production
'FAREWELL LEICESTER SQUARE'
Directed by
ALEXANDER BERMAN

CHAPTER TWO

FLASH-BACK: BRIGHTON

There were some things, he thought, which one would remember always. The smell of those rooms in Lansdowne Road. Coming in out of an unbounded night – the sea, hedged between green-sleeked breakwaters, surging with prolonged thunder upon the empty clattering stones; and the lights all along the front, blown, winking before the breathless night-riding winds – to find this immured warmth: solid, motionless. To stand, eyes dazzled, flesh still ringing from the exterior cold, before this quiet room, warm with the accumulated fires of winter and the intimate life and breath of human bodies, with gaze as bright and alien as that of some animal come momentarily out of another existence. And conscious, of course, of his own voluntary isolation; of this new and priggish desire of his to rupture the dull bondage of flesh making him one with these people.

'Well? What're you standing there like that for?'

His father looked at him; and a flash of familiar irritation passed instantaneously back and forth between the nerves of both, as between two systems sensitive to the same current.

'Go on, for goodness' sake, stop looking as though you'd dropped out of the moon! Go and take your things off, unless you want to sit about in them the whole evening.'

'And shut the door after you as you go,' said Violet. She often inserted herself thus, in the wake of a parental remark as it were, and infuriated her younger brother by the air of authority that she thereby managed to take to herself.

He went out without a word. The hall was in darkness; for Mr Berman, who in his business life would endanger large sums with an unbelievable serenity, had a passion in the domestic sphere for imposing minor economies upon his household. Alec groped his way to the horned and rickety hall-stand, hung up his coat, his limp school cap, and returned precipitately (he disliked the dark) to the warm haven of the dining-room.

His entry was more noisy than he intended. Mr Berman lowered the evening paper. His brown eyes, which had a confused bluish rim at the iris, fixed Alec with a gaze that reminded the latter of the cold watching eye of a fowl which the lid periodically shutters, then reveals again, intensity unaltered. . . . 'Like a bear out of the woods,' he muttered: and went back to his paper. Isaac Berman had managed, during the course of the thirty-odd years of his residence in this country, to combine in himself with outstanding success the characteristics of the English Victorian father with those of the Lithuanian-born Jewish patriarch; one result of this not altogether inappropriate alliance being an idiom which was at all times peculiarly lively and stinging. Alec dreaded his father's tongue almost as much as he dreaded his steady contemptuous gaze. He was totally unable, in those days, to understand the nature of that contempt: the fact that, if his father despised him at all, it was for not being able to accept this banter as the expression of a deep-locked affection that disdained more sentimental outlet. But Alec, as long as he could remember, had always been afraid of his father: even in the days when, as a very young child, he had enjoyed his father's favouritism for a while. He had feared then the very expression of that favouritism: the painful way in which his father would pinch his cheeks when he was in good humour: the way in which he would catch him up from the floor to throw him high above his head. Alec could still feel those iron thumbs spraining his arm-pits, his own complete helplessness and that dreaded sensation when, having been tossed up, the intolerable moment came in which his innards seemed to swoon away, to leave him, as he fell. . . .

He sat down quietly at the table. The red woollen cloth had been turned back at one end and here he and Sydney sat, beside their open attaché cases, occupied with their homework. Or so it appeared. Actually, beneath the mealy-smelling exercise books, the inked-over text-books, the scarred rulers and chewed-up pencils, Alec had a folded copy of a film publication and, with the cover of his case propped up to shield him from the gaze of his family, he sat furtively reading this. Also reading, and aloof from them both, Violet sat with parted knees, warming herself at the fire, hypnotized by her novel: she was eating nougat, at the same time keeping her jaws carefully suspended so that she should not be called upon to share her pocketed store. Alec was aware sometimes of

a curiosity about Violet: about her different, feminine life. . . . But she rejected with casual, elder-sisterly scorn any emotional preoccupation that he might have with her. He was only a brother, a younger brother. . . . Occasionally, however, a brother proved better than nothing at all: and then, having spent nearly an hour dressing in her bedroom, she would emerge to invite him unexpectedly to go for a walk with her: as a bribe, buying him sweets at the little shop at the corner, toffee or sherbet-drops that suddenly fizzled upon the tongue: his whole being, as they descended together towards the front, towards the two piers, expanding in pleasure at this sudden amity, truce. . . . Until they came among people, among passing groups of young men; and she began talking, smiling in a curious exaggerated fashion, glancing about out of her dark eyes; whereupon he was instantaneously aware that he had been asked merely as excuse, as pretext for all this smiling, this glancing, this display. So much for elder sisters. . . .

The door opened and Mrs Berman came in: up from the big ill-lit kitchen in the basement where she had been working.

'Get up, Violet, and let your mother sit down,' said Mr Berman who, while never moving himself, exacted a rigorous code of politeness from his children on such details.

Violet removed herself ostentatiously to a far corner. Mrs Berman came and settled down with a deep sigh into the arm-chair. Her short-sighted eyes began to search the table, the mantelpiece. Violet watched her intently: she knew what was coming. Here it was. . . . 'Oh! Violet, run and fetch me my glasses, there's a good girl; I must have left them downstairs.'

Violet looked up: lips pressed together. 'Why can't Sydney go?' she said.

'I'm doing my homework; you're only reading,' Sydney said virtuously.

'Well, I don't see why I'm always the one who has to run. Ask Alec, he's not doing anything, only reading a newspaper under there.'

Alec stared, taken aback by this betrayal.

Mrs Berman looked at the three of them for a moment: then without a change of expression stood up: 'Don't bother any of you, if it's too much trouble,' she said quietly. 'I'll get them myself.'

But now that matters had reached this stage, there was as usual a confused scramble. They all started up at once. All broke in together: '*I'm* going!' 'Sit *down*, Mother!' 'Stop it, *I'm* going!' (Ultimately, of course, they would always give in, cede their will to her – but never under any circumstance to each other – complicated feuds of adolescence which they fought out between themselves and which seemed so meaningless, so startlingly envenomed, to an adult observer.)

The glasses were fetched at last by a conscience-stricken Sydney and Mrs Berman opened her work-basket. She sat there quietly sewing. Her needle flashing in and out of the seam made a long untroubled rhythm. As always, intent upon a job, there was a look, isolated yet satisfied, about her. She was a silent woman, lacking the volatility which all of them, even Violet, possessed to a marked degree. Her life had not been an easy one: she looked considerably older than her years. The colour had long faded from what had been deep

and flower-like eyes: their beauty was withered now, never to bloom again, not even in the careless memory of the man who had loved her. What was left in place of that departed lustre was a composure, a fidelity, undisturbed now even by sadness. She was very short-sighted: perhaps because the radius of her interests was utterly narrowed down to the confines of this home. Eyes lowered, she sat sewing, with blunt apt hands. The hands of an artist, in the nearest sense creative, they had fashioned the whole life of this household. Daily, year in, year out, they prepared for them all the food that was to knit together bone and muscle; they kindled, with unfailing regularity, the frail blonde light of the Sabbath candles; they patiently unravelled each morning stale sheets and blankets to lay them out anew, immaculate; they swept, polished, dusted: they were hard and roughened from the ceaseless régime of housework – but how strangely, how *poignantly* soft, a veritable balm of tenderness, upon a burning forehead, upon sick eyes at midnight when the dying firelight casts strange shadows to the wall. . . .

Mr Berman owned two small tobacco shops in Brighton: grandiloquently named: *Havana House* and *The Emporium*. As soon as they were of an age to be useful in either, the two boys were 'taken into the business.' Syd was perfectly amenable to this change. He was already developing that type of personality, the keynote of which is a desire to play up to, amuse a fellow-being. Alec had long ago noticed at school the fact that Syd, who had very good brains and could easily have come out top of his class in any subject, chose deliberately to

throw away his chances for the sake of fooling. Knowing full well the right meaning or pronunciation of a word, he would hesitate comically, or laboriously mispronounce, for the sake of the amusement this provoked in class. Deliberate at first, this had soon become second nature with him; a persistent clowning, which had the effect of rendering him popular – but with a dangerous, useless popularity, which he could not find it in himself, even for the sake of advancement, to forgo. This disposition, however, which had hindered him in his scholastic life, promised to become an asset as soon as he was installed at Havana House. By the age of sixteen he was already slick, clever, facetious, the commercial traveller *par excellence*: a shrewd buffoon, flexible in word and spirit, with a brazen indifferent surface that did not, for those who knew him, entirely conceal the tender and sentimental heart beneath.

But for Alec things were not so easy. Even apart from the long established ambition which woke with him every morning, paced the streets by his side and occupied all his private thoughts, he would never have made a business man. And as it was, these inward musings totally inhibited all practical ability: gave him, too, a peculiar dazed lost look which, not unnaturally, alternately infuriated and alarmed his father. Being in the shop was useful to him only in so far as he now had a small regular wage from which he was able to put apart a certain sum each week; with, of course, the ultimate idea of buying himself the motion-picture camera which he craved as the means of fixing indelibly all that his senses and his emotions, inflamed by puberty, so acutely experienced.

What remained went, as Sydney put it, to the upkeep of the cinema industry in Brighton (there were four or five picture-houses already in the town); and to buying every conceivable variety of film publication. Behind the brown varnished counter of Havana House, with its lift-up flap, its packet-stacked shelves and pictures of fat-bellied monks smoking through long clay pipes, he would sit for hours amid the dry vegetable odour of tobacco, his head buried in these papers, utterly oblivious of the external world. '*Packet of Woodbine and two ounces of shag.*' '*Twenty Goldflake, please.*' '*Fifty Players and a box of matches.*' He would rouse, vague-eyed, from his entranced perusals behind the counter. The sight of customers, their brusque demands, the necessity of handling money, giving change, always threw him into a panic. He was hopeless at figures: never a day went by but that he found himself out at the end, or that he was called to book by a suspicious customer, returning to the counter with the insufficient coins on his palm. Mr Berman was, justifiably as he considered it, outraged at this peculiar deficiency in his son's make-up. After all the money spent on Alec's schooling, the latter seemed congenitally incapable of distinguishing between a two-shilling piece and half-a-crown. The fact supplied Mr Berman with material for many a long discourse. He was never tired, for instance, of telling how he himself, a lad not yet fifteen, had come over from the Lithuanian village where he was born, with only the clothes he had to his back, five pounds in money, and a smoked salmon wrapped up in grease-proof paper. All he had achieved in life, he had accomplished entirely by himself, by his own efforts he told

them. He had no one to thank but himself: a duty, according to Sydney, that he performed unstintingly. . . .

* * *

Saturday nights had about them always a sense of excitement, of adventure. For one thing, the long Sabbath day, with its constrained visit to the Synagogue in the morning, the tedium of a two-hour service in familiar but largely incomprehensible Hebrew, the enforced inaction of the afternoon in which tempers usually grew a little frayed, was over at last: and in its mere passing gave rise to a sense of freedom. The ban of its sanctity lifted, they would escape out into the dark night: and the lights of the town which were thrown in a glow against the sky, were for all of them, in their different ways, Violet, Syd and Alec, a signal, a calling to adventure. The excitement of the lit streets was in their blood already before they left the house: a sharp illicit excitement that over-rode even Sydney's compunction at his mother's sad resigned face as he put his head round the door of the dining-room, to say hurriedly – soft hat tilted upon young brows, muffler swagger-knotted about his throat – 'Well, I'm off now. . . .'

But although the two brothers often started out together on these occasions, they very soon took their separate paths. Each had his own world; inadmissible to the other. This was tacitly understood. 'Well, so long, Alec. Got a friend over there waiting for me.' The usual formula. A half-sheepish grin and Syd was gone. They were down already in that part of the town where yellow and red hoardings blared out details of motor-coach tours; where whiffs of hot oil floated out

from the steamy swing-doors of the fried fish shops which stood cheek-by-jowl, here, with dancing places, fun fairs, grill rooms, shooting galleries. Young men, surprisingly like Syd most of them, stood about in groups; hats at an angle that expressed a deliberate gesture: of daring, of knowing gallantry: an angle that, casually and courageously, delivered a salute to life. Girls passed up and down in couples; their blonde heads perm-frizzed, outrageously curled; lurid with henna-tinge, or silver-sleek from hairdresser's blue. With clothes that were an exciting caricature of the current mode. Shoes with ribbons. Skirts skin-tight over an undulating hip. A rouged, loud-laughing, common mouth that would give, uncaringly, urgent untutored kisses. This was Sydney's domain, his playground, all that he demanded of life as release from the daily grind and routine.

But Alec, alone, walked through it all with a different excitement, a different awareness. Alec was able to experience the glory of being spectator; of seeing all this unrolled for him as entertainment to his senses, his understanding. And there was something in that experience, the supreme thrill of the artist, which rendered by comparison such pleasures as Sydney might know, poor, confused and meaningless: a clarity, an intensity of awareness in which the eye saw every detail in high relief and the emotions gave the scene an artistic unity: a pleasure so intense and complete as to be in itself, like the religious experience of which he had no knowledge, a justification of existence. . . .

He stopped short at the door of a café off West Street. 'The Orient', the place was called and tried to give some congruity

to the name by the use of beaded fringes and a show of dubious brass pots in the window. Alec pushed frosted swing-doors and entered amid a clatter of beads. The café was usually deserted at this hour: but even full of strangers it would have given him a type of privacy upon which he could not count at home, where no door, except that of the narrow inhospitable lavatory on the first floor, possessed its component key, and solitude was nowhere else respected. He sat himself down in a far corner, against chocolate-coloured panelling. A quiet, very pallid waitress appeared, tray in hand, and he gave her an order for coffee and cigarettes (smoking at home was forbidden). When she left him, to vanish for a long time behind a screen at the end of the room, he fumbled in the pocket of his overcoat and brought out a box of matches, a notebook containing addresses, a few sheets of writing-paper carefully folded, and some envelopes.

'Thank you,' he said, as she set down a small tray before him. He lit a cigarette and balanced it nonchalantly between his fingers. The dry, short, spice of tobacco filled his lungs. He laid a sheet of notepaper beside his saucer. As he sipped the grey-looking coffee, he sat considering for some moments, eyes speculatively fixed under puckered brows. Then he shook his fountain pen at the floor to revive the ink and began, very carefully, to write a letter.

The hands of the grey marble clock on the mantelpiece hung with tantalizing slowness between one minute and the next. The pendulum clucked to and fro, uncaring. Tic, tic, tic, tic. In her arm-chair, Mrs Berman was breathing slowly, somnolently, hands relaxed; her darning lay untouched in her lap. Tic, tic, tic. The moments crept away. The dark eyes of Alec secretly opportuned the clock. Frowning as she concentrated, and wearing a new pink jumper that set off her rosy, swarthy good looks, Violet, at the table, was occupied in writing a letter to a Mr Jack Goldberg, of Manchester: two rough copies and an ultimate fair one that would have to pass the maternal censorship. For there were, at last, for Violet, really serious 'intentions', actual 'prospects', in the offing; the handling of which, at this stage, required a little adult discretion and guidance: Violet and her mother, the same end in view, finding themselves for once in complete sympathy and alliance. Meanwhile, at the back of the room, his jaws slowly tugging a cube of elastic and resistant gum, Sydney was occupied in studying the advertisement pages of a popular magazine. There were women, Sydney learned, who desired to put an end to 'worrying irregularities'; who did not realize that popularity with the opposite sex was uniquely due to the possession of a 'full firm bust' (which could be acquired in three weeks by the use of Madame Rosa's Miracle Cream): nervous men who desired to prolong their vitality, give up wearing a truss, increase their height by inches, conquer baldness, blushing, inferiority-complex or nail-biting. . . .

The room was silent. The clock ticked. And suddenly, so long awaited as to have over-shot expectation, there was the sound of feet shuffling on the white-washed porch outside: the scraping of the letter-box; and then a loud double-knock. Electrified, Alec sprang to his feet, forgetting caution. 'Like

a bear from the woods,' Mr Berman muttered, as his son brushed past him unceremoniously on his way to the door. But Alec was in the hall already. Without pausing to switch on the light, his eager hands gathered from the bristly mat under the door the scattered oblongs. Instantly, by touch, by the crease through the centre, he recognized one of his own envelopes, then, almost immediately after, a second one.... A painful thrill went through his joints. He stood there as if hypnotized, not moving, holding the unopened letters in his hand....

'Are you going to stay out there all night? Come on with those letters!'

An irascible voice from the dining-room. Alec, the letters in his hand, came back into the lit and overheated room. All raised expectant faces, even those who awaited nothing. Their eyes searched him over with bland and possessive curiosity. Reacting, the muscles of his face hardened; presented a composed blankness; his reply to importunity. He handed his father one of the letters; then retired to a corner with his own. But he need not, as it happened, have hunched up his shoulders so dourly, so defensively: the elaboration was wasted, for the centre of interest had suddenly shifted. The family had recognized in the buff envelope now between the hands of Mr Berman the quarter's telephone account.... Four major scenes occurred annually at Lansdowne Road; each one following the arrival of this envelope; when, after a preliminary, and general, harangue upon the situation, each member of the family was called separately to book and forced, as it were, to disgorge the number of secret and illicit

calls made during the past months which must have gone to the making up of this monstrous, this unheard-of total. . . .

Alec slit up one of the envelopes. His hand was trembling with nervous excitement. He parted the letter out of its crisp folds.

The Van Chandos Film Company, Ltd.,
Great Missenden,
Bucks

Alexander Berman, Esq,
10 Lansdowne Road,
Brighton, Sussex

Dear Sir,
In answer to your letter, I regret to state that we have no vacancy at the moment.

Yours truly,

A. J. Hearn
(*Studio Manager*)

He turned quickly to the other one. His thumb ripped up the envelope.

Europe Films Inc.,
Kew, Surrey

Dear Sir,

We thank you for your letter of the 4th inst., and regret that we have no vacancy in our studios.

Yours truly,

p.p. George Evans
(*Manager*)

Alec read both letters through again; slowly. When he had finished, he folded each one back inside its envelope with extreme care.

There was silence in the room. The clock ticked.

Mr Berman slowly, incredulously raised his head. He looked round at his family. '*Two hundred and sixty-seven 'phone calls!*' he said. A pause: he took a deep breath. '*Two hundred and sixty-seven 'phone calls! . . .*'

A month later, the *Jewish Chronicle* contained the announcement of the engagement of Mr Jack Goldberg, elder son of Mr and the late Mrs Morris Goldberg, of Manchester, to Violet, only daughter of Mr and Mrs Isaac Berman, of 10 Lansdowne Road, Brighton, Sussex.

The 'prospects', nursed with such hope, care and secrecy, had materialized; the chrysalis of the intermediate stage was over and all was now open to the light of day. A delighted, a transformed Violet was the proud possessor both of a diamond-crusted wrist-watch and of a beautiful solitaire ring, whose fire was no less bright and steadfast than that which now seemed to illumine her own nature. There was a reception on the following Sunday for sixty people in what were known as the Tudor Rooms of a restaurant in North Street, at three shillings a head, including ices: Violet standing by the door with her arm in that of her good-natured and commonplace fiancé, being congratulated by newcomers; her hair, that was jet-dark and crisp as a horse's mane, washed and set for the occasion, a dress of wine-coloured satin sheathed like a glossy skin about her young and well-developed body. Following that, and a few days later, Violet herself had to go to Manchester to visit Jack's relations there: an excursion which necessitated a new travelling coat, a new suitcase, an embroidered nightdress-case: all of which Mr Berman, as Alec and Sydney noted, bore with surprising fortitude. And indeed, during the whole period of the *fiançailles*, Mr Berman exhibited an unexpected liveliness and good nature which seemed to indicate that he enjoyed, more than they might have suspected, a touch of excitement, of festivity in the house: becoming at times jovial and uxorious to a degree that astonished and embarrassed his children. . . .

At week-ends, Jack Goldberg came down to Brighton to see Violet. They had him there always now on Friday nights. In consequence of which Mrs Berman had bought Alice, the

'daily', a cap and apron, and she was being paid extra to stay on late and wait at table whenever the visitor was expected: an innovation which the family tried to pass off nonchalantly; as though all their lives they had been used to having Alice's red trembling hand holding the salad dish at their left shoulder while they scooped uneasily with the servers; as though her staring presence at the sideboard had nothing in any way unusual about it to embarrass either her or them. Jack, unaware of machinery back-stage, was impressed by this evidence of breeding: and reacted by exhibiting a gentility that sat a trifle oddly upon him: over-daintily manipulating his teaspoon with a hand that was no less red than Alice's and if possible even clumsier: assiduously wiping his upper lip with his serviette; always ready to throw off a casual 'Mercy beau-coo' when anyone passed him the butter.

Alec, if he experienced anything at all with regard to this stranger who had claimed a place in the hitherto exclusive family circle, was conscious only of faint dislike. A dislike based entirely upon Jack's physical appearance: in those days Alec was as intolerant and obtuse as any other self-conscious young man of his age. . . . Jack Goldberg was very plump: his crinkled hair was black and rendered blacker still by the glutinous and fragrant brilliantines with which he anointed himself. His overcoats were both too long and too tight: he wore narrow yellow shoes. He had what Sydney liked to call 'prolific eyes'. He had, too, a broad Manchester accent; and, more native, a faint lisp to his tongue. And yet, had Alec but realized it, underneath all this, under his bravado – which was in reality very ill-assured – there was a humbleness

in his nature, a genuine simplicity, which Violet perhaps had sensed, and which gave her the unspoken assurance that there was waiting for her a kind of fidelity which the years, whatever they might bring of joy or sorrow, could never fundamentally impair.

Upon each silver-bracketed candle in the centre of the table there trembled an eye of flame. The meal proceeded in familiar sequence: with preliminary helpings of chopped herring, redolent of onion and vinegar; slices of the sweet twist loaf: golden-brown triangles of fried plaice; savoury fish balls; well-seasoned salad of diced celery and beetroot; stewed pears soaking in cream; and a rich cheese-cake, the final crumbs of which were finished up with a cup of good milky coffee. After which, the meal over at last, Sydney was sent to fetch the hats from the hall, and, heads ceremoniously covered, they embarked, Mr Berman leading, on the lengthy choral grace, so familiar to all of them, although it was in Hebrew, that they could sing their way faithfully through its every verse without for a moment being aware of what they were saying: 'When the Lord turned again the captivity of Zion, we were like unto them that dream. Then was our mouth filled with laughter and our tongue with exultation: then said they among the nations, The Lord hath done great things for them. Bring back our captivity, O Lord, as the streams in the south. They that sow in tears shall reap in joy. Though he goeth on his way weeping, bearing the store of seed, he shall come back with joy, bearing his sheaves.'

The last syllable was pronounced; died away. There was a slight silence. Then hats were briskly doffed, and ordinary conversation flowed again. Alice came in with her tray to clear. They left the table with its festive white cloth and now low-burning candles, and came and sat about the fire: Violet with her hand complacently linked in that of her fiancé. No smoking was allowed once the Sabbath was inaugurated: but little dishes were passed round with chocolates (best ones laid carefully to the top) and toffees. And at ten o'clock, when the conversation at last was beginning to flag, a tray came up with glasses of lemon tea and little cakes. Tea in tall glasses, weak, with a wheel of lemon floating at the surface, pale and venomously juicy. They all revived at the first sip of this piping-hot aromatic drink.

It was then that Jack, searching for gossip, said out of the blue: 'Oh! By the way. Did I tell you that I travelled down here with a *film magnate*?'

All eyes switched automatically towards Alec, who felt, to his fury, the blood mount behind his cheeks. Mr Berman observed the tell-tale signal.

'You tell that to Alec,' he said, with malicious satisfaction. 'He's the one who's film-struck here. An actor he wants to be! Douglas Fairbanks, if you please!'

Alec ignored this deliberate misconception. He turned towards Jack. 'Who was he?' he asked in a matter-of-fact voice.

'Nicolls, I believe his name was. A fellow I got talking to was telling me. They say he's worth any amount. He owns – oh, what is it? – some film company or other.'

'Ladywell Films,' Alec supplied.

'Hey, hey,' cried Mr Berman loudly. 'Listen to the expert!' His eyes narrowed; and something grim came into his expression. 'I only wish you knew half as much about the tobacco business,' he said.

Violet said quickly: 'What was he coming to Brighton for anyway? Are they going to make a film here?'

'No: it appears he lives here. He comes back every evening on that train.'

Alec's face was impassive.

'Can't imagine what he wants to live in Brighton for,' Violet said. 'Of all places.'

There was something a little pettish in her tone which revealed how irked she was by this slow tedium of family conversation.

Jack looked at her. 'You wait till you know Manchester,' he said: his eyes lingered in hers for a moment. A message flashed between the nerves of the two of them. Satisfied, Violet smiled faintly. . . .

Remote still, but approaching, something became perceptible: the gust of excitement a train seems to sweep before it along the line. At the grilled gates in front of the platform the ticket-collector got himself ready; the crowd surged expectantly forward. There was a roar, a crescendo – and the train came slowing its way into the station.

Doors were ripped open along the whole length of the train. Already, before it had well come to a standstill, people were stepping off. They slung themselves off the footboard; they came hurrying down the platform. They were streaming forth now, thick as bees from an overset hive. Business men, season tickets automatically displayed. Men in dark city

clothes met, some of them, by sunburned, light-clad women to whose arms they were smilingly linked. They came through the barrier and Alec, standing there, rapidly sifted the passing faces: let them flick through his consciousness like a player fluttering a pack of cards through his hands. Face after face passed and registered negative: and then, just as he was beginning to fear that this search was to be, after all, unavailing, a face detached itself: authentic, familiar. Richard Nicolls. No need for Alec to consult the by now familiar newspaper cutting in his pocket. That face (the prematurely grey hair, the too-narrow patrician face) was unmistakable.

He passed out through the barrier within a few inches of Alec, folding his season ticket away into an inner pocket. In the station yard he stopped in front of an old-fashioned blue Daimler and spoke a few words to the chauffeur, who, small and agile as a jockey in his uniform, had raised his cap in greeting to him. Then he climbed in, relaxing against the dove-grey padded seat: the chauffeur slammed the door smartly; settling his cap tighter upon his head and shooting one hand into his leather glove before he took the wheel; and off they went at last, gliding noiselessly out of the station yard into the streets of Brighton.

Alec turned to go. . . . As he did so, he came upon the row of newly-installed telephone booths. On a sudden impulse he went over to one, and, stepping in, let the heavy door swing to behind him. At once the noises of the outside world were muffled. Beyond the glass pane, people went noiselessly past; unimportant; with no reality, no existence beyond that which his careless attention momentarily bestowed upon them. He

picked up the directory and began to turn over the flimsy pages. H, I, J, K, L, M, N – . *Nicolls, Mrs Nancy. Nicolls, Oswald. Nicolls, Raymond, Physician and Surgeon. Nicolls, Richard, Oldwood Lodge, Rottingdean.*

Richard Nicolls, Oldwood Lodge, Rottingdean. The words stared up at him. He took out a note-book from his breast-pocket and, uncapping his fountain pen, copied the address down carefully.

Syd and Alec came to a halt at a juncture somewhere mid-way between the two piers. Sydney, his navy blue overcoat voluptuously padded in the shoulders, a soft hat tilted upon one ear, swung round, grinning cheerfully. 'Well, don't do anything I wouldn't do,' he said.

And he was gone to his own affairs. . . . Affairs about which, whatever they might be, Alec noticed, he was becoming daily more secretive. For all his expansive manner, on certain subjects Syd was not to be sounded: he had a strong inter-layer of shyness, of moral sense in his make-up which rendered him at times curiously puritanical and unapproach-able. He was still, of course, the same old Syd Berman of school days, who would sell his birthright to provoke amusement among his fellow-beings – no mess of pottage being dearer to his soul than this clown's privilege: but with it all he possessed a strong sense of reality: a curiously dis-illusioned sense, indeed, for one habitually so facetious, of the limitations of life and the consequent necessity of making the immediate best of any surroundings into which one happened to be born.

The afternoon was fine and sunny. Alec walked along, leaving behind him the heart of the town with its rabble of hotels and amusement-places, and coming out onto the cliffs at the other end where the long terraces stood with dignity against a pale clear sky. He loved the orderliness and cleanliness of these fine, big houses not yet degenerated into hotels or boarding houses: the graceful hooded balconies, the creamy stucco, long fluted pillars: and the gardens beyond, sloping close-shaven lawns, tight-packed privet hedges: the general air of graciousness, of serenity. His young impressionable senses devoured this English scene, its tones, its nuances, made it all a part of himself, of his deepest emotions: so that, later on, years later, even if this culture by which he had been seduced should ultimately reject him, he would yet be incapable, like a man fixated upon the charms of the one woman he has loved, of turning elsewhere for spiritual life, or even consolation.

The sea lay full in, to the right of him, as he walked: motionless and dazzling, the horizon neatly defined, blue upon blue. The salt of it was in his nostrils when he breathed, a cleanly incense. Under lids that were full, always slightly hooded and now more than usually drawn in protection against the bright light, his eyes, half revealed, glittered darkly; there was a faint colour beneath his cheekbones. It was warm walking: he heard his own footsteps beating the asphalt, saw his elongated shadow slanting off at an angle. He followed the pathway of the cliffs: chalk-white and brilliant, linked together, mile after mile. Now and then seagulls flew upwards, wheeling upon one wing, or came soaring down so that he was able to see, for

a moment, their sharp wild faces. Their strange creaking screams from on high were in his ears as he walked.

By the time that, through a break in the undulating cliff, he perceived at last the first roof-tops of Rottingdean, his eyes were blinded by the glare of sun upon livid staring chalk. Gratefully, he sought the shade of the narrow village street which opened at one end on to the green. The whole place seemed to be basking in this day of premature summer: held in a Sunday afternoon stillness. In the middle of the green, an ancient plane tree with a tall speckled trunk harboured the shade under its outspread wings. There was a wooden seat at its base, time-eaten, initial-scarred; and here Alec came to sit: opposite the house which, he recognized instantly, must be the one which he had come to find.

Oldwood Lodge was a long, white-painted house with two floors and, on each, windows framed with green jalousies; standing back from the road behind a tall wrought-iron gate. Through this, Alec had a glimpse of a sunken garden: crazy-paving seamed with moss, a hedge clipped in the form of a peacock. He examined the discreetly veiled windows of the house, trying to divine from them the inward pattern of the place; guess something of its life: but window after window returned his scrutiny with blankness. The reserve of the house was not to be penetrated. Its exterior presented a correct formality, unrevealing, which seemed to rebuke his curiosity.

He sat there: waiting. To the right of him he could see a pond with a file of ducks lazily breasting its mild and slimy waters: and behind it, the church, sun gleaming brazenly on

the flat round disc of the clock. In the pure sky above, big clouds, blown, silvery-white, were becalmed as in a picture. The only other beings visible, two small boys, sat on the edge of the grass beside a perambulator: over gaunt upraised knees, they swapped cigarette cards and argued; while the baby sat upright, sucking its thumb, hair glinting like a nimbus of thistledown in the sunlight.

There was the sound of voices suddenly: and Alec, looking round with a start, saw that there were people at the gate of Oldwood Lodge. An electric shock hit his nerves as he recognized Richard Nicolls. Bareheaded; wearing tweeds. He was smiling and talking to two children; a boy of about sixteen and a girl perhaps two years younger. The boy was fair; but the girl had long auburn hair, clasped at the back of her head in a slide. Boy and girl were equally slender in their jodhpurs and pullovers. They came out all three into the road and Alec, at whom they had not even glanced, could hear every word as they spoke.

'Why don't you gird up your loins and come with us, Dad?' the girl was saying: she looked up at her father, smiling. In the sunlight her red mane was like a fox's brush. She was indeed not unlike a young fox herself: looking up with her narrow face: sly, fine and sensitively on the alert.

'It's no use: you won't get Dad to budge,' said the boy. 'He'd rather sleep and cultivate his paunch.'

'Run along with you!' said Nicolls serenely: unperturbed, apparently, by a disrespect positively staggering to the listening Alec, who had never before heard a father addressed as an equal. 'Mind you don't break your necks, that's all.'

'Don't you worry.'

The girl took her father's arm with impulsive affection. She said something which Alec was unable to catch and they all three burst out laughing. They turned to separate and the girl called out 'We'll be back for tea, Dad.'

'Good,' Nicolls said briefly. He waved to them and went nonchalantly back into the house.

The two children came across the green, walking together, the boy flicking carelessly at his ankle with the thong of a riding-crop. They came towards Alec and, as they approached, he was able to receive a closer impression of their personalities: the grey level eyes of the boy; the girl with her exotic hair, red as that of a martyr in an old painting: and her attenuated face, fair and yet yellow-tinged like the narrow bell of a freesia blossom. They were now, both of them, within a yard of him: and this time their eyes came suddenly to rest upon him. He felt his heart stop. . . .

Their gaze passed him over, up and down, idly; without interest or curiosity. Then they continued on their way as though nothing were. Walking together without speaking: at one in their natural intimacy. Moving with the unconscious assurance of young animals under the sun. Alec, looking after them as they went, felt down to the roots of his being the contrast which emerged between himself and them: and it was at that precise moment, for the first time, that something new, the sense of racial distinctness, awoke in him. . . . A sudden knowledge of the difference between these two, who could tread with careless assurance a land which in every sense was theirs; and himself, who was destined to live always on the

fringe: to exist only in virtue of the toleration of others, with no birthright but that toleration. . . .

* * *

The bedroom which Alec had now, for many years, shared with Sydney, was a large bleak one, heterogeneously furnished. Its character was due to Mr Berman's passion for frequenting sale rooms: from these bringing home articles which (he admitted it himself), though not always exactly useful, had intrinsic merit in his eyes for the sake of the 'bargain' they represented. He had brought home in his time, and presented for the approval of an ominously silent family, a variety of articles that ranged from an exquisitely carved mahogany music stand (they none of them played any instrument) to a huge wine-cooler that partially blocked up, below in the basement, one of the entrances to this teetotal household.

The table at which Alec was at that moment sitting was of old-fashioned bamboo, very aged, which squeaked, as if in despair, whenever he leant upon it. It was cold in the room, for Mr Berman, who all his life had never known a day's illness nor what it was to wash save in cold water, would not hear of such luxuries as gas-fires in bedrooms: forcing his sons, even in mid-winter, to undress shivering in their big damp room and dive for warmth between unwarmed sheets: a method conducive of celerity at nights, but producing, unfortunately for the peace of the household, the opposite effect in the morning, when the process had to be reversed.

Alec lifted pen from paper. Leaning back, he surveyed this, the fifth version of his letter, with nettled brows. It was still not quite as he would have it, but he felt incapable of further alteration. He sighed and began the task of copying it out neatly word for word.

Richard Nicolls, Esq,
Oldwood Lodge,
Rottingdean, Sussex

Dear Mr Nicolls,

Believe me I am fully aware of the liberty I take in writing to you when you do not even know me. I am also aware that there is not the slightest reason why you should read this; let alone bother to answer or consider it. You must get hundreds of these letters and I am afraid that, when you read that what I want is a chance to make good in the film industry, you will throw this into your already replete wastepaper basket.

I have no qualifications and no experience. Nothing but the wholehearted desire to put myself at the disposal of a company that might be able to find use for me, in any capacity, however subsidiary, so long as I may ultimately acquire there the experience I now lack.

Yours truly,
Alexander Berman

He read it through once again, quickly, and then bent it across with his thumb-nail and slipped it into an envelope. He got up: mechanically, as he reached the door, pressing off the electric light. His parents were in the dining-room: he could hear the sound of his father's voice as he passed. He turned the knob of the front door soundlessly and, letter in hand, slipped out into the dark friendly night.

The pillar-box was at the top of the road under a lamp post. He came forward into the radius of light. About to drop the envelope through the square slit, his fingers paused for a moment. . . . He let the letter drop suddenly from his hand. And with that small additional weight, the scales of chance were, once and for all, tilted down. . . .

He was walking down a long cream-painted passage, preceded by a plump and homely maid in a black dress and white apron. She opened a door for him at the far end; and he passed into the room. 'Will you please take a seat,' she said. 'Mr Nicolls will be along directly.' He murmured his thanks and the door shut, leaving him alone.

Acutely conscious of the personality of a strange household, he sat awkwardly upon the nearest chair. When no one arrived at once to interrupt him, he was able to remind himself, incredulously, and yet without surprise now that he was here, that he was actually inside the walls of Oldwood Lodge which a week ago had seemed so impregnable. . . . He looked round him. He had imagined, but never seen, a room like this before. At one end there were tall french windows, curtained with gold brocade; and the same faded pattern was repeated on a deep couch pulled up before the fire. Upon low bookshelves, china pots and jugs were crowned with

the stained petals and black-fringed eyes of anemones. Bulbs were everywhere, growing in bowls: plantations of daffodil, the furled and pallid flower slenderly breaking forth; hyacinths; flower after flower peeled open, radiant as a star. He had at once the feeling that this room, in which so many things had root and were growing, was not entirely separated like other rooms from the garden that lay beyond: but was an extension of that; invaded by the same seasons: and the green pungent savour of spring was in it now; just as, in September, filled with brilliant rust-eaten leaves, it would hold for the senses the dry and subtle bouquet of autumn.

The door opened.

'Good evening, Mr Berman. Sorry to have kept you waiting.'

It was Richard Nicolls. Alec rose to his feet. In his self-consciousness, he knew that he was blushing and that unaccountable blush of his seemed to colour the whole horizon before his eyes. . . . At the same time he discovered that his palms were moist: whereupon, seeing that Nicolls was about to shake hands, he hurriedly, furtively, wiped his own upon the flat of his thigh. . . .

Nicolls indicated the chair from which Alec had just risen. 'Do sit down again. . . .' Seating himself in turn, he slipped an old-fashioned cigarette-case from his pocket: under his lean thumb it divided and he presented to Alec this indispensable weapon of civilization, loaded with its nicotine cartridges. 'Will you smoke?'

'Thank you, no.'

Alec shook his head in polite disclaimer and, as Nicolls

proceeded to light his own cigarette, he watched him with the unconscious narrowed-down intensity, that camera-vision of his, which he brought to bear upon all objects which interested him: the way Nicolls took the cigarette upon a protruded and elastic under lip; then, lids drooping, mouth puckered, struck a match and brought forward the creeping tag of flame. His face, as he did so, was momentarily illumined. What a long and narrow head he had: how distinguished (felt the blunt-headed Alec) were those lean cheeks, with the deeply incised lines running from the nose to the edge of the lips: the sparse, well-groomed hair; the pouched and aquiline eyes: even the strong discoloured teeth that were re-built with gold. There was no sensuousness, no mobility about those nostrils; they were correctly winged; narrow, firm. He was a man of different race. . . .

Nicolls, with reiterated movements of his wrist, shook off the flame from his match and flicked the dead stick into the fire. He leant back, crossing his narrow pointed knees and let his head rest against the tapestry of the tall chair in which he was sitting: 'And now, Mr Berman,' he said. . . .

They talked. Nicolls listened, nodding at intervals. Now and then his eyes, pale and grey-ringed above the deep pouches, came to rest discreetly upon the face of the young man. He observed the characteristic blunt head, prominent ears; the black tough hair. It was a commonplace mask, slightly vulgar, with the energetically coiled ambitious nose. The eyes alone had distinction: dark, unusually intense, and hooded, in a fine romantic way, by heavy lids. His voice had about it a trace of racial sibilance: but that, thought Nicolls, seeing how

adaptable, how anxious to conform was this young man Berman, he would soon lose. Five, ten years would see him talking, acting like the English public-school Jews whom Nicolls periodically encountered at the board meetings of his companies. Men who always gave him a slightly odd sensation as he conversed with them: who had succeeded in the extraordinary feat of ousting all trace of their origin, not only from their accent and behaviour, but actually from their physique. Despite which complex achievement (for which he was not without admiration) they struck him always as essentially unreal, hollow men. They existed in a curious limbo between the two races: their reality lost in the rôle they had adopted, and that rôle itself without reality. . . .

A slight silence established itself. Nicolls nodded absently several times. 'Yes, I see; I see,' he said. He leaned forward to tap off a thimbleful of ash into the fire. Then abruptly he seemed to rouse himself: 'Well, now!' They were coming to business at last. Nicolls coughed perfunctorily into his fist. 'I should certainly like to help you, Mr Berman, if I can. But. . . .'

But . . . ? Alec felt his heart sink. Now would come the hitch, the hiatus; the gentle but decisive letting down of his hopes. . . .

Nicolls had risen, motioning to Alec to retain his seat; he went over to a small walnut desk at the side of the room; '. . . but, of course,' he continued, 'it will have to be in a very small way, you understand,' letting down the flap, 'in a very small way, to begin with, at least.' He rustled through papers. 'I gather that all you want anyway, at this stage, is a

chance to prove yourself. Am I right? Yes. Well . . . ah, here we are!' He picked out a paper; and, closing the desk again, came back to the fire.

'I want you to take a look at that,' he said, passing the paper across to Alec. 'Yes, it's a contract. You may, or may not, have heard that Ladywell Films have inaugurated lately what they call a Practical Training Course: for enlisting likely candidates and teaching them the ropes. As it happens, Mr Berman, this year's vacancies are not yet filled; principally because the committee exercises great discretion in the choice of its candidates. It wastes their time, you understand, to train men without sufficient enthusiasm or ability.'

'Yes,' Alec murmured, keeping his eyes on the other's face.

'Well, now, if you care to study that agreement you have there in your hand, you'll see that by the terms of it, you get a year actually in the studios, training, working at the different branches. The point is that after that time Ladywell Films have the right either to take you on at a salary to be arranged, or dispense with your services altogether. You have no redress, it's at their entire discretion. The salary you get during the year is little more than a retaining fee; so that unless you have some backing, someone behind you who is willing to allow you to take this risk, give you a year's sporting chance, as it were – I'm afraid this isn't going to be much use to you. A good many of our candidates are young men down from the Universities with incomes of their own: or parents willing to support them. You understand me, don't you, Mr Berman?'

There was a pause. 'I understand, Sir,' Alec said. He felt the other's grey eyes upon him speculatively and he wondered for a second whether, divining, perhaps, the circumstances of Alec's environment, he appreciated something of the enormity that this answer, this decision meant. Was there a hint of approbation about that faint smile? . . . Nothing was said, however, and Nicolls went on briskly: 'Very well, Mr Berman. Now I am going to leave this agreement with you: I want you to study all the clauses carefully before you decide. When you do, sign it and send it on to . . .' He took out a card from his pocket and wrote on it with a silver pencil '. . . Mr Goodge at the Ladywell Studios, Vicar's Hill, Lewisham. I'll speak to him myself about you, meantime. And then you can fix up with him details of when you start and so forth.' He glanced discreetly at his watch. 'And now you must forgive me. . . .'

Alec was on his feet at once. 'Mr Nicolls, I don't know how to. . . . I can't thank you enough. . . .'

Nicolls's right hand sketched a gesture: negative, disclaiming. 'You've nothing to thank me for. Everything depends on your own ability.' Then he himself rose. The interview was at an end.

Alec found himself once more in the cream-painted passage, hung, he now noticed as they went through it, with old sporting prints soberly framed. At the end was the heavy hall door, flanked by small recessed windows, in each of which stood a yellow china parrot. Nicolls opened the door; and the light from the house, escaping, shone out into the garden; giving it a curiously bleached unreal appearance amid the surrounding darkness.

'Well, good-bye, Mr Berman. And good luck.'

Their hands met. There was an unexpected warmth in this handclasp of Nicolls's which Alec, very much later, and from the vantage-point of the years, was to look back upon frequently with satisfaction and a certain awe. But so myopic are we about the appearance of our own future that neither of the two men standing there that night could discern anything of the intimate sealing together of destinies implicit in that handclasp taking place between strangers.

Towards morning he must have dozed off: for, when he awoke with a start, there was an unmistakable pallor abroad, visible through the yellow blind that masked the window. The room was silent: a humped form in the next bed was Sydney; crouched up, imprisoned in sleep. Alec looked hastily at his watch. It was not yet five o'clock. He lay back on the pillows: shutting his eyes in a spasm of weariness, as though to obliterate all the painful events of the previous night which had come crowding back to harp upon nerves still sensitive and overstrung. The disastrous scene with his father. Why had he risked telling him at all? . . . he might have known. He should have gone off quietly without saying a word to any of them. Instead of which, when the long-awaited letter arrived, over-elated, foolhardily, he had dared to break the news – and brought the storm down on his own head. . . . Alec still dreaded childishly the impact of his father's temper: the petty and yet stinging sarcasms in the expression of which Mr Berman was so unpleasantly adept. 'So he fancies himself a *fillum-star*, does he?' Alec was seeing the whole scene again vividly: too vividly. The family, all except Violet who was in Manchester, sitting round. The red cloth on the dining-table and the glare from the overhanging lamp in its flounces of singed silk. Mr Berman was slowly reading his way through the contract: his right hand holding his pince-nez at a distance; his face screwed up in that grimace of arrogance so peculiar to him. Alec waited silently. Mr Berman came to an end at last: he lowered the screen of his pince-nez. Then without a change of expression he flicked the paper away from him. 'Very clever,' he said. 'Very clever indeed. . . . You work for them for a whole year, for nothing: and then they push you out and get another fool to do the same thing!' Alec protested. Mr Berman banged his hand suddenly upon the table. 'I've heard quite enough of this nonsense: let's talk of something else, for goodness' sake.'

'But, Father . . .'

'There he goes again!'

'But Father, you've got to listen! I'm trying to tell you. I've signed that contract: I'm *going* to London!'

A pause. Mr Berman looked at his son out of his little bright eyes. 'Oh!' he said. 'So you've signed that contract, have you? You're going to London, are you? How nice. How *very* nice.' Mimicking, baiting, as only he knew how, and watching all the while with a sort of benign satisfaction the pale desperate face of his son. . . . It often seemed as if Mr Berman had some sort of a grudge against the generation that was to displace him: as if he took for this reason a special pleasure in thwarting while the power still was his, before he himself was finally thwarted by the process of time. . . . It was therefore almost an hour later before he condescended even to admit that Alec's proposition was serious and not characteristic 'moonshine'. The change then was abrupt. Pushing his chair away from the table, he said deliberately, with the ominous quietude that with him always preceded a complete abandon of control: 'Very well: *Ve-ry* well! . . . If you don't care to take the advice of those who love you best in the world, you needn't. You can do *as* you like! Only remember this . . .' (the veins swelling up dangerously on his forehead) 'if you go, *you don't come back!* Understand? It's no use writing when they've thrown you out! You understand? You've had your chance. Either you obey my orders – or you keep away from this house and all of us for the rest of your life!'

It was perhaps typical of the awe in which Alec held his father that, even now, he did not for a moment think this to be an idle threat. . . .

He roused himself abruptly. No use going over all that again. He looked quickly at his watch: there was not much time to lose if he wished to get out of the house without risking another encounter with his father. He cast aside the tangled bedclothes and left the familiar bed which had been a rack to his sleeplessness. Sydney, in the next bed, did not move as, standing upon the strip of drugget, shivering, Alec slipped off the coat of his pyjamas and bent forward to step his lean shanks out of the trousers. Flesh contracting against the naked cold, he pulled his vest rapidly over his head, elbowing his way into it: and had the familiar sight of his bare toes, with their misshapen and yellow nails, gripped convulsively against the floor. His trousers felt cold as he shot

his legs into them. Tugging the yawning elastic of his braces over each shoulder, he went cautiously, sock-footed, to the basin: where he had to wash in icy water with a cake of soap that refused to lather. The house was silent. He wondered whether his parents were asleep. He had a vision of his mother: lying very still, concealing her sleeplessness from the husband towards whom unquestioning loyalty had for so many years been her religion. She had preserved in front of the situation last night a silence the complexity of which Alec could not fully appreciate. Indeed, he might have gone in total doubt as to his mother's true feelings towards him that night, had it not been for one incident. He had been alone upstairs in the bedroom; very pale, hands trembling with nervous exhaustion, but determinedly packing his suit-case, when she came in. He looked up, arrested, as she came towards him. She had on her arm a pile of his underwear which had been airing in the linen cupboard – which he might, therefore, have forgotten. She put these silently on his bed: and, still without a word, went from the room. . . .

Alec was dressed at last. He reached up and took his overcoat from the door. Then, irresolutely, he went towards Sydney's bed. Sydney gave no sign. He looked down. 'Syd!' Sydney's head came up instantly: revealing the fact that he had been awake – how long? His hair was tousled, his eyes puffed from the nocturnal hours. 'What is it?' he muttered thickly.

Alec indicated his case. 'I'm . . . I'm going now.'

Sydney, his warm sallow-skinned chest masked in faded stripes, raised himself up upon one elbow. Hair awry on his brow, eyes irritably squinting, he examined his brother. Then he shrugged his shoulders and said huskily, 'Well: don't expect me to cheer. I think Father's perfectly right and you're a God-forsaken fool. But . . .' He fumbled in a drawer of the bed-table and suddenly, unexpectedly, produced a five pound note: 'take that, if it's any use to you – and mind you spend it in a Kosher restaurant, you heathen.'

'Sydney ! – ' Alec stood speechless, the large crisp note in his hand. He recalled vividly the fact that Sydney had been saving-up to buy a second-hand sports car. . . . And before he could speak again, a curious sense of shame, of self-revealing shabbiness came over him. It was not so much that he was accepting this money: but that he had, up till now, kept himself insulated from his brother's life: kept himself egotistically from any sympathetic unity with him: from respect or understanding of his personality. Because of this he stood now rigid, shamed, the note in his hand, not knowing what to say.

'Syd, listen. . . .'

But Sydney was invisible again: bedclothes hunched defensively about his ears. . . . He did not move as Alec, weighted down by his suit-case, went at last towards the door. Then suddenly, he popped his head up.

'Alec!'

'Yes?'

'Give my love to Mary Pickford,' he said: and vanished again. . . .

Heart beating thickly, Alec was descending the stairs, his right arm strained in the grip of the suit-case. The hall was

deserted and through the door of the dining-room, left idly ajar, he could hear the slow ticking of the mantelpiece clock. He listened for a sound from his parents' bedroom: there was none; but his spine, as he descended the stairs, was electric with apprehension – what if the door should brusquely open and the familiar figure appear (brown woollen dressing-gown roped about a swelling waist, hair irately tufted) to summon him back at this last moment? But nothing of the sort took place: Mr Berman considered the spiritual ban of his word to be sufficient in itself; to be more effective than mere force, which he disdained, therefore, to employ: and knowing this, Alec trembled, not so much for his own sake, as for the magnitude of his father's pride and the blow he was now inflicting upon it.

He opened the front door cautiously and the bright light of outside day seared his eyes. Stepping out across yesterday's traffic-dingied porch which Alice had not yet arrived to whiten, he pulled the door to and began to hurry up Lansdowne Road towards the bus stop. The morning air blew bright and cold about him. Here was the bus. It ground to a standstill before him and he hoisted his case on to the footboard. 'Come along, please!' The bus started again. On the next seat was a workman with chalk-whitened boots, smoking a short acrid pipe, which stung in the nostrils. 'Station, please,' Alec said to the conductor. The bus rattled along the deserted street; unpliant springs bouncing the occupants uneasily one against the other. Now they were turning the corner. Alec kept his eye on his suit-case as it swayed perilously on the grooved floor. . . . It fell with a slam. Before Alec could move, the conductor indifferently hoisted it up again: and stood, one foot upon it, whistling, staring out at the morning sky, at the streets and shop-fronts that successively rode past. They were coming to the Clock Tower now. The next corner would be the station.

The bus ground itself finally to a standstill; the passengers began to descend. Above them was the façade of the station with its clock; long fingers telling off the minutes. Early as it was, there was already a bustle of cars, porters, taxis. Alec lugged his suit-case into the tall dark hall.

'Return, Sir?' asked the clerk at the booking-office.

'No. Single.'

Alec gathered up the ticket and made his way to the waiting, soot-tarnished coaches. This one would do. He mounted the steep boards. 'Excuse me.' Lurching against a woman's tardily withdrawn knees, he received, in acknowledgment of his apology, a silent grimace of exoneration. In the narrow upholstered pew of the carriage, he sat and stared up at the enormous dark spine, glass-ribbed, of the station roof. Now that there was nothing more to be done, he found himself becoming aware of his own imminent depression: the weight of anxiety looming at the back of his mind. . . . A whistle blew shrilly. He started and looked at his watch. The hands were just on the hour. Doors all along the train slammed to. He roused himself abruptly. Why, they were moving! The gentle fluid sense of motion was in his limbs at that moment. He leaned against the window-pane, staring out avidly. He was in time to see the porters, the platform gliding noiselessly past. Light flooded the carriage suddenly, like a revelation, making the red plush cushions look faded: they were out beyond the

dome of the station. Perceptibly rocking, the train accelerated; the passengers leaned all to one side as it rounded a bend. The serried houses of the town became visible at a new, unfamiliar angle: close-packed, steeply inclined. The houses seemed to rotate past the window; suddenly very close; then dwindling, vanishing. The train whistled again, gathering speed: the rhythm of its wheels beat up through the floor. They could see the travelling shadow of the engine, the flying smoke, upon the dwindling countryside, the hedged-in fields.

In the middle of one of these, upon a hoarding for Beecham's Pills, a sign said '*London 50 miles.*'

* * *

He lay in the warm soap-milky water, his body stretched out before him: a narrow elongated body that seemed to float slightly, released from the thraldom of gravity. Intense abstraction clouded his mind; chin sunk on his chest, he did not move. He lay unresisting, enveloped in warm liquid. In that benign and fluid environment, adjustment became so perfect that the smallest action was superfluous. Lapped in the mild womb of waters, he lay there, totally relaxed, immersed in an ethereal drowsiness.

. . . Somebody was saying something, calling. A brusque warning rap on the partition. Then: 'Time nearly up, sir!' He recognized the attendant's voice. Footsteps receded noisily along the resounding tiled corridor.

He came back to himself, with difficulty: to the circumstances of his own being. Half an hour, he remembered, was the maximum time granted at the Lewisham Public Baths.

He dragged himself together unwillingly; he sat up and at once the warmth, the kindly water, his weekly drug, slipped from him, leaving him bare. Back in the world of reality, he looked at the clock. As late as that! Hastily, hands on the curved edges of the bath, he raised himself. At the same time he noted with some disquietude that he seemed to be getting thinner: there was a certain ominous slackness about thigh and forearm that a month ago had not been perceptible. Was he eating enough? Too many cold meals; tinned things, sausages, tea and bread-and-butter. Only on Sundays that hot meal: the tray that Mrs Stepney, for an extra ninepence, brought up and left outside his door: two slips of underdone meat, boiled greens, dark roast potatoes, Yorkshire pudding: and another plate with a pale crust of pie cupped over some sugar-stewed fruit. The gastric juices spurted suddenly, painfully under his tongue, as he thought of the joint inside the oven, trickling salt red wine from its sinews as it browned and spat. His jaws began to ache slightly, under the ears. . . .

He stood up and, letting the intimately discoloured water drain from the bath with a gurgle, rubbed his body down with the coarsely laundered towel. With a sense of newness he resumed his clothes: ducked his head into his shirt: combed wet hair flat. Sitting on the edge of the bath, he tugged his socks over flushed damp feet. He wrung out his flannel, water splattering into the empty bath, and wrapped his piece of soap inside, stuffing the parcel into his raincoat pocket. Now he was ready.

He emerged at last through the turnstile into the noisy

evening streets. The trams were keening their way along Lewisham High Street, swaying slightly as they went, top-heavy vessels, with masts aslant. He paused for a while to admire their oncoming grandeur; sailing up: to savour once again the peculiar quality of that diapason, swelling, metallic, which he found so disturbing when he lay awake in his room at night, eyes listening through the darkness. . . . He looked about him. Daylight still persisted but dusk was imminent: about to fall. The voices of children playing alongside the small banks of the Quaggy had something of the remote sad quality associated always in his mind with summer evenings. As if to shake off this intangible nostalgia, he glanced up at the rise of Vicar's Hill in front of him, where, half way up, on the left hand side, Ladywell Film Studios occupied a site between Hilly Fields and what had once been a Bird Sanctuary. The corrugated sides, glassy shed-like roof of the studios rose strangely above the small serried houses of the neighbourhood: a ramshackle building, somewhat resembling the dome of a railway-station. Sordid chrysalis from which emerged, evanescent, radiant, the butterfly of illusion . . .

He turned a familiar corner: and Marsala Road was before him in the wan evening light. He walked down that road of small grey two-storied houses: semi-detached, all of them: coupled, like Siamese twins. They had, each one, a ground-floor bow window draped with Nottingham lace curtains, in the aperture of which stood a glossy drooping aspidistra engulfed in a china pot. That of number fifty-eight had instead a number of other plants; searing red geraniums, white-rayed marguerites, an astonishing variety of ferns; all crowded

behind the glass, so that the small window had about it something of the baroque and humble beauty of a shrine by the wayside. . . . Alec opened the low iron gate and heard its familiar plaint at his back as he reached the front door, two yards away. Whi-i-ine . . . clang! That meant heads raised inquisitively within the house; in the houses on either side. Who was it this time? *Oh, young Mr Berman, Mrs Stepney's lodger. Been to the Baths, by the look of him.*

He shut the door cautiously behind him. The smell, not entirely displeasing to him now, in its familiarity, of beeswax, of cabbage, of stuffy plush sofas, rose faithfully to greet him: more than an odour – an emanation from a specific mode of life, peculiar, and which he could have identified anywhere. Before him was the narrow passage, the polished linoleum with its design of yellow and brown squares. Two steps at the far end led into the small back kitchen, through which he was regularly constrained to pass on his way to the rickety wooden lavatory outside. On the left was the parlour: small, incredibly over-furnished, full of plush, of china ornaments, of bamboo stands, of birdcages, gilt-framed pictures, presents from Margate, and poker-work texts from the lesser poets. Withal, it was an intensely snug, personal room, intimate as a kennel, and Alec was often aware of a desire to linger there on the rare occasions when he paid it a visit, passing its closed door even now with a sense of being excluded. This parlour was Mrs Stepney's particular sanctum, in which – Delphic Muse of Lewisham – for the price of one shilling, she illicitly told fortunes to the local housewives: reading, in a sequence of work-cracked palms, tales of great wealth imminent, of a journey

across water before the year was out. On these occasions, Mr Stepney, dispossessed, was forced to retire to the kitchen; where he remained, studying the thumbed pages of a sporting edition, or staring moodily into the small overgrown garden. Mr Stepney was by profession a plasterer: and chronically unemployed. He was a large bald man, extremely fat. There was a deceptive air of dignity, of melancholy about his features. He had, as Alec soon discovered, an unlimited capacity for small talk. Conversation, indeed, of any kind, was meat and drink to him: it was his sole creative effort: his release: the means by which he conquered his universe; rose above it. It was his Art. And like all Art, necessitating an audience. . . . Alec looked about him warily. Mr Stepney was in: his greasy cap hung upon the hall-stand: a danger-signal. Seeing which, Mr Stepney's lodger quietly, guiltily, tip-toed his way upstairs to the sanctity of his own room. . . .

With tapping fingers he sought along the mantelpiece for the cube of the matchbox. He scraped a match, opening a hole in the darkness: then reached above his head to the pale cone of the gas-mantle. There was a plop: the room softly ignited; he saw the tall brass bed with whose austere geography he was intimately acquainted; the washstand with its china jug and cotton apron shrouding the slop-pail: the rickety fumed-oak wardrobe that sheltered his two suits, the table draped in its pall of dusty plush. He washed his hands in cold water at the washstand, then went across and opened the cupboard under the gas-meter. From it he drew out a loaf of bread, a quarter of butter still in its greaseproof paper, a teapot, a tin of sardines and a banana. By the side of the gas-stove was a small ring and on this he put a tin kettle to boil, endeavouring, meanwhile, to furl the lid off the top of the sardine-tin with the key provided. He emptied decapitated sardines on to a plate: smelling their oily pungency with hunger. From the stale loaf he cut himself a slice of bread, scooping butter carefully from the creases of the greaseproof paper. He wetted the tea. Then he sat there, eating his evening meal and staring out at the row of poplars along the railway line at the end of the garden.

Still eating, he took out a small notebook and proceeded to study it with absorption. Mr Berman, who used to complain so bitterly about his son's inability to cope with simple arithmetic, would have been surprised to perceive the intensity with which the latter studied the figures which that book contained. Alec received ten shillings a week from Ladywell Films and would do so for the six months of his probation there: added to this, he had nineteen pounds of his own and the five pound note given him by Sydney. He knew that his position was hazardous in the extreme. He had neither guarantee of re-employment, nor the possibility of support in any form, financial or moral, from Lansdowne Road. . . . There were times, particularly at night, alone, looking at a strange ceiling and listening to the whine of trains in the darkness, when the contemplation of these facts caused a sudden sweat to spring out upon him. Abjectly, then, he felt himself crave for familiarity: for the voices about him that he knew: the sound of his mother laying the table in the dining-room. Sudden tears, fierce, unbidden, would gall his eyes at the realization of that lost security. Rolling over, he would turn his mouth into the pillow to stifle pain and

longing. . . . But even at such moments the memory of his father was sufficient to pull him up short: the thought of his unending triumph if he were forced to return (always supposing, that is, that his father would consent to receive him). Only someone who understood the complexity of that father-son relationship could know what that would really mean: the degradation, loss of integrity, such a defeat would entail. He was in more danger, therefore, from the security offered by that family life from which he had wrested himself than from the precariousness of his own hard-won independence. That he realized. Nevertheless, he had permitted himself to write once: a postcard containing, in case *they* wished to avail themselves of the knowledge, his new address: Marsala Road, Ladywell, Lewisham, S.E.16. It evoked no response. He wrote no more. And now, every day that he stayed away from them rendered more impossible his return: every day of silence increased and confirmed his distance from them all. . . .

A terrifying and peculiar sound, as of an animal being butchered, was let loose upon Marsala Road. Alec hurried to a small side window and, forcing up the sash, craned his neck out. Nothing untoward met his gaze: except that in the road below, at the gate of the Stepney home, stood an open Ford tourer, mud-spattered; the flabby khaki hood folded back, engine still running. A dark young man at the wheel was gazing inquiringly up at the house. He pressed the bulb at the side of the car and once again that inhuman bellow startled the road. Alec leaned further out: 'All right: I'm coming!' he shouted. Lewis (known as Lew) Solomon looked up, grinned

and touched his forehead. Alec seized his hat and, without bothering to clear away, hurried out: leaping the steep narrow stairs three at a time. The front door slammed loudly behind him as he reached the kerb.

Lew made a frame of his two hands. *'Long Shot,'* he said. *'Door opens. Berman appears and staggers unevenly down garden path.'*

Alec leaned upon the side of the car, one foot on the running-board. 'Hullo,' he said: pleased.

'Caption,' said Lew, undeterred. *'Coming for a drive? Close-up of Berman's face looking dubious. Cut to view of sumptuous limousine standing in the drive.'* As he spoke, he opened the door on the far side: Alec skirted the car and climbed in. Lew watched for a moment his ineffectual attempts to shut the door; then reached unceremoniously across him and with one movement smacked it sharply to. 'They're off!' he said, pressing the accelerator. There was a sudden snort and the car shot forward. Alec bounced on his seat: his lower jaw rose and dealt him a sharp blow. 'My mistake,' said Lew cheerfully. It was a fortnight since Lew had acquired a driving licence, and permission to use the family Ford. Lew's people were in tailoring; comfortably off: they lived in a ramshackle stucco house in Brondesbury Villas Road. Alec had visited the house: diffident at first of accepting Lew's casual invitation: reassured at once, and as soon as the front-door opened, by a familiar smell; the sight of the hallstand piled untidily with coats, the telephone balanced on a tattered copy of the directory, a pad with its pencilled numbers: *Joe, Sadie, Mrs Bramson, United Grocers*. . . . Lew's father, Jacob Solomon, was a kindly man:

small and wizened and hard-working, speaking broken English: and yet tolerant enough, or wise enough, to allow a son incongruously bitten by the 'fillums' to test his ability for six months before coming finally into the family trade. Thus it was that in that year Lew Solomon and Alexander Berman, along with two young 'varsity men, Brian McKay and Denis Ponder, were all fellow apprentices at Ladywell Films, Lewisham. . . .

The car made headway: they skirted the mean grey streets: the women gossiping at their doors; the children playing with skipping ropes around lampposts. Lew whipped the wheel over: they shaved round a corner without an inch to spare: Alec felt the breath lifted out of his lungs. He watched Lew's foot, in a pointed yellow shoe, tread the accelerator: observed, at the same time, the width, the perfect hang of Lew's family-tailored trousers: the slick fit of his coat, with its sharply built-up shoulders. Out of this rose Lew's neck: broad and squat, with small thick ears sticking out on either side like handles: black frizzy hair embalmed in a rich oil. On first meeting him, Alec (as, to a lesser degree, Brian McKay and Denis Ponder and others at the studios) had been repelled by Lew's appearance, to the extent of feeling what amounted to actual hatred for him: but it had taken only a few days of acquaintanceship and the mollifying effect of habit, for him to realize how misleading that appearance was: to become aware of the mildness, the intrinsic human innocence beneath the foibles of Lew's personality. The realization, then, of his own former intolerance startled him. Why should he find Lew more offensive than, say, some tow-haired youth, low-browed and

spotty-faced, with a dangerous animal vacuity in his light-blue eyes? Did Englishmen feel as much resentment at the sight of unpleasing Englishmen as he did, confronted with the minutest failing of his own race? But Englishmen had status, security. Jews had the first on tolerance only: and therefore little of the latter; one reason why Alec was always faintly uneasy at being seen in Lew's company: afraid that the enmity invoked would include him. . . .

'Didn't see you all the afternoon,' Lew was saying. 'Where were you?'

'Where do you think I was?' Alec roused himself. His voice became grim. 'In the office of Mr Fat Pants, licking stamps.'

Lew grimaced in disgust. 'Why don't they advertise for a combined bell-hop, bottle-washer, and between-maid? Instead of putting on this ridiculous act about apprentices and contracts! Contracts. Fine chance of getting a contract we've got, haven't we? I'd like to give that man Nicolls a bit of my mind.'

'It's not Nicolls's fault. I'm quite sure he doesn't realize what's happening,' Alec said; as always, defending the man he regarded as his patron. He cherished an obscure hero-worship for Nicolls.

'Doesn't he? Well, he should come down and take a look round now and then. He might learn something. Do you know what I've been doing to-day? Showing a couple of gaping school-children round the studios. That is, of course, when I wasn't running messages for Tom, Dick and Harry. Oh, and ordering a special tea up for Fat Pants: and running to the post for him, to send a registered letter to his lady-love.' He sighed deeply. 'At this rate, I shall be making waistcoats again before the year's out.'

Alec was silent for a moment. 'And I shall have to start looking for a nice cosy spot on the Embankment,' he said.

Lew glanced at him quickly. 'Not you!' They passed under the lee of a tall rocking tram. 'You don't know what I heard to-day.'

'What?'

'I was speaking to Masie, you know Masie, and she told me she heard Shepherd telling Fat Pants that you were the most promising one of the whole lot of us.' This Lew really believed: and not a flicker of his eyelid revealed the fact that the story itself was a kindly invention.

'Lew! Really!' Alec had come alive again. As always, at the slightest hint of encouragement, his hopes rocketed: he was convinced at once of his own ability: of the fact that he was destined for success. He tried to conceal this elation; but in spite of himself a smile leaked out at the corners of his mouth: his eyes shone.

'Thought that would please you,' Lew said modestly. At the same moment down came a yellow-shod foot upon the accelerator. . . .

They fled through street after street, the engine ripping up noise in its fierce wake. Ahhhhrrrr! The night was theirs. The streets whipped past them: lamp-posts whirled by. With a long whining scream the engine accelerated: Alec felt the wind flay one side of his face. He crouched lower in the seat: seeking the shelter of the jointed windscreen. With one hand he tugged his hat down on his head: his ears were icy-cold.

The lights of a big picture palace suffused the night. The doors were open, and a crowd, still buttoning their coats, heartened by the final strains of 'God Save The King', were coming out after the end of a performance. They began to stream across the road. Lew reached for the handbrake: there was a harsh squeal: the car sobered up suddenly. . . . Lew turned in his seat and winked at Alec:

'Bad policy to exterminate your public,' he said. . . .

CHAPTER THREE

AFTER THE SHOW

'Bad policy to exterminate your public,' said Hetty Follet. 'Look out!'

An inch from the silver arrow on his radiator, a woman darted for the kerb. His foot jammed down and brakes squealed a living protest. Hetty grimaced sharply, drawing up her delicate painted face.

'For God's *sake*, Alec. . . .'

He smiled and said nothing.

More than an hour after the performance (they had supped, meanwhile, with much publicity, at a newly opened restaurant) traffic was still congested in the vicinity of the Piccadilly Dome. They crawled slowly forward. In the shifting files of traffic, the pointed nose of his car greedily trailed every inch of ceded-up space; sniffed impatiently upon the heels of great lumbering buses. Every now and then the alternation of lights intercepted their progress: and, as they hung there, obedient to this mechanical will, there were always passers-by to recognize Hetty Follet – a sudden halting, coagulation of people about the kerb, stooping, peering; then the abrupt pressing forward of faces in which the lust of curiosity stood brazenly expressed. Hetty's eyes (remarkable eyes, like some pallid jewel of enigmatic quality) watched the signals ahead: she continued speaking to him without a change of expression. A light but unassailable detachment, at this stage of her career, preserved her integrity in such situations. She was neither confused nor debased by this strange amorphous passion of which she was the object: a hint of frostiness, that actually added glamour to her mien, preserved her from contact with it; from these tongues, mouths, eyes, obscure desires that sought her.

Lights flashed to green, signalling release. Thankfully, through a sudden oasis of space that opened out in front, the car raced forward. Speed blurred the faces of passers-by: inside the car they were alone again. As he drove, Alec had her faint perfume in his nostrils, his mind. Beside him, above a sleek edge of ermine, was that shallow, subtle profile, the nuances of which a camera could detect so perfectly: the slight fluting of the nostrils, tender pout of the upper lip. The perverse contrast of deeply blackened lashes accentuated her transparent eyes, the bouquet of blonde hair coiled back beyond her ears. She was beautiful: more beautiful, he realized, than she had been, even a year ago: experience, and the expression of that experience, had added to her: moulded, refined her face into planes that, for all their purity, could express, now, a curious intriguing duplicity. And yet, looking at her, he experienced, not pleasure, but a slight jading, lassitude of his senses. . . . The beauty of Hetty Follet was an end in itself: it was static; meant nothing, forbade any natural

conclusion. Her rôle in society, that of the actress, demanded that it remain at that pitch: perfect, and infertile. She was virgin of all her lovers: in the last instance responsive only to the exiguous demands of the camera; at her most intense only within the sterilizing glare of the arc-lamps that separated her from normal living. Although they had been lovers so long that they had reached something of the casual understanding of married people, there were times, lately, when he felt a sense of panic, of imprisonment in her company. Her beauty led nowhere. It was a prison, a cul-de-sac, from which he must escape, retreat; get back to life.

They discussed the *première*. There was no doubt, of course, had been none, from the first moment that the production went on the floor, that *Farewell Leicester Square* was going to be a success. The sort of picture of middle-class London life that Alexander Berman could be trusted to do with his eyes shut. A trivial but well-constructed story, adapted from a recent lending-library success, redeemed, brought alive, by his loving insistence on detail, his genius for putting the commonplace on to the screen and somehow illumining it with his own passion of observation. Hetty, the heroine, blonde waitress in a Corner House restaurant, improbable, but lovely. A curious contrast to his other characters: his dowdy suburban housewives, typists, shopkeepers; belonging, despite – or perhaps because of – her technical polish, to quite another dimension; remote from the realism that was the keynote of the rest of the picture. For she was already Hetty Follet, *the* Follet: a recognized integral quantity, not divisible; and as such becoming subtly and increasingly director-proof. He sighed. He had a sudden memory of her, six years ago, practically unknown, as he also then was, walking about his room in her old green dressing-gown, making toast and coffee. . . . Ah well ! – a great deal had happened since those days.

Lights changing again. He swung the wheel over, turning the car abruptly into a side street, shuttered and nocturnal at this hour, with a policeman sauntering idly past back doors and garbage tins, thumbs hooked in his belt. Beyond, was a large silent square, around which the lamp-posts stood solitary, each in its own circle of light. Massed behind railings, tall plane trees branched out obscurely; here and there a gaunt speckled trunk, a crown of boughs, dipping low, was blanched theatrically in the radiance from a lamp-post beneath. He glanced up: remembering, as he always did, how, when he first came to London, the beauty of these dark squares at night had held him transfixed. Remembering precisely, even now, the quality of such emotion, he found himself wondering (and with a strange biting jealousy of that former self) whether he was losing his sensitivity to experience. . . . Ten years ago, looking at lamplit trees at night, he was possessed, in acknowledgment of their beauty, by a sort of exalted agony. Looking up at these same trees to-night he felt in himself a disturbance of a different quality: a sharp unavailing nostalgia for the pain which he no longer experienced.

CHAPTER FOUR

PARTY SCENE

Alexander Berman had, for several years, now, occupied a flat overlooking Regent's Park Canal. It was on the first floor of an old, beautiful and very dilapidated house, the interior of which, under the pressure of economic circumstance, had been converted; but with a view rather to exterior discretion than to internal comfort. Thus, although the main room was unusually large and perfectly proportioned, with three tall windows that framed the vivid banners of trees in the park beyond, the bedroom at the back of this was small and cramped; and bathroom and kitchen had entered into a peculiar misalliance in which, from one side of the wall, a small gas-stove and a smaller sink faced, on the opposite side, not more than two yards distant, one of those baths upon which the disguise of a wooden flap can be let down when not in use. Alec had become, during the course of time, extremely attached to everything connected with this flat: to the spacious front room with its lofty windows: to the view, a certain formation of trees against the skyline that he gathered from the latter; and even, since these were just as much an integral part of his existence, to the familiar scheme of discomforts offered by the whole. With regard to these and despite the expostulations of certain of his friends, including, of course, Hetty, he refused to seek improvement by moving elsewhere. He preferred Regency Road, dignified and flyblown, a last backwater of individualism, to the standardized comforts that tried to lure him into one or other of the great barrack-like blocks of luxury flats at that time invading the neighbourhood.

Big folding doors off the main room opened into his bedroom which was occupied practically in its entirety by an over-size divan bed, such as he had taken a fancy to at a very early stage of his career and since, through sentiment or apathy, had neglected to dispose of, despite the fact that his present humour was for something much less ostentatious. The divan was masked in daytime by a heavily embroidered mauve spread, the work of some Central European peasant woman, and presented to him by a Roumanian actress. Here, at nights, he slept, always peacefully, and always in solitude. . . .

Nevertheless, occasional (and at one time, many) afternoons had been spent, in congenial company, upon that embroidered spread. The spread itself never came off for these episodes: and it was typical of each one of them that this disguise should remain between it and his own personal life. He had no desire, in those days, for a between-sheet intimacy: love with the covers on, disguised, exciting, ephemeral was all he sought or accepted.

As to his domestic arrangements, always a source of curiosity to feminine visitors, these were very simple. A

certain Mrs Monk arrived every morning at seven-thirty to clear up and make breakfast. Having given Mr Berman a very good breakfast of porridge and cream, kippers, toast and coffee, brushed his overcoat and soft black hat and seen him off the premises, she remained for two hours to clean up the place: empty innumerable ash-trays, get rid of an accumulation of newspapers, remake his bed ('big enough for a family of six' as she told her neighbours in the Marylebone tenement house where she lived); pile up the refuse bucket with tea-leaves, empty bottles, stained food-cartons from the delicatessen-store, cigarette ends and, once even, a more scandalous article, the discovery of which, beneath the folds of the couch, provided Marylebone with several hours of enthralled conversation. Mrs Monk, being a woman of experience, was naturally able to deduct, with a fair accuracy, the nature of Mr Berman's life, from these fragments, in the same manner as a geologist can reconstruct an unseen monster from a thigh-bone. Nevertheless, and despite her incurable penchant for gossip at his expense, she was genuinely devoted to her employer, in whose service she had been since the first week he moved into Regency Road. This fidelity of hers had, so far, remained unimpaired, both by his exigences and, what was more remarkable, by his benevolences. Alec never quite realized, perhaps, as, at Christmas or on a birthday, he slipped a pound note into her palm, how this facile generosity of his, by decreasing suddenly the value of her earned money, threatened to corrupt both her own integrity and the honesty of their mutual relationship.

* * *

There were already half-a-dozen cars at the kerb: empty, lights muted: faithful shells that, until three or four in the morning, would await the re-animating touch of their occupants and owners. A lamp-post shone down, solitary, upon Regency Road: and opposite, in the darkness, laced about by railings, the park was rich with maturing autumn, invisibly rustling with dried leaves, that sometimes dropped and, floating soundlessly, were borne away on the dark waters of the canal to accumulate, perhaps, in the wake of a blunt sleepy barge, bound, with hoarse pulsing engine and one oil-lit eye awake, for Manchester and the North.

Another car slid round the corner, proceeded slowly up Regency Road to the right number. It stopped, backed, stopped again: the door broke open and a party of newcomers emerged on to the pavement. They were in evening dress: and in Regency Road, at that hour empty as a stage, the sound of their voices came up clearly, magnified: blank faces partially illumined, cigarette points burning holes through the darkness like small dangerous weapons. They were people who had come on late, after a show, another party. They pushed open the iron gate, passed through a small leaf-smelling garden and went up the flight of hospitably worn steps to stand beneath the portico. A squat male thumb pressed commandingly upon the button; and at once a muffled trill came to their ears.

The door opened. Mrs Monk, translated from her habitual régime of dingy overalls to the formality of a black dress and apron, her greying hair plentifully frizzed by the action of

curlers, smelling of starch, of serge, of the obscure perspirations of her age and class, led them into the long dignified hall. In front of a low oak bench, she collected indiscriminately, hats, wraps, coats. Then, through long custom more agile than any of them, she preceded them nimbly up a flight of dark Turkey-carpeted stairs to the first floor where, in a burst of noise and talk and laughter, they found the party in progress.

. . . The host. Where was the host? They stood, momentarily at a loss: their presence unsanctioned. Then, through a barrier of alien heads and shoulders, they glimpsed him – there he was! Confidence returned: the pilot was there, to navigate, discriminate for them amongst the unknown, the potentially hostile. Alec! A-lec! He looked up at last; caught their eyes, their smiles. Oh . . . recognition broke over his face. 'Excuse me.' He came towards them, glass in hand. Rupturing a momentary intimacy for their benefit. Smiling, animated; in extra good form to-night, obviously. Suavely shaved for once, sprucely dressed in a new suit that outlined, flattered the masculinity of his short vigorous figure: a fulsome silk tie pouched upon his chest. His black hair glistening and healthy under a bloom of hair-oil, black eyes alight. It was obvious, but not too obvious, that the convivial infection of alcohol was in his veins. . . . There were handclasps, greetings. A few introductions: but now that the first strangeness had gone, they discovered that they knew each other: scenario writers, actors, designers: from British-Alliance or other lots. They found themselves in the vicinity of the buffet: taking the dwarf glasses in which tilted, through some colourless liquid, a chit of lemon peel, a pallid and disembowelled cherry. The cool stinging kiss of alcohol came like an initiation. With it, the grip of inner tensions relaxed: they were ready, with a sort of feminine and amorous receptiveness, for the contact of other human beings: warm bodies, or the kindling intercourse of minds.

Behind the buffet table stood Lily Monk, Mrs Monk's daughter: slim, in black, with a frilled apron; her hair incredibly curled, eyebrows like antennæ chalked on to a pallid Cockney face. She presided over an array of bottles, sherry, gin, beer, whisky, bitters, rinsing returned glasses in a trough of water before loading them up to send back into circulation again. To her right were dishes heaped with pungent cheesy biscuits, baby sausages impaled on toothpicks, verdigris-tinted olives, salty, fragile crisps: the black watery globules of caviare and triangles of sandwiches, sprigged with parsley. Mrs Monk, meanwhile, indefatigable, relentless, and just a little terrifying with her long black dress, frizzed grey hair and ill-applied patches of powder, circulated with the tray, ministering to the thirsty, and regularly, unremittingly, importuning the teetotal or the satiated. . . . The big room, with its lofty painted ceiling, crystal chandelier, low couches and scattered creamy-shaded lamps, was crowded, warm. To the mingled aromas of cigarette smoke, flowers, alcohol, feminine perfume, the heat gave a sort of tropical intensity: the climate, recognizable anywhere, of a successful party. Whenever there came a slight lull in the noise, in the piercing macaw-like urgency of a multitude of personalities striving for self-expression across

others, no less urgent, ranting from the perch of Ego, there could be heard, strangely percolating up through the floor, a sort of distant moaning, a persistent musical neurosis. This emanated from a room downstairs, specially lent for such occasions, in which couples could dance, if they so chose, to the strains of a large radiogram. Further along, on the same floor, there was another room, some sort of a small sitting-room, apparently, with a big low couch: the initiated, or the venturesome, had discovered this fairly early in the evening: the unguarded walked in carelessly, glanced round in the obscurity, the sudden stillness, then muttering 'Oh, I beg your pardon,' backed out, a little precipitately, a little foolishly. . . .

Brian McKay took Alec by the arm in his warm predatory grip. In the other hand he held a glass of whisky: when he leaned forward to talk, as he always did with an air of unnecessary confidentiality, looking earnestly at the other person's face through thick horn-rimmed glasses, a betraying spirituous vapour momentarily infected the air. Alec, who disliked to be reminded of another's more intimate exhalations, could not avert his head: but he pinched his nostrils together against the invasion. His arm jerked restlessly in the other's grip. Brian was altogether too warm, too good-natured, too human. . . .

'Now, about that idea we were discussing,' Brian began: he persisted in trying to pin down Alec's wandering attention.

'What idea?' Alec often had a perverse desire to obstruct Brian in some way: perhaps because he knew it was part of Brian's policy never to allow himself to lose his temper.

Brian smiled patiently. 'The book, the memoirs, the *autobiography*, old chap,' he said persuasively. 'You know. What we were discussing the other day at lunch. I told you then I knew the agent who would handle it for you. Well, I've been dining with him to-night, and I've brought him along here. He's very keen on the idea. Will you speak to him?'

'Not now, Brian: not now. There's a time and a place you know. . . .'

'Well, let me introduce you, at least. He's very anxious to meet you.' Brian steered a way through the crowd; a warm persistent hand on Alec's arm. 'He's a nice chap,' he said. 'You'll like him. He's been wanting to meet you; I told him about you.'

'Where have you parked him?'

'Here he is; over here. . . .' They stopped. 'Basil,' said Brian, 'let me introduce you – this is Alec Berman.'

There was a sudden pause: a moment in which Alec, examining the face before him, became aware of a strong, immediate interest: of something else, akin to an attraction, which he found himself totally unable to analyze. . . . He shook hands with a slight young man, fair-haired; quizzical: his palm was shortly gripped and then released. It was, in its way, a handsome face that confronted him, with a high forehead and fine jutting nose: but there was a hint of cruelty in the face's exaggerated narrowness: the unconscious cruelty, perhaps, of a nature too finely tempered. . . . He spoke, and his voice was soft, distinctive. Alec, sensitive to social intonations, knew at once the measure of his own inferiority: this man, with his lackadaisical appearance, easy manner, was one

of those to whom culture had come as a birthright: the Oxford accent, that of his father and grandfather as well as his own, informed his personality: he was marked, unmistakably, by the privileges of his own birth. Alec sensed this, and the thought which invariably flashed up into consciousness when he was introduced to a new or distinctive personality – *Does he mind I'm a Jew?* – lit in him now. He glanced at the other man as though to seek his answer. There was always this moment before he could permit himself to seek intimacy with another: never knowing whether, despite his individual worth, he might not be, in the eyes of the other party, discredited at the outset by general prejudice. . . .

Nothing appeared at the surface: they made their way together to the buffet: Brian guarding the newly-formed relationship tenderly: listening with approval to what fell from the lips of each: taking to himself the credit of their mutual interest. Brian lived in a curious manner: with intensity, and yet almost entirely through the lives of his friends. He hovered, now, on the outskirts of the conversation: patently unincluded, the ordinary sensitive person would have made some excuse and retired: but it was part of Brian's nature, of his indiscriminate *bonhomie*, to be at any juncture impermeably snub-proof. Despite this untiring display of good feeling, however, Alec was never certain whether Brian did not harbour resentment at the fact that, whereas, starting out together in the old Lewisham days, Alec had become a star director, Brian, on the other hand, had been relegated first to studio management, and then to publicity, where he now was. If he did feel such a sense of injury, he managed to hide it

well: but it may, too, have been the source of this perverse amiability that he forced himself to display: a display which must secretly outrage his own nature all the while.

They stood, Alec and this newcomer whose name he had not yet learnt, under the big crystal-ringed chandelier, clasping each a glass in the right hand. Strangers, they tacitly searched for a contact, straining their ears to catch each other's intonation through the unrelenting din. Alec, looking at the other's face, was teased, all the while, by a strong sense of familiarity, which he would not, however, allow himself to investigate: he had long ago recognized (whenever this feeling rose in him at the sight of an unknown woman, for instance) that it was merely a trick of the mind: the *desire* to become acquainted with a certain person being projected as the impression that one has already done so. . . .

There was a sudden insinuation of perfume, rustle of material. They looked up. It was Hetty Follet. Her fairy-coloured hair was in curls upon her brow: she wore a lavender taffeta dress, tight at the waist and spreading about her feet, which, the toenails silvered, were bare inside lavender-silk sandals. 'Hello, Alec!' Her hand slipped, a shade imperiously, into the crook of his arm. 'Oh, hallo, Brian!' she said coolly. Her pallid eyes, ringed with dyed exotic lashes, sought Alec's, and he saw there that something dilated, soft, about her expression which only alcohol could produce in her. It was because she was now, in a slight degree, unsober, that her eyes promised him acquiescence, sensuality. . . . Despite the years that had trained them both to a perfunctory acceptance of each other, he was aware of the quick response in his nerves. At

the same time he was able to reflect, not at all cynically, upon this power of a woman to recreate virginity, the lure of the unobtained, from the very ashes of the preceding occasion: a phœnix-act at which Hetty, certainly, was particularly adept. . . .

'Oh, Hetty,' said Brian, 'just a minute. I want to introduce you. . . .' Once more in his element; the *deus ex machina*. The young man bowed. His eyes, that were suave and attractive for all that they were too narrow, too close-set, met Hetty's; very discreetly appraised. Her hand was still resting upon Alec's arm: a visible claim. The young man seemed to have taken in the implications of the situation. He did not obtrude himself. Hetty gave him a faint smile in acknowledgment of his bow, his reticent admiration: of Brian she took not the slightest heed. A necessary, but distasteful, tie bound these two: the star and her publicity manager. Brian it was who, on her behalf, disseminated photographs, gossip, intimate life-stories: tickled interest, lured custom: well-paid and indefatigable pimp. . . .

'Let's dance, Alec,' Hetty said. Her hand tightened a little within his arm. He had to comply, but he was aware of a slight reluctance. 'We must meet again,' he found himself saying to the young man. Again he met those intelligent, remote eyes: again received a baffling impression of familiarity. 'Arrange it with Brian,' he said: and then: 'make it soon.' As he moved off, finally, with Hetty's arm slipped through his, he was aware that he tried to arch his back, his neck: Hetty was taller than he and he did not care that this disparity against him should at that moment be obvious.

Downstairs, in the long white-panelled room, with the chintz furniture and embroidered framed samplers, a few couples were dancing. A radiogram maundered softly from a corner. 'Come back to me, dream lover.' The words unwound upon an insistent, throbbing background that treacherously incited the nerves. Subtle, Hetty's body trained itself against his: his hand held the warm stem of her waist. He received the gradual transfusion of her warmth, her personality into his own being; and was himself in that moment recreated; like a plant suddenly glorified by the warm sunlight. This miracle, mere contact could always effect in him: even promiscuous contact, with which the spirit was not associated; and it was, perhaps, at that time, what he sought most of women: the promise of that sensuous peace, satisfaction, strange amorphous comfort. . . .

The telephone was ringing. Alec, still adrift in sleep, did not move. Perhaps it would stop. . . . It went on and on. He lay there, eyes sealed, waiting for Mrs Monk to answer it from the other room. It still blared maddeningly: and then he awoke sufficiently to reach out one arm and drag the receiver from the bracket, silencing it. He laid the cold ring of the receiver to his ear. 'Hullo?' he said huskily.

. . . 'That you, Alec? Good morning.'

'Oh, my God, what on earth do *you* want?'

'Now I ask you. Is that nice?' said Brian, pained.

'What d'you mean by it? Ringing up at this unearthly hour. . . .'

'Oh, very well, very well: I apologize: we'll take all that as said. . . . Now listen, Alec. About that book business. . . .'

Alec groaned. 'Don't you *ever* go to sleep?'

'All right, all right. Don't start again. Tell me this: are you by any chance free this week-end?'

'This week-end? What on earth for? Who wants to know?'

'Let me speak, can't you? If you are, would you like to come down to Middle Bay? I'm going, too, as it happens and he suggests. . . .'

'Who does? What in hell are you talking about? Oh, why don't you go away. I've got a headache.'

'Now don't panic. It's all quite simple. You know who I mean. The fellow I brought to your party last night. You spoke to him. Don't you remember? Christ, what a hangover you must be having!'

Alec paused. 'Oh, him,' he said.

'Yes, him. Is the light dawning?'

'What does he want?'

Brian said patiently, 'He wants to know will you come down with me and spend the week-end at his place in Middle Bay? Did you get that all right or would you like me to spell it out for you?'

'Oh.'

Pause. . . .

Brian: 'You still there, or have you passed into a trance?'

'No, I'm here.' Alec's voice sounded suddenly more alive. 'All right, Brian, thanks. Tell him I'd like to come.'

'Well, now we're getting on! Splendid. I'm driving down late on Saturday night: you can come with me, if you like. Bring a bag to Oxshott and we'll go straight on from there: or I'll pick you up somewhere if you prefer it. It's all the same to me.'

'Hum, got it all taped, haven't you? By the way you might at least tell me the fellow's name.'

A sigh came ostentatiously along the wires. 'I did tell you. Several times. He's Basil Nicolls. Of Nicolls and Brice, Literary Agents.'

'Nicolls,' said Alec. 'Nicolls. . . .' He saw that face before him again. 'Any relation to *our* Nicolls, the old fellow, I mean?' he asked suddenly.

'Yes,' said Brian patiently. 'His son. I told you that, too.'

There was a pause.

Alec, unconsciously, was smiling into the telephone. Then: 'Well, I never,' he said softly: 'well, I never. . . .' Eyes unfocused, he found himself looking beyond the haphazard paraphernalia of the present, into the unvarying past: Lansdowne Road, the Oriental Café, Rottingdean, Oldwood Lodge: lengthening synopsis to the present moment. . . .

'Brian,' he said eagerly, incautiously: 'there's a girl there, too, isn't there? A sister? With red hair.' He stopped. At the other end of the wire, Brian was wheezily laughing. 'What's the matter with you, you old goat?' he said irritably.

Brian's voice was laden with innuendo. 'Talk of a one-track mind. . . .' he began. He was preparing to enjoy himself.

Alec softly, deliberately, slipped on the receiver: closing communication.

CHAPTER FIVE

AT MIDDLE BAY

It was dark by the time that they approached Pulborough. A faint rain was falling; coming out of it, the lights of other cars wavered towards them, liquefied. At the corner, the policeman held out a mackintoshed arm like liquorice. The windscreen grew mottled: and the wiper, set going by Brian, began to sweep a fan of clearness on the glass. Twin headlights opened up the long country roads for them: their misty glow flawed with the falling rain.

It had been a long day at Oxshott: in the unnaturally heated and muffled atmosphere of the set. Soon after they started out, Alec, eyes slightly filmed, yawning deeply, sank into utter torpor. His body adjusted to the deep well of the car, he did not move a muscle, a limb, as they travelled: the breath went gently in and out of him in a small tide of life, peaceful as his thoughts: but he was not asleep: a focus of consciousness watched, as if at a display, the dim pageant and flow of his own thoughts, as well as, and without any sense of separation between the two, the countryside climbing past beyond the rain-blurred window. He was savouring that state, inactive but

intense, and of all others most pleasurable to him, of pure æsthetic awareness: himself the medium upon which all experience was recorded. . . .

Beside him, sheathed in a big leather coat, Brian hummed to himself interminably some song in which the refrain 'She-was-a-Good-Girl-but-He-took-Advantage-of-Her' recurred with frequency and with varying effect; while his hands, in oil-stained gloves, nursed the wheel. Small eyes, under lids that were betrayingly sensual and nervous, looked out under the brim of a greenish pork-pie hat. That hat, and the angle at which it was worn, revealed something to Alec: the fact that Brian cherished as his secret ideal the current conception of the Tough Guy: hankered after the flesh-pots of the successful extrovert. Alec, casually watching him, noticed for the first time that this man, this six-foot adult, energetic publicity manager for one of the biggest film concerns in the country, this being who, for some reason, inspired a host of conflicting legends concerning his private life, had the mouth, tender, unformed, of an acquisitive and frustrated baby.

Darkness fled by: the road raced away beneath their wheels. On the windscreen, the razor-edge of the windscreen-wiper continuously shaved away the drops of moisture that sprang up between its strokes: it ticked from side to side like a metronome, punctuating drowsiness. Alec stirred at last, to seek the ease of a new position; breaking up the cast, the mould, that prolonged apathy had made about him. He felt the new blood, released, springing through his limbs. Abruptly he yawned. A-a-oah-ho. . . . He turned to Brian;

revived; inclined now for a little conversation. . . . 'These people – what's their name – ' he said, casually rubbing the waters of lassitude out of his eye-sockets: 'Nicolls and Brice – they a good firm?'

Brian shot him a glance. 'One of the best. Best of the small ones, anyway. All due to Basil, too: old Brice is about as useful as an outsize pumpkin. It's Basil who's got the brains there: *and* the business instincts, too, surprisingly enough. Brice is just ballast.'

'But it was Nicolls, I suppose, who put capital into the concern in the first place?'

'Not a bit of it,' said Brian. 'Basil hadn't a bean to his name when he started.'

Alec looked surprised. He thought that Brian, who liked to give an impression of omniscience where the lives of his acquaintances were concerned, was talking glibly: misinformed. In this case, and without Brian's being aware of it, he himself knew something of the circumstances of Basil's youth. 'But surely old Nicolls . . .' he began.

'Hadn't such a vast amount either,' Brian said triumphantly. 'A lot of directorship fees from various companies, of course: but those stopped when he died. He was a pretty poor sort of speculator, too, I believe. Ladywell Films was his biggest venture: and you know what happened to *that* when sound came along. Basil was at Oxford at the time; he had to leave. He got a job as a journalist – that's how I first came across him. When all the mess was cleared up after the old man died, they found there was about five pounds a week left: and that Basil handed over to the girl.'

There was a pause. 'Oh! And what does *she* do?' Alec's tone was non-committal.

'Cathy? She's some sort of an artist, I believe. Makes a bit at poster-work, or illustrating, now and then. Don't suppose you've heard of her, have you? Catherine Nicolls.'

'Catherine Nicolls?' Alec repeated carefully. He shook his head. 'No. . . .' he said.

In silence he watched the headlights invading the darkness in front: the blanched and spectral hedges, cottages and tree-trunks riding swiftly past.

A long narrow veranda ran the whole length of the house: upon it rain could be heard faintly, melodiously ringing. The rain was everywhere: a persistent undertone, unvarying. It was too dark to distinguish shapes beyond: when he pressed his forehead against the cold palm of the glass, trying to peer forth, he was intercepted by his own reflection, hanging mysteriously before him. He knew, however, that they were close to the sea; he remembered the sudden unmistakable bite of salt, the lung-stinging freshness that had assailed him out of the darkness as he made his way over a knuckled gravel path to the lit hallway. His senses unprepared for that sudden invasion, in those few yards between the car and the door, it had seemed to him that he struggled, not with the unruly wind, but with some up-welling impulse from time itself, which sought to displace his hold on the actual – Brighton, childhood, the past, released, seemed to surge up in him, threatening the supremacy of the present moment: emotional anarchy as sudden as it was unexpected. . . .

Rousing himself, he came away from the window. This bungalow of Nicolls had at one time been an army hut: moderately converted, it still retained most of the features of such. The walls were flimsy: in the next room he could plainly hear Brian clicking open the locks of his suit-case. His own room was narrow: simple in the extreme: a camp bed with a faded blue spread, a shelf of books, a pink-painted chest-of-drawers from which the salt air had gradually eaten the paint, a pink wooden chair in a similar condition. Looking at the dinginess of that paint, he saw again evidence of that subtle tarnish which, too soon, becomes imposed upon all things, objects as well as emotions. . . . How continuously, he thought, while we lived, while we were sane, we had that to fight. Cease but a moment, give in, and with horrible swiftness, inevitability, like a spring running down, wits degenerated into laxity and impotence, dust accumulated, the flowers withered, moths bred, and stale water stank in the slimy pot. . . .

Abruptly, collecting himself, he hoisted his suit-case on to a chair. Under his thumb, the latches flew up, releasing an odour of tissue-paper and shaving-soap. He threw his pyjamas, still in their slim laundered folds, on to the bed: hung up his dressing-gown on the door and undid the noose at the mouth of his sponge bag. As he let the soiled water gurgle out of the basin and began to rub his face briskly in a clean worn towel, there came a perfunctory knock on the door. He raised a glowing face. 'Yes?'

Brian lounged in, sucking an unlit pipe: his hands in his pockets. 'You ready?' His eyes darted round: examining the nature and disposition of Alec's possessions. The silk pyjamas,

dog-eared leather slippers, the dressing-gown, the various flasks of hair-fixative and tooth-powder all came in for scrutiny. He sat himself down finally, amid a creaking of springs, upon the bed: and, noticing the half unpacked suit-case, began to cast furtive, almost hopeful glances into it, as though, against reason, it might contain something destined for him. Alec was suddenly reminded of the fact that whenever Brian heard the rustle of paper, he at once glanced up; a child expecting a bag of sweets to be produced. . . . Pavlov's dog still salivating at the sound of the bell . . . and Brian, for whom life was full of titillating rustles, unproductive, ringing of bells that heralded deception, learning nothing, it seemed, from failure; but still, to the distaste or embarrassment of his friends, hopefully salivating: always, whatever the situation, ready with a bewildering variety of superfluous responses.

Alec, leaning towards the mirror, massaged his scalp briskly with a pair of ivory-backed brushes: then he clapped the two together, bristles mating, and swung round. 'Ready,' he said. The bed creaked again as Brian relieved it of his weight. He groaned as he stood up, one hand on the small of his back. 'Rheumatism,' he said sadly. 'Getting old.'

'At thirty-four?'

'Thirty-five, old chap, thirty-five. And if the Psalmist is right, that's half the allotted span. Precisely half. I've already embarked on the decline. Grim thought, isn't it?' He shepherded Alec through the door, taking his arm as they went along a narrow hair-carpeted passage. Male or female, Brian must always manage somehow to touch, fondle, the person he was at the moment in conversation with. Brian was

a *Pawer*, confidentially said to each other the typists in the Publicity Department at British-Alliance: one and all, despite their avowed opinion of such, secretly flattered, at first, by the hand casually, intimately, laid on: then all the more chagrined when they realized that this was simply a mannerism of his and too widely employed to have any specific implication in their own favour. . . .

'And now let's go and find mine host,' said Brian.

Basil stood, looking much younger in flannels and an old tweed jacket; one hand tentatively on the beak of the syphon. 'Brian, what's yours? Berman?'

Alec accepted a whisky and soda. He sat, clasping the big tumbler; not yet attempting to drink, but as though savouring through the palm of his hand, the cordiality in store. He watched a line of suspiring bubbles stream gently to the surface. The syphon gasped once again: and then Basil picked up his own drink and came back to the fire with it. Behind him, a lamp was lit within its round parchment cage: it illumined a room which, with its sagging chintz-covered arm-chairs, its long book-cases, its gramophone records piled up haphazard in their paper sheaths, had about it something of the atmosphere of undergraduate quarters. An effect accentuated by the presence of Basil in his flannels, looking very young, precociously intelligent: no maturity about that narrow face, but wisdom there as it were, *a priori*. And yet, if one looked closely, there was a sowing of grey already in that distinctive head: a hint of frost within the fairness. The fact suggested, curiously, as did several things about Basil when one got to

know him better, a withering of that which had not yet grown old. . . .

The three men sat talking. Beneath the surface of that conversation, of their mutual interest, each one caught up, involved in the private labyrinth of his own mental and physical metabolism. . . . Their faces flickered uncertainly in the firelight. From time to time a gust of wind raided the window-panes: then, its assault broken, retired, limping and whining. They could hear its retreat. In the quietude that ensued, Brian stretched out his long fattish limbs complacently: with his fist curled before his mouth, he quenched a rising yawn and then, unexpectedly, he brought out the query: 'Cathy not here this week-end?'

Alec stared down into his glass. His heart suddenly confused its beat: and as suddenly righted itself: like a soldier double-stepping to regain the rhythm.

Nicolls got up and put an empty glass back on the tray. 'She'll be coming down, I think,' he said. 'Either to-night or to-morrow, I'm not sure. I spoke to her on the 'phone before I left. She was rather vague.' He said nothing further. Robbed of more precise information, Alec found himself irrationally annoyed: he stared intently at his host's back as though, by the pressure of his will, he could compel him to be communicative. But the topic was not re-introduced. Basil's attention was engaged by Brian, who had already embarked on a favourite theme of his and one which has always, in any company, a particular appeal: the subject of Personalities. 'Been seeing anything of So-and-So lately? . . . Have you heard that . . . ? Between you and me and the lamppost,

of course . . .' During the course of this essentially human interchange, words were casually spoken that, overheard by the person concerned, would have caused undying mortification and resentment: and indeed the speakers themselves (instinctively confident of the sanctity of their own personalities) would, in the same circumstances, have been no less outraged to think that any should presume, offhand, to discuss or pass temerarious judgment upon their private affairs. . . .

There was a sudden rattle from the other end of the room. A serving-hatch in the wall was lifted and a man put his head through. 'Ready now, Sir, if you are,' he said.

The table was laid in the corner of the room. Informally, with a check linen cloth and, in the centre, an earthenware pot of mimosa, downy, canary-bright, that breathed forth a tender and penetrating fragrance of vanilla. Alec, sitting before the open dial of a grapefruit, uneasily nested in its green Woolworth glass, surveyed the picture, the still-life, these things made, with a momentary inner satisfaction. (Only a few years ago he could have lived in that satisfaction alone: the texture, the appearance of the material world. And now . . . ? He was uneasy that the former intensity should be slipping from him: and suspicious of that which was coming to replace it: an interest in ideas and values. Were these, perhaps, only a second-best?)

The meal had started. Deftly, amid conversation, they sat spooning into the sockets of the grapefruit: shook the silver castor and passed it politely on. Hazlitt (who was an ex-serviceman and lame) limped behind their chairs doing discreet service: a wizened kindly Cockney, in a grey alpaca

coat. He collected the plundered rinds, his hand obtruding: a short hand with the small stunted nails of the labourer. He returned a few minutes later wheeling a trolley over the floor and, with it, the smell of roast meat came savoury through the air. Off came the covers of the vegetable dishes, beaded with moisture: the vegetables lay steaming underneath, butter dwindling from the top: a belt of roast potatoes enlaced the joint. Behind their chairs again, he offered green flecked mint-sauce, tart red cranberries: and – 'What will you drink, Sir?' – poured a foaming rivulet of lager into the tall glasses.

Basil all the while had the air, interested and yet diffident, of being a guest at his own table. Without seeming inhospitable, he yet appeared to take upon himself none of the manner of a host. It was as though there was at the root of his nature some aversion to the responsibility of personal relationships. He was already the confirmed bachelor: aloof from emotional or practical burdens. Equally, Alec saw, he was without ambition. Ambition was a liability: it involved facing competition, and this Basil, perhaps through lack of emotional stamina, sought to avoid. And yet, thought Alec, competition was healthy: the natural condition of life. Seeking to excuse himself: for, absurdly, he had the feeling that his own success branded, degraded him subtly, before this elegant will-to-obscurity.

Hazlitt limped behind their chairs, collecting used plates. He brought to the table an apricot tart, a glass with the long pale braids of celery, a slab of cheese, a dish of fruit and nuts: and then a tray with a Cona on it. They got down to the enjoyable bric-à-brac that ends a meal: nicked slices off a cheese so pungent that it seared the tongue: crushed walnuts between

the tongs of the nut-cracker. Basil struck a match and touched the wick of the spirit lamp: presently, over a pansy-shaped flame, water was bubbling inside the transparent globe. Up rose the burnt incense of coffee. Alec began to peel an apple, allowing the green scale to lengthen under his knife. Basil was speaking about films. 'I always enjoy your pictures, Berman: they're so essentially *London*. You're a Cockney yourself, I suppose?'

Alec continued to peel his apple with precision. 'No. I was born in Brighton.'

Basil, as he had known he would, looked up. 'Oh, that's interesting. I'm Sussex born, too. Just near. Rottingdean. You know the place, I suppose?'

'Very well,' Alec said.

Brian was on his toes. 'Of course, he does! Alec was one of the original apprentices at Lewisham: your father himself got him the position. It was in Rottingdean they met. Isn't that so, Alec?'

Alec let the spiral of peel collapse on to his plate. 'Yes,' he said. He waited a moment. 'As a matter of fact,' he said with a sort of detached interest, 'I once visited your house, Nicolls.'

There was a pause. Basil looked as though he ought to have some recollection of the incident and was obviously a little embarrassed that he could find none. 'When exactly was it?' he said at last. 'Oh, then.' A look of relief crossed his face. 'That explains it. I wasn't there. Let me see, I must have been in my last term at Harrow.'

'Alec and I,' said Brian, tactfully opening up the way for autobiographical discussion, 'are veterans of the industry.'

Basil did not follow it up. He was reaching for the little glass cap of the spirit lamp. 'Place has changed very much since those days,' he said. 'Rottingdean, I mean. You'd hardly recognize it, would you?'

'I don't know,' Alec said. 'I've never been back.' He was conscious that Basil looked at him for a moment in surprise. But the latter made no comment. He carefully lowered the glass cap, and at once the purple flame vanished: the genie of the lamp was gone.

* * *

He pushed open the door and stepped out on to the veranda. As the morning air smote him in its keenness, he drew a deep breath, looking about him. It was a beautiful autumn day: the light bright as a blade: the grass and leaves of the garden freshly dyed with dew. Out on the horizon was the sea, sparkling: and clouds which, all night, had been wind-swept, now lay scattered, sparse and motionless.

He went down the wooden steps of the veranda and crossed the long untidy garden: the wet grass licking his shoes. At the end of it, a low gate opened on to an edge of sandy cliff. He jumped down from this, thudding into the soft firm sand. To his right, a groyne stretched away down to the sea: it was encrusted with immovable shells, with ancient seaweed that smelt of drains. He climbed over it and went striding briskly along the sands: upon the small frilled shells that crackled underfoot, upon round chalk pebbles each smoothly sunk in its navel of sand.

A dog, a large red setter, bounded violently in front of his feet, barking. A voice called 'Sulphur, Sulphur!' The dog continued to bark: it flounced up and down before him, with vigorous forepaws assaulting his knees. *'Sulphur!'* He looked up and saw a young woman coming towards him. She was holding a dog-leash. 'Sulphur – come here.' She looked at Alec. 'He *is* naughty.' Then with a smile she held out her hand. 'You're Alec Berman, aren't you? I was so sorry I couldn't get down last night.'

Light broke on him. 'Oh, you're . . .' Catherine, he had been about to say. 'Miss Nicolls.' A slim dry hand went into his: gave him, quickly, a sort of sharp, no-nonsense handshake that disappointed him slightly. 'I should have recognized you,' he said. 'The family resemblance.' His eyes were upon her, openly searching her face.

She did not seem to notice. She gave Sulphur a short slap on the flank: 'Get along with you.' He bounded off, looking foolish but rejoiced. By tacit consent they fell into step side by side. Sulphur was puttering along and sniffing the sand. 'I had to take him out for a run,' she said; 'after being cooped up in the car most of the night.' She had driven down late, she told him; after a party. 'I've had four hours' sleep.'

He glanced at her. 'You look fine. I should be all in. I need my eight hours.'

'Oh, I've trained myself to do without it,' she said. 'You can, you know. Like fasting. It's only habit.'

'Ah, but I happen to be very bound by habit.'

'I should have thought you were too enterprising to let yourself fall into a rut.'

'On the contrary,' he told her, smiling, 'I have the rut mentality. I revel in routine.'

All the while he was watching her. She walked along beside him: the wind lifting her hair. It was still red: not perhaps the sharp foxy gold that he remembered (but every seven years, they say, the substance of our bodies undergoes complete change; and that was fourteen years ago: she was twice altered since then), a duller red, and crisply, coarsely curled, as such hair is by nature: combed back to reveal the small pallid ears, the narrow face so like Basil's; but sallow and with restless red-brown eyes.

'You came down with Brian, didn't you?' she said.

'Yes. He gave me a lift.'

'I suppose he's a great friend of yours.' It was not put as a question, but there was an edge of query to her voice. He wondered whether she liked Brian or not and, before committing himself, tried to sense what her attitude was. 'I've known him a great many years,' he said.

'So Basil was telling me.' She looked faintly amused. 'Personally, I think he's poison,' she said.

Alec was impressed by such uncompromising directness. There was a certain integrity about a person who could give forth any opinion or prejudice regardless. 'Basil seems to like him,' he said. She shrugged her shoulders: 'Goodness knows why!' But Alec understood very well the nature of Basil's affection for Brian. It satisfied him, gave him some peculiar type of pleasure, to have about him people that he knew were second-rate. It was perhaps a lazy way of affirming, maintaining his own superiority. Himself, as he chose to consider it,

above the battle, he had the detached connoisseur's interest in human nature; in its cracks and subterfuges: passing no judgment, merely collecting, assessing. . . .

Further along the beach, Sulphur had encountered another of his kind. The two dogs were engaged in a sort of personality contest, trying to outstare each other and growling ominously through their jaws. Catherine summarily interrupted them: 'Come *here*, will you!' She slipped a hand inside Sulphur's collar, restraining him, and bent down to fasten the leash. Alec watched her. Her figure was slender and wiry. She must be about twenty-eight, he calculated: but the narrow breast, narrow hips, gave a look of immaturity. He saw her hands as she fumbled with the leash: they were small hands, muscular, freckled and the nails unvarnished. Alec, who could not remember when he had last seen nails in their natural condition, discovered their pallor with surprise. There was for him such strong novelty in her lack of glamour, that he found her very ordinariness (her plainness, her freckles, her faded jumper and heavy coat) a stimulant. That which was strongest in him, his æsthetic sense, was roused, not by the beauty, but by the actuality of her: no specious bloom of powder, no mask of lipstick: her hair untransformed by dye, her eyelashes soft and human. Her face was as naked and innocent to his gaze as a flower, a plant: he had forgotten that the human face, the texture of a human being, could have that appeal. . . .

The beach was wide and empty: it stretched flatly for miles, here and there marred by a rock, a half buried lobster-pot with its ribs open, a cluster of desiccated egg-cases, yellow as sweetcorn. The tide was coming in, wave after wave; unloading its bales of water, that came flying out across the sand like a carpet unfurled. The gulls kept squeaking high up in the air.

'It's so lovely here at this time of the year,' she said.

'I suppose you come down a lot.'

'As much as I can. When I'm not too busy.'

He took that up. 'Oh, yes. You paint, don't you? Brian told me you do poster-work.'

She shrugged. 'Oh, that,' she said. 'Yes. One has to live.'

'Now don't affect to turn your nose up at commercial art,' he told her, (surprisingly at ease). 'In the not so distant future most of the best work will be found on hoardings! Where it should be. . . . No more stuffy galleries at a shilling a time. Instead, a democratic open-air exhibition extending from one end of the country to the other!'

She considered this. 'Yes. Very nice. But who's to pay for it?'

'The big advertising firms, of course.'

'Oh, I see,' she said. She made a slight *moue*. 'Would you really like to see Picasso advertising Celanese?'

'Wouldn't I? . . . Imagine what the walls of the Tube are going to look like when Salvador Dali advocates beer. Or Stanley Spencer portrays a dish of military pickles. Think what a fine impression the foreigner will get as he passes our railway hoardings! Why, it gives Art a justification.'

'Do you think it needs it?'

'Well,' he said, 'Plato wouldn't have an artist within a hundred miles of his ideal State. . . . I suppose that's why artists have to compensate themselves with the idea of Art for Art's sake – Pirandello's madman holding mock court, while the real world goes on just outside the door.'

‘I think you’re quite wrong,’ she said. ‘As a matter of fact, the artist has always been the pet of society.’

‘So has the gigolo. They’re both in the same position. They’re being kept for their charm.’

She laughed. Her mouth pulled slightly awry, exposing the pale bed of the gums. Usually, he disliked this characteristic, but in her it was a flaw that seemed, since it was undisguised, to add to her, to give her honesty.

‘Well,’ she said at last. ‘I think we ought to turn back, now, or we won’t get any breakfast. Come on, Sulphur.’

They turned about and the wind now was on their faces. She was wearing a scarf that must have been Basil’s: striped green and mauve, college colours, probably: it fluttered out behind her head. She looked best in profile, with the line of hair from her brow rippling out, red and thorny, to the curly mass on her nape. Strange how that dull red hair had about it an emotional, almost a spiritual aura: contradicted, anyway, by the rest of her, which was forthright and wiry.

‘Basil tells me you once came to our house at Rottingdean,’ she said. ‘Do you know, I believe I remember someone coming to see Daddy, late one night, after dinner. It might have been you.’

‘It might.’

‘Well, I suppose the appropriate comment is that it’s a small world.’ She looked at him with friendliness in her eyes. ‘Rottingdean was a lovely place in those days, wasn’t it?’

They were walking easily, their stride matched, their arms almost touching. Alec was feeling extraordinarily happy. The clarity, the radiance of the world about him seemed to enter into him with every breath he drew. He said, 'I'm told it's changed a lot since those days.'

'Alas, yes. All that new stuff they've built.'

'The March of Time,' he quoted. 'I suppose we have to accept progress.'

'I suppose we have. But one can't help doing a little *hankering* from time to time.'

'I know.' He gestured. 'The Present is like your legitimate everyday wife, but the Past is a sort of remote half-dream mistress. . . .' He looked up. Sea gulls were skimming the empty tide of air: claws gathered, the tabernacle of their wings unfurled. He watched one soar: a piercing white joy.

She sighed faintly. 'Funny to think you came to Oldwood Lodge, that you knew Daddy. . . .'

'I had a great admiration for your father,' he told her.

She looked at him quickly: pleased. Then she smiled with a sort of deprecating tenderness. 'Poor lamb,' she said. 'Of course, he was hopelessly unpractical and idealistic. . . . We used to call him "The Last Liberal."'

'He wasn't the last,' Alec said.

'You?' she said, surprised. Then, 'I shouldn't have thought any doctrine would appeal to you that needed so little energy.'

'Ah,' he said, 'but – on the contrary – it needs almost superhuman energy to sort out and control our instincts. . . . And until that's done it's waste of time to think of social reconstruction. These moderns all put the cart before the horse. Look at Russia. At the cost of the most immense and admirable efforts she's built herself a fine modern house – and where? – bang on top of the old insanitary foundations.'

'Oh, dear,' she said, smiling. 'And I thought we were all good communists these days.'

'Ultimately,' he said. 'But not yet. The ideal gets discredited if it's applied too soon. . . . Humanity has got to learn its table manners before we can all eat amicably out of the one bowl.'

Catherine seemed to be pursuing a train of thought of her own. 'Of course, there's a snag about Liberalism,' she said thoughtfully. 'So often it's the people who aren't quite up to par themselves who advocate it. They *have* to uphold the Liberal idea, because they need it for their own protection.'

Abruptly, Alec was silent. . . .

* * *

It rained again towards noon. Brian picked up an American magazine which had, on the cover, a pair of silk-clad feminine legs bestriding the Eiffel tower, and, armed with this, retired into a prolonged coma upon the living-room couch. Catherine had gone to another room at the far end of the bungalow, where there was a piano: she could be heard, indistinctly and intermittently, playing. Alec wondered whether or not she played well: since he himself was indifferent to music, he hoped that she did not: not desiring her to excel in a realm from which he was excluded. He was a fish out of water where musical experience was concerned: it seemed that he lacked, somewhere, the necessary gills which made this element habitable. So he explained to Basil, who sat lounging in another chair: his bony feet thrust into a pair of slippers: mouth puckered upon the stem of his pipe. Alec noticed, with the interest which he invariably accorded to detail, the way in which the muscular play demanded by the act of pipe-sucking altered Basil's expression; gave his face a sort of hollow sternness which quite spuriously ennobled it. Whereas Brian with a pipe looked rather disgusting: unctuous-mouthed: a baby with its dummy. Alec himself never smoked one: his mood requiring only the flimsiness of a cigarette which, as he drew on it, seemed to be consumed, not by its own fire but by the nervous energy within him demanding something to feed on.

'And Miss Nicolls?' he said. They were still talking about musical appreciation.

'Oh, Catherine *likes* music; but she plays very badly,' Basil said.

'What about you?'

Basil spread his fingers. 'I also like music: I play equally badly.'

Alec, exploring the Nicolls's taste, mentioned tentatively the names of a few composers. But he saw at once from Basil's expression that these were not Basil's cup of tea. Basil looked curiously apologetic: he was excusing himself for the stringency of his own taste to which such popular names were anathema: embarrassed by his own high standards in front of one who did not share them, as a man of wealth might be in the company of the needy: humorously, therefore, behaving as though the exquisiteness of his own taste were some sort of idiosyncrasy with which he was afflicted and which others must be indulgent enough to pardon in him.

'Bach,' Alec said at last: and saw Basil's look of relief. Obviously, as Brian would say, Bach was the goods. They could face each other as equals again. And Alec had his clue.

(All the while, because this was second nature with him, something automatic, apart from personal feeling – he was studying Basil; absorbing his personality with the cold æsthetic relish of spider at work on fly: only in this case the fly gives unlimitedly without itself sustaining any loss, or even being aware of the process.) Basil had an aversion to the inchoate; the emotional. He sought, never the direct experience, but its abstraction. Refinement: essence. For him, the actual was always the vulgar: Alec understood now Basil's frequent condemnation of modern feminine novelists with their 'tedious catalogues.' He understood, too, this curious room in which they were sitting: its meaningless furniture and effects. Basil would not commit himself to anything so impermanent as a definite pattern. It had become for him superfluous and wearisome, bad taste, in fact, to exhibit any taste at all.

There was a hoarse explosion of laughter from Brian on the couch: the springs quivered rhythmically beneath him. They looked across at him tolerantly. He levered himself up on one elbow and peered at them over the page. 'Listen to this,' he said. 'It's a husband coming home one day and finding his wife in bed with the window-cleaner . . .'

When he had finished, Basil said without any change of expression, 'It's curious, but I invariably become depressed, almost alarmed, when I see someone preparing to tell me a joke. It paralyzes me. I get a sort of stage fright. I *know* I won't be able to laugh at the end.'

'It works the other way round with me,' Alec said. 'I'm so desperately anxious to laugh, I unleash a sudden bellow of mirth before the point has been reached at all.'

Brian turned away from them in disgust. 'The trouble with you two, you're too damn intellectual,' he said: and relapsed into his magazine.

'Our friend Brian,' said Basil in a dispassionate voice, 'represents an interesting phenomenon. . . . Himself congenitally an intellectual, he spends his time trying to conceal the light of his own reason under a bushel of he-manship. He's as shy of disclosing intelligence as a man formerly was of revealing his baser parts.' He paused: they could hear the faint bubbling of his pipe. 'That's the new fashion, of course,' he said. 'The retreat from reason. Somersault: humanity's new attitude: heads down, organs up.'

'I hope you're wrong,' Alec said soberly.

'I don't think I am,' Basil replied. 'No, I don't think I am,' he said gently. He smiled, then, in what struck Alec as a new fashion: his teeth gripped on the stem of his pipe looked for a moment curiously naked. Alec was suddenly reminded of his first impression of Basil Nicolls: the sense of latent cruelty he had received. . . . A sort of uneasiness seized him: for the first time he wondered, since the book had not been mentioned again, what exactly were the other man's motives in getting him here: whether he was perhaps extracting some peculiar pleasure out of his own hidden enmity towards a guest. The impression was gone before he could fix it: a faint creeping of his senses; no more. He listened again. 'The gunman has become the modern ideal,' Basil was saying. 'Public Enemy No. 1, is also Public Hero No. 1. And hence,' waving his hand slightly in the direction of Brian, 'we have the diverting spectacle of intelligent and humanitarian men doing their utmost to look as though they might shoot at sight.'

Brian was unperturbed. 'Yah,' he said: and turned an indifferent shoulder.

Alec got up to look for a cigarette. He said, casually, dispatching a charred match into the fire, 'There are still a few of us who intend to keep the banner of reason flying.'

Basil shook his head. 'Forlorn hope,' he said. He struck his hands behind his neck, interlaced, and stretched luxuriously: 'Attila is at the gates.' He seemed to take a strange sensuous pleasure in the prospect of devastation.

'We can keep the gates shut.'

'Can we? When Reason itself enjoys tampering with the lock?'

'Oh, boy,' said Brian with relish. They turned to him and he held up for their inspection a page-long drawing of ineffably slender titillating legs sheathed in exotic stockings. They looked at it with a certain amount of appreciation. 'So much, much lovelier than the real thing,' Brian mourned. 'That's the devil about these artists. They create a standard no flesh-and-blood female can even emulate: that simply doesn't exist. And you see it all over the place: open a paper, a magazine, there it is again. No wonder we all go about with an itch these days. It's about time the Censor turned his attention to the advertisement columns of the public press.'

Basil reached out and examined the page. 'Exquisitely fine . . . clinging . . . dream-like . . . glamorous,' he read. 'Hum,' he said. 'And what a text! Reads like a seduction scene. No wonder they sell the things.'

Brian yawned suddenly, cavernously; rubbing his face. Then he swung his legs over the edge of the couch and came to stand before the fire, warming his buttocks. Swaying slightly from his heel towards the ball of his foot and back again. (Like Father used to, Alec thought.) He yawned again: 'Oh, Lor', Oh, Lor',' revealing, unashamed, his cracked yellow teeth, his nose wrinkled into a snarl like an animal's. Then his face relaxed; became human again. He looked furtively at his watch. It was twenty to four. No tea going yet. That long, long, twenty minutes. . . . He sighed.

Basil, too, as though suddenly weary of the situation they formed there between the three of them, rose abruptly. He went over to the window and stood staring out at the rain-swept garden, the remote blurred sea. In the silence which had fallen the rain could be heard: on the veranda, in the garden, multiplied, persistent. Sulphur, the dog, who had raised his head at Basil's movement, now rose from the spot where he had been dozing by the brim of the fire and padded across the room on deliberate velvet paws. He stood staring up at his master: ardently switching his tail: waiting. 'He thinks I'm going to take him out,' Basil said. He stuck his hands in his pockets. 'Well, what about it? Anyone game for a tramp?'

Brian groaned. Into Alec's mind, concealed from the other two, there flashed an old, a very old, joke of Lew Solomon's. The would-be English Jew saying (Lew's incomparable pronunciation) '*Vee Englishmen go out in all kinds of vedders.*' He suppressed a sudden inclination to laugh. For a moment Lew had been present with him, sharing something the

others could not appreciate: it was as though, in some other dimension, they had exchanged a secret smile. . . .

The door opened, instantly sucking a draught into the room. Catherine turned and pinned the door to behind her. She came forward into the warm fire-blazoned room. Alec rose to his feet, but she seemed not to notice him. She went over to the fire and stood, crisping and uncrisping her fingers, her face serious still from the solitude of music.

'Been practising?' Brian said, unnecessarily.

'Yes.' Then she sighed. 'I'm rusty. No good any more. . . . Ah, well!' She slipped down on to the low couch, drawing up her legs in a familiar, comfortable attitude. 'Any tea going?' she said.

'I'll ring.' Basil crossed the room to the bell. She threw her head back, leaning it upon the arm of the couch. 'I expect we could all do with a cup,' she said. 'There's nothing to do in this weather but just eat and go on eating.' She yawned and sleeked both hands through her hair, casually: her head still supported against the faded chintz of the couch. Alec watched, through the mingled dusk and firelight of the room, the tense cord of her throat: the prow-shaped jaw. Of course, she was thin: far too thin: but this extreme refinement of the flesh, and its consequent detailing of the bony structure, had its own beauty: distinctive, if a little arid. She was wearing her tweeds: a checked skirt and faded green woollen jumper. Still no powder: no make-up of any sort. He was aware, this time, and to his own surprise, of a faint pique upon perceiving this: the fact that in no way, apparently, had she endeavoured to make herself attractive for his benefit. She treated him with a sort of friendly disregard which he was unaccustomed to meet in women. Or was this apparent lack of wile the symptom of an intelligent coquetry on her part? A campaign, in fact? *He knows so many beautiful, exquisitely groomed women: let him meet a plain simple one for a change. . . .*

There was a joyful rattle of china. They all turned their heads. Hazlitt came in, wheeling the tea-trolley across the floor. He placed it accurately in front of Catherine . . . 'Thank you, Hazlitt.' 'Thank you, Miss,' . . . and quietly withdrew. She sat up, pushing a cushion into place behind her. 'Now then.' Basil stopped wandering in his silent fashion about the room and came and sat on the couch beside her. 'Ah, crumpets,' he said. 'Good.' He paused. 'Help you, Cath?'

'I can manage.'

Alec, watching them together, was struck by two things. First of all, the intimacy of their tone, revealed in this adept casualness; as though they understood each other so well that half words sufficed. Basil had, for her, a manner totally different to that which he adopted with the rest of the world; he seemed, in speaking to her, to be indulging in a sort of self-communion. . . . Then there was the resemblance between them. Alec had not thought at first that they looked alike, but now, the two faces seen together, the mutual basis was apparent: the key form that set them apart; the special Nicolls pattern. Alec was aware of a curious sensation: he realized that he was averse to that resemblance. He disliked seeing the originality of Catherine's face duplicated, detracted from: disliked seeing it caricatured, as it were, in a male setting. If there was more to his feeling than that, a jealousy of that

pre-established relationship, he was not prepared, just then, to recognize the fact.

'Brian, you take sugar, don't you?' Catherine was serving the tea: her arm bent over the tea-pot. The forked mouth poured forth its beautifully rounded stream of amber. Alec watched. Enjoying keenly that which was missing so often in his life – the ritual of being served by a particular woman: starved of this, day after day, by the impersonal receipt of his meals over a restaurant table. He took his cup from her humbly: held it out to her while, delicately, from the tongs, she dropped one, two, lumps of sugar into it: feeling, in the pleasure of accepting her small ministrations, that, childlike, he was surrendered to her: that she took from him the burden of his own independence.

'Crumpets?' Brian, already chewing, offered the dish round. There was a smear of butter on his cheek. Sulphur stood with his long head and elegant famished flanks watching the interchange of cups, of food. Basil dropped a rubbery strip of his crumpet. Down went the setter's head, browsing after it along the floor: his jaws snapped it up. 'You'll lose that Gossard Line of Beauty, old boy,' said Brian. He shook his head as Sulphur came round to him expectantly. 'Registers perfectly, doesn't he?' he said to Alec. 'Look at that expression. We ought to give him a screen test. What do you think?'

'By all means,' Basil said. 'Sign him up.'

'Unknown Dog Leaps Into Fame Overnight,' quoted Brian. He passed his cup again. 'Not *quite* so strong this time,' he directed gently. 'That's it. . . . Thank you.' He sat stirring the contents of his cup thoughtfully. 'You coming back to town with Alec and me to-night?' he asked suddenly. He was addressing Catherine.

Alec looked up: unexpectedly, his glance met Catherine's. They both looked away, as though startled by that impact. . . . Catherine seemed to hesitate. Then Basil cut in abruptly, 'No. Cathy's staying the night. I'm driving back with her to-morrow.'

'Well, why don't you two stay also?' Catherine said, busy over the tea-trolley.

'Alec's got to be on the set at nine to-morrow,' Brian explained. 'I could stay,' he added vaguely.

No one seemed interested in the fact. The subject was simply dropped. In the obvious silence Alec stole a glance at Brian. His face was expressionless. Because he represented himself so often as the social clown, people were only too ready, accepting him at his own estimate, to treat him as such: as a man who could take all rebuffs and humiliating slips in his stride: saved by an inhuman rubbery bounce that shielded him from discomfort; and others from the necessity of considering his feelings.

Catherine reached out languidly and selected a cigarette from the box. There was a movement: simultaneously, three men tendered lit matches towards her. She smiled: then, her face brightly illumined, she bent forward to kindle her cigarette from Alec's flame. 'Hey – steady.' She closed her left hand firmly round his wrist. He was taken aback. But the action was so casual, so deliberate, that it might equally well have been an invitation, or (proof that the contact was meaningless to her) a rebuff to intimacy. . . . He could not judge.

Hazlitt appeared again. He went to the windows, each in turn, and drew the curtains: obliterating the darkness. He lit another lamp in the corner of the room, then wheeled away the trolley with its littered cups and plates. The fire roared cosily in the wide red-brick grate. Alec was reminded of another fire, another room. He said at random, 'What happened to Oldwood Lodge? Does it still belong to you?'

'Lord, no,' Basil answered him. 'It went with all the goods and chattels when the old man died.'

Alec was startled by the irreverence of his tone. It revealed to him at once the fact that, from the established cult of admiration for Richard Nicolls, Nicolls's son was a secret renegade. He was distressed, but not altogether surprised, by the discovery: he felt, now, that he could imagine the young Basil, silently, cynically, nursing his treachery even as he sat in the very heart of the fold. . . . He was about to say something, then he changed his mind abruptly. Instead he asked: 'And who has the place now?' Catherine was looking at him. In the firelight her eyes were sombre and warm: the colour of mahogany. 'Oldwood?' she said, replying to his question. She exhaled smoke slowly. 'Heaven knows. Oh! yes – some awful dago, I believe.'

A sudden familiar shock went through him. The careless contempt in that expression. . . . Me, she means. Dago: Jew: Outsider. . . . Unconsciously, she had made a thrust at his pretensions, at his emotional preoccupation with her. She might just as easily have said 'Some ghastly Jew. . . .' He could anticipate the scene. Her sudden violent flush. Oh, I'm so sorry, I didn't mean – And then the usual smoothing over. Of course, *you're* different. Or else: Some of my best friends are Jews. . . . They always said that. And one was supposed to be humbly grateful, quite bowled over, in fact, by the astonishing thing. *Jews*, just fancy! Some of my best friends are chimney sweeps, performing seals. Oh, Lord. Their tolerance. Their damned shallow self-satisfied *tolerance*!

Basil took his pipe from his pocket and began thumbing tobacco into the bowl. He looked gently at Alec. 'Penny for your thoughts, Mr Berman,' he said. . . .

They drove back to town the same night. The rain had not abated. The roads were churning with mud; and dangerously greasy. Again and again the car swung out of control; waltzing gaily from one hedge to the other, while Brian, at the wheel, cursed man and circumstance; and Alec, on one occasion, at least, really alarmed, made as though to rise in his seat.

'Hold tight, sucker,' Brian said. 'I never yet met the steer that could throw Broncho Bill.' He eased, coaxed the car back to sobriety. They splashed forward again; their headlights looking pale and diluted; the windscreen so blind with water that it was like seeing out of focus. Now and then, the dazzling rain-blurred lamps of other cars waxed up ahead of them, then wheeled past and were extinguished. Darkness resumed; and the heavy running of rain upon the sunshine roof.

One of the windows was leaking slightly: Alec found that the elbow of his overcoat was sodden. Normally, he would have concentrated upon this fact (for he was always very concerned about his physical well-being and the possibility of illness) but now he sat, preoccupied, unheeding. He replied in monosyllables to Brian. Once he failed to answer altogether.

Brian looked sideways at him. He was perfectly aware of Alec's absorption and at the same time puzzled. What was up? . . . *Cathy*, he thought: surely it's not Cathy! No – hardly his type. Still, you never can tell. The things people see in each other. . . . What would our Hetty say? He grinned faintly. She'd refuse to believe it for one thing. Be insulted at such a rival. But it can't be. Why, it's a notorious thing, Alec Berman has hundreds of the loveliest women in England at his beck and call – one of the perks of being a director. As for Catherine – well, most people wouldn't look twice at Catherine. Still you never know. You never know.

On his face was an expression familiar to him: the half furtive, half avid look of a man constrained to fasten upon the lives of others for emotional sustenance. Born of this, and at least equally strong, was the ever-present fear that those others, his friends and acquaintances, might somehow better themselves, steal a march on him; and behind those thick amiable-looking glasses, therefore, he was perpetually on the watch; torn by a strange acute jealousy: resenting any advancement in status, in friendship, in worldly goods: as though every new success achieved by others robbed him somehow, unfairly, of his own part in the universal share-out. . . .

END OF PART I

PART II

CHAPTER SIX

CATHERINE AND ALEC

He was standing under a lamp-post in Frith Street. He wore a dark overcoat, a silk muffler and black Homburg hat. He had not, however, had time to shave (they did not finish on the set, that evening, until past seven) and, a little anxiously, he kept touching a gruff chin with his finger-tips. Can't be helped, now, he thought. He shot his wrist out of his sleeve: ten to eight. She was late.

It was a November evening; unexpectedly mild. Rain had ceased: but the road still glistened and pavements were laced with mud. The lamp-posts were ringed in mist. A man passed with a bundle of newspapers: a placard, worn like an apron about his waist, gleamed dully; saturated with moisture. From a grating in the road, steam rose up. The big plate-glass windows of the *Chien Andalou* were mantled in a mist through which the lights, the figures of the diners within, appeared remote and blurred.

He glanced at his watch again; then, tired of standing in the one position, began slowly to pace up and down. His eyes, full of her image, kept trying to place her, superimpose her,

as it were, on the physique of any passer-by who remotely resembled her. Foiled each time by different, alien features. Momentarily foiled: next time, the image would fit: it would be her. . . . Which way would she eventually come, he wondered: from this corner – or that one? The whole street was alive for him with the potentiality of her presence. Under the dark brim of his hat, his eyes darted restlessly. Every taxi that appeared, that seemed about to slow down, caused him to stop in his tracks; expectant. But as taxi after taxi paused only to discharge strangers, or went by, unheeding, his mood altered: he became suddenly apprehensive. Why didn't she come? He stared up and down the street, which was, now, alarmingly empty of her presence. Doubt began to gnaw. Surely the arrangement had been explicit enough. He reviewed, frowning, the brief conversation that had ensued between them; saw himself, telephone receiver at his ear, his free hand drawing triangles on the woolly pink of a blotter on the desk. What had been said? Tormented by the possibility that his directions had been inadequate, he wished he had been more precise, insisted fully on details of time and place while the opportunity yet was his. Now if he had only said. . . . Aware of futility, he stood trying to reconstruct the past, so that the present moment might come to satisfactory issue.

Another taxi appeared. Anxiously, he watched the course it was taking. To his joy, it began to slow down, it was stopping: smiling, sure this time, Alec took a step forward. . . . It pulled up, almost at his feet: to disgorge an elderly gentleman in evening dress. He stood fishing for sixpences, while Alec watched him with despair. The matter of the tip successfully

negotiated, intent on his own affairs, he went past Alec into the *Chien Andalou*: leaving the latter standing there, with a fixed expression; motionless, right knee flexed, like a marionette with one string broken. . . . She was more than twenty minutes late. He continued to stand there, both as an assertion that the arrangement between them still held and because he was unable to do anything else: paralysed by the certainty that she was not now coming at all.

A figure slipped up behind him. 'Here I am,' said Catherine Nicolls at his elbow.

* * *

He had reserved a table. They were up in a corner, where an alcove seat of padded red velvet encircled the small table, standing immaculate in its stiff white drapes. Catherine ignored the officious ministrations of the waiter and slipped off a camel-hair coat. She was wearing a dark green dress laced up to the neck with rust-coloured cord. Her hair, that auburn, brambled mass, was combed away behind her ears. She sat opposite him, pale face inclined, examining the menu card. He had time, in this momentary interval, to correct, adjust, the disparity between his first impression of her, to which memory had tentatively added here and there a false colour, untrue line; and this, her new, her actual appearance.

She put down the menu and glanced across at him. There was a quizzical look in her eye. Indicating his black tie: 'I'd no idea you were putting on Soup-and-Fish,' she said. 'I understood you were coming direct from Oxshott.'

'I changed there.'

'Oh!' she said. 'And I expected to find you in shirt-sleeves, chewing a cigar. Or with a sweater and megaphone.'

'Life is full of disappointments.'

He turned away to summon the wine-waiter. Catherine could not see it, but he was faintly put out. There was something just a little ridiculous in the situation; for him, at least, since he was aware that her lack of formality was quite as deliberate as his own assumption of it. . . . He was certain that she had been brought up to change for dinner every night: whereas he himself, all the time he had lived in Brighton, had seen dress clothes only behind plate-glass in the larger shops in North Street. . . . The waiter put a greasy leather-jacketed list before them. Catherine ordered a Martini. Alec had tomato-juice and sat sipping the soupy redness with the slightly smug pleasure which he derived always from consuming that which reputedly was 'good for one.' Catherine nursed the transparent shell of glass in a sensible freckled hand. The green dress she wore was skin-tight about her flat nervous frame: the frail crescent of each breast outlined. Her shoulders were wrong, too wide, gaunt: but there was a certain elegance, if a disproportionate one, about her waist, her sharp, spare hips. It was not a physique that, normally, he admired in women. But because this was she, Catherine Nicolls (the girl out of his own past, the girl from Rottingdean: a symbol; unforgotten), that fact was without importance: physical contour became a triviality; something deeper had been established and, as a result, no fault, no defect of hers, however clearly perceived, could ever alter the meaning she possessed for him.

Catherine slipped him a glance. Then she dropped her eyes.

Twisting the stem of her glass, she confessed: 'I haven't *dared* to look at the time. Was I shockingly late?'

He sensed at once, from her voice, that there was more to her embarrassment than regret at having kept him waiting. Intuition visited him: he knew suddenly why she was late: with whom she had been. He said, with assumed lightness, 'Well, you're here now – that's all that matters.' She said nothing. He put both elbows on the table and brought his hands together, locking the fingers. With the nail-edge of two thumbs he caressed his lower lip, musingly. There was a very slight pause. . . . 'How is your brother?' he said.

Colour flushed up slowly, accusingly, into her face. She kept her eyes from him; ostrich-wise, as though, by not seeing him, she concealed herself from his gaze. 'He's all right,' she replied briefly.

Alec had not moved. His thumbs pinched at his lower lip, pulling it forward. Over linked knuckles, his eyes observed her: steady, dark, behind hooded lids. Then he dropped his hands and said in a matter-of-fact voice, 'He doesn't approve of me, does he?'

'What? Why, how absurd!' She was indignant.

'But he doesn't – does he, now?' He spoke gently, softly, as though coaxing the admission from her. . . .

But she had regained a measure of self-possession. She resisted his intention. 'What on earth makes you think so?' she said.

'I don't know. Instinct, I suppose. . . .' Deliberately he kept testing his finger upon the upturned prong of a fork. 'It's true, isn't it?'

'No, of course, it isn't!' She was betrayed into speaking more sharply than she intended.

'Not?'

'Of course not. On the contrary! He's very interested in you. He thinks a lot of you. He admires you.'

'But he doesn't like me.'

'Oh, *well*,' she said; and deliberately shrugged her shoulders; 'if you've made up your mind about it, there's nothing I can say. . . . But you're wrong – quite wrong.'

'There are some things one isn't wrong about.'

'Look here,' she said then, and there was a perceptible heat in her voice (for such an apparently trivial matter they were both surprisingly intense, concerned), 'I think I know Basil just a little better than you do. You admit that, don't you? Basil and I are like twins. I know exactly what he thinks and feels, just as he knows what I do.'

'Oh?' Alec's tone was not altogether polite. He was angry, resentful of that parade of intimacy. Furthermore, although it was not his place to say so, he considered that Catherine was misled. Basil might know everything about her – as she alleged: but he was quite certain that she, on her side, was far from being aware of all there was to know about Basil.

She threw her head back. 'What an absurd argument this is,' she said. 'Of course, if you *insist* on the privilege of being disliked. . . .'

Alec was taken aback. He could think of nothing to say for the moment. He smiled, but his expression was a little wry. 'All right,' he said at last. 'You win.'

'Thank you.'

'And now – do we eat?' He raised his hand and the waiter, who had been whisking dreamily at an adjoining table with a folded serviette, became aware of their presence with a start. 'Sir?' Sallow, incredibly concave within his toil-worn dress-suit, he hovered above them. As he hung over their table, he surreptitiously tweaked at a spoon here and there, like a veteran player unable to refrain from intervening in someone else's game of chess. . . . Then he composed himself, with stoic patience, while they wavered through the ritual of selecting a meal. 'Women always like meat underdone and men like it well done, have you noticed?' Alec said. It proved to be so in this case. They ordered blue trout: and then, for Catherine, two cutlets, frail little sticks on which the tender heart of meat was scarcely varnished from the grill, with creamed spinach and straw potatoes: while Alec had his favourite point steak, sturdily browned. The waiter departed and a young Italian, with aproned knees, wheeled up his trolley of *hors d'œuvres*. 'Anchovy, Russian salad, sweet-corn, Spanish onions, herring, olives, sauerkraut?' he intoned. Spoon and fork were nipped ready in his agile fingers.

Alec had smoked salmon instead. Skilfully, he squeezed a chit of lemon over the rosy slivers on his plate. 'What would you care to do afterwards?' he said, separating the oleaginous petals with his fork. 'We could get in to the ballet, I think. Would you care to? . . . Anything you like.'

'The ballet, of course. What are they doing tonight?'

They recalled the waiter; and after some negotiations he produced for them a limp copy of the evening paper.

'Now let's see.' Alec flattened out the sheets. Intent, he followed his index finger down the columns of the entertainment page. Across the table, Catherine watched him. His head was bent: she could see clipped black hair bristling between the two thongs at the back of his neck; and for a moment, as she smelled the faint violet odour of hair-oil, her finger-tips yearned to learn the sense of his hair: there, where it bristled, and there where it became abundant, coarse black under the glossiness. . . .

Alec looked up. 'Sadler's Wells have got ballet, too,' he said. He paused. She saw his expression. 'Do you know, you look like a Rossetti,' he said. 'That dress. You only want a turquoise comb in your hair. . . .'

'Goodness!' said Catherine easily (this was not for her a new compliment). 'I'm much too skinny. I can't aspire to those voluptuous, goitrous throats.' How attractive he was, she thought, with his dark, screened eyes: the matt, foreign skin. And his mouth. He had a beautiful mouth: firm and suave. She was aware of feeling within her a guilty weakness each time that her glance strayed to that mouth. . . . She had, of course (she moved these days largely in artistic circles), known other Jews before she met Alec Berman. She recognized now that each, to a greater or lesser degree, affected her in the same way. She enjoyed being with them: felt at her best in their company. They were so appreciative, so vital; and at the same time curiously humble. One felt a being apart: ardently desired: no less ardently respected. Taboo gave its mystery, its emotional intensity to the situation. It was, too, an easy, a flattering situation, for whatever one's value to a male of one's own race, with these men one was, at the outset, heavily at a premium. . . . The waiter appeared again. He scooped away their plates and stood holding them on the flat of a rusty black arm. 'And a sweet, Madam?' he said dispassionately. His voice suggested an immeasurable remoteness from any world in which the choice of a sweet was a matter of importance.

Alec passed her the menu. 'Ice Cream,' he asked, 'or the ubiquitous Crême Caramel?' Catherine shook her head, indicating the clock. 'All right: two coffees, then,' Alec told the waiter. He folded the newspaper again: but instead of studying it, looked at Catherine with a sort of abstracted absorption. She rapped on the table with mock severity.

'Alec!'

'Catherine!'

'You're not concentrating,' she said.

'I am, I am,' he said. 'It's – the colour of your dress and your hair against that red velvet. . . .'

'Go on,' she answered severely. 'Or we'll never get in anywhere. Look up the times.'

'I remember you with a plait down your back,' he said.

'Nonsense,' she said.

'But it's true.' He smiled across at her. 'And now here you are. . . .'

She gave a sigh of resignation. 'All right,' she said. 'No ballet.'

He snapped his fingers in the air. 'Waiter! Check, please.' He turned back to her. 'All right. We're going places,' he said.

She saw that he was, suddenly, in a pleased, light-hearted mood. He slipped his hand into an inner pocket and brought

out a morocco-leather notecase: at the same time, covertly studying the folded slip the waiter had presented to him on a plate. Of course, there were defects to his face, she thought: the ears, in particular; vulgar, misplaced. And he was small; smaller than her. That should have mattered. Surprisingly, it did not. There was something different about Alec Berman. A certain purposefulness. She had sensed it the week-end at Middle Bay. Sensed it and been afraid of it, for it seemed to threaten something in her which she valued. . . . Her immunity. . . . That emotional detachment of hers which had replaced actual virginity and come to acquire for her the same value: a protection, a guard against life. . . . A young man, a Welsh novelist, who for some time had been in love with her, once referred to this as her 'essential integrity.' Integrity. She was grateful for the refuge of that word. She herself alone knew, without ever admitting it, what fear, what void, such integrity really meant. During all these years of emancipation, of free life among the cultured and the intellectual, she had spent her time imprisoned within the magic circle of that integrity, in the last resort, as inaccessible as the most inveterate of spinsters. A certain thorniness of manner, indeed, was due to the constant fear that, some day, someone would guess what a small strange death-in-life she was living in the midst of her lovers.

Alec allowed the waiter to hoist his coat on to his shoulders: submitting without pleasure to that impersonal solicitude. Then he came round the table himself to assist Catherine. 'Let me help.' 'Thank you.' She slipped into her coat. As she did so, she felt the warmth of his hand on hers for a moment;

and, suddenly, she shivered. A queer pain, that was not altogether pain, went through her: vibrated in the pit of her stomach. . . . 'Ready?' he said softly. She nodded. By an effort, since they seemed tranced, weighted with a new awareness, she raised her lids. Yes, Alec Berman was different. . . . She looked at him, and he was at a loss to understand the expression, half pleasure, half fear, that he saw on her face at that moment.

Alec signalled peremptorily; and a taxi swerved out of its course; to stop at their feet. He spoke to the driver, hand upon the door; then climbed in beside Catherine. 'We'll just do it, I think,' he said. His coat hung open: the white of his shirt-front gleamed; then the edge of a cuff, as he raised his hand to wind up the window: shielding her from draught. Lamplight flashed and darkened as the taxi began to move.

'Will you smoke?' he said. A cigarette-case snapped apart in his hand.

'Thank you.'

She slipped a cigarette out from the elastic band. He noticed that she seemed to be keeping her distance from him, hedging slightly to the corner of the taxi. This surprised him; since hitherto she had shown no awareness of accidental contact. . . . His thumb switched the wheel of his lighter: and he tendered towards her the frail flame. Her face came close: lit and shadowed; like a mask, the eyes downcast. Then she sipped quickly at the flame and leant back, exhaling smoke. 'Thank you, Alec.' Her voice was subdued. Cigarette smoke came drifting across to him and he inhaled deeply that which she had inhaled: taking a daring intimacy, unknown to her.

In a few minutes they were near the theatres and caught up, with countless other vehicles, in the turgid, fitful stream of theatre-going traffic. The taxi crawled forward, stopping, hooting. Progress became infinitesimal. In front of them, was the stolid neck of the driver, involved in a woollen scarf the colour of pea-soup. In the strip of mirror inclined over the windscreen, they could see one somnolent eye. Alec was beginning to fidget. He mentioned, several times, the fact that it would be quicker to walk. . . . They jerked forward a few yards: then stopped again. Vainly, on all sides, horns sounded. Alec leant forward abruptly and tapped on the glass partition. (He was one of those individuals, Catherine recognized, who become a prey to anxiety in taxis: watch the meter and the route taken with a restless, paranoid eye.) 'All right – we'll get out here,' he indicated. The driver nodded: as though he knew all about these people who get seized with a sudden fever to economize that last threepence. . . . They broached the kerb; and, before they had well come to a standstill, Alec was handing Catherine out: then he stood there, with a palmful of silver, uneasily calculating. 'Thank *you*, Sir,' said the driver. 'All right – good night.' Alec looked relieved. He never tipped a cabman without the feeling that he was paying a sort of ransom to be allowed to go free. . . .

'Now then!' Gaily, he took Catherine by the forearm. They made their way to the open doors of the theatre through which, a minute before the performance was due to begin, people were still streaming. In the foyer, Alec craned his neck

at the small grill of the box-office: like a man occupied in looking into a peepshow. Catherine waited with the detachment becoming at such a juncture. He joined her in a moment, the perforated slips in his hand. 'O.K.' he said. 'We were lucky. Two just returned.' As they made their way through gilded corridors, they could hear the strains of the orchestra. They pushed open swing doors and stepped through, to a burst of music, into the warm, murmuring arena. A painted, matronly woman with an enormous bow on her discoloured hair examined their tickets, then led them down the sloping gangway. 'Chocolates, programmes?' Alec negotiated rapidly: then – 'Sorry' – they shuffled, askew, past frigidly averted knees, to two empty seats. He helped her off with her coat: gave her the programme to slit apart. The lights began to dim.

A hood of darkness came up over the audience; quenching the murmur of voices, effacing individuality. Then, like an eyelid opening on to brightness, up went the curtain. . . .

Music slowly swelling, swelling out: and suddenly, upon the tide of it, the white aerial-robed beings, translated, moving, radiant, through their own strange element: birds in the empty ether, fish coiling through the green unbreathable waters. Like a ring of sea-foam they broke upon the boards, as quick swept back upon the magic tide of sound: tossed and exalted; swept, low and hurrying, under the cloud's dark menace, thrown up in a crash of brilliant white spume, as soon to melt away, wholly dissolve and reform under the impulse of new and sweeter harmonies. Not human, these girls, these boys, these slender springing children; fire-darting fingers outstretched, loins pregnant with dance: but wild new beings set free of gravity, exquisitely purged of consequence and reality.

In the darkness, Catherine sat rapt, face upturned. Alec sensed her concentration. He stole a glance at her, knowing that she was unaware of him: her whole being held, magnetized. He himself, once the first surprise of pleasure was over, was conscious of a growing aloofness. He was outside the spell. . . . Perhaps he was beginning to lose his aptitude for the ballet, he thought. This evening, for instance, he felt what amounted to a definite repulsion for the mechanics of the whole thing: the grotesquely painted faces, the quivering muscles, the gleam of sweat. . . . That in him which was hardily matter-of-fact (and which he himself did not readily acknowledge, since it derived from his father) was always, whatever æsthetic sensibilities might be tickled, a little surly before the fantastic: suspicious, too, as in the present instance, of all this intensity about something so alien to every day reality. He decided, watching the stage, that the attitude of extreme tip-toe was an unlovely one: that he disliked seeing women teetering along on their toes like maimed birds. . . . He sighed. There were moments, this evening, in particular, watching a group of male dancers seriously posturing, when he felt almost ashamed for humanity. . . .

It was over at last. The bright-lit group on the stage sinking into stillness, into finality. The music drained slowly from them: leaving them marooned, static: human again. There was a pause – then the curtain came running to the floor. Light grew up slowly in the auditorium: and with it, the focus of interest was transferred: they were restored to themselves again. Applause broke out: hand clapping into hand in prolonged acclamation. A clattering ecstasy. The house seethed with beating hands like a startled dovecot. Alec gave a perfunctory tap or two. 'Come on, let's get a drink,' he said. They stood up and plush seats sprang to attention behind them. People were still clapping, persistently; from every part of the house. 'What enthusiasm!' Catherine remarked. But Alec had his own theory about the applause of an audience. A great part of it, he believed, was simply reaction from having been kept silent so long: more a need for movement than a specific appreciation.

'Coming?' They made their way into the foyer: up a passage which sloped under them like a deck. The bar was at the end: crowded already. Mirrored walls held a fresco of animated faces: washed and limber Englishmen with blonde well-clipped hair and immaculate voices; clear emphatic young women, bare-backed, trailing silver fox: here and there, tweeds and a beard: but expensive tweeds, and a beard the cultivation of which was a luxury, not an economy. Alec and Catherine stood waiting their turn, watching coffee-cups slop their way across the counter, uncorked bottles foam briefly into tilted glasses. 'Well?' said Catherine.

'Well?' Alec wrenched himself from fascinated contemplation of a young man in white kid gloves rouging his lips at a mirror.

'How did you like it?'

He considered: pursing his brows. 'Not as much as I would have done, even a year ago.' He broke off to receive two glasses from the barmaid: to pass one on to Catherine. 'I know,' he said, forestalling her, 'I'm becoming a Philistine in my old age. . . . But there you are. I find it increasingly hard to take the arts at all seriously.' He lifted the glass. 'Well – here's to us. . . .'

The slam of the taxi door, the hum of the engine, was startlingly loud in the silent road. The silence seemed to become more intense as the driver righted his flag and drove off; leaving them standing there, alone with the blind windows and downward looking roofs. A lamp-post burned above their heads; pitched about it for the night was a round impalpable tent of radiance. Catherine's face appeared blanched in that soft glare, her eyes glittered. He was watching her: his gaze ambiguous in the shadow of his hat-brim. Aware of that gaze, of his intent proximity, she felt curiously helpless: at a loss, too, before his sudden purposeful silence. At last she put her hand on the green-painted gate; the other was thrust away in the pocket of her camel-hair coat. 'My third late night this week,' she began: trying to speak lightly. He said nothing. She had recourse to the muffled, ostentatious yawn. Still he did not move. Then she said, as she had already said to him that evening, only this time it was not a challenge but a gesture of helplessness, 'Well?'

'Well?' He spoke gently, as if to a child: softening it with a smile. Inexorable, all the same.

She accepted his will, then. Gave the password he had extorted from her. 'Are you coming in for a drink? . . .' He nodded. Without a word, she pushed open the gate with its rusted notice discouraging hawkers and canvassers. So that was that: the die cast. . . . As he followed her, he glanced about him quickly, trying to get his bearings. They were somewhere in St. John's Wood. Detached stucco houses; smug under cream paint. Not one of the best parts, though: no encroachment of modern Georgian: small average houses running comfortably to seed before demolition. What was she doing here? He picked his way with difficulty along a narrow passage that seemed to skirt the house: and then his footsteps went soft: they were walking on grass: there was a garden at the rear. 'This way,' Catherine said. He murmured something: his eyes were distended unseeingly. He disliked the dark perhaps more than most people: robbed of the data of sight, he had an immediate sense of suffocation, which, if prolonged, could turn to acute panic. They stopped, a moment later: and he could distinguish the outline of a long low-built house. Standing at her elbow, he heard a latchkey scrape into the lock. The door swung open. She stepped in, preceding him: and he followed cautiously: one hand spread, as if exploring the face of the darkness. 'Here we are,' he heard her say. A flick of her thumb flooded the place with light.

The pain of that sudden transformation died out of his eyeballs and he looked about him with keen interest. Of course. It was a studio. A large one, with high white-washed walls. In one corner, near a jutting anthracite stove, a Chinese chair stood on a dais: in the other, was a divan, sown with multi-coloured cushions. A row of small cacti in pots lined the mantelpiece; along with post cards of Japanese prints from the British Museum, anemones in a drug-jar, a small clay head; a litter of invitations to art shows and sherry parties.

He stood, without moving, in the centre of the room: looking around; his hat in his hand. 'You live here?' he said.

'Most of the time. I'm sharing it with a friend.'

He paused. . . .

'A girl called Venitia Rowton.' Smoothly, she gave the reassurance. 'You may have heard of her. She does wood-cuts, mostly.' She paused: a certain measure of confidence had returned to her now that she was back in this familiar setting: 'She's in Paris at the moment,' she added. . . . Alec made no reply. (Indeed, thought Catherine, turning from him, the deliberate way he had passed that up, without even a flicker of expression, was just a little insulting. . . .) She smiled wryly: and slipping out of her coat, flung it on the divan. She was the emancipated woman again: efficient, casual in her acceptance of the situation: and not admitting, even to herself, how untrue, how secondhand, was this manner one adopted as appropriate to the circumstance.

'Do take your coat off,' she said. 'It's sweltering in here. It's that stove. I have to stoke it up whenever I go out.' She began to comb her hair at a small mirror on the wall. 'The blessed thing rules our lives,' she said. 'We spend our time ministering to it, feeding it, coaxing it. It's as bad as being married, Venitia always says.'

He sat hunched on one of the low chairs. She had her back to him, her weight on one hip: he saw her slim irregular legs. Under the light, the coil of her hair became the colour of old copper. Her skin had the unrelieved pallor that goes with such hair, the irregular freckling: as though the element of tawniness in her, not confined to hair, must break out again,

stippling the surface of the flesh. She began to comb the small coarse ripples off from her face: one ear was revealed; mushroom-pale. He watched her: absorbed in a sort of dream in which, hearing the rasp of hair through the comb, he found himself, without transition, thinking of his mother: of the way she would sit, hooded in her hair as in a living mysterious garment, and methodically groom out the long strands with her old gap-toothed comb. Something within him remembered with painful intensity the sense of her faded gentle hair. It would hang in a long tapered plait at her back when, soft-footed, at night, she came into the children's room to assure herself of their rest before seeking her own: always ready, night or day, to exchange her own peace of mind for theirs. Separated from her, he marvelled, now, at that which he had always taken for granted. Was she, he wondered, utterly selfless? Possibly the explanation was simpler than that: merely, indeed, that her children were to her the cherished selfishness. She gave them life: and in turn lived through them. A happy, hopeful woman therefore: sustained by this intimate reciprocity. He let his thoughts dwell for a moment on the familiar picture of her, sitting at the head of the table, ceaselessly watching their plates, their appetites, their well-being and ignoring her own: carelessly; with impunity: as if she were sufficiently supplemented by their lives. His heart contracted. My God, he thought, how well he remembered that scene: she sitting there, himself next to her and Sydney; Violet opposite, admiring her face in the glass of the side-board, and Father at the other end, browsing unlimitedly on rye bread and the leading article; the old lamp hanging over

them all in its singed petticoats. Yes, and the radiant white cloth on Friday night, the pointed flames on the candles, the curtains cosily drawn, the meal waiting, the sense of family festivity. . . . He put his hand suddenly over his eyes, as though shading them from a too sharp light. A paralyzing loneliness, such as he had not experienced since the first days at Lewisham, had fallen upon him. A pain of regret for his mother, for that old life. For the sense of being one in a community again; for that protection, that solidarity, that oneness. . . .

He roused himself with a sort of violence. Shocked and startled. What had happened that he had permitted himself this slipping-back, this retrogression? . . . He got up and began to walk about the room; pacing up and down obsessively. Catherine turned to look at him in surprise. His sudden pallor was perceptible to her. She watched him, curiously. It did not suit him to be so pale, she thought; it altered him, gave his face a pinched look, as though some spiritual distemper were appearing through the flesh. . . . She wondered what had happened to cause this change. Whether in any chance remark of hers, she had been tactless: touching on that complex of sensibilities that lay so near the surface. It was difficult to know how to deal with him. He was in many ways quite incalculable. There were moods, she knew, from which she was excluded: a whole part of him that was unavailable to her. At the moment, she did not resent the fact: indeed, it lent to him an added attraction. A certain mystery, a concealed power, lacking in the men of her own kind, whose mentality was familiar, whose reactions she could foretell as she might those of a brother, a relative. . . .

'Alec,' she said meekly, 'you're wearing out my carpet.'

He stopped. 'Pardon?'

'Why the Man of Destiny act?' she asked.

He stared at her uncomprehending.

She put her hand on his arm and shook him. 'Oh, come, wake up, lad. . . .' She smiled at him: her hand still on his arm. 'The question is, what are you going to have to drink? If it's alcohol, you'll find the all and sundry in that cabinet over there.' She released him. 'Alternatively,' she said, 'I could boil up a kettle and produce a nice strong brew of tea. Does that say anything to you?'

The mood vanished. He was himself again. He smiled: his dark live eyes upon her face. 'Now you're talking,' he said. 'Tea – of course!'

'And biscuits?' she said.

'And biscuits.'

'What about a savoury sandwich?'

'A savoury sandwich – certainly.'

'Anything else?' She smiled back, provocatively.

'Anything else,' he said, 'that you like to offer me. . . .'

While she was busy in what was, apparently, a small kitchenette off the main room, he permitted himself, for the first time, to examine the canvases piled up against the walls. He always avoided, if he could, considering a work in the presence of the artist, for, although all artists beg for candour, it is, in actual fact, the last thing that they can tolerate: and he knew too well what really lay beneath the casual-seeming exterior: the painful craving for praise: hunger of the

exhibitionist child. . . . Moreover, the administration of this praise, in the guise of considered criticism, was an exhausting and often a thankless job. It was not enough to praise: one had to praise the right thing: disfavour fell at once if one admired that which the artist had decided to discard: or a work done a few years ago and already established, instead of the newly executed one. Since the latter, in turn, was liable to fall into disfavour once the heat of creation had cooled, it was important, even then, not to commit oneself too finally, for it would, under the new order of things, be a ticklish task to erase, diplomatically reverse, the old judgment: it being a recognized fact that an artist, however mild in everyday life, becomes a terrifying Nero when holding court with his own Art.

He picked up one or two canvases and examined them closely. They were of that type of modern work which makes little demand on technical ability; and has become, therefore, a happy hunting ground for those who can conceal in it both lack of originality and uncertainty of draughtsmanship. The effect aimed at, he realized, was a child-like simplicity of perception. He distrusted both the intention and the effect. The cult of infantilism had no appeal for him. He looked at the canvas he had in his hand: the distorted outlines, the deliberately naïve perspective, the bulbous legs, oversimplified face. 'School of Truby King,' he thought. He put it away gently, its face to the wall. He was both disappointed and relieved to discover that the artistic impulse in Catherine Nicolls was merely a derived one. Without roots, it might, in time, even, be gently extracted from her system. . . .

In the darkness, nested in some invisible steeple, a church clock gave forth its sudden ringing wail – emphasizing their solitude: the smallness of the hour. They each listened to it: to this tongue speaking impersonally out of the night: but neither of them stirred. The sound died away and left their intimacy undisturbed. Behind the bars of the stove, the coals glowed brazen; transparent with heat. Their faces, as they lounged on the cushions Catherine had spread for them on the floor, were illumined: a deep steady radiance enclosed them both.

Catherine stirred. She bent over the tray that lay between them, a dumpy brown tea-pot presiding over the cups. 'I should think this must have brewed by now,' she said. She put her hand on the sleek flank of the pot. 'How do you take yours?' she asked.

He smiled. Abstractedly he gazed up at the ceiling. Without moving he remarked. 'It always strikes me as a portentous moment when a woman asks a man for the first time how he takes his tea. . . .'

'Tut, tut,' she said deprecatingly. 'What a very romantic disposition you have.'

Her manner was a little too easy: he was not deceived. Propped up on one elbow, he turned to look across at her. She diverted his attention to the tea-pot: 'Medium,' he said in response to her gesture. 'And two sugars: that's perfect.' He accepted the cup from her and set it down on the floor by him. She poured another for herself; sitting upright to do so, her legs curved under her. Lit by the fire, her hair made a startling aura about her sharp pallid face. He thought: she looks like some old painting: a martyr saint. But it was only the hair, the pallor, that gave that effect: for the expression was wrong. Neither exaltation nor serenity informed that face. Here and there it was, already, faintly lined: the insidious, frittering effect of time, or dissatisfaction. . . .

He said, his eyes still upon her, speaking softly, 'I wonder what you're really doing in this place.'

'What do you mean? I live here.'

'No,' he said. 'Not the real you.' He explained: 'I see you otherwise.'

'How mysterious. How do you see me? A Rossetti model, living in a sort of junk-shop, surrounded with peacocks and pearls and corals?'

'By no means,' he said, stirring his tea. 'I see you in a spacious respectable house. Preferably double-fronted. With a large garden and a greenhouse. . . . Two maids, probably very neat in their uniform. A nursery at the top of the house. And a desk in the corner of a room somewhere, where you do all your house-keeping accounts and make out the menus for the week.'

She raised her eyebrows. 'How too, too suburb!'

He put away his cup. 'Catherine,' he said soberly, 'don't be Noel Coward. It doesn't suit you.'

She flushed at that. The rare colour transformed her face momentarily: she looked young and angry. He understood what he had done. He had shown her that he realized exactly to what extent she was posing: to a woman, whose emotions, pretensions, are intimately bound up in her pose, this is always the unpardonable brutality. . . . He got up suddenly; on the pretext of fetching a cigarette from his coat. Opening his case, he slipped one between his lips. There was a momentary silence as he scraped a match. She did not look round. He came back towards her: and stood prodding the mantelpiece with the charred end of the match. 'I'm sorry,' he said. 'But I want to talk to you about real things.'

'Oh, no, Alec.' She was, now, formidably composed. 'Not at this hour of the night. Not after all that tea.' She looked at him maliciously. 'Too, too Chekhov!'

Abruptly (but not entirely without memory of the countless actors who had performed this gesture under his direction), he ground out the unused cigarette. Left it splayed in the ash-tray. . . . In a movement, he was beside her. She turned – startled: but all he did was to take her hand with extreme gentleness. 'No, Catherine; please don't,' he said. 'You and I don't have to talk to each other like people in a third-rate modern comedy.'

She did not relent. 'Film Director Slates Snappy Dialogue,' she said.

'Catherine.' He spoke pleadingly.

'Alec?' She looked innocent.

'You know I – that I. . . .'

'Yes, Alec?'

He was silent, looking down at her hand imprisoned between his fingers. 'Catherine,' he said at last. 'Be a nice girl. . . . I know it's your feminine due, but don't force me into the ridiculous position of having to declare myself in words.'

'Declare what?' she asked. 'You speak as if I were a Customs official.'

'That's not funny,' he said. 'It's merely tiresome.'

'Oh, well, if we're going to quarrel, I'd like to have my hand back.' She tried to withdraw it. His grasp tightened with violence. She was unable to disengage herself. She gave up the attempt and looked at him evenly. 'So what?' she said.

She expected what came next. She was pulled roughly against him: held relentlessly at an angle that produced excruciating discomfort. She experienced the brusque infliction of his mouth, quick, seeking tongue: her cheek burned against the hard bristles of his face. In the midst of this, she had time to register once again the disheartening fact that all kisses taste alike. Her sense of his personality, far from being intensified, was diminished by proximity: blurred, put out of focus; in the blind anonymity of a kiss he was momentarily lost to her. . . .

He released her. His hair was disordered: he tried to smooth it back: his hand was shaking. She looked at him curiously: seeing him, for the first time, altered, as others had been altered, at such moments; the calm, superficial personality of social occasions surprisingly belied. . . . As always, she experienced two things: that smug feminine satisfaction which takes pride in being able to effect this: and a childish fear of the resulting consequences. . . . A certain regret, too. Something had gone. Something which hitherto had been intact between them, and, as such, of unique, of incalculable value, had lost its quality.

'Catherine,' he murmured at last. His voice sounded strange after that impersonal silence. 'You're not angry?'

'Angry?' She smiled a little. She leant back against the cushions, one elbow crooked under her. She continued to smile; looking up at him. He came close. 'Catherine.' He took her hand again. 'You know, don't you, what I feel about you? . . .' He lifted her hand to his mouth and she felt the warm pressure of his lips against her palm. His dark eyes were upon her: his warm living breath within her palm. A faint exquisite shudder ran through her. Her lids drooped. 'Catherine?' She shut her eyes; and nodded. . . .

There was an unexpected pause. A sudden blankness. Alec's expression underwent a change. He stared at her, incredulously; not understanding, at first; not wanting to understand. Then realization broke on him: the full implication of her gesture. His jaw dropped: he looked foolish, like a man who has, gratuitously, been slapped in the face.

She opened her eyes. A little surprised. He had permitted himself to miss his cue. . . . She found herself disinclined, in the circumstances, to act as prompter: with her, apathy was always quick to set in. . . . She waited, but with a certain amount of indifference, now, for the initiative to come from him.

He did not move. The first raging disappointment died out of him. There was nothing for him to say. She had been ready to surrender to him. Because of that, he was abased: made nothing of. Defeated by the light worthless victory she offered him. . . .

She sat up suddenly. Her manner changed. She looked at him with concern. 'What's the matter, Alec? . . .'

He averted his face; as if he were ashamed. 'Oh, nothing,' he said.

'Don't be silly.' Her voice was half sharp, half kindly. 'Come on. What is it, now? Tell me.'

He shook his head: and she reached out suddenly and tugged at his elbow. 'For goodness' sake, Alec!'

He shrugged his shoulders. Then he said huskily, 'Just that one of us made a slight mistake, that's all.'

'A mistake?' Her eyebrows contracted.

'Yes.' His eyes met hers for a brief moment. The look in them explained much to her. 'You see, I wanted to marry you.'

'Oh!' She stared at him. He fancied that she drew back a little. 'Marriage?' she said. Her voice was hard. She would not let him realize how startled, how deeply moved she was. . . .

He said bitterly, 'Does it amaze you so much that I should even have thought of that?'

'No, of course not.' She tried to justify herself. 'It's only that I've never considered marriage. Never thought of it.'

'Not with me, at any rate.'

'Not with anyone.' She corrected him quickly. 'Please don't flatter yourself by imagining that I discriminate specially against you.' He made no reply to this. There was a look on his face that she did not then wholly understand: but with which she was about to become familiar. He had accepted his own defeat. And now he was clinging to it: forbidding her to wrest it from him or mitigate its effect. . . . 'Don't be absurd,' she said impatiently. 'Do you think I don't mean what I say? I've never thought of myself as a married woman: as a wife; as a Mrs Somebody- or-Other. . . .'

'As a Mrs Alexander Joseph Berman. Obviously, that would be out of the question.'

So that was it! Light dawned on her. It was not her he was

despising, but himself. She had misread the whole situation. 'Alec!' she exclaimed: and her voice was incredulous. 'You don't for a moment think that I could have anything to do with such an absurd prejudice!'

He shrugged his shoulders. He was carefully noncommittal. 'The prejudice happens to be a very widespread one,' he said.

'But Alec! *Darling!* Don't be absurd. It means nothing, nothing whatever to me.' The sincerity in her voice was unmistakable.

He looked at her, then: and, seeing her candid eyes, his expression altered a little. 'I suppose I ought to be grateful to you for feeling that,' he said. 'But I don't want to be grateful. . . . I don't want to have to feel grateful for being accepted.'

'But why on earth should you?' she said.

He did not answer for a moment. When he spoke again it was in a new, a curiously elaborate manner: as if they had touched, now, on a subject which he found difficult to discuss naturally. 'You see, Catherine,' he said, 'I'm afraid you can't possibly have the remotest idea of what it means to be born a Jew.'

'Is it so different to being born an Englishman?'

'It shouldn't be. But it is. Very different.'

'I can only repeat that I feel no difference between us that matters.'

'But *I* feel it,' he said violently. He got up abruptly and began to pace up and down the room. He was deeply agitated. 'Let me try to explain,' he said at last. 'Look.' He stopped in front of her. 'You've never, have you, Catherine, felt intensely gratified, happy, if someone happened to mistake you for other than what you are? Have you?'

'No, of course not.' She was slightly at a loss.

'You've never had to. . . . You don't know, either, what it feels like to walk about on earth that doesn't belong to you, speak a language which isn't really yours (although you know no other): live every second of your life among people who at best tolerate you: be dependent for life itself upon those people. . . . You haven't – you can't possibly have – the slightest conception of the perpetual uneasiness in which a Jew lives – the terrifying lack of security: the sense that all one has yearned and striven for (the every-day happiness which any human being is entitled to) is entirely at the mercy of politicians, is challenged by every hostile word, look, gesture. . . . The sense that everything, Catherine, that a Jew builds, is built upon quicksands. . . .'

'Wait a moment, Alec.' She interrupted him. 'What you say may be true in general – I don't know. I can't pretend to know, as you say. . . . But we're concerned now with a particular case: you yourself, Alec. And after all – you live in England. . . . Don't forget that.'

'Forget it? The country I was born in? Catherine, my dear, I'm so little likely to forget, that (unlike my ancestors who wept when they remembered Zion) you'd find me sitting on the banks of a river in Zion weeping when I remembered Babylon. . . .' He gave a short laugh. 'So you see, if I'm pushed out, I shall be doubly disinherited,' he said.

'Since at the moment,' she began patiently, 'there seems to be absolutely no prospect of that happening. . . .'

'I know.' This time it was he who interrupted her: quickly. 'I'm one of the lucky ones. Do you think I don't know it? Treasure my momentary good fortune: tremble for it? . . . the fact that I'm allowed for a while to live more or less as other people. . . .' He paused. 'Even then, Catherine,' he said, 'I don't think you quite realize the peculiar sort of psychological existence the *lucky* ones lead. The way one's mind and emotions are continually worked on. . . .' He began to pace up and down the room again. 'I can give you some trivial examples,' he said. He walked up and down without looking at her. 'You, for instance,' he said, 'have never faced the moral dilemma of inclining, say, to a particular political party; at the same time knowing it expedient, for the safety of your fellow Jews, to uphold, instead, a more socially popular one.'

'No,' she said: 'and I can't see you doing it either.'

'Don't idealize me,' he said. 'Don't miscalculate what the force of circumstances can do to one. . . .'

He stopped. 'Say a vacancy occurs at the studios,' he began again after a moment. 'Some candidates come up for the job: Jewish and otherwise. I have the casting vote. Well, in those circumstances, merit should be the only criterion. On the other hand, my own job is safer, myself less conspicuous if I'm not too surrounded by others of my kind. . . .'

'But what you say applies to all of us!' she cried at once. 'In one way or another, we're all in the same boat: we're all guilty of hammering on the fingers of those who try to climb in and threaten our own security. . . .'

'Something that doesn't apply to all,' he said, 'is fear – a very special type of low-grade fear that's always there, behind every situation. You don't know that – you can't. The walking in the street and wondering what the content is of the glances you receive. . . . The way a Jew lowers his voice to pronounce the word Jew. . . . You don't know the sixth sense which tells you that the man behind the counter, the boy who sells you a newspaper at the corner, has sized you up; the fact that even such a momentary relationship is qualified. You don't know the constant sense of inferiority. Before even the most inferior of your race, before anyone who really belongs. . . . One's gratitude if a bus-conductor, a waiter, a navvy, seem to accept one naturally.'

'You don't feel that in the company of cultivated people.'

'People who say that their best friends are Jews?' He gave a sad, wry smile. 'That's another thing,' he said. 'You've never had the experience of warning people who seemed about to become friendly with you that you were Jewish: warning them in time, so that they could, if necessary, withdraw their overtures of friendship without too much difficulty or embarrassment.'

Catherine was silent.

Alec said, staring before him, 'You've never had the experience of hearing your own race casually vilified; and allowing the remark to pass . . . smiling even. . . . Degraded, again and again, not by the insult, but by your own reaction to it.'

Catherine did not know what to say. She made an effort. 'Oh, but it *isn't* as bad as all that, Alec. . . . As I said before – this is England.'

He looked at her. 'Yes. The concentration camp is only *spiritual*, here.'

Catherine rose. She went towards him, as he stood there, and took both his hands: forcing him to look at her. 'Alec,' she said, 'don't be offended at what I'm going to say. Are you sure that the concentration camp isn't something subjective – that it doesn't exist largely in your own mind?'

He said incredulously: 'Good Lord, do you think we *want* to be in it? That it's a sort of masochist's pleasure-resort? . . .' He controlled himself. 'No,' he said bitterly, 'it's circumstance that has made us what we are. Not our own choice.'

'You don't have to accept circumstance,' she said. Her hands were still tightly locked in his.

'I don't accept it. My life is one long struggle to overcome it. To prove that it can be overcome.'

'What do you want, then, Alec?' she asked.

'I want a chance to be *allowed* to be normal. To be *allowed* to be as other men.'

'But, my darling,' she said softly, 'to me you are as other men. More than other men, perhaps. You diminish yourself by insisting on this difference.'

He gripped her hands more fiercely. 'Oh, Catherine, I wish you loved me. That would make all the difference. That would make me whole. I'd belong then: like the others. I wouldn't be outside, any more, if I only had that.' His face was entirely altered: all that was trivial and sensual seemed to have faded from it; leaving it like a mask that expressed, not individual anguish, but an impersonal sorrow, inbred through generations.

She went very white. Her hands were still imprisoned in his. She made no effort to withdraw from him: resist that

claim. The situation was stronger than her: it was as if she were compelled to play her part in it. She heard herself say, 'How do you know that I don't love you, Alec?' And, having spoken the words, she became aware of an exquisite sense of irresponsibility; of gladness: some deep tension released at last in this, her first surrender. Doubt vanished in that new emotion: in the answering emotion she saw in his face. 'Catherine!' She saw his exalted look: she was unaware that tears glittered in her own eyes. They stood there, holding each others' hands: like two creatures suddenly and miraculously freed of barriers: sharing a brief, a unique moment in which they discovered themselves united in an unbelievable and healing simplicity.

CHAPTER SEVEN

OFF THE SET

Green lights over the studio doors changed to red. RECORDING: KEEP OUT. Within, the unit were grouped about the brightly lit set. One of the sun-arcs sizzled and spat in a last minute adjustment. Rudi Schlesinger glanced at the foreman electrician; and received a nod. He murmured, 'All right, now, Alec.'

'Okay for sound?'

From a booth at the side of the set, 'We're ready, Sir.'

Wilson, the first assistant, shouting, 'All right. Settle down for a take. Hold your hammering at the back.'

A bell rang warningly.

'Everybody quiet! Dead quiet, please!'

'All right – turn 'em over, Steve.'

An intense concentrated silence fell upon them all like a trance. The clapper boy dodged neatly out of the way. Under the ear of the microphone, Hetty Follet spoke, with a surprising air of conviction, the words which she had been repeating on and off, without variation, the entire morning. *'I tell you I've*

never seen that letter! I know nothing about it, I tell you. Now leave me alone, can't you, leave me alone!' Her silver hair was wrought into a myriad of curls: her face masked in a tawny-golden make-up that erased all flaws of skin. Long artificial lashes starred her eyes.

'Aw come to, sister: quit stalling. Hand it over.' This was Drew Fosters, the American actor: feeding Hetty her lines: himself not being filmed at the moment.

'I know nothing about it, I tell you! Can't you get that into your head? I've never seen it – I didn't know there was a letter!' Hetty's restrained hysteria: infinitely competent; and infinitely unconvincing.

Alec suddenly intervened. 'Cut it! No good.' He stood up. Instantly the scene broke up. People on the set and about it, assistant directors, hairdressers, prop men, came to life again. Somewhere at the back, the heavy hammering was resumed. Alec and Rudi Schlesinger went into conference. Hetty came off the set indifferently; and, finding her chair under some disused props, sat down and continued filing her nails. Drew Fosters returned to his absorbed perusal of the script girl's *Daily Mirror*.

Alec, having explained what it was he wanted, came off the set: leaving Rudi and the lighting-expert despairingly scratching their heads. He pushed open heavy padded doors and went through into his office to have a smoke. The real world, noisy and drab, burst about him again. He sighed with relief: free of the desiccated and timeless atmosphere that prevailed on the other side of the padded doors. . . . He scratched a match and, gratefully, inhaled cigarette smoke

into his jaded lungs. Through the open window, he could see Oxshott spread out, gentle under the morning sunshine: people going about their daily business. Occupied with life; not with plaster props and make-believe emotion: with reality, and not with this peculiar child-on-the-floor-with-his-box-of-bricks business of simulating reality.

When his cigarette was reduced to a stub, he returned to the set and found Rudi, Steve and the sound-men who had now become involved, still hard at it. He groaned inwardly. There were times when he found the whole film-medium intolerably unwieldy and cumbersome. Rudi glanced at him: he saw his kind mild eyes behind the thick glasses. 'Won't be long now, Alec.'

'All right. But step on it.' He tapped the face of his wrist-watch. It was a Wednesday, which meant they had to finish early: both stars had matinées in the West End. He dropped into his chair. A few yards away, Hetty sat, studiously intent. He would have liked to have gone over to her and spoken a few casual words: but he knew that she would not welcome, now, this simulacrum of an intimacy which no longer existed. Strange, he thought, how little physical intimacy means in the end: looking now at Hetty he felt a complete stranger to her: found it hard to re-create the idea of her body in his arms. The thought, even, seemed impossible; emptied of all its former content. How little, he thought, one is bound to a person with whom one has merely slept. Whereas an emotional attachment. . . .

There was a call for 'Edna!' Hetty's stand-in appeared, to take her place on the set. She was wearing clothes that were an approximate and cheap reproduction of Hetty's: she was approximately Hetty's height and colouring. She stood obediently on the set, while men in shirt sleeves shifted her indifferently here and there and the focus-puller measured with a tape the distance of her face from the camera. Alec found himself wondering why she was prepared to accept this rôle of dummy, this amoral reduction in her status as a human being. He was always, despite years of familiarity, curious about the mentality of that strange population known as 'extras'. There were about twenty of them, now, lounging at the back of the set. Browny-yellow make-up on every face; eyes bright, lips reddened. Heads of silver, platinum, henna. Eyebrows ruled in at perverse angles: teeth which had been artificially faced for whiteness; faces, breasts, surgically remodelled. They talked desultorily among themselves (always of the bits they had played or just missed the chance of playing) but they never seemed inclined to eye each other with interest, attraction: they never flirted, these beautiful young creatures, these broad-shouldered young men. They were curiously dead to each other: insulated each by his private and consuming ambition.

Alec observed them idly. Why, he wondered, had they left circumstances in which they had an individual meaning, a personal rôle, to endure this glaring anonymity? To live in this horrible limbo lost to their own real identity? (But I forget, he thought, the compensation; that other reality: the fact that in the personal drama of the very humblest, everybody else, even kings and queens, figure merely as extras. . . .)

'All ready to go, Sir.' Deferential third assistant. He roused himself: came forward and resumed his canvas seat under the camera. Hetty was back in her place: the scene re-composed. They were waiting for him. He spoke to Hetty: trying to explain what he wanted of her. She nodded rapidly. 'I know – yes, I know what you mean.' Hetty had both the merits and the drawbacks of her long experience: she was quick at picking up the inflection required of her – too quick: too ready, in response, to trot out one or other of the stereotyped set of tricks, emotions. 'All right,' Alec said at last. He knew he was wasting his time. He was perfectly conscious of her faint implacable resistance.

Green lights outside the doors changed to red. RECORDING: KEEP OUT.

'Quiet, please. Everybody quiet!'

'All set, Bill?'

'Okay for sound.'

'Quiet now, please! Quiet! We're shooting.'

'Ready, Alec.'

'Right! Roll 'em, Steve.'

Brian, Drew Fosters and Alec stood waiting in the courtyard for the car to be driven round. It was a mid-summer day: a stilly heat was abroad. Out on the common, the scorched bracken curled, dry as ash: occasionally a bird dipped through the blue, wings pulsing, swart tail outspread. The grey factory-like walls of British-Alliance looked strangely bleached, impalpable: its futuristic Mercury squat above their heads as they stood there. Carpenters and electricians streamed across the yard on their way to the canteen; shirt-sleeved: the extras, bound in similar manner to their own feeding-place, with tissue-paper tucked under their chins to protect their clothes from make-up, screened their faces from the devastating reality of the sun. Brian stood, face a-grin against the brightness. His upper lip, his forehead gleamed. 'Phew,' he said. 'What a scorcher.'

'And I've got to wear a fur-lined overcoat in Act II,' said Drew Fosters.

'So you've already informed us.'

The car, its dark surfaces flashing back the sunlight, came gliding up to them. Wragg, Alec's chauffeur, opened the door. He looked at Alec. 'Drop Mr Fosters and Mr McKay at the Criterion, first,' Alec told him.

They climbed in: Brian straddled on the flip-up seat in front of them. The yard, the big portals of British-Alliance receded from them: old Saunders, at the gate, conscientiously wagging his forefinger to his right temple. A light breeze fluttered in through the window: bland and soft. Drew took his hat off and smoothed his forehead with his palm. He was always, like the characters he portrayed, immaculately dressed: charming, with that peculiar type of charm which makes it so easy to approach a man in the first instance and so hard to feel that one has made any real headway with him in parting. It was not known that he took an interest in women.

A countryside, so familiar to all of them that its every aspect had become routine, went by on either side: they saw the full-rigged summer trees becalmed against a doldrum sky: the fields of grass, shabby from the heat. Alec, conscious of

Brian's knees before his own and displeased with that proximity, moved slightly. As he did so, he recalled for his own benefit the fact that Catherine often said to him, 'I can't think why you remain so thick with Brian when you really dislike him.' But in the long history of his relationship with Brian McKay, he reflected, that dislike, which he never denied, had become a curiously irrelevant factor. In no fundamental way did it affect that relationship. The fact that he had known Brian more than fifteen years, that they had roots in a mutual past, rendered him necessary; likable or not. He had acquired value as a prop, an essential part of one's environment: which accounted for the fact that, although Alec could discuss his faults in detail with Catherine, he discussed them dispassionately and without any real desire to see them remedied, as one might some long-standing anomalies in the British Constitution. The truth was that, having known each other since youth, they had now reached a stage in which they regarded each other's merits and demerits, successes and setbacks, with the jaundiced and tolerant eye of what was virtually family feeling.

The car rounded a corner: they all swayed in the one direction. Brian grasped the grey padded strap. He was looking across at Alec. 'How's Catherine?' he asked.

'Very well,' Alec said. He added nothing to that brief reply. Alec's marriage had set up between him and Brian, as, to a lesser degree, it had between him and all his unmarried friends, a new and ticklish sort of barrier. The difference that separates the initiate from the non-initiate. Alec now belonged to an order: he had taken the marriage vows: Brian

remained of the world, the laity. . . . The difference in status produced its slight inevitable strain. This was evident with Brian in the way in which he laboriously suppressed the names of women whom he supposed Alec to have been intimate with: as a layman might guard his tongue against casual blasphemy in the presence of one newly ordained. At the same time, he was full of curiosity, of unspoken questions; and much put out in this regard to encounter in Alec the impenetrable modesty of the married man. He had not yet recovered from his surprise that Alec, whom he regarded as a confirmed bachelor, should have foresworn this state so unexpectedly. The news had had a surprising effect upon him. As always, the discovery that any two of his acquaintances considered themselves in love depressed him unreasonably. To a man of his mentality, it meant at once something from which he was excluded; an emotional world created by two people in which he himself counted for nothing. It was for this reason that, as somebody once said of him, he seemed to take the news of his friends' engagements and marriages as a series of personal affronts.

Drew turned his costly profile away from the window. 'Are you coming to lunch with Brian and me?' he asked Alec.

'That's right,' said Brian. 'Share a lettuce and a beaker of iced water with us.'

'Sorry.' Alec shook his head. 'I'm lunching at home to-day.'

'Oh, yes,' said Drew: he looked at Alec with his fine blue eyes in which the lower lid sagged too much, giving a certain laxity to an otherwise perfect face; 'You've moved into a house, haven't you? Where is it?'

'Addison Road,' Alec answered.

'*Très* upper-middle-class,' said Brian.

'I don't know the district,' Drew said. 'Is it a nice house?'

'We like it.'

Brian grinned. 'You know the sort of thing,' he said to Drew. 'Detached. Newly painted. Tiled bathroom; tasteful W.C. Wood-block floors, antiques. Trim parlourmaid. . . . Ultra-respectable, like Alec himself.' He waved his hand. 'Look at him,' he said. 'Britain's most highly-paid film director. Success written all over him. We don't hear so much, these days, about justice and social equality. His emotional arteries have begun to harden. Symptom of an enlarged bank balance.'

Alec was faintly annoyed.

'He's even got fat,' Brian went on. 'Have you noticed? He's lost that lean and hungry look. He sleeps o' nights.'

'Don't you?'

Brian ignored him. 'Seriously, Alexander,' he said, 'you're putting on weight.'

'The pot-belly calling the kettle black,' Alec said suavely.

Brian had, in fact, become of late very stout. That air of shabbiness, bagginess, so characteristic of him, was markedly accentuated. In spite of the fact that he was now a comparatively wealthy man, he still looked curiously down-at-heel: as if some obscure moral bankruptcy had to work its way with him and come to the surface, whatever disguise he wore. His black wiry hair was vividly streaked with grey: he appeared far older than his years. But to Alec, he was still the Brian McKay of Lewisham days, the tousled, slouching undergraduate: and these progressive changes in him he scarcely noticed; or

noticed them with superficial interest, as he might some new and eccentric suit of clothes that Brian had chosen to wear. The essence of a person, he was beginning to find, remained irreductible, absolute; the changes that time effected in physique being astonishingly irrelevant. He felt indebted to Brian, if only for the reason that his existence demonstrated so conclusively this fact, that the paunchiness, the wrinkles, the greyness, were a sign, not of time's victory, but of its impotence.

Before him was the beautiful pale blue door: flanked on each side by yew-trees in pale blue tubs. His latchkey gripped the lock and the door swung inwards before him. He stepped in: and at once the smell of home, indefinable but positive, entered his being: that atmosphere natural to his own existence which every animal recognizes in its own lair. . . . The hall was before him: the cream panelling, the old flower prints, the pale rose carpet. On the hall table, in a low wicker basket, were massed small flowering plants from the garden. He stopped here, putting down his hat and gloves; flicking through the letters on the tray. On the telephone pad he saw Nancy's laborious even handwriting. *Mr Nicolls 'phone for Madam, he says no message*. Basil; what did he want? . . . He put down the pad. Through the half-open door on his right, he could see the dining-room, with the table laid for two: the gleaming walnut, fringed rose-coloured mats, smoky Scandinavian glass. A remote clink of china came from the basement. As he stood there, breathing in the piney fragrance of furniture polish, that aroma of orderliness, he had a moment of still, private joy: he loved this sense of the house spread out and ready for him: the smell, at this hour of the day, of open windows, of clean curtains softly billowing; a house renewed and tranquil.

At the far end of the hall, there was a glass door. Pushing this open, he stepped out on to a little wrought-iron balcony, which had a flight of steps leading down into the garden. The brilliant sunshine greeted him: the sweet warm smell of grass, like a waft of happiness. All along the wall, rhododendrons were hung, as for a carnival, with flowers large as lanterns. Roses were blooming everywhere: the delicate yellow sort that Catherine especially preferred: the branches seemed to spray forth like the streams of a fountain, spilling the savour, the radiance they had drawn up from the bountiful earth. He looked down. On the lawn at the end of the garden he saw cushions, newspapers: and Catherine lying flat on her stomach, her chin cupped in her hands, eyes downcast, reading.

She did not hear his footsteps across the grass. She was reading the film page of the daily newspaper. Lightly he smacked a sparse, shapely bottom. She rolled over: furious. Then smiled up at him: 'Alec! I never heard you.' He dropped down beside her. 'Move up – give us some room,' he said. The newspaper crackled as he leant on it. He put his arm round her neck and drew her head towards him: kissing her pale warm cheek. 'Hullo,' he said.

'Hullo!' She gave him her characteristic smile of reserved, almost reluctant, tenderness.

'Home is the hunter,' he said, 'home from the hill.'

She thought of something and looked at her watch. 'Why

you're early,' she exclaimed. 'And I told them lunch at half-past.'

Forcefully, he put his hand on her wrist, covering the watch. 'Pleased to see me?' Like a little boy begging for sweets, he thought.

'Of course.'

'Then why the hell don't you say so?'

'I am pleased, you fool,' she said.

He turned suddenly, sighing deeply in content, and laid himself flat out on the earth, his hands clasped behind his head. As he stared up at unlimited blue, he had a sense of freedom, of being released, along the wings of his own vision, into that insubstantial vastness. 'Gosh – what a heavenly day!'

She was looking down at him. In the sunlight her face was pale, her hair brilliant. Seen from this angle, her eyes looked like slits; gleaming down seriously upon him. 'Alec,' she said, 'I sometimes think you look a little like Eddie Cantor.'

He did not stir. 'Oh?' he said indifferently. 'It was Harpo Marx last week.'

'That was in your bath.'

He put out his hand and tried to pull her down beside him. She resisted. 'No, Alec. They can see us from the window.' He gave up the attempt: instead he put his hand on her leg: he moved it: and encountered the coolness of her thigh.

'Alec! There's a time and a place for everything.'

'True,' he said dreamily. . . .

She pulled herself away from him, a little sharply.

He opened one eye and squinted up at her. She was sitting back on her haunches, very upright. Lazily, he admired, from a new angle, the way her neck went up, straight and clean from her shoulders: the assurance in that line, in the poise it gave her head. He admired this assurance, this definition about her: even when it expressed itself, as it sometimes did, in a certain abruptness; an unexpected sharpness. To him, who was so bound inwardly to his complex of sensibilities, there was something admirable about a being not thus inhibited. Insensitiveness was sometimes a hall-mark of superiority. People of a certain breeding, assured in their position, have no need of such refinements: they have their roots: they have simplicity, wholeness. . . .

He murmured, 'I like you in that dress. It suits you.' It was a striped silk washing frock, rainbow-coloured, very simple, perfectly cut. The narrow belt about her waist accentuated the litheness, hare-like quickness of her body.

'What, this old thing?' she said dubiously. Then she shrugged her shoulders. 'Oh, well,' she said. 'I know I can't compete with your Glamour Girls.'

'You don't have to.'

'No? Don't imagine I accept the job of being a film-director's wife with an easy mind. It's no sinecure.'

'You'll always be a sinecure with me.'

'Oh, thank you, darling.' She plucked up grass by the roots and showered it methodically over his face. 'You have hair growing in your nostrils,' she remarked.

He rolled over on to his right arm, to watch her. 'Well,' he said, 'tell me. What have you been doing with yourself since this morning?'

'Nothing,' she said. 'I bought some oilskin curtains for the bathroom.'

'Anything else?' He waited to hear if she would mention to him that Basil had telephoned her. But she said nothing. A slight uneasiness took him. Why did she avoid that topic? . . . He had a sudden memory of Basil, as he had looked that morning at the Marylebone registry office: unexpectedly smart, dandified almost, with a flower in his button-hole: and on his face, all the while, a curious faint smile, as though he were aware of some joke implicit in the situation. . . . They rarely saw him nowadays. He had visited them once for dinner: bland and ambiguous, very amiable: but Alec noticed that throughout the evening brother and sister avoided each other's eye. . . . He sensed very well that Catherine was uneasy when the three of them were together: that she was altered, not at her best; that she was actually unhappy, even, since, in the effort to hold the balance between them, she could be true neither to Alec's conception of her, nor to Basil's. She was, too, on the defensive the whole while: anxious to protect each from the other's implicit criticism. As a result, she appeared aloof, almost hostile: for she could not give a look of private understanding on the one side without instantly feeling that she betrayed the other. In many ways, this was only natural: it was difficult enough, Alec realized, to effect these adjustments in ordinary marriage, but when, into the bargain, the brothers-in-law were not only of different blood but of different race. . . . Catherine had chosen to ignore this frontier for the sake of a man who loved her: it was too much to expect that Basil should make the same effort. . . . The best he could hope for from Basil was quiescence. He thought again of that 'phone message, the import of which Catherine had withheld from him; and he wondered fleetingly whether he was getting even that. . . .

A white oblong lying on the grass attracted his attention. He reached out for it. It was Catherine's sketchbook. 'Hullo, been working?' he asked.

'Trying to,' she said. He turned over the pages: it was mostly old stuff: sketches of arms, hands, casual profiles, nudes sitting, spine askew, upon their flattened buttocks. He saw that she had begun a charcoal sketch of the back of the house, with its pale walls and tall blank windows. 'That's rather nice,' he said, relieved to discover that he really thought so. 'Why don't you finish it?'

'Too lazy,' she said. She sighed; and then suddenly reached out and took the book away from him. When they first moved into this house in Addison Road, Catherine had made a great point of setting apart what was to be her studio: a square room built on to the side of the house, with a glazed roof and large sliding windows. Here, with her easel and her clay heads, her grotesque colony of cacti lining the windows, her canvases and her bric-à-brac, she had tried to recreate something of the atmosphere of her former studio. Alec suspected that her intention in this was to stake out a claim, at the outset, to her own independence: a suspicion that was confirmed when she said to him one day (it was shortly before their marriage) 'I hate the sloppy way that people, when they marry, think that they've got to "merge," don't you? – all that unpleasant "one flesh" idea. It's so dull for one thing. Do let's try and remain what we are and not turn into Siamese Twins, one waddling obediently in the direction the other wants the whole party to go.' Alec, as is usual at such a juncture, had agreed. As with all modern young couples, in fact, on the eve of marriage, like two countries on the verge of war, they made elaborate

non-intervention treaties: they solemnly guaranteed each other's independence and their own neutrality in the event of a third party's claims. . . . Curious, thought Alec, once you were actually married, how superfluous all these precautions seemed. Catherine's studio, that sanctum of Pure Art, that symbol of her selfness, her integrity, which marriage was not to alter or undermine, became gradually littered up with White Sale catalogues, clippings of furnishing fabrics, tradesmen's books and bills: and the canvases, Alec noticed, seemed to lean week after week, neglected, against the walls. . . .

There was a sudden stillness abroad. The sense of solitude that reigns when most of the world has retired indoors for a meal. Catherine experienced it; she turned her wrist to look at her watch and her eyebrows contracted. 'Whatever can Mary be up to? It's not like her to be late.' Catherine hated unpunctuality. She had what amounted to a nervous aversion to disorder. She demanded scrupulous punctuality on the part of anyone in her employment. Punctuality and a corresponding efficiency. The it-came-to-pieces-in-me-hand school of maids found short shrift at Addison Road. Catherine was a realist in the routines she worked out for her household: an idealist in that she demanded that there be no 'accidents.' She permitted neither the encroachment of intimacy nor 'fluffing' over duties. Oddly enough, she got good service by this: even devotion: it seemed that she was actually respected for her intolerance. Alec, who was always secretly ashamed of being waited on and compensated for his own sense of guilt by a sporadic lavishness, had occasion at times to urge Catherine to be more indulgent: more 'human' as he called it. She replied

'My dear Alec, I find it just as grotesque as you do, this system of relying on other people's hands: but since that's the convention, the only way of making it at all tolerable is to keep it as impersonal as possible.' The wealthier you were, Alec once reflected, the greater the degree in which you were able to relapse into the irresponsibility of babyhood: you were dressed, bathed, fed, put into your car as into a pram, the rugs tucked round you: and all you had to do was to fill in your playtime with a variety of quickly-palling toys. . . .

Catherine was restless: her head in the air, she seemed to be sniffing out domestic breakdown: insubordination: sabotage. To prevent her from going in person to ascertain the nature of the delay, Alec heaved himself over and laid his head in her lap. 'Don't,' she said instinctively, then looked embarrassed: she was always afraid that he was about to become demonstrative; and equally afraid that he would discover her fear of this. She touched his dark eyebrow with the tip of her finger and said lightly, 'How you love laying your head in women's laps. I believe you've got a mother-fixation.'

'Haven't we all?' he said. He sighed comfortably. 'We're every one of us trying to hitch our umbilical cords back on to something, whether it's a woman or a philosophy. . . .' He was gazing up at her: at the underneath of her chin, rarely seen, paler than the rest of her, soft as the breast of a bird. There was a constellation of freckles across her forehead: her forearms, he noticed, were scalded from the sun. 'Darling,' he said, 'I have to inform you that you're looking adorably plain.'

'Thank you.' She gave his face a slight push. 'Am I supposed to register pleasure at that?'

'Yes,' he said, 'because you don't ever have to feel that you've got to look your best to please me. I like you just as you are: real.'

'Plain,' she said. 'Penny plain.'

'Well . . . I get so much twopence-coloured in my sort of life – so much gilt and so little ginger bread. . . .'

'Oh, I see.' She interrupted him. 'I'm to be the emetic after an overdose of glamour. The bread-and-butter in your life. In other words, your offer of marriage was not a compliment, but an insult.' She bent down: he felt her mouth sudden and soft on his. 'Confound you,' she said.

He reached out for her hand and held it against his cheek. They said nothing for a moment. Her palm was dry and soft: unemotional. He could smell the familiar fragrance of the soap with which she washed. 'Your hand smells of lavender,' he said.

'Does it?' She spoke absently. 'When I was at school, there was a girl there who used to tell us that if we rubbed the palms of our hands together hard, they would smell of sulphur, like dead bodies.'

'How revolting!' He opened his eyes indignantly.

'Childish prattle, you know.'

'What sort of child were you?' he asked her: still holding her hand to his cheek, as if he were sleeping against it.

'Very average. Lean and stringy and keen on games. What about you?'

'I don't know.' He paused. 'Pretty bloody, I believe. My father certainly thought so. I didn't agree with him in those days; but I'm not so sure now that he wasn't right.'

Catherine laughed. 'I believe I should have liked your

father,' she said. 'From all you tell me about him, he sounds a regular Barrett. My father was perfect, of course, but you could never quarrel with him. He was always reasonable and always in the right. I sometimes think I should have enjoyed a few rip-snorting rows.'

'Oh, no, you wouldn't.'

'No, but I mean it,' she persisted. 'I've often thought that Basil and I had it too easy. We got *too* much care and understanding. If there had been a few more obstacles, perhaps we'd have gone further – Basil, anyway.'

'All right,' he said. 'If we have children we'll persecute them once a week, just to develop their talents.'

Long awaited, the low humming of the gong could be heard from the house. 'At last,' Catherine said. She withdrew her knees. Displaced, Alec sat for a moment, gazing up at the sky. 'What a glorious day,' he said. 'What shall we do this afternoon?'

Catherine laughed.

. . . The quilt had fallen to the floor. Under his head were Catherine's peach-coloured pillows. He opened his eyes a fraction: he could see the painted ceiling: and sunlight blooming within the long muslin curtains. As he lay there, his left arm under her neck, his right about her waist, they were so close as to be almost unaware of each other: they lay, drowsy; not sleeping, not wholly awake; sharing the peculiar, the indescribable sensation of a common identity.

Alec stirred: and as though the movement were her own, she adjusted to it without breaking the sameness between

them. There was an indeterminate silence. . . . Alec said presently, 'You know, I hate to admit it, but there's *something* in all that Lawrence stuff. Not a lot. But something. . . .'

Catherine said in a remote voice, 'I think it's a lot of waffle.'

'I expect it is, really.'

. . . He shut his eyes again, contentedly. Lapsed back. Finding again that amorphousness: the exquisite diffusion of thought and senses. After a while, Catherine began to slide her hand softly up and down his bare back. 'Read any good books lately?' she quoted. She laughed; and he felt the warmth of her breath against his shoulder.

'Can you breathe down there?' he asked.

'Only just. Mind: I'm coming up for air.' She sat up, within the circle of his arm and pushed her hair off her brow. Her arms were a different colour to the rest of her body: her breast-bone had a weathered look. 'That's what comes of sun-bathing in bits,' she said. 'Lord, don't I look awful.'

'Like a patchwork quilt,' he said.

She stretched, arms rigid, as if tugging the creases of sleep out of her muscles. 'I wonder what the time is,' she said. He looked at the watch incongruously strapped to his wrist: 'Twenty past four.'

'Heavens! Let me out of that clinch a moment.' She swung her legs over the side of the bed and thrust her thin feet into mules. Reaching out, she put on a velvet gown with trailing sleeves. She went over to her dressing-table and examined her face. 'My goodness!' she said. 'I wish you'd shave before you come to bed.' She sat down on the silk buttoned stool. In the baroque gilt mirror, she had a glimpse of him, behind her, on the bed: his arms linked under his head, lazily surveying her. Familiar face upon the less familiar body. He was matt and dark-skinned, and in design, his body had that sort of simplicity which was for her both essentially male and essentially unlike her own disparate untidy female entity. She began to powder her face: putting on the stuff with a big lambskin puff: lifting her head to pat it under her jaw.

'Catherine,' Alec said. 'Are you happy?'

She stopped powdering for a moment. Then went back to it with a slight laugh. 'Alec,' she said, 'do you really think it's necessary to ask me that question – right out of the blue like that?'

'Why not?'

'Well, it's so – . You're like a man who sees someone cycling along a road and knocks him off the bike to ask him if he knows how to ride.'

'Don't follow that.' He abandoned his supine attitude and sat up, absently scratching. 'Are you?' he persisted.

She coloured. 'Yes. Are you?'

'Very,' he said simply.

She looked down, embarrassed with pleasure. To her own surprise, her eyes suddenly suffused. She felt deeply, astonishingly tender towards Alec because of this fact that she was able to bring him happiness. He had given her that; rehabilitated her: in a few months, all the unhappy sterile years were forgotten: here in this house, with its beauty, its warmth, in the atmosphere of his appreciation, his sensitive persistent appreciation, which so favourably revealed her to herself, she often found herself thinking, 'It is as though I were at home again,' and the thought would strike her again during one or other of those interminable and entrancing discussions which had already become quite a feature of their married lives and which resembled so closely those she used to hold with her father in the far-off magic days. . . . Thinking of this, she was silent: the puff still in her hand. Then, because she was always reluctant to dwell upon an emotional moment, perhaps because she feared that it would lose its value if prolonged, or that she herself, as too often happened, would somehow mismanage it, she exclaimed with unnecessary brusqueness (she was curiously unable to modulate her reactions and knew that Alec was often taken aback by this) 'Okay. We've checked up on each other for the time being. Now don't you think you ought to go and make yourself respectable?'

'What for?' he said.

'Tea.'

'Oh, yes. Tea.' He did not move. 'I'm admiring my manly figure in the glass,' he said. He was.

'You're too fat,' she told him.

He was hurt: and pulled in his stomach muscles; squared his shoulders.

She began to pull on tailored satin cami-knickers: wriggling her shoulders to adjust the strap over each in turn. 'Oh, I forgot to tell you,' she said. 'A friend of mine sent me tickets for a show to-night. Would you care to go?'

'And who's this "friend of yours?"' he said.

'Never mind the laboured tone, dearie. It's only Venitia. For that thing at the Criterion.'

He looked up. 'Oh, Drew's play. I've been wanting to see that. Let's go.' He reached down for his slippers and began to put them on. There was a new energy in his movements. Very often, after they had been intensely immersed in each other like this, they found it expedient to turn their interest on to something outside themselves: so that they seized on such an opportunity as this with an unconcealed relief which nowise betrayed that which was between them, since everything that they saw, that their minds and senses could gather from outside sources, all went, ultimately, to enrich their own intercourse when they found themselves alone once more.

She drew her frock over her head and meticulously pulled the belt to about her waist. Alec, his dressing-gown suspended from his shoulders, went past her into the bathroom. As she sat down to comb her hair, to kick off her mules and stick her feet into suede court shoes, she could hear him moving about in there. Presently, he began to whistle an old dance tune.

'So you met someone who set you back on your heels,
    goody-goody.
So you met someone and now know how it feels,
    goody-goody.
Hurrah and hallelujah, you had it coming to ya,
Goody-goody for him, goody-goody for me
And I hope you're satisfied, you rascal you!'

CHAPTER EIGHT

PICCADILLY CIRCUS

There was one other person, besides Brian McKay, with whom Alec had consistently kept in touch since the already remote Lewisham days. This was Louis Solomon. Lew, as he was still known, had years since given up any interest in the film business and was comfortably, and to all appearances, quite happily, established as a partner in his father's tailoring firm. The Solomons were prosperous, in a mild sort of way: they still lived in the same house in Brondesbury Villas Road to which Lew had first taken Alec in their apprentice days. Lew was the only son: he had four, or was it five, dark good-looking sisters, all married, and all residing among their rising families in various provincial towns in England. Lew himself had not married: he remained, very typically, the son at home: whenever Alec visited him, there he was, in the same old shabby sitting-room, lounging comfortably in his slippers, cigarette-ash lodged in the folds of his waistcoat; turning off the wireless as Alec came in, or slipping a marker into the pages of his detective novel. 'Hullo: how're you?' He would rise to his feet, with the inelegant shambling gait, which was a

product more of apathy than of actual diffidence: greeting Alec casually, without bothering to shake hands. If Alec had changed in appearance very little since the old days, in Lew there was a perceptible alteration. His scalp had begun to gleam through his top hair. His suits were no longer conspicuously accurate in cut, nor were his shoes waspish and yellow: on the contrary: with the turn of the years, that old foppishness completely vanished, he exhibited an increasing tendency to retain his old clothes; an aversion to adopting, himself, the innovations in style which his firm propounded: he began to appear month in, month out, in the same suit, glossy of cuff, degenerate of pocket: a suit, as it were, subdued, trodden down by the routine of his own personality. Always a good son to his parents, he had remained just that: he was still the dutiful son in the home and perfectly comfortable in the unaltered family atmosphere; in the unaltered affection of his ageing parents. Perhaps because he was assured of that affection, because the triangular relationship was so serene and natural, he had never had any impulse to marry: indeed, he resented the intrusion of eligible young women whom his sisters, from time to time, in the hope of arousing his interest, introduced into the home. He was not really happy until, the unfamiliar presence removed, the slam of the front door proclaimed the restoration of the *status quo*. Jealously, he guarded the sameness of his existence: as though he suspected that the outside world, whatever its lure, could never offer him in exchange anything to approach that safety and comfort. . . .

Unaltered throughout the years, he had retained for Alec Berman a genuine, if singularly undemonstrative affection.

He regarded Alec's successes without the remotest trace of either malice or envy: indeed, in the partnership of their friendship, he seemed content that it should be Alec who won all the laurels: he himself sitting back and, in the ease of obscurity, taking a paternal and vicarious enjoyment out of Alec's efforts. Very often, months would elapse before they actually met. Lew had an exaggerated opinion of the brilliance of Alec's social circle. Too modest to impinge upon such grandeurs, he never presumed to 'phone Alec, or to initiate a meeting himself. He was content to wait until the move came from Alec. As it eventually always did. If Alec was at a loose end, or feeling a little depressed and not wishing to go anywhere where he need pretend to be other than himself, he would find himself, sooner or later, reaching out for the 'phone and beginning to dial the Solomons' number. . . .

Naturally, Lew and his parents (who, sharing their son's pride in their distinguished friend, had, like him, taken out emotional shares in Alec's success) expected a 'brilliant' match, when Alec eventually married: an internationally celebrated actress, or some lovely and highly-connected débutante. But it was obviously not on that account that there ensued such an awkward silence when Alec announced to them his intention of marrying Catherine Nicolls. It was in the quality of that silence that Alec was first able to gauge the feeling that in the average Jew is aroused by the thought of a mixed marriage. . . . He knew that they were inexpressibly shocked. Lew, no less than his parents. He had never been embarrassed before Alec; but he was embarrassed now. Alec felt the brunt of an instinctive, unreasoning prejudice. What he

proposed to do was, in Lew's eyes, nothing short of perverse. Natural and inevitable as it seemed to him and Catherine, so in equal measure did it appear unnatural and unnecessary to this man who was (Alec recognized the fact) his best, his only friend. Confronted by this diversity of outlook, for the first time Alec found himself experiencing a sudden violent irritation with Lew: how should he, who had never been able to cut away from the emotional apron-strings of his own family, presume to judge someone who had graduated from such an infantile level and sought out an adult love? The anticipation of criticism always made Alec fiercely resentful, and he opened his mouth to say something sharp: then checked himself abruptly. What was the use? There is no reasoning away the unreasonable. The best thing was not to discuss it at all. He saw that Lew himself had come to the same conclusion. And on that basis, which involved the tacit avoidance of the dangerous topic, their friendship was resumed. It had pained Alec at first, this necessity for silence: but he saw that there was no other way for it. Possibly there were friends of Catherine, he thought, with whom she had been forced to make the same adjustment: and without telling him: as he in turn would refrain from telling her of the rift that had ensued between him and Louis Solomon on her account.

They were to meet at Oxford Circus. Alec, confident, as he always was when his appointment was with Lew, that he would not have to wait long, leaned upon the head of his stick and politely avoided the glances of young women. He watched a tough old man, with a Late Night Final poster aproned at his knees, trying to hawk news which, at this hour, had already wilted. 'Armaments Question in House' said the poster. Another instalment in the unending serial: the penny dreadful of history. *Look out for to-morrow's Dramatic and Blood-curdling Chapter. Will Mankind succumb to the Deadly Poison Gas? Can War be Averted? Do not Miss the Next Great Hair-Raising Instalment!*

Here was Lew. Hat at an angle, sloping along, scanning faces, shop-fronts. He looked like a middle-aged commercial traveller. Alec, as he went forward to greet him, was aware that Lew's company did not do him credit. The fact no longer disturbed him. Alec was older. He sometimes even fancied that he was wiser.

'Well,' said Lew, without preamble, 'where shall we eat – Chinese, as usual?' Alec nodded his assent. Catherine had gone that evening to dine with Venitia, lately embarked on a new love affair that required the exhaustive discussions that they accorded to such matters: Alec had seen her off with the injunction that, concerning these feminine confidences, there was to be no exchange in kind. She laughed: and he knew then that Venitia was already in full possession of the details concerning his marital temperament: a fact which explained, perhaps, the appraising looks she was wont to bestow upon him when they met. . . . They began to walk up Regent Street. There was that mingling of daylight and electricity characteristic of summer in cities. Regent Street was crowded: people going from one lit window to the other, as if visiting exhibits at a show. The shuffling of feet along the pavement went on unceasingly. There was no break in the double stream of cars filing in both directions along the broad curved street. They came towards Piccadilly Circus: and then Lew gripped Alec's arm suddenly. Alec looked at him interrogatively. Without saying anything, Lew, with a jerk of his chin, indicated something a few yards ahead. Alec turned his head. At the kerb, a man with a badge was selling newspapers. Alec recognized the badge; his heart dropped a beat. 'See?' said Lew. 'I see,' Alec said briefly. A state of intent communicativeness existed suddenly between the two of them. They came nearer: and now they could hear the formula that the man was calling out as he tendered a folded paper towards the passers-by: 'Buy the only newspaper not run by Jewish finance! . . . Clear out the Jews! . . . England for the English!'

Lew said without a change of expression, 'How does it sound, Alec?' In some queer way, neither of them was surprised nor even taken aback. It was as if, unconsciously, they had always expected this: been on the look-out for it, distrustful of the long truce. . . . Alec had a sudden, a compelling desire to see the face of this man: an impersonal, declared enemy. He turned to Lew. 'Just a moment.' Without further explanation, he left Lew standing, too startled to remonstrate, had he been inclined to do such a thing. A few steps and he was at the edge of the kerb. He saw the man glance quickly at him. They were face to face. Alec tendered a coin. 'May I have a paper, please?' he said quietly.

The other hesitated. There was a moment in which they looked at each other: in which Alec searched the glance of a man of his own age, with fair, thinning hair and a weather-beaten face: a moment of curious, still intensity in which something passed between them which was almost a recognition: and then Alec, who had wished to look at an enemy and experience the relief of hatred, became aware, instead, of a sudden deep discouragement. . . . This was merely another human being: one like himself: seeking, like himself, like everyone else, a means to live, some sort of personal fulfilment. At the same time, like everyone else, fundamentally insignificant: too full of the small everyday pathos of being merely human (his teeth were broken, the cuffs of his coat frayed) to merit hatred. . . .

The moment passed. Alec held out his coin: silently received a paper in exchange. 'Thank you,' he said. Conscious now of the cynical glances of passers-by, he folded the paper under his arm. He rejoined Lew. Lew looked at him, dark brows inquiringly pursed. 'Come on,' Alec said shortly.

Red traffic signals flashed through amber into green; and they crossed Piccadilly Circus; at this hour already ringed about with eccentric lights. At the entrance to the Chinese Restaurant was a newsvendor with an Extra poster, which proclaimed a new record long-distance flight. They entered; and in the same moment a notice within caught their attention. 'No Japanese Served Here.' Abruptly, Alec laughed. . . . 'What's the use of inventing machines which can bring the farthest countries close together, when this sort of mania keeps them more isolated than they were in the time of Christopher Columbus?' he said. They mounted the marble steps. Emotion checkmating reason, he thought. That's why we progress in circles. Science proposes – man disposes. . . .

On the first floor, they found their favourite table. It was in a corner by the big low windows from which diners, looking directly down on to Piccadilly Circus beneath them, could watch, at their ease, the circling cars, the crowds, the motley orchestrated lights: Eros winged and fanciful, presiding over the rendezvous. The whole thing was like a gigantic stage set; and always fascinated Alec by this exciting approximation to art. He could sit watching it for hours without speaking a word. Unconsciously enjoying that sense of power, of possession, which the artist experiences before that which is to become his material: that sense of pure experience which precedes the travails and disappointments of re-creation and so much transcends it. Alec was perhaps, happiest at such moments: most himself. But to-night, looking at the familiar scene, he knew a sharp uneasiness. Suppose that his material (the streets and characters and shadows of this city which he loved) were denied to him – even his right to appreciate it questioned? That would be exile, suicide in the midst of his own living. Where then should he turn? To what horizons native to him? But palm trees, sand and burning blue were as alien to him who had never known them as they were to anyone in that crowd passing and repassing there below in a security they could not appreciate. He knew only the colours, the accents of this one culture which he had absorbed – to which he was passionately attached – and to which, it seemed, he had no right. . . .

'Wake up,' said Lew. The waiter was standing by their table. Alec listlessly turned the thick pages of the menu. Finally, Lew gave the order for both of them. The waiter departed. The restaurant was crowded already: a warm and spicy smell hung on the air. Every now and then the swing door opened to admit another couple, courteously greeted by the tall formal-looking Chinaman on their way to a table. Alec had not yet unfolded his paper: it lay at his elbow. Lew reached across and took it. He sat studying it, holding it at a distance from his eyes as he always did of late when he read. Then, abruptly, he flung it down on the table. The gesture was violent; but when he spoke his voice was as mild as ever. 'It seems,' he said, 'that they don't like us. . . .'

'No.' Alec's tone was grim. 'Well, we can't do anything about it, either. I've long ago discovered the fact that it's no use trying. No use whatever. Our faults and our virtues inflame them equally.' He broke off, as the waiter leant over them to place a variety of small round dishes on the table: untidily covered, some of them, with a blanket of crispy noodle. Lew muttered something. 'What's that you say?' Alec asked.

'I say be damned to them,' Lew answered. He was eating rice with a spoon and fork. 'Lot of copy-cats. Who thought up this race-purity campaign, anyway? When we were running it, we made quite a respectable thing of it. Look what they turned it into when they got hold of it at last – only about two thousand years behind the times!'

'They plagiarize,' Alec said. 'And we have to bear the brunt of it. First Jesus; and now this. Hoist with our own petard every time.'

Lew served himself liberally. 'Well,' he said, 'nobody wants us and we've nowhere to go. Short of some particularly classy form of Euthanasia I don't see any way out.'

'Oh, they'd never allow that,' Alec said. 'We're too valuable. . . . We make the best persecutees ever . . . absolute *cordon bleu*. And I can quite see the necessity . . . somebody's got to be the whipping boy. Only we've held the post so long, I think it's about time they gave us a Sabbatical holiday. The Aryan world ought to pension us off.'

'Special seats in the park for disabled Ex-Persecutees. Hitler awards Israel the D.S.O.' said Lew through rice and bamboo shoots. He poured ginger beer, grey and soapy-looking into a tall glass.

'The trouble is,' Alec said, 'we're so infernally convenient. Psychologically and politically. The role of the Jew in society is that of a Standard, Guaranteed-to-give-good-results Electric Hare.' He paused then said irrelevantly, 'Hell! I hate tendentiousness . . . in myself as much as in anyone else. . . .'

'Have some more noodle,' Lew said soothingly. But Alec shook his head. He pushed away his untidy-looking plate and picked up the paper that still lay between them. He began to read; then altered his position slightly, putting his hand over his forehead as though screening from the other people in the room an inward shame. Lew opened his mouth to say something, then checked himself. He shrugged his shoulders. Philosophically, he went on eating: mixing the contents of the various dishes upon his plate and liberally spattering the whole with an ink-black sauce from the metal container.

'Lew,' said Alec, 'the Jews are International Mischief-makers. Did you know? . . . Do you number many International Mischief-makers among your friends?'

'No,' said Lew amiably. 'But then I haven't many friends.'

Alec turned a page. He looked up. 'Mr Solomon,' he said in a contained voice, 'are you given to drinking the blood of Christian children?'

'Oh, give it a rest,' Lew said. 'I want to eat my dinner. You spoil my appetite with all that highbrow Aryan stuff.'

'Lew,' said Alec, 'I regret to say that you've deceived me. You've been concealing your real nature from me. You led me to believe that you were a decent average human being. You played on my credulity. Now what do I find?' – he looked closer at the print – 'in reality you're a degenerate, devoid of normal human instincts; a sinister parasite; an effluvium from the ferment of rottenness.'

Lew's eyes swam obliquely towards the bridge of his nose; he waggled his ears. 'Bogey, bogey!' he said: sepulchral. Two women sitting at the next table glanced at each other uneasily.

Alec suddenly put the paper down on the table with an expression of open despair. 'No – but what in Heaven's name *is* all this?' he exclaimed. 'I'm beginning to wonder if I'm on my head or my heels: to doubt myself. Am I what they say? Are you? Which of us is mad – the people who write this, or you and I?'

'That, I take it,' said Lew, 'is a purely rhetorical question.'

Alec was looking out of the window. 'Don't you find that there are moments when it's *intolerable* being a Jew?' he said abruptly. 'All these ridiculous, impossible complications on top of the normal complications of merely being alive. . . .'

Lew shrugged plump shoulders. 'Every now and then,' he said in a disinterested voice, 'some individual takes it into his head to make a remark about my profile. . . .'

'Yes?' – Alec turned to look at him.

'But there aren't any complications,' Lew said. 'Or at least, none that I can't deal with. . . . I simply get up, walk over to where he is standing, measure the distance very scrupulously and spit in his right eye.'

'No, no.' Alec turned away with a gesture of irritation. 'We gain nothing by adopting their methods.'

Lew looked at him in surprise. 'What do you expect me to do then? Turn the other cheek?'

'If you can.'

'Well, I'm afraid I can't,' Lew said, decidedly. 'Not any more. I used to be able to. But not now. Now after what I've seen. . . . I wish nobody any harm but, if a man hits me on one cheek, I consider it my elementary duty to give as good as I got.'

'Yes. That's the easy way out – and it's the wrong way. Because it isn't a way out at all – in the end it puts you back where you started. Violence always breeds more violence.'

'What the hell do you expect me to do then?'

Alec did not answer at once. After a moment he said quietly, 'The meek shall inherit the earth. That's not religion – it's first-class *Real-Politik*.'

'Yeh,' said Lew. 'It is. . . . Six foot four of earth.' They were silent: turning away to watch the crowds on the pavements below. Couples strolling arm-in-arm, or youthfully enlaced: men and women talking, smiling as they passed: hailing taxis, climbing on to buses: moving off to join the queue outside a cinema or find a table at some neighbouring restaurant: intent all of them on their individual relaxation after the day's work. It was hard to believe that potentialities of evil and violence lay beneath that surface of good humour and good manners. 'Why in the name of sense don't we throw up the sponge and go to Palestine,' Lew said suddenly. 'We're mugs to stay on here. Put up with all we have to. . . . I get fed to the teeth with it at times. I see more of it than you do, of course, working down in the East End. . . .'

'Oh, I get it too.' There was a wry look about Alec's mouth. 'I can claim my little share. It's more rarefied perhaps – but all the more invidious for that. One's got a sort of sixth sense by now – always on the alert for attack. Not physical attack: but other things – things that cut away one's self-respect – a smile – a silence. . . .'

Lew cut him short. 'I know. We all know. Do you think there's a Jew outside Palestine who doesn't know? The trouble is, we get acclimatized to it. We accept it – as a cripple accepts his condition and forgets the normal. . . . But just imagine for one moment standing on earth that really belongs to you, being in a position to challenge anybody. Being able to hold up your head. *Belonging*. . . .' He checked himself; and then said in a calmer voice, 'I tell you – we're mugs to stick it here.'

'You forget,' said Alec, 'the fact that there's only an area about a quarter the size of Wales for sixteen million Jews to redeem themselves on. Even spiritually, that's overcrowding. . . . And if you and I were to go there (and I agree that would solve everything for us), it still wouldn't solve anything for all the millions who've got to find their salvation elsewhere. . . . It's them I'm thinking about. Not those who're persecuted even: that's another case. But those like you and me: the fortunate ones. Tolerated; and yet not tolerated. Living in a sort of civilized limbo. . . .'

'If you're not careful,' Lew said, 'we shall find ourselves discussing the Jewish problem.' He turned round and beckoned

to the waiter. 'Check, please,' he said. He pushed back his chair. 'Come along, let's go to a news reel and cheer ourselves up with pictures of high-explosive bombs,' he said. He put the slip of paper between his lips and fumbled about his person for change. 'There's one consolation anyhow,' he said, through the paper: 'the Jews seem to specialize in surviving.' He took the check out of his mouth. 'What is it they say? "The Jews have always stood by the graves of their oppressors."'

'That may be,' Alec said. 'But it's a bloody melancholy occupation!'

CHAPTER NINE

GYNÆCOLOGICAL

The door opened; and she was shown into a wide marble-paved hall. 'Mr Whitstable, please,' she murmured. The butler permitted himself a discreet smile of recognition. 'This way, please,' he said. He opened the door into the stillness of the waiting-room. Two women, thumbing the *Tatler* absently, looked her over with a penetrating and knowledgeable stare. She sat down, at an angle to the polished mahogany table and lost no time in subjecting them in turn to the same scrutiny. The silence resumed; the reserved aware stillness that binds strangers like an intimacy: uneasily they listened to each other turn pages, breathe, or creak on their chairs. The clock on the mantelpiece seemed to click its tongue reprovingly. In covert glances, they gathered data about each other's condition, social and gynæcological: noted the clumsily camouflaged specimen bottles; the ambiguous wrap-over gowns: the incongruously smart hats and sheer silk stockings. There was an obscure sort of jealousy in all this: they resented each other's claim upon the great Mr Whitstable: disliked this reminder that they were not the sole object of his attention. . . . But, thought Catherine, looking at distorted snapshots of people supping at the Café de Paris, or dining, upon leopard-skin, at the El Morocco, surely these others did not share with him that indefinable warmth, that easy understanding that had existed between herself and him from the first moment, and which made her feel that, whatever the number of his other patients, she herself was his *especial* protégée. . . . Or was that merely a mechanism of his: the way in which, with his sensitive patients, he managed to evade the onus of his own popularity?

One of the women had already been summoned; she departed with an air of triumph; the look of a favoured courtesan. Catherine ostentatiously glanced first at her watch, then at the French gilt clock on the wall, and back to her watch again, as if unsure which was deceiving her. She listened to the slam of taxi doors along Harley Street. Stared listlessly at the familiar fresco, associated in her mind always with waiting-rooms, of goblins and fairies interlaced upon the cover of *Punch*. . . .

The door opened. 'Mrs Berman, please,' the butler said. As Catherine rose in response, she was conscious that the other woman looked at her quickly. She was used to this by now: the way that people, on first hearing her married name, would glance her over, puzzled by the apparent discrepancy between the name and her own appearance. . . . She never failed to find this amusing: to see people momentarily at a loss, not knowing, as she put it, which prejudice to stand on. She said to Alec, 'My one regret is that you're not called Finkelstein. You can't imagine the kick I should get out of being introduced as that.' Alec was a little taken aback at this

insouciance of hers; she seemed to take the shadow of discrimination which lightly lay upon her with the greatest of good humour. As though the whole thing were an excellent joke. Perhaps it was.

She followed the butler down the hall: stepping carefully over Persian rugs, each one, she recognized, a priceless specimen, but as treacherous, on that marble floor, as banana skins. He stood aside and opened the door. 'Mrs Berman,' he announced; and withdrew, soundlessly shutting the door behind him. Catherine came forward, across a room that seemed immense, to be received by that cool, firm hand. 'How *are* you, Mrs Berman?' he said; looking as surprised and gratified as if she were paying him an unexpected social call. Mr Whitstable had in a marked degree that peculiar graciousness of manner which eminent obstetricians share with stage ambassadors. Catherine, who came always vowing that she was not going to be taken in by this indiscriminate amiability, yet always found herself succumbing: going under at once, flags flying and all hands on deck: perhaps, she thought, because she really wished to be captivated: longed secretly to believe in this fiction of the omniscient being tirelessly solicitous on her behalf. . . .

She allowed him to lead her to a chair. He presided, behind his beautiful writing table; his inkwells, his case sheets, his Georgian silver; the silver-framed photograph of two little boys in ruffled silk shirts. His sons. . . . He had, of course, a private life. Was he, she wondered, as benign, as omniscient, there: off-stage: or did he on the contrary, divested of black coat and stripes, scowl irritably at the children, bellow at the

servants: even, in glorious reaction, smash things? . . . The disparity between the private, the natural man, and his over-size public figure always fascinated her: the ability of human beings to seem, at times, and particularly in the uniform of their professions, more than human. . . . The giraffe, she had read, owes the configuration of its neck to a constant ambition for the higher leaves on the tree: it thrilled her to be enabled to witness the same process at work in men, for whom the standard of public conduct is always a few inches higher than their own private necks. . . .

Like examiner and candidate in a viva voce they proceeded to the usual syllabus of questions: exercise: nipples: cramp: bismuth. 'Good,' he said each time: 'good.' He had once told her she was a model patient, and she would rather disavow all her symptoms than have him forgo this opinion of her. As she stood up to pass into the examination room, she placed on the edge of his table her awkwardly wrapped parcel. 'Thank you,' he said: politely. . . .

In the small white-painted cubicle, she undressed partially and assumed the required position on a sheeted couch. When she was ready, she pulled the coarse brown blanket over her. After a discreet interval, Mr Whitstable appeared. 'Right,' he said. He folded down the blanket. His glasses gleaming on his pale suave face, he bent over her. 'Relax,' he said. 'Don't hold your breath. Good.' His eyes were intent. 'Been to any shows lately?' he asked.

'Yes,' said Catherine, staring at the wall. 'We saw *Hamlet* last night.'

'Oh – the new production. Was it as good as they say?'

'It never is, is it?'

'I suppose not.' ('Oh!' she interjected involuntarily: 'Sorry,' he said.) 'Still he's a fine actor in spite of his mannerisms. . . . Just lie on your back for a moment, will you?' She turned over. She felt his cold firm fingers knead her stomach. 'Head seems to be down all right,' he said. 'Mind you,' he said, 'I can't say I care much for Shakespeare in the ordinary way. I mean I couldn't go to a "straight" performance. It's got to be gingered up with lights and trick costumes in the modern idiom.' He took, as he spoke, a small instrument and, placing it on the dome of her belly, inclined his ear to the other end. She held her breath: he was searching for the heartbeats of her child: listening-in to the future. . . . 'That's all right,' he said, straightening up. He replaced the blanket. 'You can dress,' he told her.

She found herself once more walking along Harley Street, admiring the impressive front doors, the variety of brass-inscribed names. As always, she had a feeling of relief now that the ordeal was safely over: another milestone passed. . . . The time, she found, went very slowly; but she was aware, as yet, of no impatience: on the contrary: she savoured the distinction of her state: the glances of acute interest from women merely normal in silhouette. . . . The peculiarities of her own silhouette, as viewed in the bathroom mirror at Addison Road, had become with time a source of mild awe to her: her slim legs and thighs unaltered, and then this smooth rotundity; her navel protruding like the butt-end of a lemon. . . .

She crossed Marylebone Road, into Regent's Park. The world was turning green. All along the chestnut avenue, the trees were putting forth young leaves furled up like a chicken's claw. Stone swans spouted water from their beaks. The sweet English grass was mottled with fickle sunshine, with a bank-holiday litter of crocuses. This time last year, she thought, she and Alec were still on their honeymoon: she saw them, on their way to Venice, the pine-covered mountains rising up and falling away, as they sat, knees meeting under the small table, eating rolls and honey and grapes in the restaurant-car of the Simplon-Orient Express. What a lot of things they had not known about each other, then: how different, even looking back, seemed the aspect of the dark stranger smiling at her across a variety of restaurant tables, leaning over and speaking to her against foreign settings, in suits she did not know, to the Alec she knew now; the man become as familiar as a member of her own family, all intimacies, the most exalted as well as the most sordid, explored; all failings, the trivial mannerisms no less than the deeper character flaws, known and accepted in the scheme of a relationship as solid as it was, at this stage, altogether unglamorous.

With her new gait (she felt these days, she told Alec, like a man trundling a wheelbarrow), she walked along beside the lake and paused at the bridge to stare down at the ducks tippling in the mild and shadowy water. At a swan, with a neck like a tulip, gliding past in dreamlike slow motion. . . . This period of growth, of waiting, she thought, was, in the relationship of the two people implicated, something unique: these mysterious months in which a man could love, in the

one person, wife and child without distinction. She herself had never felt so much at one with any being as she did now with Alec: with this man, she reflected, who a little while ago was totally unknown to her. A few years ago, they might have passed each other in the street and never known. And now, through their separate lives, which so arbitrarily had been grafted together in marriage, a common blood was beginning to pulse; partnered, flesh conspiring with flesh, they would never be able to feel that separateness again; they who in this blood-pact had inextricably and finally mingled temperament and personality, race and family. . . . She stared at the lilting water, with its facets of hammered silver. What pattern, she wondered, would finally emerge out of that jig-saw puzzle even now shaping itself, dove-tailing its way into a completion to which both had contributed but which neither could foresee?

A young man, saddled on a light swift boat, shot out from beneath the bridge. She watched his arms and legs straining as he wrestled with the waters: the patina of sweat on his forehead gleaming. Upraised for a moment, his glance sought, not hers, but that of the young girl standing with her companion on the bridge and brooding down into the shifting element which this strange young man so powerfully rode. Watching in turn these slender young girls, their wistful crude faces brushed with the pollen of a cheap and scented powder, Catherine had a sudden sense of her own ponderousness, her maturity. . . . This thought, that she was no longer very young, had the power, of late, to affect her unpleasingly. She saw, in nature, how swiftly the corolla, its work done, withered away

to give place to the fruit: and, since she was always relentlessly honest with herself, she was quite aware that the restlessness, the fretful attempts at coquetry which she, like many women, experienced at this time, was an effort to deny that process; to refute it with new hats, exotic make-up, permanent waves, an accumulation of frilly lingerie for the *accouchement* stage. . . . How cruel this whole process is, she thought: this game in which we are given all the trump cards at the beginning, only to have them one by one inexorably withdrawn again. Until nothing remains. Until one is left *sans* eyes, *sans* teeth, *sans* everything. At least animals suffer the process without awareness, fore-knowledge: but human beings, she thought, have to submit to the cruel and fantastic operations of time in full consciousness, see themselves dismembered, disintegrated, helpless and without an anæsthetic. . . .

She walked away from the bridge. Stared unseeingly at the trees crowned in their green youth. Nothing, thought Catherine, *nothing in the world* compensated for one's own ageing. . . . The key to this passionate refusal of hers to accept age lay in something deep in her nature. Catherine would not accept age because she still wished to think of herself as her father's young and loved daughter. Under that surface of efficiency, of aloofness, she craved, still, the unaltering, undemanding love, the utter sense of protection, which his presence had meant to her and which life everywhere else so uncompromisingly and bleakly denied her. Or had denied her, she thought, until she met Alec Berman. . . . Now, strangely, through him, she seemed to sense something of that old relationship again; to be finding her way back. It was as if she had been given the past again; as if, through some trick, time, which withheld so much from her, had been defeated. She derived a sort of passionate happiness from this illusion. Paradoxically, that which drew her near to Alec, that element which she most cherished in her marriage, was something entirely unconnected with Alec: something not of him, but which he was able to evoke: as if his presence in her life were the lightning conductor which drew down and canalized a dangerous, homeless emotion. It was for this reason that she never tried to explain to Basil the nature of her attachment to Alec: Basil who had always, even in the old days, stood outside the harmony that existed between father and daughter: relinquished his demands upon her then, as he relinquished them now, wordlessly, with an ambiguous smile. . . . She worried a good deal about Basil: always without telling Alec. For she could not betray him, even to Alec. Alec must go on thinking Basil successful, unassailable. Only she knew something of the carefully concealed emptiness in his life: an emptiness which he forbade her, with that bland and yet terrible smile of his, to mention or betray.

Some children came running towards her, calling out in the high mincing voices characteristic of the better-class young. She looked questioningly into their faces. She had never liked children, hitherto: babies she feared and the imperious egotism of older children always roused in her a sort of jealous resentment. On the rare occasions when she encountered the children of other people, she took a small unworthy delight in quashing this juvenile egomania. How, she wondered now, was she going to react to a child of her

own? She could only hope that some blind pride of maternity would descend upon her at the psychological moment, that she would never resent this rival that had squeezed its way, unbidden, into the foreground. . . . Thinking of this, she made once again the passionate wish that it should be a boy. That, for her, would make all the difference, she knew. Not a girl, a daughter: but a boy, a son. Please goodness, it would be a boy. . . . As though disturbed by her thoughts, the child moved in her: gave a plunge, a convulsive wriggle, like a fish caught in a net. When it moved like that, if she quickly put her hand to her side, she could feel distinctly the point of an elbow, a knee; she had the intimation of something that seemed, already, blindly to battle with life. . . . She remembered the first time she had felt the child. Walking across a room, she had stopped dead. Arrested by something never before experienced, out of another dimension. It was as if, at the core of her, a harp string had been tentatively plucked. . . . She would never forget that, she thought. In the as yet unplayed symphony of a human being's life, that first faint pluck of strings; . . . the opening note. . . .

CHAPTER TEN

DINNER FOR FOUR

Alec stood before the big fire, one hand bracketed upon his rump, the other holding up before him a folded copy of the evening paper. On a table near him was an untouched glass of sherry. He drew on the cigarette hanging lax from his mouth, frowning away the rising smoke. Satin curtains had been pulled to across the windows: the room was diffusely lit with fringed ivory lamps. In a square greenish tank, chrysanthemums gave out their earthy fragrance: their petals matted like animal fur in the rain.

The door opened. He raised his head. It was Catherine. He allowed the evening paper, still clasped between his fingers, to drop to his side. 'And very nice, too,' he said.

'Pooh,' she said, coming forward. 'Yes,' she said, in response to lifted eyebrows; 'you say that so very much in the tone of a man who knows what's expected of him – a husband.' He complained indignantly, 'Why the admiration of a husband is always suspect, I don't know,' and affected to take to his paper again. She went across the room to pour herself a glass of sherry. She was wearing a striped yellow house-coat that buttoned beneath her chin and opened in deep folds from her waist. Her red hair had been brushed back and Alec's present, baroque turquoise ear-rings, hung upon the dead soft lobes of her ears. She was still feeding her baby, and her breasts had an unwonted roundness that gave her figure a new poise and balance. Maternity, so people said, had improved Catherine: that slight hawkish look had disappeared from her face; she no longer had muscles that nervously twitched in her neck, nor the sudden blotchy patches of colour that used to stain her skin under the influence of excitement. She looked at the same time both younger and more mature, a combination that, momentarily at least, enhanced her personality.

Behind her back, a big Venetian mirror seemed to absorb the room, surfeit to its glass brim with images. Her red head passed across it momentarily as she stooped towards the tray. She lifted the decanter, with its fanciful garland of shell flowers. 'Well . . . cheers!' Seeing his expression, she stopped. 'I know, dearie – but this little drop won't hurt, truly it won't. Besides, it's hours before the next feed.' She refused to take seriously Alec's uneasiness at her partiality for liquor. She came across the room, nursing her glass. 'Pretty good sherry, at that. Where did you get it? Wait till you see the old man lap it up.' They were expecting to dinner that evening Venitia and her father, Colonel Rowton, up in London that week-end to see his daughter. Colonel Rowton, whom Catherine, Basil and even Venitia always referred to as 'Bunny', had been a friend and neighbour of Richard Nicolls in the old days: out of England at the time of Catherine's marriage, he had yet to make Alec's acquaintance. Hence this formal invitation. Venitia,

constrained, as Catherine had it, on these periodical visits from her father, to wash her face and rid her environment of some of her more disreputable lovers, had been on the 'phone to Catherine half an hour ago: giving a list of names that were strictly taboo; explaining complicated alibis that had to be maintained; inquiring as to what Catherine intended to wear and then exclaiming with dismay over the poverty of her own wardrobe. 'I shall have to find myself an oriental film-magnate, too,' she said; and was a little taken aback at Catherine's limp silence at the other end. . . .

Alec put his paper down. He began to finger the lay of his tie: to question his wrist-watch. 'They're late, aren't they?' he said finally.

'Holding Up the Whole Unit,' Catherine said mockingly. She came over to him and twined her arm under his. 'Try and be nice to Venitia, my love. I know you don't like her.'

'I don't dislike her. I merely feel that her girlish gaze sees right down to the ultimate fig-leaf. Her interest is so exact and clinical, it's not even stimulating.'

Catherine said thoughtfully, 'I think I shall have to start weaning Dave. I believe he's getting a tooth.'

'Mazzeltov!' exclaimed Alec involuntarily. Catherine looked enquiring. 'An old Spanish custom,' he told her: he grinned suddenly. . . . She saw that he was thinking of things of which she had no knowledge. For a moment he was far from her: it was as if she held the arm of a dummy. She sensed this and sensed, too, that he was extracting a sort of bittersweet flavour from the situation; from the fact that he would never be able to share with her the humour of these memories.

She said abruptly, 'I think I shall have to get rid of that cow of a Nanny. I can't stand the patient air she puts on when I want to handle Dave. And the possessive triumphant way she grabs him back again as soon as I've finished.'

Alec was recalled to the present. 'I shouldn't take the slightest notice of her,' he said soothingly.

But Catherine was not so easily diverted from that topic. 'Of course, they can't *stand* her in the kitchen,' she said. 'And she knows it, too. Edith resents having to turn out the nurseries for her. And Mrs Wylde never bothers to have her trays ready for her when she comes down to fetch them. She keeps her hanging about on purpose.'

Alec's expression of interest and commiseration turned a little glassy. He had long become accustomed to the fact that his apparently peaceful home was the seat of a relentless internecine warfare, the bulletins of which he had to be posted with each day on his return from work. He had become accustomed, too, to the strange process whereby an individual, lauded as a paragon of all the virtues on her arrival, became progressively transformed with the passage of time into a monster of all the vices. What he could not resign himself to was the passion with which Catherine scented out and apprehended these flaws in her domestic structure: the way she allowed trivialities to work upon her, consume her peace of mind. Edith had neglected this. . . . Nanny had said that. . . . The kettle was left boiling away for hours on the gas. . . . A plate had been smashed and thrown into the dust bin without a word being said of it. . . . These were sufficient to cloud her face completely for a whole evening: shut her up in a silence which excluded both Alec's attempts at conversation and the serious consideration of any other topic.

To divert her train of thought now, he said quickly, 'Oh, I forgot to tell you. I saw Schwab to-day. We're definitely going to make "The Two Lakes."'

'Do you mind?' she said, concerned. 'I thought you didn't like the story.'

'Not at first. But I'm pleased now. It'll be a complete change from aspidistras and pubs.' He grinned. 'Don't forget our good friend the *Observer*. *"It is high time Mr Berman rid himself of his æsthetic fixation on the Kilburn High Road."*'

Catherine moved away from him and began to rearrange the flowers in the glass tank. 'Will you be going on location for it?' she asked.

'Obviously. It's nearly all exteriors, you know.'

'Who's playing the girl?'

'Hetty Follet, I suppose.'

'That *dear* girl,' Catherine murmured. 'What would the British film industry do without her. . . .'

'Of course,' cried Catherine. 'You two haven't met.' Her hands still linked in those of Colonel Rowton, she turned back to her husband. 'Bunny, let me introduce you at last – this is Alec.'

'How do you do.'

'How do you do.'

A cold strong hand closed on his: but the handshake was, as it were, out of focus: Alec's knuckles ground awkwardly within the other's grasp. At the same time he was aware, as always

when introduced to certain friends of his wife's, of the look of surprise turned upon him: a surprise quickly concealed by the mask of affability, unconcern. So *this* was what Catherine had married. . . . Well, he thought, it was only fair to remember that Catherine, introduced into his Brighton *milieu*, would have produced the same questioning looks. But he could not help feeling that the quality of the surprise provoked by her appearance was potentially more flattering than that which actually fell to his share. . . .

'What's everybody going to drink?' Catherine was saying. 'Come along, Bunny – Venitia.' Alec went dutifully towards the tray. Venitia, whose appearance was at all times her most effective alibi against scandal, came over to the fire; wisps of not altogether immaculate chiffon trailing from her, her soft hair turning up like a child's about her shoulders. She was smaller even than Alec: with entrancing limpid eyes. She spread her hands at the blaze and it was surprising, on a being of such fragility, to discover the prehensile efficiency of those hands, the squat curved thumbs. . . . Alec passed her a brimming glass. At his approach, her lash-weaponed eyelids fluttered, startled; then settled down over her cheeks, like a butterfly composing itself upon a flower. Alec examined the display coolly, then turned away. 'And you, Colonel?' he said. 'Oh – thanks very much.' The Colonel bent forward: there was a civilized crackle of starched linen. Colonel Rowton was a tall good-looking man of fifty with a perfect complexion and finely-groomed grey hair matched by a grey moustache that looked like a small neat bow upon his upper lip. Behind the ambush of straggling eyebrows, his fine frosty eyes scrutinized

a host, thick-set, in a too perfect dinner-jacket, with black oiled hair, fleshy prominent ears and a social manner with which no fault could be found but that it must have been acquired of recent years. . . . It seemed, after that scrutiny, that he had nothing to say and accordingly he relapsed into silence. He sipped at his sherry. Alec, perfectly conscious of all that the Colonel experienced, saw the dubious way he approached the glass to his lips: his involuntary look of appreciation as he realized its quality: and he wondered privately what the Colonel's emotions must be at finding himself in the position of having to accept hospitality from one whom he himself must instinctively class as an outsider. . . . It was a situation, on the other hand, which Alec himself was used to, if not resigned to: to entertaining men who, while eating his food or drinking, as now, his wine, regarded him with a hidden reservation in their expression. Men very often many times his inferior in character, in achievement. . . . That was the real rub, he thought. Anything he had done was automatically discounted because of what he was. . . .

Turning, Catherine caught Alec's expression. She understood at once: she was beginning, these days, to understand a great deal. . . . She said, 'Come on lovey, have a drink' and put a glass into his hand before he could speak. As he took it from her, she moved slightly, so that he alone could see her face: at which moment she winked broadly. Then she turned back to continue, with an outrageous suavity of manner, the conversation she was having with the Colonel. . . . That was all: but it was sufficient to alter altogether the tenor of Alec's mood: she had conveyed to him the simple and illuminating

fact that in the relationship of herself to Alec, it was Colonel Rowton who figured as the outsider. She was satisfied, she let him know, to betray her friends, the people of her own kind, for him. This was characteristic of her. Impatient of what she was beginning to call his 'touchiness' on these matters, her scornful mind was continually demonstrating to him the fact that barriers exist only when we recognize them; that there are two sides to every question; that your world is what you make it. . . .

Venitia accepted a cigarette from the box Alec proffered her, with the air of engaging him in a compromising situation. Alec once said to Catherine, 'I can never make out precisely which it is that your pal Venitia is trying to convey: that she's eminently bed-worthy or merely eminently *photogénique*.' 'Perhaps one, as a preliminary to the other,' Catherine suggested. She was secretly, smugly amused at Alec's reaction to her hitherto all-conquering friend. Long before she had permitted Venitia and her husband to meet, she had prepared the ground by casually informing him of those traits in Venitia's nature which she knew were the least likely to endear themselves or their owner to him. Then, safely conditioned, after an operation of a type familiar to most wives, she left him without a tremor in Venitia's company, sure of his immunity. . . . 'The unglamorous woman is forced to live on her wits,' she would say sweetly to Venitia: who was well aware that Alec's strange blankness towards her could only be due to some good spadework put in by Catherine before they ever met.

* * *

Conversation crept its way painfully along the fuse of such topics as the weather and what-shows-have-you-seen to a welcome explosion of spontaneous interest; in this case released by a discussion on the personalities of film-stars. But this was not until they were back, all of them, in the drawing-room again: nursing balloon-shaped brandy-glasses or fragile beakers of coffee. The meal had been good: complexions were a little higher: eyes more animated. There was less awkwardness now in the conversation. A common level had been established. Momentarily, the material beings of Alec Berman and Colonel Rowton were related by the assimilation of identical food.

'There are no *women* any more,' the Colonel was saying: 'only girls. . . . *Les Girls*. The ideal of Anglo-Saxon immaturity. Whereas with Frenchmen, who demand an adult relationship, their actresses are always *Madame* So-and-So. Women with a figure and a personality: with the dignity that the title implies.'

Alec tapped off the pale flaky ash of the cigar he smoked on such occasions with a minimum of enjoyment. 'Hollywood,' he said, 'has standardized a female eunuch for the occidental world.'

'Alec!' Venitia, who elected whenever possible to sit underneath a lamp so that her hair might be illumined to best advantage, now leaned forward impulsively. 'Do tell us, Alec. Is it true what they say about Hetty Follet?'

'I expect so,' Alec said shortly. She opened her mouth to speak and he gave her a level look. Catherine interposed: 'Have some more coffee, Venitia,' and extracted the cup from her. Passing Alec she gave him a jab in the ribs that meant, Behave Yourself. . . .

The Colonel had been to see a film. 'What was it called, Venitia?' he said. 'Eh, what? "The Glamour Queen."' His expression changed. 'Glamour!' His ridiculous little bow of a moustache quivered as he pronounced the word. 'The whole word, the whole conception's decadent. Sublimated sex, nothing more.'

'Admitted,' said Alec. 'But what's wrong with that? Shepherd's Pie is sublimated mutton. The further we get from the original mutton, the higher the degree of civilization. It's a thoroughly desirable sign. It isn't decadent – on the contrary. It's mankind's Excelsior!'

'Meantime,' said Catherine standing up, 'I expect the future generation's howling its head off in the nursery wondering why I don't come.' It was a quarter-past ten.

Venitia began to giggle. 'I simply can't imagine Cath with an infant!' she said to Alec. 'I can't believe it even now.'

'Why not?'

'Oh, well, of course you didn't know Cath as I used to know her. In the old days I mean. . . .'

'Here,' said Alec grimly to Catherine, 'you'd better take this young woman upstairs with you and demonstrate some of the elementary facts of life to her.'

'Oh, can I really come?' Venitia cried unabashed.

'Of course. He's used to an audience.' She turned to Alec and to the Colonel. 'Come up in about twenty minutes, if you like. He'll probably be on his pot; but the natural functions are always excused in the very young.'

'Tough luck on Alec leaving him alone again with Dad,' Venitia said in a different voice as they made their way upstairs. 'Poor Dad gets so very prosy at this hour of the night.'

'Venitia,' said Catherine indignantly, 'why do you always talk like the village idiot in front of Alec? It reflects so badly on me – as a friend of yours.'

Venitia was unperturbed. 'I've discovered that it doesn't pay to be brainy,' she said. 'It puts men on their guard. Hide the light of your intelligence under a bushel every time.'

'But you hide yours under a positive haystack. I warn you – Alec's beginning to think you're M.D.' They were at the door of the night nursery and, as she spoke, Catherine tapped lightly before putting her hand to the knob. A subdued voice said, 'Come in.' They entered, quickly lowering their voices: inhaling at once, along with the characteristic odour of milk, urine and wool, the tender meadow-sweetness of *baby*. . . . The nursery, with its sentimental pink walls and blue-painted furniture, its china rabbits and frilly gingham curtains, was softly, dimly lit: the gas-fire making an oasis of warmth at the heart of the room. On a low chair, next to a table full of cotton-wool, safety pins and creams, Nanny sat, with the baby laid out in her lap in his long white nightgown.

Catherine advanced into the room. 'Hullo, young Davey. . . . Isn't he *good*, Nanny; he isn't making a sound.'

'Of course he's good, bless his pretty heart!' Nanny, a small carroty-haired Scotswoman, was modestly wrapped in a blue woollen dressing-gown, her peculiar knuckled feet thrust into rabbit's wool moccasins. She got up now and began some complicated transaction with a weighing-scale: laying Davey, rolled in a shawl like a diminutive mummy, on the wicker pan as she fumbled for the weights. 'Venitia – sit over there, will you?' Catherine indicated the covered divan that was Nanny's bed. She herself sat in the low chair Nanny had vacated, tied a flannel apron about her waist and undid the first few buttons of her house-coat. With the efficiency, the serene lack of modesty that characterizes the nursing mother, she bared her breast – 'Left first this time, is it, Nanny? I always forget' – and swabbed it with cotton-wool. Venitia saw the strange new nipple: full-blown, carnation-dark. 'That's got it,' said Nanny, lifting the baby from the scales. Catherine extended her arms. Already the baby was turning, lapping the air, nuzzling his way towards the bounteousness to come. . . . 'There,' said Catherine: 'there.' Gripped to the nipple at last, he began to suck and, as the milk came surging up, Catherine felt the familiar painful tightening in her breasts. Involuntarily, she winced.

'Does it hurt?' Venitia asked respectfully.

'Only for a moment.' She turned. 'All right now, Nanny.'

'Then I'll just pop along and have my bath. See he gets his full time, won't you, Mrs Berman? Keep him to it.'

When the door had closed behind her, Venitia smiled: 'Keeps you in your place, doesn't she?'

'Oh, my dear. It's impossible to preserve any dignity when you're regarded merely as a human feeding-bottle.'

Davey, at the breast, sucked firmly, regularly, noisily. 'Is that him?' Venitia asked, astonished. 'He sounds like a horse at a trough.'

Catherine laughed. 'You always were a poetical soul, Venitia.'

Composed and gentle, her arm wreathed about the child, she was looking down at his head, as small and fluffy as a coconut. A tiny claw-like hand rested on her breast, pinching her convulsively from time to time. 'He really is rather a pet,' Catherine said serenely.

'I've seen so many pictures of women suckling babies,' Venitia remarked, 'that now when I see the real thing I think it's just a pose.'

'Do you?' Catherine spoke absently. She was staring at Nanny's leather travelling clock on the mantelpiece. 'I believe he's had his time on this. I'd better change him over.' She placed two fingers on his small jaws and firmly detached him. He sat hanging over her arm, lips dewed, head helplessly bobbing. 'He looks completely cock-eyed,' Venitia said: 'You shouldn't have had all that sherry.' Catherine began to massage his back. 'Bring his windies up,' she said in a tone that made Venitia stare incredulously. 'Come on now, *Windies*, pet.' The baby responded with a sudden deep-fetched 'U-u-u-H . . . U-u-u-r-r-p!' 'Clever boy!' Catherine regarded him radiantly and transferred him to her other breast.

Venitia was getting a little restless: the process threatened to lack variety. . . . She reached out for her bag and, delving into it, produced her lipstick; unfailing solace at such moments. Carefully, she accentuated the raspberry tinge upon her lips and, mirror raised, regarded the result from all angles with a satisfied expression. Occupied thus, she said languidly, 'So his name's David, you say. . . . It usually is, isn't it, when it's necessary to combine the Semitic and the fashionable.' She lowered her mirror. 'The best of both worlds, in fact.'

‘Perhaps that’s precisely what we hope for him,’ Catherine said. She spoke soberly, looking down at the small ambiguous countenance. There was a slight silence.

‘Well, of course, no mixed marriage is altogether a bed of roses – ’ Venitia began. Catherine interrupted her. ‘Oh, people *madden* me when they insist on talking about *mixed* marriage!’ she exclaimed vigorously. ‘As though every marriage weren’t mixed – fundamentally and of its very nature: as though that weren’t the whole meaning of marriage.’

‘There are degrees of mixedness,’ Venitia pointed out. ‘The sort of marriage Dad expects me to make, to some lusty blue-eyed subaltern . . .’ (‘The Mixture As Before,’ Catherine murmured.) ‘. . . and yours.’ She paused. ‘I can quite understand the lure of – of – ’ she hesitated, ‘men of Alec’s race: but I still think it was very courageous of you actually to marry one, the world being what it is.’

‘The world being what it is made me keener than ever on making this marriage,’ Catherine said serenely.

‘How quixotic of you,’ Venitia said disbelievingly.

‘Not at all. One’s just recording one’s vote, that’s all.’

‘Oh, yes, of course,’ said Venitia. ‘That’s what all the more distinguished Aryans feel about it, naturally.’ She paused. ‘At the same time,’ she said, ‘I wonder how much of that liberal fervour of yours is just a result of your falling in love – and how much it depends on your *remaining* in love,’ she added shrewdly.

It was very late. Catherine and the servants had already gone to bed. Alec, with reminiscences in his mind of straying

on to deserted sets late at night at the studios, stood alone in the drawing-room, looking about him; listening. He heard the clocks throughout the household take on a life of their own; whispering stealthily across empty rooms and then joining all together in a sudden ribald outburst of chimes. Silence again. A stale sweet odour hung in the room; of cigars, of brandy, of flowers: a nostalgic aftermath. The cushions of the couch were disarranged: chairs pushed aside: on the mantelpiece the ash-tray was rammed with dead cigarettes. He went over to the end of the room and drew aside the heavy curtains. The garden lay as if entranced under a still frosty night in which the configuration of every twig was important, distinct: beyond, the moonlight lying white as snow along the roof-tops. He approached his parted mouth to the dark pane. He loved this wintry scene. It was to him like a mental state: after the spring of arising emotion, summer's sensuality, and the autumn of consequence, this was the period when all was gone but the consciousness of what had been: pure, unemotional, clarified; held in a cold peace by the intellect: one cycle of experience completed and another, implicit, far-off, about to begin. . . .

He stood like that for a long time, looking out. Then he dropped the curtain and went upstairs to bed.

END OF PART II

PART III

CHAPTER ELEVEN

FAMILY GROUP

The white glare of the portable arc lamp seemed to isolate, and at the same time magnify, the two who sat there, enduring the heat of its rays: Dave, his limbs obediently set in the dictated posture, yet looking, unmoved, into the dark eye of the camera; and Catherine, in black, of course, with pearls, encircling him with one arm: the palm of the other hand lying idly upturned in her lap in that attitude dear to the heart of Bond Street photography. 'That's got it,' said the man, signalling to his assistant: 'that'll do nicely. Still, now. . . .'

Catherine was bending over Dave. The light beat down on his youthful head, on the lank blond hair, newly polished, Alec noted (he had surprised the scene by returning home early that afternoon) by Nanny's vigilant hairbrush. He was wearing a cream silk shirt; brief knickers; and his slender bony ankles were encased in white socks. Looking at him, Alec was irresistibly reminded of the glances which he and Syd, in the old days, used to cast upon the little boys they met along the front dressed somewhat after this fashion: the incredulity; the derision mixed with envy: the sense, in it all, of a quite

immeasurable distance separating such children and themselves. And here, now, was his son, his own flesh-and-blood, turning up as one of 'them': white socks, high-pitched accent, Nanny and all. . . . (*Nanny*! – to this day the word affected Alec as secretly blush-making.) He had very often these days to suppress in himself an irrational and wholly unworthy desire to tease Dave upon his accent, his clothes, his manners. He was both proud of the niceties exhibited by his son and obscurely irritated by them. He thought of the way he himself had been brought up: the big damp home in Lansdowne Road; the way he trailed, a child in dirty overalls, from room to room, unattended for hours, or hung at his mother's skirts in the kitchen; ate food that would have sent Nanny into a swoon, wore boots and long woollen stockings and slept with all windows hermetically shut. . . . He discovered in himself an increasing desire to take with Dave this gambit: 'When I was your age, I never had this . . . or I never had that,' emphasizing, with a new and unexpected pleasure, the more meagre and stringent aspects of his own upbringing. And aware, all the while, of the extreme illogicality of his attitude, since what it came to was that he was reproaching Dave for the benefits which he himself had striven to confer upon him.

'Look!' cried the man, dodging out from behind the camera. He clapped his hands, waggled his ears, grimaced. David Berman watched the performance with detachment. Nothing, they discovered, would induce him to smile. They might change his attitude as much as they fancied, put him sitting, kneeling, standing, his expression remained invariable. Alec was impressed by this display of recalcitrance. It struck him anew that his son was, even at this early age, possessed of an integrity that could resist quite effortlessly the blandishments of the outside world. As he stood there and watched the boy, he was all the more conscious of the presence of that quality in him, since it was something he had often felt to be lacking in himself, who was invariably more-than-needs-be susceptible to the personality of others. Whereas Dave, thought Alec with a sudden sense of conviction, whatever his handicaps, is well equipped for life in that he will always know how to resist the demands of others. ('Oh, not so stern,' the man pleaded: 'Come on, now, let's see you laugh.') There was something about the boy's slight inexpressive profile in that moment which persuaded Alec of the justice of his intuition: here was a nature, he thought, not without faint apprehension, that would not easily be swayed by others; that would know exactly how to resist, and with equal impartiality, their flattery or their pain. . . .

They began to move the camera, the lamps. They wanted, this time, a head-and-shoulders study. Alec watched the preparations with the sense of indulging in a busman's holiday. 'Now look up,' the man told Dave, in that voice of studied tolerance which he used in dealing with child sitters: 'raise your head a little – tha-at's it.' Obediently, Dave lifted his face. He was looking at Catherine: and in that moment Alec could see clearly the Nicolls pattern in both faces: that in his son which was not of himself. It reminded him of the fact, which he contemplated always with awe, that this child was Richard Nicolls's grandson. . . . He wondered what the old man would have thought of this group: of himself, in particular, the

stranger, the interloper, who had stolen that family inheritance, the Nicolls look, to embody it within his own family: who had altered forever the Nicolls strain: made of Richard Nicolls's grandson a Jew. . . . Not that, as far as appearance was concerned, the facts of Dave's paternity were at all in evidence. The boy was exaggeratedly slender, even for his age: he had the elegant Nicolls head; a shallow immature nose and shallow coldly-modelled lips. He was fair. His eyes were neither those of his mother nor of his father. Grey narrow eyes, a little meagre in their spacing. Basil's eyes. . . . The fact was, the boy resembled Basil to a striking degree. So much so, that it seemed to Alec at times incredible, and even subtly wrong, that this being, his own son, should be cast in the mould of a stranger: should look at him through the eyes of a quite alien and even hostile entity (for such he had come to regard Basil). It was as if Basil, who had been gradually and, he thought, hitherto successfully, excluded from the domain of his life with Catherine, had managed now to re-establish himself in their midst in a new and ineradicable form.

The arc lamp was switched off and normal daylight filled the room again. Alec helped to push the couch back into place. The photographer and his assistant, accompanied by Catherine, went to the door, where they collected the couple of sleekly felted hats the sight of which had intrigued Alec on his arrival earlier in the afternoon. Dave had already disappeared upstairs. Alec lit a cigarette and leant back on the couch. He tilted open his mouth and let cigarette smoke meander upwards into the air, watching it swim and twine above him. Catherine returned. Without saying anything, pointedly, she took an ash-tray from the mantelpiece and placed it next to him on the couch. He accepted the rebuke with a grin. 'Oof, what a day!' he remarked, stretching. 'Young Wilson fell on the set and broke his wrist, and one of the girls in the crowd managed to set her dress alight. B.-A.'s going to have a nice old bill for damages, I can see.' A faint rattle of crockery made itself heard from the basement. He raised his head. 'What have you got for tea?' he asked with interest.

'Nothing unusual,' Catherine said. 'Nursery tea. I didn't know you were coming.'

He realized from her tone that she was put out: and felt guilty. He suspected, and not without justification, that the slight domestic hitch involved by his return outweighed in her mind the pleasure she might have felt at his presence in the home at this hour. He was not, however, unduly chastened by her attitude: since he knew it to be dictated, not so much by paucity of affection, as by that characteristic and unyielding orderliness of hers which tended, of late, to govern, not only her actions but her whole emotional outlook. Catherine loved to have everything cut-and-dried: extracted some sort of deep pleasure from the exercise of precision. System, she always said; with system you can get anything done. . . . She could not tolerate blunderers, and increasingly, these days, the slowness or inefficiency of others (which, perversely, she found herself watching out for) set her teeth on edge, like a discord. Any interference with the routines she planned disturbed her to a quite disproportionate degree. For this

reason the variability of Alec's working hours were a distinct source of irritation: she expected of a husband that he 'stay put' at fixed hours. She suffered, in fact, the penalty of so many energetic efficient women in that, if her efficiency or her energy were contradicted in any way, she was thrown completely out of gear into a useless self-devouring fret, like an engine racing with its wheels off the ground.

Alec glanced at her. 'Come and sit down,' he said. He spoke casually, because he knew that she was in that unresponsive mood when the slightest pressure on his part served only to drive her further into herself. He simulated, knowing that, a detachment he could not feel: having learnt, this past year or so, the fact that there were times when she resented passionately his solicitude, his questioning: the importunity of his concern. 'What's the matter, Cath?' he would say: repeating the question when she brushed it aside. And then: 'Oh, *nothing's* the matter, I tell you! Let it rest, for Heaven's sake. With you, everything has always got to be dragged out and examined and analyzed. . . .' He had learnt his lesson: he did not insist. Only 'Come and sit down,' he said lightly.

She obeyed: and then, without speaking, gently, as it were absently, he touched her wrist with his fingers. She gave no sign. Neither awareness, nor that sharp withdrawal which sometimes protected the inviolability of her mood. 'You're tired, aren't you?' he murmured. 'Yes . . .' and in response to his questioning look: '. . . the usual.' As always, at these times, she was so pale that the freckles looked dark on her skin: her eyes hollowed: visibly, it seemed, the whole chemistry of her personality altered. Alec felt a sudden pity for the instability of

womankind which he knew it would be injudicious to show. Catherine, he found himself thinking, should have had more children. But she had never wished to: she was not built for promiscuous maternity, she told him: and, after the birth of Dave, she had found such a complete satisfaction in him, that she desired no other child: indeed guarded jealously, for his sake, against the possibility of that second one: keeping at bay the unknown claimant – the rival to Dave.

'Schwab called me in to see him to-day,' Alec said. 'He's thinking about "The Two Lakes" again.'

'They've been thinking about it for the last four years,' Catherine said. 'One day they'll find themselves actually making it, if they're not careful.'

Alec laughed. 'Oh – and I met Brian, too,' he said: 'ambling along, looking rather forlorn. He sends you his love. I think we'll have to ask him round for a meal one night.' He saw, too late, that he had walked straight into the ambush. . . .

'We can't ask anyone for a meal at the moment,' Catherine said, instantly. 'I've given Mrs Swift notice. I was in two or three registry offices to-day and no one they have on their books seems the slightest good. It's all very well your complaining about the cooking here, but the trouble is that no first-class cook who can do the fancy bits you like is going to go into a place without a kitchenmaid. I can get "good, plain" cooks galore, of course, but I know only too well what you think of good plain cooking.'

'All right,' said Alec. 'I'm the villain of the piece. I apologize for causing such deadlock in registry offices.' He spoke lightly, but there was an underlying resentment in him

('I pay the piper, but I mustn't call the tune') of which he was conscious and which he tried, at times successfully, to suppress: as he did this obstinate and trivial craving of his palate for old tastes, old sensations, long ungratified. . . .

The door opened and Nanny, like a warder setting a prisoner at liberty for an interview, let Dave into the room. 'Hullo old boy.' Alec rose to greet him. Boisterously he picked him up; and, because his frame felt so slight between his hands, lifted him high above his head. Dave endured for a tense moment the sensation of the iron thumbs spraining his arm-pits, of his own complete helplessness, before Alec released him, set him to the floor again. . . . He feared and hated these, what he felt to be, physical contests with his father: with this man of careless, superior strength: feared above all his father's jovialities, the marks of his favour. . . . Catherine looked up. 'Come along, come and sit down and we'll all have tea,' she said: and Dave came across to her instantly, seeking, as she knew, the shelter of her calm, of her apparent indifference, in which temperate atmosphere he seemed to be at home, to thrive.

Alec came too and sat himself down. Absently. He was staring at Dave with a familiar frown of concern over his brows: and Catherine told herself that she knew word for word what his next remark would be. . . . Sure enough: 'He's very skinny,' Alec said, turning to her – 'All that malt doesn't seem to make much difference. I should like to see a bit more fat on him. Look at his legs: like drum-sticks.'

Catherine said with forced patience. 'He's all right. It's not his temperament to put on a lot of weight.' You worry too much about him, she told Alec, increasingly conscious of the necessity of shielding the child from the unrelieved pressure of that love, that concern, of which he was the object: as well as of the anomalies of her own position in endeavouring to do so. . . .

The door opened; and this time it was Edith with the tea-trolley, wheeling it carefully across the parquet. Smart in her uniform, coquettishly frilled at apron and wrist with organdie: but wearing, Alec noted, cheap broken-down shoes. 'Ah, *tea*,' he said, with unnecessary cordiality: as if this cordiality of his might stand for the apologies he felt he owed her: for the quality of her shoes, for the fact that he remained seated while she wheeled in his tea. . . . 'Thank you, Edith,' Catherine said briefly. She gave the contents of the trolley a searching look. 'You haven't brought the sugar-basin,' she said. When Edith disappeared to fetch that article, she gave the sigh of patience infinitely taxed. 'These girls!' she said. 'She'll forget her head next.'

Alec ate wholemeal bread, spread with bramble jelly. On the trolley was a fruit cake, a plate of sponge fingers and a plate of biscuits with animals in iced sugar. 'This nursery tea?' Alec asked. 'I think you do yourself jolly well, young fellow. When I was your age I had cocoa and bread and butter for tea, day in, day out.' Dave looked guilty; as if he were personally responsible for the simplicity of fare on which his father had been reared.

'Take your milk, Dave,' Catherine said a little impatiently. She passed him his silver mug. He held it in both hands, carefully, intent on not spilling a drop. Alec, watching the

complete absorption in his face, was aware of a certain emotion. A child's face: the innocence of all experience therein was almost terrifying. Its very blankness was a sign that here was a being marked out; waiting to be tracked down by experience. Sorrows yet unborn were startlingly marked in that milky blankness; so much more awesome, for that reason, than the commonplace lines of maturity achieved. And yet, thought Alec, why should I be more afraid for him than I have been for myself? I came through: so will he. Is it pride or pity makes us feel that others may not endure successfully what we have endured? For instance, he thought, and his gaze still fixed on the boy darkened so perceptibly that Dave, conscious and uneasy, turned his head away: the familiarity with ostracism – can that be acquired painlessly? Or must it come as an irreparable shock to a being born innocently, as other beings, into a world of his kind, to discover himself the target of an accepted, unyielding and inescapable prejudice? A man born crippled has to discover the fact of his condition and learn to accept it: but, thought Alec sombrely, it is harder to accept what amounts to an analogous condition when it is artificially thrust upon one by the malicious, or merely complacent, determination of others. Dave, he thought, a creature unborn in that he has not yet left the cosy-fitting shell of his home life, knows nothing of it yet. Can his nature learn sufficiently early, sufficiently easily, the tricks of adaptation: the peculiar fifth dimension in which the Jew, over and above the normal four of other people, has to live? (He thought of Lew: 'While everybody has problems, the Jew always has an extra problem on top of those he shares with everybody else.

He's perpetually like the Shell advert – *Plus a little something some others haven't got* – to worry about. . . .')

Unaware of following so closely upon his train of thought, Catherine said, 'I forgot to tell you. I got the prospectus of that school I was telling you about this morning. I like the look of it. I want to go along and see Miss Thwaites and, if everything is satisfactory, Dave might start there in the autumn.'

Alec was aware of the mixture of feelings with which he received this news. He was always saying that Dave had been kept too long at home, should be seeing more of other children: and at the same time he was curiously reluctant, afraid of making the decisive move. Afraid, he thought now, for Dave's sake: wanting to protect him a little longer, let him preserve the illusion, which yet was not an illusion, that he was no different from the other children he was going to meet and mix with. . . . And it was true that he was no different, now, Alec thought, before that contact had been made, before the knowledge of their attitude began to mark, to deform him – if only he could retain that wholeness, that natural confidence which was offered him as a human being and denied to him as a Jew. . . . Would it be kinder, Alec wondered once again, to warn him of what was coming: or would that merely predispose him to defeat?

'I must look at the prospectus,' he said mechanically. 'We must discuss it. We'll see. . . .'

'Timothy goes there,' Dave said unexpectedly.

'Who's Timothy?'

Catherine explained. 'He's Dave's friend – a boy he meets in Kensington Gardens.'

'What's his name – Timothy what?' Alec asked. Dave had it off pat. 'Timothy Hope-Sewell,' he said proudly. Hope-Sewell, thought Alec. Pukkha sahibs, what. Wonder if they mind their boy playing with Dave. . . . And for the first time he was aware of a desire that his son should have a Jewish friend, be surrounded with Jewish people, people with whom he was at ease; secure. . . . Almost at once, he was indignant with himself for the thought. That attitude's too easy; it's cowardly, he thought. Either you live in the ghetto and be done with it, or you come out and insist on your right to live as other human beings. That's what I've done and that's what I hope Dave will do; always. I hope the world will accept him and that he won't have to make himself conspicuous by insisting on these rights; but, if it doesn't, I hope he will know how to make plain every time that he intends to live precisely as other people: that he will, in the last instance, succeed in creating himself a normal average human being by a sheer act of will.

CHAPTER TWELVE

THE AGENT

'If you'll wait a moment, I'll just inquire,' said the girl. She spoke into a telephone. Catherine waited, looking at the brown varnished wall from which signed photographs of the firm's more successful authors returned her a satisfied and Olympian smile. 'Mrs Berman to see you,' said the girl; briskly impersonal. There was a pause, while Catherine contemplated a row of ash-blonde curls; then the girl looked up: 'Mr Nicolls will see you now,' she said.

Catherine made her way through a room filled with the clatter of typewriters, up a flight of stairs to another room, with a sombre brown-varnished door. She tapped and, without waiting for an answer, walked in. Basil did not move, did not rise as she pushed the door to behind her. He sat in the middle of the room, behind his untidy heaped-up desk, and looked at her. He did not speak. She came deliberately over across the room, lifted a pile of books from the seat and sat herself down on the chair next to his desk. 'Hullo,' she said.

'Hullo,' he said then.

'Well, Mr Nicolls?'

'Well, Mrs Berman? . . .' And he raised an eyebrow. 'What can I do for you? Royalties not satisfactory? American sales falling off?'

'Oh,' she said carelessly, 'I was in the neighbourhood, so I thought I'd drop in and see you.' The fact that she thought fit to give some sort of explanation underlined the character of the occasion: recalled, to the momentary discomfort of both of them, the months that had elapsed since they last met. It was a new thing this, that they should be embarrassed when they were alone together. Unless it was that since the traitorous admission, by Catherine, of a third into their lives, they could never, now, be altogether alone again. . . . And, as if the thoughts of both of them had converged at that moment, Basil said casually, 'Alec's at Oxshott, I presume.'

'Yes.' She spoke with a certain defiance, because her answer was so patently an admission that she was here only in virtue of his absence: of his ignorance of her movements. To recover herself from a not altogether dignified position, she changed the subject. 'Well,' she said lightly, 'tell me about yourself. How's good old Ten Per Cent?'

'Thank you.' He inclined his head courteously. 'We manage to keep the wolf from the door.'

'Been lunching with any female novelists lately?'

'One to-day, as it happens. . . . *Sole Bonne Femme* and Chicken Paprika. And you should see the way we waded into the wine-list.'

'Hum. You do them proud,' she observed.

'We feed them,' he said; 'in order that they may feed us.'

Catherine laughed. She was beginning to feel more at her

ease. As she had so often done in 'the old days', visiting Basil at her fancy, bringing him a posy for his desk, or some confidence to be dissected, she put her gloves and her bag on his desk: calmly claiming his working time: knowing herself privileged as none other was privileged; and warmly, complacently satisfied in that knowledge. She gave a deep sigh. 'Gosh! . . . It's good to see you, Bas.'

'It's a pleasure you might accord yourself more often,' he remarked in a detached voice. She looked at him. 'I know. . . . I know. . . .' A shadow fell on her face: she looked downcast. 'But you don't understand – there are so many things. . . .'

'Quite,' he said. He leaned forward to take a cigarette and he said deliberately: 'You don't have to apologize to me, Catherine. Have you forgotten? I'm the only person in the world you don't have to apologize to, whatever you do.' There was no emotion in his voice. Brother and sister, they had this amoral acceptance of each other's character traits; an acceptance which no wise blinded them to each other's faults; but which made them ready to accept such faults, and even perversely cherish them, against what they knew, at the same time, to be the more correct standard of the outside world. Family love is not so much blind as complacently without standards. Hence it was always in the nature of a self-indulgence for Catherine to find herself in Basil's company: a moral holiday; which could be shared with no one else in the world since no other member of the family now existed.

'How's the boy?' Basil asked her.

'He's all right. He goes to school now. I don't see so much of him.'

'Does he still look like me?'

'More than ever.' She smiled. 'Odd, isn't it?'

'Odd, I suppose, that Alec, thinking to perpetuate himself, should instead perpetuate a Nicolls. Moral: Cuckoo in the Nest, or Heredity makes Cuckolds of us All.' He pushed the box of cigarettes over towards her. 'Smoke?' he said. 'It's on the house.'

She picked out a cigarette and he reached for the matches; extending to her casually, between the tips of his fingers, a match flagged with flame. She lit her cigarette and leant back, fondling the newness of it between her lips. 'That's a nice bit of goods you have at the telephone downstairs,' she said, irrelevantly. 'Bed-worthy, or not?'

He shrugged his shoulders. 'Come, come,' he said: 'you know that the bed-worthiness of my staff has never been a subject of preoccupation with me. You've been seeing too many films.'

'I suppose I should resent that,' she said speculatively. 'But I don't. . . . On the contrary: you can't imagine how much I enjoy the luxury of not bothering to resent it.' At her words, the tone of her voice, he glanced at her quickly. She did not look away. Instead, she stretched, sighed deeply and permitted herself to say with what was obviously a quite voluptuous candour, 'Oh, it's such a *relief* being with you again, Basil!'

'Is it? . . . I'm both flattered and perturbed to hear it.'

'I can say any darn thing I like and it doesn't matter! No one cares a hoot, no one crawls away to nurse their wounded sensibilities. . . . I can say what I like, how I like and when I like!'

He looked at her keenly. 'Why all this craving for Free Speech?'

'Oh,' she said recklessly, 'you'd know soon enough if you lived with Alec.' She paused for a moment, half repentant; but she was already too far committed to draw back now; had, in any case, wanted, intended to commit herself in this regard. . . . Basil looked at her uneasily, aware of that intention, and afraid; not wanting to be involved in this betrayal: unwilling to allow her (entirely for her own sake, this) to abandon standards of reticence which hitherto she had respected. Once she was alone again, he knew, out of the special climate that their mutual presence created, that part of her which belonged, not to him, but to the external world and its standards, would begin to suffer; worked on by the toothache of remorse. It was this that he wished to spare her: it was of this that he sought to remind her by his apparent unwillingness to listen.

But Catherine was not to be denied: she chose, intentionally, he could see, to skirt that refusal. . . . 'It's like a sort of perpetual Inquisition,' she said. 'I've got to keep a watch on my tongue, keep my wits about me all the time. Because if I do let a word slip out, you should see the way it's pounced upon. It's not directed against him personally. Oh, no, that's much too simple: it's the black heresy, anti-Semitism, of course. . . . You think I exaggerate? But I daren't even *look* at any Jews we see casually in the street, or I'm looking at them coldly, or with repulsion, or something. He's always saying that he wants Jews to be treated like any other human beings, but at the same time he's like a cat on hot bricks all the time about himself and all the others.'

'I know; I know,' said Basil: and his intention was not to encourage, but to restrain. . . .

'He never forgets the thing for one moment, I've discovered: it's always there, at the back of his mind, whatever he does and wherever he is. It haunts him; and now it's beginning to haunt me. . . . I'm not only afraid of what I may say, but of what other people may inadvertently say when he's present: I try to steer the conversation out of dangerous channels: I blush for his sake in theatres when someone makes an unflattering allusion: I actually feel guilty when we happen to meet some really ugly or ill-behaved Jews, as if it was obscurely my fault. . . .'

'Catherine,' Basil protested.

'But I mean it! I can feel him disapproving of what he supposes to be my disapproval. . . .'

'What do you expect?' Basil said then, shrugging his shoulders. 'That's the minority mentality.'

'But it's so absurd,' she cried out. 'It's not *me* who's conscious of the difference between us, but *him*: he's the one who keeps on insisting on it, keeping it alive, refusing to allow me to forget it.'

'Surely he realizes that?'

'No,' she said, 'that's just it. He doesn't. He's so clever about so many things and I can't get him to face up to that in himself.' Her hand lying in her lap tightened involuntarily. 'It's awful and I hate it. I've no patience with it! I hate the way he watches out, almost greedily, for a sign that I'm tired of the situation, that what he chooses to consider are my real feelings are beginning to show through. . . .' She dabbed at an ash-tray with the dead butt of her cigarette; there was something a little shrewish in her look. 'Anyway, I'm wise to him now,' she said. 'I refuse to gratify him. I insist on behaving as if nothing were: I won't budge an inch. He's not going to get any change out of me on the subject any more.'

'But is that altogether wise?' Basil said. 'Surely some sort of a discussion on the matter would be more profitable.'

She gave a short laugh. 'I've had some of those discussions with Alec,' she said. 'Never again, thank you.'

'That's not like you, Catherine.'

She looked at him and looked away. 'I know,' she said. 'When I was young I used to believe in having everything out (although there's a difference in that and going over the same ground again and again *ad nauseam*). . . . But I'm older, now: I find I haven't the time or the patience any longer.'

Basil was silent. He picked up a pencil from his desk and began to draw a face on his thumb nail. He said quietly, 'Why are you telling me all this? You still love him, don't you?'

The frayed cigarette became still between her fingers. . . . She stared out of the window at the houses of Fleet Street opposite: at a man she could see working at something behind one of the windows; crouched over his task, intent, oblivious. It seemed that she derived a sense of balance, of stability from the sight of him working there; entirely unconnected with herself and the facts of her own existence. . . . 'Yes,' she said and, surprisingly, her tone, now, was gentle: 'I do love him, I know that, however much I'm capable of forgetting it at times. . . .'

'Then it seems to me,' said Basil, and his voice was icy, 'that you have nothing to complain of.'

'He loves me, too,' Catherine said, oblivious; 'that's why all this is so absurd. It's threatening to break up a perfectly good relationship – ' She stopped short: alarmed at the nature of that involuntary admission.

'I seem to remember that there were people who warned you of the peculiarities of mixed marriage,' Basil said, his eyes fixed on her.

'But I don't mean that we weren't right!' she said instantly. 'I can still see what we ought to have made of it; if we ourselves, perhaps, had been better material. . . . It's we who went wrong. We failed the ideal: not the ideal us.' She gave a sigh. 'Human, all too human.'

'Did you expect to be more than that?' he asked wry-lipped.

'Yes,' she said seriously. 'In a sense we did. . . . There was a time even when we were exalted in the thought that we might prove ourselves so.' The light, tender, introspective, of reminiscence died out of her eyes. She roused herself and reached for another cigarette. 'That's part of the trouble, of course,' she said. 'We can't help feeling that we're in the limelight all the time; to ourselves; and to others. We know only too well that there are people *watching* for the first cracks to appear: all ready primed with their *I told you so . . .*'

Basil's face was impassive.

'We have the feeling all the time that we've *got* to justify what we did and I think that puts an unfair strain upon us.' She was interrupted by the 'phone at her elbow ringing sharply. She stopped: Basil reached out for the receiver. He pursed his lips for a moment, then: 'All right, put him through,' he said. He

covered the mouthpiece momentarily with his palm. 'Sorry,' he said. 'Business.'

'Go ahead.' She heard him, voice totally altered, speaking with professional amiability to the unknown person at the other end of the wire. She got up, while he was so occupied, and strolled restlessly about the room, looking at the dust-jackets of momentarily celebrated novels framed on the walls. '. . . he's a better publisher, of course, from the point of view of prestige,' she heard him say; 'but I doubt if you'll get those terms from him. . . .' The man over the way framed in his window was still bending over some invisible task. A subdued rumble of traffic came up from Fleet Street; the stray bleat of horns. Some quality in the daylight made her conscious of the passage of time; and brought to her, as that always did, a sudden sense of loss, of panic. . . . She looked at her watch, like a mariner out of his bearings, consulting his compass. Five o'clock: she located, with relief, her position in time again. She must be thinking about getting back. Dave would be expecting her. And at the thought of Dave her heart warmed. She saw him, as she so often found him, leaning over the banisters, straining eye and ear for the first intimation of her presence. . . .

'. . . all right. I'll expect the manuscript in a day or two. No, I won't forget. . . . Yes, of course. You leave it to me. . . . Good-bye.' Wearily, as if the receiver had become too heavy for his hand, he dropped it – *ping* – on to its bracket. 'I feel like a headmistress interviewing proud and anxious mothers about the progress of their young,' he said. 'They come with the same pride, the same fussiness, the same deadly jealousy. . . .'

He sighed gently. 'Catherine, my love,' he said, 'there are times when I am very very tired indeed of the whole kindergarten of literature and *littérateurs*.'

'Poor sweet!' she said.

'I am also tired,' he went on in the same voice, 'of occupying what you might call a Ten Per Cent position in the universe. . . . Of living always on the margin: on ten per cent of other people's lives. Grudgingly accorded. And no less grudgingly received. You see before you a congenital but unwilling parasite: a victim, as well as a beneficiary, of human symbiosis.'

'What's that?' Catherine asked with interest.

'Have you ever seen that greenish look on certain inferior specimens of animal life? It's caused by a lowly weed that lives on those animals and uses up their carbon dioxide in return for supplying them with oxygen. That's symbiosis. Need I say more?'

'Give-and-Take,' said Catherine. 'What could be more equable and civilized?' She came forward and picked up her gloves, her bag. 'Basil – I must go.' He saw her restlessness: knew that the claims of her other life were making themselves felt; observed the strength of those claims, he who had no other life. . . . He stood up at once. He did not ask her when he would see her again, because not she, he felt, could determine that, but the train of events. He was constrained to bide his time: perhaps, even, after to-day, content to do so.

He saw her to the door without speaking. Only as she turned finally to go away from him, he recalled her. 'Catherine,' he said briefly.

She looked back at him. 'Yes?'

He paused for a moment before saying it. Much, he knew, for him at least, hung upon her reception of these, the first tentative words. . . . 'Middle Bay,' he said, 'the bungalow there – it's always ready for you. If you ever want it. . . .'

CHAPTER THIRTEEN

MORNING OFF

As Alec sat there at his ease in the window-seat, backed by a cushion, one knee hung comfortably over the other, he had the delicious sensation of the February sunlight warming the nape of his neck: a gratuitous embrace, that he endured with a still and cat-like happiness. The house was peaceful: Dave had not yet returned from school and Catherine was occupied with her gardening (he could see her at it if he craned his head), solicitously crouched over the bleak-looking flower-beds. He had before him the pile of newspapers which, in the expansive mood induced by the prospect of a morning's idleness, he had gone out previously to buy: but he had not yet got down to the unrestrained browsing he had promised himself when he collected them at the newsagent's: he was content, just now, to appreciate with a calm and subtle pleasure the mildewy smell of printer's ink, the sight of the neatly folded sheets, immaculately laundered, fresh from the press, with a glaze almost of starch upon them. . . . As he sat there, there came to him from other quarters of the house the sounds of the domestic routine following its course: he could

hear the faint knock of the housemaid's brush on the stairs: the swing of the tradesmen's door as the milkman arrived: Moffat, the butcher: then a greengrocer's van. He followed, fascinated, the entrances and exits of this domestic scene, of which this room afforded him a reasonably good view. It was a small room at the side of the house known as the morning-room: the room, in point of fact, in which all the innumerable odd jobs of daily life came to be transacted. And as such, perhaps particularly sympathetic to Alec; with its reminiscence of the living-room in Lansdowne Road. . . . It smelt of coal and of sunshine; of damp maturing earth from the innumerable bowls of bulbs roosted in every corner; and of something else: what Dave called a 'dressmaker smell': for Miss Hornby, the sewing woman, used this room twice a week, sitting enthroned here with her whirring machine, her cup of tea, her pile of sheets to be hemmed and her pin-cushion formidable as a porcupine-at-arms. There was a cheerful coal fire in the grate; a big oak table at which Dave did his home lessons; and a wheezy chintz-shrouded chair in which Catherine sat reading or knitting, while Dave (who sought out her company on every conceivable occasion) lay on his stomach on the floor, painting with the water-colours she had given him, a jam jar of muddy water at his elbow and his tongue roving from side to side in his mouth, like the erect seeking tip of a cat's tail. . . .

Catherine came in; sniffing from the cold air. She was wearing a very ancient tweed coat. She had no hat on and her ears were pinched, scarlet. There was an unwonted colour in her cheeks which made her look young and animated. She began to draw off her gardening gloves. 'Hullo, lump,' she said.

A little absently, he put out his hand and caught hold of her. 'Brr,' he said, as the cold, slightly rough fingers came into his. 'Ice maiden. Come and thaw down to human temperature.'

She took her coat off and appeared in the clothes she wore 'about the house' in the mornings. An old green jumper with a red belt; and an even older skirt which, scrupulously tailored, had retained, even in age, the original intention of its lines; as, indeed, all Catherine's clothes did, however long she wore them. In this respect they were very strenuously tested, for Catherine had developed what amounted to a mania for retaining her old clothes: appearing in the same thing day in, day out without variation. She liked even to lay the garments down on the chair by her bed in a certain order every night; to know them there, ready for her, like that, when she chose to assume them again: a process which also had to be carried out according to plan. . . . She came over towards the fire; polishing the closed fist of one hand in the palm of the other. The cosmetic the chill air had applied to her cheeks (slyly overcoming her rigorous defence against coquetry) began to die off in the warm indoor atmosphere. To Alec, watching, she seemed in a certain degree to fade, to wither before his eyes: resume the drab garment of her years. . . . He saw again with concern the fine irritable lines on her brow; the new shadows that were pitted here and there on her face. Unmistakable signs of time's distemper: the fret of laughter or of tears branded in, like an identification mark, so that, privileged anonymity of youth lost, the secrets of personality might be read on the face

at first glance and by every indifferent passer-by. . . . When one was young, he found himself thinking, one looked on time as an ally; the agent of one's own desires (in time I shall have this, in time I shall have that). One achieved these things and then there came a pause, a slackening. A moment ominous and still. And between that moment and the next, fine as a knife-edge, all was changed. Time was no longer an ally but an enemy. Not a benefactor whose gratuities were unthinkingly accepted; but a creditor, coming to claim what he had given; inopportunely pressing the recovery of his loans: and ready (how unbelievable!) to leave a one-time favourite bankrupt even of teeth, of sight, of hearing. . . . With a calm and terrible justice, withdrawing his bounties one by one. Altering, despoiling, capriciously filching the lustre first of this faculty, then that. Systematically destroying what he had been at such pains to build up: insatiable, not content even when he had picked and rifled his way down to barren bone, but hounding his victims still further, into powder, into dust, into inconceivable and rarefied nothingness. . . . All gone: bones, blood, genitals, friendship, banking account, laughter, learning: all gone, the poetry, the French, the arithmetic, the technique of batting ball from wicket: liquidated the wisdom, gone all the images (the buses, the bridges, the policeman at Oxford Circus): the unique Private Collection that is a human personality lost, disbanded forever; the whole complex house of bricks collapsed, reduced to zero, *caput*, finished. Time, the Great Scavenger. . . .

He shivered slightly. . . . There was present a certain element of exaggeration about that shiver: he was aware of

a small vain desire to acquaint someone with the tenor of his emotions which, while they harrowed, also held for him a secret enchantment. . . . But Catherine took no notice. She was used to what she liked to call his 'fanciful fits' and had no intention of acting as stooge. . . . She stood over by the fire, rubbing her hands; as if laying them in that warmth. Her pose was almost aggressively unaware. It was typical of Catherine, this unaccommodating refusal to respond to any emotion that she suspected to be tinged, even in a remote degree, with the bogus, the self-conscious. Very gradually, and indeed in spite of herself (because her pride would not at first allow her to see, to accept this, in the man whom she wished perfect), she had come to suspect, at certain times, the integrity of Alec's responses: suspect the self-indulgence beneath the mood, the emotion. She withdrew, then, with anger, with an almost æsthetic distaste, from that in him which might not be altogether genuine. Anger, because she felt that he was letting her down; betraying that which she wished him above all things to be: flawless, infallible; like that figure out of her own past, her childhood. . . . She had no talent for compromise: at such moments she merely became silent, remote; turned altogether stony: so that Alec, caught up in his own mood, was at a loss on occasion to understand why, abruptly, she would look away from him as if he had insulted her. . . . Still without saying anything, she took her work-bag on her knee and sat down by the fire. She was making a sweater for Dave. She took out her ball of wool, the needles, the dog-eared pattern book, and silently began to knit.

Alec sat staring before him. He was, this time, really unaware of Catherine and of this room. A memory (of his childhood;

of the old synagogue in Brighton) had taken possession, not only of his mind, but, it seemed, of his limbs; so that, translated, he could feel the leather seat under his youthful knee-bare legs: see before him the tedious dust revolving in the shafts of sabbath sunlight: see, too, his father, glasses clipped severely midway down his nose, turning over the pages of the prayer-book: he could hear in his ears, like something more than merely actual, the monotonous sing-song of the man reading from the Scroll of the Law; the familiar discords, diapasons: the sudden murmur and rustle as the whole congregation prepared to get to its feet. . . . On the Day of Atonement, the way the old people would shake and moan and cry; the children looking at them with round eyes, not knowing that they, in turn, would inherit these incomprehensible sorrows. . . . 'Lord, what is man that Thou regardest him, or the son of man that Thou takest account of him? . . . His days are as a shadow that passeth away. In the morning he bloometh and sprouteth afresh: in the evening he is cut down and withereth. . . . Oh, God, take us not hence in the midst of our days. Let us complete in peace the number of our years. . . .' He could hear the very break, the quiver in the old minister's voice. . . . It happened to him increasingly these days that things which had not passed the frontier of consciousness for years would suddenly rise up in this fashion, to claim him: as if there was no progress, no real sequence, he thought, and he was travelling backwards (with an accelerated speed now that he had passed a certain age), towards the events of his own past; which seemed, in these visitations, to be advancing to meet him. Or was it, perhaps, not a grandiose metaphysical question at all, but merely the subjective fact that, with age, certain controls were insensibly slackened; that one permitted all sorts of things, hitherto rigorously suppressed, to come again into the foreground? He could see it in himself: he was, for instance, becoming very much more indulgent towards the circumstances of his own past. He hankered, actually, in a restless unacknowledged way, after the events of that past, which seemed, through the lapse of years, to have acquired some new quality which rendered even the most trivial occurrence of a peculiar and incalculable value. . . .

He laughed suddenly and turned to Catherine. 'Did I ever tell you about my father and his illicit still? . . . He read somewhere or other a recipe for making beer for next to nothing. (We none of us drank, of course; but that was beside the point: for my father, economy was something in the nature of Abstract Art.) Well, he made the stuff according to formula, but he corked up the bottles too tight and, one night, we were all wakened by the most shattering explosion from the basement. . . .'

Catherine listened: she permitted a slight smile to tinge her lips. She did not really enjoy, any longer, the stories of his youth in Lansdowne Road: she had heard them all before, she told herself: and she disliked, too, the inverted snobbery in it all, which made such cramped conditions right and normal, and obliquely reproached the ease, the cultivated atmosphere of her own home life. She was tired of hearing the words 'not up to Oldwood Lodge standard, I suppose,' whenever she disapproved of something. And she who, in her studio days, had herself been the first to laugh at such standards, now found that, instinctively, she seemed to defend them, to refer to them, in any crisis that might arise. . . .

She reached over and pressed the bell. 'I'm going to have my mid-morning cup of tea. You can join me if you like.'

'Of course, I like.' He watched with interest as Edith came in with the tray: dressed, not in the brown and *écru* of afternoon, but in an unfamiliar drab blue, and baggily aproned; her fingers chapped and seamed with black. . . . Catherine lifted the tea-pot: passed him a plate of small biscuits. He stirred his tea happily, meditatively. 'This, I suppose,' he said, 'is the psychological moment when housewives all over the country tune in to *Radio Luxembourg*. Listen to nostalgic *passé* dance music and recipes for making Queen's Pudding. . . . The ideal programme in fact: indulging the emotional, and, at the same time, equipping the practical life. Baking-powder and *Ramona*. . . . Withal, a secret bitterness in it all. *Ramona* and romance disappear forever, but baking-powder and scouring-soap remain, the eternal verities of suburbia.'

Click-click, went Catherine's needles: *click-click, click-click, click-click*. It was a sound which (since Catherine could never sit with empty hands but must be always at this queer frittering activity) was beginning to punctuate Alec's waking hours: a perpetual undertone to their hours of intimacy. These knitting needles of hers had come to seem to Alec like instruments, not of creation, but of aggression: sharp, pointed, they seemed to engage in some interminable and unrelenting battle: rapidly, venomously to fence, and without ever losing or gaining the advantage. . . . That, of course, in a way, was Catherine's intention: at all costs to maintain the *status quo*;

and therefore avoid, as best might be, the glances, the topics that might jeopardize the delicate balance of circumstance. . . . She seemed, now, to know that his eyes were upon her; for she did not look up. How well he knew it, that obstinate refusal to become conscious of him. . . . He could not see her expression: steadfastly, her eyes remained lowered. He knew what it meant, that blankness. A curt and unmistakable signal. Blinds Down: No Funny Business. . . .

Rebuffed, although no word had been spoken between them, he picked up the newspaper: a shield to his pride. He read what was written on a certain page: but at the same time he was following the train of his own thoughts; a sort of mental double exposure in which, through the story of reported mobilization on a foreign frontier, he found himself thinking: She has never really accepted me; that's what it is. Never deep down. . . . He was accepted up to a point; but when he sought to press that point closer, then something out of her deepest nature rejected him, just as, he thought, in a sudden painful flash of illumination, every race rejects the Jewish one on the point of assimilation. . . .

Catherine distrusted his silence. Although she affected to be self-sufficient, unaware, in point of fact she was always acutely and nervously conscious of what might be going on in his mind. Without looking up: 'What's in the paper?' she asked casually. She would take refuge from words in silence; and then alarmed at his corresponding silence, be forced reluctantly to emerge into the open again. . . .

'Oh, nothing much,' he said. He roused himself. 'Except, of course, an account of the "frenzied enthusiasm" that greeted

the Dictator's last speech. You know the sort of frenzy, of course: you get a sample of it on the wireless sometimes, when you twiddle the knobs and alight on a foreign station. As a woman of experience, you can't mistake the quality of it.' He dropped the paper. 'I've nothing against orgasms, as such – in fact, I'm all for them – in the proper place. But that place is not in politics.'

This time she laughed. She was immediately at her ease when they discussed impersonal topics. In these she seemed able to release the warmth and the spontaneity that she denied their converse about private matters: so that, perversely, it was in the realm of the abstract, these days, that they were at their happiest, their most intimate. . . . 'More tea?' she asked him. 'Thanks!' He passed her his cup. Strange, he thought, as he watched her pour it out for him, how one can accept almost anything, if only it happens slowly enough. . . . He and Catherine had been married seven years, now. If he had had presented to him, at the outset, a picture of what his life was to be with Catherine (say what it was at this moment), he would have been, he knew, violently distressed. And yet, now that he was living it, that it had established itself slowly and therefore, it seemed, inevitably, it did not appear to him intolerable. On the contrary: it seemed to him that this was the natural order of things; the sort of reality every husband and wife had to face up to in the intimacy of their private lives. . . . After all, he thought, the consciousness that a marriage is not what might be called a successful one, is actually quite intermittent. Even then, the sun does not shine less bright, nor food taste less well. The ordinary things of life, in fact, go on precisely as before: the small joys, the small interests which go to make up the major part of living get woven in and about the circumstances of marriage, so that, in time, the whole thing comes to constitute the fabric of the normal, the accepted. So long as one was healthy, there was almost everything to be thankful for. Only occasionally there came the restless consciousness of some light, some quality gone from things: and even then, one was always ready to attribute that to the impersonal factor: the passage of time; the slow inevitable loss of youth. . . .

There were sudden quick footsteps along the corridor outside. Catherine raised her head sharply. Then the door burst open and Dave appeared; flushed, dishevelled. 'Mummy . . .' He stopped dead; seeing Alec. 'Oh . . .' he said, unguardedly. His reaction was, for once, quite obvious: his hostility towards the man whom he found thus taking his ease in the very room which he (Dave) liked to consider dedicated to intimacy with his mother. . . . His eyes fell. 'I didn't know you were here,' he said lamely. Visibly, he hesitated: uncertain whether to come in or to go away.

'Well, you know it now.' Alec spoke a little sharply. He was deeply wounded and no less deeply irritated by that which he had read in his son's expression. He felt in his turn that there lit up in him some old half-forgotten quality of hostility; reminiscent of the father-son relationship from which time had emancipated him and, in which, rôle reversed, time now involved him again. . . . 'What on earth have you been up to?' he said. 'Look at you – look at your face.' (Like a bear from the woods, he nearly said.) Yes; the quality of the thing was the same, whichever rôle one played. First one was dominated; then took in turn a pleasure out of dominating. Thus the sins, not of the fathers but of the grandfathers, were always in one form or another visited on the grandsons. . . . Don't you know it's not the thing to burst in on your mother like that?' He noticed at that moment that Dave's lip was cut: there was dried blood on his chin. 'What on earth have you been doing to get in such a state?'

Dave did not answer.

'Dave! Have you become deaf by any chance? I asked you a question. How did you manage to cut your face about like that? What have you been doing?'

There was a pause. Dave looked at his father with a very peculiar expression before he said softly, but with a quite appalling distinctness: 'I'm not going to tell you.' Then he turned and walked out of the door. Alec rose instantly to his feet, but Catherine was quicker than he. 'Wait – I'll go,' she said. 'Please, Alec. . . .' He was silent. She went out, closing the door behind her.

She was away a long time. When she came back, she walked into the room with a quick firm step and at once sat down and took up her knitting. She wished, it was obvious, to convey the impression that the whole incident, having been adequately dealt with, was now closed. . . .

Alec ignored this. 'Well?' he said.

She did not look up. 'What you might expect, of course,' she said briefly. 'He was fighting.'

'Hum! He seems to have become very pugnacious lately.' Alec paused. 'Fighting, eh?' he said thoughtfully. He looked up. 'What was it about? I'd like to know what that boy considers worth fighting for.'

She shrugged her shoulders. 'What do boys fight about? . . .' Warned by something in her voice, Alec turned to look at her. He saw, then, and with a sharp unpleasant shock that her hands were trembling. 'Hullo!' . . . He stood up. 'What's the matter, Catherine?'

'The matter? . . . Nothing. Why should anything be the matter now?' But she did not trouble to disguise the deep weariness in her voice.

He looked at her. 'You're concealing something from me,' he said. *(Oh, the joy with which he said that, she thought, sickly.)* 'What is it, Catherine?'

She did not reply.

'Catherine!'

'You're making a mountain out of a molehill again,' she said.

'Not at all. I'm merely trying to investigate the nature of the molehill.'

'Alec,' she said. 'You won't do any good by this. Let it rest. . . . For once. . . . Please, Alec. . . .'

All of a sudden he lost control. 'But what the hell is all this?' he said furiously. 'I'm absolutely fed up with it! . . . What do you think I am? Anyone would think I ill-treated you – you and Dave – the way you behave when I'm about. What am I supposed to have done? Aren't I a good husband and a good father – don't I slave to the best of my ability to keep this house going – keep things in the best way I can for you and Dave? . . .'

(Oh, you do: she thought bitterly; you do, and you know it. Always the male trump card. Our complete dependence on you. . . .)

'. . . And what do I get in return? I'm treated like some sort of an ogre; an outsider. Things have got to be hidden from me. Dave has to be protected from me: I'm too brutal for him and his emotional refinements. . . .'

'That's funny.' She laughed shortly. '*Dave's* emotional refinements!'

'What do you mean?'

'I mean if anyone's a hound for *refinements* here, it's you. You refine things out of all recognition. You'll never for a moment allow that any situation can be open and simple. . . .'

'Is that so?' He did not allow her to finish. 'Well, here's a perfectly simple open situation after your own heart. . . . My son comes back from school with his face messed up. I ask a straightforward question – what has he been fighting about? – and I'm met with the most astonishing manœuvres and evasions. I'm even blackmailed into considering myself a villain for asking.' He paused. 'I'm sorry, Catherine,' he said, 'but I'm not quite such a fool as you think. And I've had more than enough of these tactics. I regret to have to force you into complete frankness for once, but I'm determined – absolutely determined, do you hear me, Catherine? – to get to the bottom of this, once and for all. . . .'

(Stop it, she was crying in herself, stop it, oh, stop it, you fool, can't you guess what I'm trying to spare you?)

'Catherine?'

She said then, and her voice was characteristic of that peculiar, unflinching calm which was these days her refuge from complete emotional disintegration: 'You're wasting your time. I haven't the least idea what he was fighting about. I never troubled to ask him.'

He saw that she was lying and he was, for a moment, completely taken aback. Catherine never lied to him. Inept for lies, too fastidious or too impatient, she retreated instead into her honest, ungainly silences. But now she thought it worth her while to lie. . . . Abruptly, he went over towards the door. 'Very well,' he said. 'I must find out from Dave, that's all.'

'Alec.' She lifted her face. She looked old and weary. 'Shut the door,' she said. Silently he obeyed her. . . . She said without expression: 'The reason he had that fight to-day was because one of the boys in the playground – in front of all the others – called him a Jew. . . .'

CHAPTER FOURTEEN

ON LOCATION

The guard slammed the door shut; and Alec, tugging at the strap, let the window down into its socket. There was still a minute to go. People were clustering ardently about the train; straining to grip hands, to express the utmost contact before the void of absence began to open, wider and wider with each revolution of the wheels, between those leaving and those staying behind. Alec pushed his shoulders through the narrow aperture. 'Write to me to Göthenburg,' he said. 'I'll expect a letter from you there.' Catherine nodded, without speaking. They were waiting, both of them, for the hands of the clock to jump forward: they could not say goodbye before that: they were like actors listening nervously in the wings for their cue. 'Don't bother to wait,' he told her: knowing that he would be ignored. There is something that compels people to witness departures painful to them: accompany their friends to railway stations or funerals. *Partir, c'est mourir un peu. . . .* Catherine's hand clung to his with an inexplicable and passionate intensity, as if there was much she might convey to him that her lips must not speak. 'I shall miss you,' Alec found himself saying. Her face was upraised to his under a straw hat that shed across it an unfamiliar, an ambiguous light. 'And I you,' she said. Her fingers tightened convulsively about his. And yet, between them, all the while, was the fact, to which neither of them now referred, that Catherine had refused to accompany her husband on this journey. This situation, which appeared to cause her pain, was yet of her own creating. The pain, then, that she experienced was not born of the desire to be with him, but of regret for the fact that she could not find in herself that desire. . . .

The whistle blew sharply. He took the parting kiss from her upraised mouth. 'Goodbye, my love.' 'Goodbye, Alec – God bless you.' He saw then what he had only once before seen: the glitter of tears in her eyes. He was, for a moment, strangely confused. He tried to speak to her, but already the movement of the train was tearing their hands asunder. Space intervened: intimacy was briskly amputated. Absence, although they could still see each other, had at this point begun. The train gathered speed. They were each borne away from the other, diminishing, impotently waving. . . .

That was that. . . . Relinquishing, on the final bend of the train, their connexions with London, the passengers drew in their heads and came back into the compartment. Human nature has no independence: bereft of one support, at once, by the chemistry of proximity, it sends out its tendrils in search of the next. Already, in the swaying corridor, there were some who glanced tentatively, questioningly, at their fellow passengers. Others plunged at once into books or papers: seeking a more impersonal refuge in the printed word. Or

a liquefaction of the personal problem, the devouring self-awareness in the shining glass, the bottle. Over the Pullman table, Hetty Follet (and with her Stephen Wynn, B.-A.'s rising young featured player) clung each one to their glass as to some temporary anchor against circumstance. Andy Wilson sat opposite them: not drinking. Andy was the unit's first assistant. He was young, very young indeed, barely in his twenties: a miracle of efficiency and good humour, he was at one and the same time altogether worldly-wise and altogether innocent. He had a flat honest face, and the inner soundness of him was to be read openly in his eyes. Scores of mature actors, actresses, extras and technicians had confided their amours, their private difficulties, their unsavoury stories in Andy; that farmer's lad freshness of eye and character remaining totally unaffected. His mental health was such that it would have thriven even on a dung-heap. Stephen raised his glass to him now in friendship. '*Skål*,' he said. The train was flying along between rows of tall brick houses; between back-gardens unequally mean or splendiferous: everywhere, it seemed, the nation's washing was hanging out to dry, a multi-coloured bunting; the banner, manifesto of everyday reality.

Rudi Schlesinger appeared out of nowhere, a monumental, a much-labelled, suit-case slung before his knees. He put the suit-case down and waved a hand towards the scene beyond the window. 'Look at that: pure Alec Berman,' he said. He turned to where Alec had ensconced himself, away from the others, in a corner seat. 'It's infringement of copyright,' he said. Alec said nothing. Rudi hesitated: he wanted, had intended to join Alec: but Alec sat unmoving, smoking, staring out of the window. . . . Rudi, who after nine years of association knew Alec very well indeed, went over and joined Hetty's group, leaving Alec to the luxury of his own taciturnity.

'The train is full of the most interesting people,' Rudi announced as he sat down amongst them. 'Swedes returning to their native land. Healthy-looking blondes with kindergarten complexions and surprisingly bold eyes.'

'Aha,' murmured Stephen. 'The shape of things to come.'

Hetty, releasing an exquisitely expensive odour of musk, turned to shrug her shoulders out of a white camel-hair coat. Stephen bent over at once to assist her: very courteously and without the slightest interest. Hetty was 'work'. . . . Hetty, equally, accepted his ministrations with indifference: the professional relationship that existed between these two rendered all personal contact meaningless: each was to the other utterly neutral. Perhaps for this reason, they were often faintly uneasy in each other's presence; as might be a married couple, conscious of some intimate failure. . . . The paradox being that every suburban cinema, every film paper in the kingdom, carried its close-up of Stephen Wynn's dark striking head bent over Hetty's frail blonde one: their perfectly-modelled lips accurately and firmly joined. Possibly from this it was that the mutual distaste sprang: there being a difference of degree only between these two, the handsome young man and lovely celebrated woman, who daily mimed love for a living, and others who, in unspecified surroundings, anonymously consented to pose for a less sentimental and more comprehensive type of close-up. . . .

At Tilbury, they saw their ship waiting for them: the *Suecia*: very tall, white and cold-looking. She was flying the Swedish colours: a yellow cross on a sky-blue ground. Once on board, Alec wandered off in the direction of the purser's cabin: hoping, without permitting himself to hope, for a wire from Catherine. There was none. . . . He went below to discover the cabin he was at his own request sharing with Rudi. A bleached-looking stewardess directed him in fluent but peculiarly intoned English. He thanked her and, stepping in, looked about him apprehensively. Alec was a land-lubber: he disliked unconditionally the whole atmosphere of ships: the saltiness in his lungs, the blankness of the sky-line: as he disliked at this moment the peculiar and, to him, instantly nauseating atmosphere of his cabin: the asphyxiating smell of blankets; the narrow berth; the flask of water anchored to its bracket: the sinister container awaiting his *malaise*. He fled the cabin and, with the tremble and throb of concealed engines in his ears, made his way up a steep flight of stairs to the deck. He found no comfort in the aseptic emanations of sea-air that greeted him there; and, threading his way unheeded through a confusion of passengers and wanted-on-voyage luggage, took refuge in the writing-room, where chintz curtains masked the obtrusive sea-view and a soft Turkey carpet belied its presence underfoot. He sat at a small desk in the corner of the deserted room and, finding some notepaper marked *S.S. Suecia*, uncapped his fountain pen and began to compose a letter to Catherine.

An hour later, looking through the porthole, he could see England slipping away with a sort of silent uncanny ease. The ship seemed motionlessly to tread her natural element: they ran smoothly, barely a throb. It was a lovely evening: the sunset only now dying from the calm sky; the land faintly veiled in the oncoming darkness. Alec thought: If it's only like this for the next thirty-six hours it won't be so bad. . . .

Rudi came into the writing-room, looking for him. He was wearing an elaborate sweater and brown and white shoes. 'Oh, there you are,' he said, brought up short at the sight of Alec in his corner. 'Come and have dinner before the stampede begins.' They went out; stepping over the high bar at the entrance. 'Andy had a cable from the others,' he told Alec as they went along the deck. 'Shooting conditions are still O.K. apparently. Everything else is fixed up. Not a hitch. Location near Karlstad: and there's an absolutely first-class hotel. Trust young Walton to make sure of the creature comforts.'

It was darker now: lights, which were beginning to twinkle all along the coast, travelled smoothly past them and away as the ship pursued her path, dividing the deep waters in her passage. People were strolling along the deck, chatting and laughing: an unfamiliar accent fell upon Alec's ears. A tall young woman, with pale yellow hair and a pale shapely face: a fair young man who wore a dark suit and bright yellow shoes: he listened to the sing-song voices. Someone was calling along the deck, 'Sven, Sven!' *Sven*: that was the name of the hero in this film they were about to make. . . . A faint despair invaded him: he felt so remote from these people, so totally unable to get the hang of their thoughts, feelings. . . . This bloody picture'll be no good, he said: forgetting that he said this regularly and with equal conviction before every picture he had ever embarked upon. . . .

In the small comfortable smoking-room, after dinner, they were joined by Stephen and Andy, both obviously in convivial mood. Stephen, who knew the drink appropriate to any conceivable latitude and had already initiated Andy into the ritual of the pre-prandial *schnapps*, ordered black coffee, punch and cigars for everybody. The punch came, sweet and potent, ice-cold, in glasses that were misted to the brim; a perfect accompaniment to the good coffee, the fragrant exhalations of tobacco that hung about them like the aura of their own complete physical satisfaction.

'Where's Hetty?' Alec asked.

'Dining in her *state room*. . . . Hetty, like Garbo, wishes to be alone.'

No one commented on the fact. In a way they were sorry for Hetty. Hetty had been a long time in films, now: there were some who had suggested latterly that she was beginning to 'slip' at the box-office: that she was finished: that this picture would be her last for British-Alliance. . . .

'Should I go and fetch her?' Andy asked uncertainly.

'Plenty of time,' Rudi said. Almost imperceptibly he shook his head. Andy saw and sank into his seat again: deferring to the other's judgment. Rudi sighed and, abruptly, lifting his glass: 'Well, here we go – Laughing and Scratching,' he said. He drained the small glass.

The sound of music, a faint throb of jazz, floated in to them from the deck. 'Hullo.' They all looked up. 'Revelry by night!' said Stephen. He pushed away his glass: 'This must be investigated.' He stood up with alacrity and Rudi, disentangling his length from the wicker arm-chair, rose with him. Andy looked at Alec.

‘Run along,’ Alec said with a smile. ‘I’ve got some writing to do. I’ll join you later.’

Left to himself, he took out from between the pages of the unread (and he was beginning to fear, unreadable) novel he had carried firmly clamped to his chest ever since setting foot on board (as a potential re-agent against sea-sickness, boredom or the intrusive curiosity of his fellow passengers), the sheets of note-paper on which he had, earlier in the evening, begun his letter to Catherine. He read through it now with a certain amount of appreciation, altering a word here and there. . . . Then, turning over a sheet, he set himself to continue. He sat for a long time with the nib of his fountain pen poised: dry of words. Endeavouring at last to seek inspiration out of his previous momentum, he read through the screed again. Even then his pen found no impulse: the doldrums continued: he began to draw faces on the pink edge of the blotter; watching the lines blur and thicken. Occupied at this soul-destroying task, he became aware of the shadows of people passing along on the deck outside: of their voices, laughter. The sound of dance-music came louder: the languorous beat of a tango. He realized that the smoke-room was deserted: everyone else seemed to be out on deck. . . . Abruptly, slipping the untouched sheets of note-paper into the novel and the novel under his arm again, he got up and went out into the mysterious light and darkness of a shipboard night.

It was pitch dark, now: sea and sky equally invisible: the sea mapped out here and there by a riding light; the sky by its stars. At one end of the ship, the hard brilliance of electricity beat down on the deck; and it was here that, to the music of a big gramophone, couples were dancing: passing in and out, from shadow into light, and back into the shadows again. The stock of records was apparently a mixed one: Alec, who, unmusical, yet never forgot a trivial tune, recognized the vintage of the tango that was being played. He had danced to it himself – how many years ago?

'Liebe war es nie,
Nur eine kleine liebelei. . . .'

The music swelled, sang out clearly into the unlimited night. Alec stood still and watched. Among the couples dancing, he presently perceived Rudi. Stephen was nowhere to be seen: Stephen, Alec reflected, was a fast worker. . . . Young Andy stood at the gramophone, amiably winding, changing needles and records: unheeded, unthanked. A nice lad. . . . Alec turned again to seek out Rudi among the dancers. There he was; his arm closely encircling the waist of the tall blonde Alec had noticed previously. They danced perfectly: without a word: strangers rapt in the utter communion of bodies at one, moving with the same impulse and knowledge.

'Liebe war es nie. . . .'

How well, Alec thought, the hackneyed tawdriness of dance tunes expressed a certain level of experience: the languors, the moron sorrows, the voluptuous abandonment of infatuation. . . . What value they set on this one thing: not sex, but sexual romanticism: glamour. And yet, he thought, cheap and fictitious as it all was, when one had lost the capacity for being seduced by that fiction, something had gone for ever. . . . Standing there, not dancing, watching the others dance, he was suddenly reminded of the fact that he was a married man; a father: that a whole part, the major part, perhaps, of his life was already over and done with. . . . Strangely enough, the thought meant little to him: it did not seem to register. Quite simply, he did not believe it. Perhaps, he thought, because one really regards youth as a component part of one's personality; one of one's gifts, permanent assets. . . .

The music was languishing to a close. The dancers paused, still embraced: then, the final note spent, in the consummation of silence, they parted, strangers again. . . . Nursing her right elbow lightly in his palm, Rudi led the tall young woman back to her seat: where he bowed and left her. He came over to where Alec was standing and lit a cigarette. There was a certain unmistakable animation in his eye. 'Not dancing?' he asked Alec.

Alec shook his head. He said, but entirely out of curiosity to discover what it felt like, 'My dancing days are over.' He listened to himself say it. More amused than convinced. For, of course, it was not true: it could never be true. Inalterably young, one assumed, indulgently, the disguises considered appropriate to one's age. *My dancing days are over*. . . . What humbug. Nothing, Alec thought, nothing at all (not the greyness, not the rheumatism, not the denture bathing in the glass of water) would ever convince one that one's dancing days were really over. . . .

Andy put another record on: the throb of jazz filled the air again. People were rising, moving off to seek new partners.

Rudi wasted no time. He crushed out his cigarette, buttoned the lower button in his jacket, and crossed the deck. He bowed once again before the tall blonde; who, until the moment that he actually presented himself before her, sat with a look of acute unawareness on her face. She rose then, with the appropriate off-hand I-don't-mind-if-I-do expression, and came into his arms. He said something to her and she smiled faintly. They moved off and were lost to view among the other dancers.

'. . . and I seem to find the happiness I seek,
When we're out together
Dancing cheek to cheek. . . .'

Alec sighed suddenly. He turned away. Pausing to smoke a cigarette, he leaned over the rail, staring into darkness, watching the ghostly foam flash and vanish beneath. Then he went below to his cabin. Undressing, he got into the lower bunk and, switching on the light above his head, took up his novel again and began to read. Behaving sensibly, a married man and a father. . . . He smoked cigarettes, waiting for Rudi. But it was very much later before Rudi finally appeared: very pale, his hair in disorder.

When the *Suecia* landed at Göthenburg two mornings later, Alec came up on deck, shivering and unsteady. He had been extremely ill during the voyage. He stood there in the dazzling sunlight, huddled inside his overcoat, the green-backed novel still clasped to his heart: his life-buoy, his plank,

his one contact with reality. . . . Wanly he looked about him, with a convalescent's eye: surprised to see how flat and placid the deck looked, how innocent the water in the harbour, sparkling in the early sunlight. All fight had gone out of the ship: she submitted to being hauled in, tied up to the quayside; tamely: almost penitently. All passion spent. As he thought so, she gave a sudden jerk and quiver: at once, some inner equilibrium shifted: he was back in the nightmare atmosphere of giddy eyes, perspiring head, the violent recurring *malaise* that lifted the heart out of him. . . . Rudi, standing by him, eyed him anxiously. 'Bear up,' he said. 'We're landing.' Alec nodded. He could not trust himself to speak. . . .

They made their way finally down the slatted gangway and set foot on Sweden. A car was waiting for them and, almost at once, they drove into Göthenburg, where Walton had arranged for them to breakfast at the Grand Hotel. Alec, conscious of land, stability, beneath him, but oppressed by a sort of mazy headache whenever the car swung round a corner, shut his eyes to the foreign-looking trains, houses, posters. He leaned back against the padded side of the car and listened to the others talking: discovering thereby the queer, slightly distorted world that emerges when hearing a conversation with lids sealed. He hoped the journey would continue like this indefinitely: in a sort of suspension of awareness, of personal participation. . . . But already the car was slowing-down; stopping. They were at the Grand. Alec opened his eyes unwillingly. He looked at the front of the hotel: the big porch. Now for it. Unconsciously, for several hours, he had

been both dreading and looking forward to this moment: steeling himself, or rather drugging himself, against the disappointment in store should Catherine not have sent him a letter there as she had promised to do. . . . Now, before he had actually inquired for it, he could still persuade himself that there was a letter: frame, even, anticipating her intention, the words it must contain. *'Away from you, all those differences that have lately overshadowed our lives together, seem to dwindle, become unimportant; and I know once again what you really mean to me. . . .'* Instantly, then, everything would be all right again: he would know that she had sent him to solitude only in order, eventually, to discover herself closer to him. . . .

'No, sir,' said the clerk behind the polished counter. (He spoke with an American accent.) 'No mail for Herr Berman. . . . Quite, Sir. . . . Oh, yes, Sir, quite sure. . . .'

Alec sat in a corner of the big dining-room; at this early hour deserted: a wilderness of starched white table-cloths. There was a cup of hot coffee before him; he sipped at it slowly. The cup trembled in his grasp: it was an effort to hold it: his wrist felt enervated, flaccid. Trains, keening a foreign note, surged along just beyond the big curtained windows. Someone passed a plate of the flat, perforated hard-bread along the table. He could not be sure, but he had an idea that Stephen Wynn, at the other end of the table, was drinking *schnapps* and eating what looked like herring and boiled potatoes. . . . Andy spoke: when Alec turned to look, he saw a face that grinned, unfamiliar, through a sort of fog. He nodded, but he had not heard what Andy said: nor did he hear what the others about the table were saying: voices, he realized, seemed to have lost their power to carry; they were muffled, they did not bite cleanly on his hearing. Sitting there, unconcerned, calm, almost, he was aware of a queer feeling: of slipping a little out of focus: losing contact with things. . . .

In the train (they were on their way to Karlstad), Rudi peremptorily hauled suit-cases off the seat and made Alec lie down at full length. He went off and borrowed a travelling cushion from Hetty's dresser. Alec, still wearing his overcoat, could find no warmth: on the contrary, warmth seemed, with each breath, to flow out of him, leaving him transparent, vulnerable. He began to shiver. Rudi was watching him. 'I know what'll fix you,' he said. He disappeared and presently came back with Stephen Wynn's ornate morocco-leather and silver travelling flask. Sitting down, he unscrewed the cap and poured out brandy with a steady hand. 'Here you are,' he said. 'A little bit of what you fancy does you good, as Marie Lloyd used to say.' His large amiable face hovered for a moment over Alec. Alec swallowed obediently, shuddering under the sudden nettling in his throat: at once, he lay down again, turning on his side, huddling his chin into his chest, as if to seek within himself some centre of warmth. After a time, he appeared to doze. Rudi picked up his detective novel: a paper-backed *Albatross* that he had bought in Göthenburg. Occasionally, he glanced out at the pine trees, the shining lakes, the red wooden houses with white window-sashes: more often, his glance came to rest on Alec. Whenever it did so, he frowned. Rudi Schlesinger understood, perhaps, more about Alec Berman than Alec Berman realized. . . . He knew, for instance, something of Alec's emotional dependency on his family life: of his uneasiness

about this, his first picture with a foreign background. He knew, too, that at the last moment, for some reason not explained, Alec's wife had failed to accompany him on the journey. . . . Rudi looked across at Alec for a moment: he seemed about to say something, then he changed his mind. He gave a slight shrug of the shoulders and went on reading.

At Kil, where others of the unit would have to get a further connexion for Karlstad, Walton, the second assistant, met Alec, Rudi, Stephen and Hetty with a very new-looking Packard car. He sounded a tattoo on the horn when he saw them; splitting the air. They came up to the car and Walton's unfailingly facetious manner dropped from him when he saw Alec. He exclaimed in concern, 'Gosh! – what's wrong?'

'Poor old Alec's suffered a sea-change of some sort,' Stephen said. He wished to cover up the fact that he had kept himself at a distance from Alec since learning of his indisposition: Stephen feared illness and was ashamed of his fear. . . . 'Come on – get in,' Rudi said shortly. Out here in the sunlight, Alec looked wan and dazzled, ghost-like. He said to Walton, who was staring at him: 'Beastly crossing, that's all: I'll be all right.' He was surprised as he spoke to hear his own voice reaching him as if through a layer of cotton wool. It gave him a new sensation: he felt remote from himself. . . . In the car, Hetty, hatless, in her white travelling coat, looked at him keenly. 'You're a nice one,' she said. But there was sympathy in her voice: her eyes smiled at him. Old scores had long been wiped out between these two; they forgave each other much, including the betrayal of that which once had existed between them: that which Time, now, held in pawn and which they could never reclaim. . . . The car started: they swung through the interminable pine-bordered roads: saw pine trees and more pine trees, like a city of spires under the brilliant blue sky.

Unnoticed by the others, Alec grew even paler. Something was happening to him. Treacherously, terrifyingly, reality had begun to slip away from him. . . . He required every ounce of his energy to hold on, not allow it to slip away altogether: he sweated with the effort. . . . Already, his hands and feet were miles from him, empty of sensation, like balloons. Walton spoke; and his voice had gone queer: it was like a buzz, a drill, wavering close, then receding again. . . . Alec tried to say something: call out, anchor himself to the others and their everyday reality. A surprising wave of weakness, different to anything he had yet experienced, went over him. He fought to regain control: summon himself back to himself. But it was too late. With a sense, then, of pure relief that he need no longer fight, he let go; and went head over heels into the bounteous soft blackness. . . .

There was a sudden blank in the conversation. A new sort of silence. . . . Had the car stopped? A pause. . . . Someone's fingers, three cold finger-tips, were sidling along his wrist; were pressed on to the cord of his pulse as on to a violin string. No part of him existed, except his wrist, like the wrist of a drowned man with these cold fingers upon it. 'He's got hardly any pulse,' he heard a voice say suddenly: quite loud, it was like a shout. He made an effort, tried to look up, open his perspiring eyelids: everything went small, far-off again. . . .

They had pulled up somewhere. He was being assisted through a doorway. He heard voices, as in a dream. Then he was

in a lift that rose, whining: he was walking down a carpeted passage, into a cold white bedroom. Then this must be Karlstad, the what's-its-name hotel. . . . Well, thank goodness for that. . . . He opened his eyes a fraction, tearing a slit in the darkness, and had a glimpse, through the rent, of big windows: a quilted bed: then cold, nausea closed on him again. 'Come on, old man.' Rudi was struggling to get him out of his coat. He was lying in bed, soft sheets piled up about his shoulders, his face sunk in the lap of the pillows: conscious that now, safely, he could seek oblivion. . . . There were voices again. 'He's here, doctor,' he heard someone say. He was being examined again: his pulse: then the cold ring of the stethoscope flattened itself on to his heart. They gave him more brandy. This time, he was aware, after a moment, of a gradual warmth expanding within him; then more warmth, as they packed hot-water bottles about him. Voluptuously, he allowed himself to bathe in the stream; that warmth which began now to permeate right through him, miraculously dissolving away the cold, the vacuousness; bringing with it a sense of returning reality, of release from the nightmare insecurity. After a time, he fell into a deep natural sleep. He slept round the clock without moving.

That was Friday. On Saturday morning he was down to breakfast with the unit at seven o'clock. Completely restored. They greeted him boisterously, accepting his recovery with relief, ready at once to forget their anxiety of the day before. 'You're a fraud, that's what you are – putting the wind up us like that.' (But Rudi had cornered him that morning as he stood shaving in his luxurious green-tiled bathroom. Saying

nothing at first, staring at Alec busy with his tube of shaving-cream. Then – 'Well?' Rudi said at last. 'Well?' Alec countered: rubbing cream into his chin: unconcerned. 'And what,' Rudi said deliberately, 'what exactly did you mean by it all?' But Alec only shrugged his shoulders. . . .) At the head of the long white table this morning, he ate heartily: with enjoyment. The food at the Stadshotel was excellent. Mouth full, he questioned Walton about the day's arrangements. They were shooting that morning at a spot near Filipstad; a small town about an hour from Karlstad. The weather was perfect: brilliant sunshine coming out of an almost cloudless sky. Walton had, without difficulty, rounded up dozens of willing 'locals' to act as extras. Everyone was good-tempered. For the moment all was right with the world from a film unit's point of view. Rudi himself had been up since six. He had managed to secure a shot of six hundred workers arriving on their bicycles at a factory in Herrhagen. . . .

Andy appeared, with an armful of English newspapers – and letters. Everyone glanced up: their eyes fastened at once on what he had in his hand. Hypnotized, all of them, by that exciting-looking bundle; long envelopes, short fat ones, typed or addressed by hand. . . . They looked at Andy as if he were Father Christmas, preparing to distribute free gifts. Alec had learnt discipline: there would be none for him. . . . 'One for you, Alec,' Andy said. Unique words! . . . Alec felt indebted to Andy even for pronouncing them. . . . Andy held out the letter. How beautiful, how thrilling was the squat shape of the envelope, the red English stamp interlaced in its post-mark. . . . 'Thank you': Alec smiled, reaching out. He saw the

handwriting. His heart dropped like a stone. Brian's finicky 'varsity script. . . .

After breakfast, there ensued that hiatus, conspicuous in hotels, when people, after dawdling in a desultory way about the lounge, disappear unobtrusively with *The Times* tucked underneath their arm: re-appearing after a short spell with a brisk satisfied air, to peer out of windows and talk of going out for a walk. The rest of the unit had already gone on: Alec, Hetty and Stephen (the latter two in their make-up) were the last to leave. The Packard of yesterday awaited them outside the hotel door. Alec looked, for a moment, with pleasure, at Karlstad: the broad river; the general air of order and cleanliness: even here, the smell of pines reached him. 'Not a bad little place, is it?' Stephen said. Alec nodded. His hostility to a strange country was ready to disappear. If only Catherine had been here with him, he thought. . . . As it was, every new sight, every hint of beauty, became a burden, since it reminded him that he was here alone to see it. He missed, more acutely than he ever thought he would, the companionship of her mind. The comments he knew she would have made; where she would have been enthusiastic; where amused. Her ghost accompanied him in this way: making of her absence a positive, present thing. . . .

They worked hard that morning. Alec, Walton, Andy and the interpreter set to marshalling the dozen or so peasants specially got up for the occasion in their multicoloured national costume. Hetty (playing a rôle that in one form or another she had often portrayed before, that of an adventuress: in this case, an international jewel-thief) was supposed to be at the wheel of her car, driving, when the car, previously doctored by Stephen (a detective, following love and duty awkwardly combined in the one person), breaks down on the road. A group of peasants, coming back from church, swarm round, peeping, trying to help. . . . The car, the usual cream-coloured roadster, was already in position and Hetty, wearing a white sharkskin jacket and an unlikely travelling hat with a flowing veil, sat in it, submitting to the ministrations of her dresser: having her hair combed out, powder patted on her face, with an impersonal air, as if she were a public statue being groomed: a comprehensible detachment, since it was not her, but Felicia, the adventuress, who was receiving these ministrations, Hetty being there only by proxy; undergoing this process on Felicia's behalf. The peasants, with their light-blue eyes, their tow-coloured hair, stared, fascinated. Equally, when Alec, through the interpreter, tried to convey to them exactly which actions they were to fulfil, they watched him, grinning, more interested in his voice and gestures than in that which they were supposed to do. The sun beat down: forcing out an exquisite smell of resin from the pine trees: the lake garnered between the trees sparkled fiercely. Alec wiped his brow and tried again. 'Explain it to them,' he said to the interpreter. 'Tell them that . . .'

At noon, Alec, Hetty, Stephen, and with them, the interpreter, left the unit exploring the contents of their cardboard lunch-boxes and went off for a meal. Stephen drove. They passed through Filipstad, with its wooden houses, its beflowered lamp-posts, its little bridges arched over glittering streams almost too shallow to cover the pebbles beneath; and began

to climb a pine-bordered road. 'There we are – Spångberget' the interpreter said, pointing. It was a big wooden chalet in a clearing in the pine woods, with the tables laid out all round on the open verandas. There was a mixed smell of pine tree and roast coffee: wholly delicious. Hetty sniffed appreciatively. 'Gosh,' she said. She took off her hat and swept back her newly-doctored silver-white hair. She still had her sweeping artificial eyelashes; her carefully composed yellow-rose complexion, as flawless and unconvincing as an artificial peach. The interpreter, a young student local to Karlstad, could not keep his eyes off her. There was respect, admiration and incredulity in his gaze. . . .

Alec, taking a solitary stroll about Karlstad that evening, saw that the cinema in the big cobbled marketplace had revived, as a gesture to his presence in the town, what was perhaps his most celebrated picture, 'Farewell Leicester Square.' *Farewell Leicester Square*. . . . To-day the words had a faintly ominous ring for him, absent when, himself younger and the world, even those few years ago, a different place, he had made that picture. *Farewell Leicester Square*. . . . Would he ever, he wondered, be saying that in earnest? Compelled, against the grain, against his most deep-rooted inclinations, to go? Go – but go where? There was no Tipperary for him: his heart held no loyalties save to this one country which might or might not (the hair-breadth balance of policies; impersonal) decide from one day to the next to dispense with himself and his loyalties equally. Impartially sacked from his dedicated, his life's job as a British citizen. . . . Where then?

He had a vision of the contemporary situation: country after country shutting its doors. Unlovely panic. . . . Comprehensible, though. The instinct of self-preservation. . . . He thought of what Catherine had said to him once: We are all guilty of hammering on the knuckles of those who try to climb into our boat. . . . That was what they were doing, those doctors, those lawyers who protested against the 'influx' of refugee doctors, lawyers. . . . What we want, he thought, is the Barnardo spirit in politics. The Ever-Open Door. No Really Destitute Person Ever Refused Admission. . . . But the morality which governs people in their private lives is not incumbent upon them as a nation. On the contrary. The policy is No Really Destitute Person Ever Granted Admission. The Ever-Bolted Door. At the same time he blamed no one. Unflinchingly honest with himself, he realized that he himself might well be equally indifferent if he were one of the fortunate; the secure. . . .

He came back to the hotel. At once he was intercepted. 'Herr Berman!' It was the clerk: a pale young man wearing startlingly bright-yellow shoes. He came out from behind his desk. Before he spoke, Alec saw what he had in his hand. 'A letter for Herr Berman,' he said.

. . . So it had come. 'Thank you,' Alec said. 'Thanks very much.' The clerk went away and he stared at the letter in his hand, at Catherine's writing on an unfamiliar envelope. He experienced something new: a sort of recoil. He wished that he was not holding this letter: that he was, instead, still waiting for it. . . . Looking idly at the post-mark, the half-obliterated stamping, he recognized the words *Middle Bay*. He thought: so Catherine had been seeing Basil. . . . She had seen him and given him her hastily scribbled letter to post; and he, equally casual, had forgotten to do so, until reaching the bungalow. That, or – He turned abruptly and went upstairs to his room, the unopened letter in his hand. Andy, passing him on a turn of the stairs and about to speak, checked himself: staring instead with a look of open surprise. . . .

The cream-panelled door: the already familiar number. His room. He let himself in and pushed the door to behind him. The room seemed to await him: enclosed in the hush of solitude. The big window framed a view of Karlstad, motionless, distinct, under the withheld dusk. He turned his eyes from the view reluctantly and opened the envelope. His hand was shaking. The first words told him. Yes, this was it. It had come, at last. . . . He read through it quickly, without a change of expression: without surprise or emotion, as though he had known it all before: the phrasing, the very commas, the fact that she chose to scribble in pencil on a cheap ruled pad. . . . He looked out of the window. The moment passed. . . . He became aware of an astonishing feeling: a sort of comfort, almost. It was as though he were, at last, safe. Safe, now that the sword of Damocles had actually fallen. . . . The event is less agonizing than the anticipation of it. There is a certain calm, a sense of security, even, in knowing the worst. One is no longer menaced. The event itself frees one of its more sinister component, the fear, the distorted shadow it casts before it; and is therefore not more, but less after its occurrence. . . .

He stood looking out at the river, lying broad under its bridge; suffused still with a sunlight that was only now beginning to ebb from the horizon. He saw the broad square beneath him, with people walking in it: the distant tufts of pine trees encroaching over the houses, standing, in the early dimness, as still as eavesdroppers. . . . Phrases from her letter repeated themselves in his brain.

'. . . Alec, do you remember you once said you were unwilling that, in marrying you, I should have to accept that "scheme of disadvantages" to which you are subject, in being what you are? I said I was ready to accept it – and I have been: it's never meant a thing to me, I've always been able to laugh at it, as you know. . . . But Alec (and do please try to understand this) *I'm not willing to accept the same scheme of disadvantages for my son*. . . . And he's the one who matters now. . . . It's different for a child, especially for a child like Dave. . . . You've seen for yourself . . . the divided loyalties . . . the fears . . . the self-consciousness. . . . He's not the sort of child to stand up to his position, unfortunately. On the contrary, it's making him ill. . . . If you want the best for him, Alec, you'll agree to part from him: at least for a while, until he's older, until he can see things for himself and make his own choice. . . . That's why I've come down here to Middle Bay. . . . I want a rest, too: how badly you don't know. . . . For myself I don't regret anything. . . . I believe you know this: that I've never loved anyone in the same way as I have you. No one at all. . . . That should have been sufficient. Apparently, it wasn't. . . .'

He folded the letter carefully in the same folds as Catherine had made and slipped it into the envelope, as she had done. So that was that, he said to himself mechanically, like a person who has made up his accounts: bewildered to find the small, the apparently trifling items adding up to make what seemed

a wholly disproportionate total. He stared out of the window: at the square beneath him; the cars, the people passing. Between that scene and himself, interposed, he saw Catherine's face: close, vivid in its most minute detail. He seemed to experience the actual quality of her presence, the everyday unvarnished reality of her, so bound up by now in his scheme of existence as to be altogether taken for granted. . . . *Catherine!* All of him went into that fierce silent invocation: his very pulses seemed to cry out her name. . . . His heart burned. He had never felt so full of love for her as he did at that moment.

Then her presence, her image, even, seemed to vanish from him. Alone, he stared down at the river, the square beneath. What did they call that Square? He had forgotten, if, indeed, he had ever known. . . . People whose very language was foreign to him passed up and down: coming out of shops, waiting on the kerb to cross, or lingering by the river. He did not know the name of that river. The scene had no associations for him: it was blank of meaning. . . . A piercing sense of solitariness filled him: unlike anything he had hitherto experienced: he shivered. Standing there, motionless in the light Northern dusk, he felt marooned from all that he had loved: an outcast from his own existence. Too clearly, and with a vision that related this to future events, he saw what he was losing; what process had begun; what exactly it was that was slipping from him. . . .

Farewell, Leicester Square. . . .

Ten days later, when Alec, accompanied by Rudi Schlesinger, came down the small flight of steps from his 'plane on to the field at Croydon, the first face he saw among the waiting group of people was Brian McKay's. Rudi saw it too. 'Hullo, look at the reception committee,' he said to Alec. Rapidly, he brushed his soft hat with the edge of a cuff. 'I hope you have some suitably improper tales to tell him about the *Frökens*. He'll feel jilted if you don't.' But Brian, when they at last got through to him, greeted them soberly. He gave a quick glance at Alec, who was looking white and tired. Then he said, and in the same moment Alec saw the orange slip of paper in his hand: 'Alec – this telegram came for you this morning, to Oxshott: Miss Travers opened it. In view of the contents, I thought I'd better bring it along. . . .'

'Thank you,' Alec said. He put out his hand and Brian gave him the telegram. Concerned, Rudi questioned Brian with raised eyebrows. Brian shrugged his shoulders. . . . Alec stood still: he read what the telegram said. *'Can you come at once Mother very ill.'* It was signed *'Sydney.'*

CHAPTER FIFTEEEN

THE JOURNEY BACK

The train pulled smoothly out of London. It gathered speed, rocking with a gentle persuasive motion: the white-coated waiter, coming down the central aisle of the Pullman car with a tray on the flat of his hand, staggered slightly and brought up smoothly again, the contents of his tray undisturbed. The suburbs went by, in a pattern that repeated itself: the lit cubes of windows, a tram crowned in light, the deserted playgrounds of county council schools. In an hour they would be in Brighton.

His head rested against the deep cushions at his back. He made no attempt to open the newspapers on the table before him. His eyes were shut. The rocking of the train caused his head to shake with a slight unceasing motion over which he had no control. He looked as if he were sleeping. People glanced at him with the slight embarrassment experienced before the sight of a fellow being publicly abandoned to oblivion. But he was not asleep. He was so utterly fatigued that even sleep was beyond him. He let his body shake with the motion of the train like the body of a dead man: utterly abandoning himself, now, to circumstance. . . .

When the train appeared to slow down somewhat, he managed to open his eyes. He looked about him vaguely. They were in a tunnel: brownish smoke mantled the big panels of the windows, the thunder of the train was muffled; the lights from the carriage reflected back on the blank window-panes: momentarily, they were in November. He saw the dark fog coil beyond the window. He shut his eyes again. After a moment, it seemed to him that he was back on the 'plane: that he travelled, floorless, in space: he heard the noise the engine made, revolving, ploughing through emptiness. . . . Equally suddenly, he was travelling, instead, in time, he was the young man on his way to London, with a big shabby suit-case and Richard Nicolls's letter in his pocket. . . . Lewisham and Mrs Stepney awaited him: he had yet to make the acquaintance of Brian McKay and Lewis Solomon, the big ramshackle studio on Vicar's Hill: British-Alliance and Rudi Schlesinger, Regency Road, Mrs Monk, Basil Nicolls and his sister Catherine. . . . He opened his eyes. They were out of the tunnel: the muffled roar of the train was liberated, the smoke no longer clung along the window-panes. A countryside he had not seen for seventeen years was flying away beyond the windows.

He began to feel in his bones the imminence of his home-town, his birthplace. . . . Rousing himself finally, he turned his head to the window, staring out for the first glimpse of what was travelling to meet him. Opposite him, a woman was beginning to grope for her coat; her bag; her gloves; and, seeing that re-assembly in progress, others about her began also to marshall their effects. The waiter appeared: to clear away ash-desecrated plates, paper wrappings shed from diminutive cubes of sugar: to present the discreetly folded bill, collect the discreetly proffered tip. The first lights sprang into view: then a chain of lights, a growing population of lights. . . . 'Excuse me,' said someone: reaching for a suit-case over Alec's head. The lights began to rotate more slowly: the train was slackening speed. Then, abruptly, they vanished altogether to be replaced by a vague dispersed illumination as they ran under the long hood of the station. Punctual on the hour, they were at Brighton.

* * *

People were pressing down the catches on the doors, stepping out on to the platform while the train was still slowing down alongside. All along the train, doors broke open: impatiently wrenched up. Liberated, the passengers streamed forth. Alexander Berman amongst them: holding the suit-case that he had packed, yesterday, in a bedroom of the Stadshotel, Karlstad. . . . As he set foot on the platform, he became aware of something at work in him: a curious repressed animation. Fatigue receded: consumed by this different fever. . . . Ignoring the porters, hauling his suit-case along beside him, he began to make his way down the platform, looking about him with excitement, as if he had reached some unimaginable land. . . . 'Tickets, please!' Recalled, he gave up the cardboard slip and passed through the grill into the hall of the station.

There, he stood transfixed. . . . The same waiting-room, the same buffet, the same big four-faced clock. . . . The trains, buses, outside. You got one from here that went to Rottingdean. And there, as before, to the left of him, was the yard with the waiting cars, the taxis: the telephone kiosks where he had looked up Richard Nicolls's address. . . . He stared about him at these things: no longer, now that he was actually here to see them, mysterious, as are objects glimpsed through time: but as dusty and commonplace as they had looked when he last laid eyes upon them in the flesh seventeen years ago. . . .

There was a brief touch upon his arm.

'Hullo, stranger.'

A shock of familiarity jolted his nerves; he turned round sharply. . . .

'Thought I'd spot you,' said Sydney Berman.

Alec felt the blood flame up into his face: he went painfully scarlet; even the tips of his ears burned. 'Syd!'

There was a moment, brief and revealing, before either of them could find words, when they merely stared: stared and, at the same time, openly took stock of each other; as wary and impersonal as strangers: which, in these instants of hiatus before the resumption of familiarity, they actually were: then, simultaneously, jerkily, interrupting each other, unaccustomed to the rhythm of each other's speech, they began together: 'Did you get the message we . . .?' 'I sent a wire to tell you. . . .' Alec stopped: he stared hopelessly at the face of his brother, comically, terribly disguised in its setting of fat: all the tone, the lustre of youth gone; dull-hued, with deep lines sunk about the mouth; the jaw-line beneath flaccid, badly shaven. (The dandified Sydney!) Even the forehead seemed altered: it looked taller, now that the profuse hair of youth had receded: hat and hairline, equally, seemed to inhabit the higher slopes of Sydney's head. . . . Only the eyes had not changed: authentic, recognizable, those were the eyes of the Syd he knew, looking at him strangely out of this altered mask.

'Well, Alec?'

'Well, Sydney?'

Belatedly, then, they shook hands and smiled faintly: at what, they did not know. Their hands fell asunder. . . . 'I'm glad you were able to make it,' Sydney said: trying to speak without embarrassment: (seventeen years is a long time: the mechanism of intimacy had become disused; intimacy itself an anachronism: and this sudden confrontal did as much violence to natures grown unaccustomed, as a sudden parting to natures deeply habit-bound. . . .) 'She'd been asking for you,' Sydney said. 'We were afraid we mightn't be able to find you. . . . We saw in the papers that you were away filming somewhere.'

The flush had died completely out of Alec's face: he looked again pale and exhausted. 'Tell me,' he said in a low voice: 'how is she?'

Sydney pursed his lips in a characteristic gesture: as if disclaiming any inner knowledge of her condition. 'I saw the doctor again just before I came out,' he said. 'He said she was much about the same. No change, in fact.'

'How – bad – is it, then?'

Sydney paused. 'Touch and go, I think myself,' he said. 'But you know these doctors. They won't give you yea or nay. . . . Father, of course, thinks the man's a quack and a robber. You should see the way he dashes to the window to spy on him when he goes off, as if he could learn something about him that way. . . .' He gave a faint, almost appreciative smile. . . . Then, recalling himself abruptly to the situation in hand: 'Well – coming?' he said. 'I've got the car over there.'

Alec picked up his suit-case and walked along beside his brother. 'I suppose Father knows I've been sent for?' he said.

'You bet.'

'Is he – fed up about it?'

They stopped in front of a battered navy-blue family saloon car. 'On the contrary,' Sydney said, unlocking the door, 'he's delighted that the decision has been taken out of his hands: that he can have his cake and eat it, so to speak: see you, without feeling that he's had to climb down first, go back on his word. . . . He's been pottering about all day, mending the broken window-cord in your room, rooting about in drawers – trying to discover the place where he hid the best cigars; worrying Amy to death about things.'

'Amy?' Alec said: since he must say something, to disguise the moment's emotion. . . .

'Oh, Amy's the maid. . . . Getting in? . . . A bit of a slut, I believe, but quite good-tempered. You'll see her. . . . Just a minute.' He stopped. 'Let me put your suit-case in the back,' he said. He took it from Alec's grip and then held it for a moment: arrested: looking at the pigskin flanks, slim brass fittings, perfectly stamped initials. All of a sudden a wide unrestrained smile transformed his face: a grin that skipped seventeen years. 'Local Boy Makes Good,' he murmured. . . .

The car started up, at last, and they slid out of the yard, past the waiting buses, into Brighton. Sooner than he expected,

Alec had before him the façade of the Regent Cinema, in the darkness of which he had nursed his early ambitions; then the Clock Tower: the streets, some of the shops, even, that had been for seventeen years only a memory. And here they were, clothed in reality once again: but a different reality to that which he had lent them: smaller, shabbier, more crowded than he remembered. . . . 'Know your way?' Sydney asked: he turned the car sharply to the right. 'This part just here hasn't changed so much – it's further along you'll see it: the big stores, Marks and Spencers, Boots. . . .' Lights intercepted them, shooting from amber to red: they waited, engines throbbing. Alec said to Sydney, who sat watching for the first returning flicker of amber, 'Why didn't you let me know about all this earlier? . . . I could have brought a specialist down from London.'

'I don't think that would have done much good,' Sydney said. (His hand on the driving-wheel was plump, quite round across the back, the knuckles invisible. The cuff of a grimy striped shirt protruded from a sleeve that with increasing plumpness had become too short for his arm.) 'You see, it's quite a straightforward case. A few weeks ago, she had a small operation, one of these women's things, nothing much in itself. But she didn't seem to pull round from it as she should have. She began to lose strength. . . . And then she got that she wouldn't eat; wouldn't look at food even. . . . These last few days she can't keep anything down, not even water. . . . It's only a question of her strength holding out. . . .'

Amber; and then the green. The car shot forward. 'Where is she?' Alec asked.

'Oh, we have her home again, now. She couldn't stick that nursing-home. I don't blame her, either. The smell was enough for me. And that sour-looking nurse, thin as a yard of pump-water. . . .' He paused. 'Besides,' he said, 'she only fretted away from the house: worried about how we were "managing". You know Mother. . . .'

'Yes,' Alec said.

'Before the operation, all she was fretting about was would Amy fry the fish and make the chicken-soup as Father liked it done. She made them bring her paper and pencil and wrote out all the instructions in detail. . . . It was almost like her will,' he said simply. 'She had nothing else to leave. Only her knowledge of how to make every one comfortable.'

'She had a hard life,' Alec said: and he was thinking with the old half-conscious resentment of his Father: the way he took her presence, her ministrations equally for granted, with never an overt word of appreciation. . . .

'No. She's been happy, really,' Sydney said, unexpectedly. 'As happy as she knew how to be. She could only live through other people. She'd have felt wasted if she hadn't been able to devote herself. There isn't room for unhappiness in her sort of life.'

'Only weariness,' Alec said: remembering how she used to sit in the evenings, dozing over the mending that still remained to be done.

Sydney glanced at him. 'Yes. That's what it is now I think. . . . She's just too tired to pick up again.' He hesitated. 'Besides, the family's grown up now; she doesn't feel she's wanted in quite the same way. . . . She's relaxing for the first time in her life. . . .'

They were silent. Alec began to look about him, craning his head to see out beyond the low windscreen. He was surprised to find how clearly he remembered the layout of the streets. Looking for a landmark, he bent forward, a small expectant smile on his face, which changed after a moment to blankness: he turned his head quickly, staring back over his shoulder: searching the street. 'Why, the Emporium's gone,' he cried.

'Yes,' Sydney said. 'We sold out last year. That's it – that shop where they've got stockings and corsets. . . . Didn't get our price for it, of course: but then things haven't been too good lately. We've extended Havana House, though; it's got a double front, now: you remember, where the barber's shop used to be. We've been doing quite well there, ever since they opened the Sports Stadium. You must come over and see it to-morrow – I don't suppose you'll recognize it.'

'Father doesn't do much now, I suppose?'

'He's there every day; punctual to the minute. Can you imagine Father retiring before he has to? He'd go potty if he had nothing to do all day but gossip on the front with his cronies. . . . We're taking Arthur into the business next year. He's a bright lad.'

'Arthur?'

'My boy,' Sydney said. He grinned. 'He had some hair-brain notion of wanting to go on the stage – he can imitate Will Hay and all of them to the life – but Father soon put a stop to all that,' he said.

Alec had not recovered from his surprise. 'I didn't know you were married,' he said.

Sydney was equally surprised. 'Why, I've been spliced for years now. Arthur's fourteen and I've got two girls; Cynthia, who's twelve, and Ruth, eight. . . . You've got a boy, too, haven't you? We read about it in the papers.'

'Yes, he's six,' Alec said awkwardly. 'Who is your wife?' he asked. 'Did I know her?'

'You must have met her once. She was a Florrie Mosheim. She says she remembers you.'

'Oh, yes,' Alec said, who had never heard the name. 'I believe I do recollect, vaguely. . . .'

He became silent as the car, swinging away from the traffic, took the familiar short-cut that in two minutes would lead them into Lansdowne Road.

'Well,' Sydney said, lowering Alec's suit-case on to the sunken white-washed doorstep, 'welcome to the old homestead. . . . I suppose that's the appropriate *Brocha* to say over a returning prodigal.' Deviously attached to one end of the chain that held his latch-key, he leaned himself forward to negotiate a recalcitrant lock. Recovering the key with a tussle ('Lock still needs mending, you see') he reached across Alec and gave the door a slight push. Then he stood back, inviting Alec with a smile, a gesture, to pass in before him.

Alec's heart was beating rapidly. He had to fight down a rising sense of panic. Face to face after all these years with that familiar shabby door, he was strangely, almost frighteningly moved. . . . *Retourner, c'est mourir un peu*. To return, to venture back on one's own tracks, was to acquire the realization of death: to be nourished on a harvest of emptiness, to find a dry stick, a withered leaf in token of the glory, the greenness, plague-devoured by Time. . . . 'Well?' Sydney said. He was still waiting: his hand on the door. 'Thanks,' Alec said smiling. As if nothing were, he crossed over the threshold. . . .

And there it was. My God, *there it was*! . . . The same long badly-lit narrow hall: the same towering hall-stand: the same series of lithographs 'thrown in' with some job lot bought by Mr Berman at a sale-room: the same unique close-knit, instantly recognizable smell of a particular family's home-life. . . .

So this was it, Alec thought, staring. So this was actually it. . . . The hall-stand where he had hung his school-cap: the brass tray his mother used to polish every week with newspapers spread on the kitchen table. . . . He looked about him. The same – and yet how altered! How much smaller, shabbier, darker, less impressive, even, than memory, unimpressed, had portrayed it! Seen now, with the eyes of the actual, curiously altered, misshapen, almost; certain objects misplaced, angles too high or too low, all proportions disquietingly shrunk, the whole looking like some second-rate, undersized version of itself.

A voice cried, 'Is he here? . . . Is it him?' Rapidly, heavily, someone was descending the stairs. He turned, to see at the bend of the stairs, where a purple and red frosted glass window darkened the small landing, a stout dark woman – his mother – no, no, good heavens, how absurd; it was Violet, *Violet!*

'Alec. . . . Oh, Alec. . . .'

Before he could move, she was down the stairs and across the hall. And before he had time to utter a word, she threw both arms about him and kissed him: without reserve, without embarrassment; with sincere and delighted affection. . . . He experienced a moment indescribable and strangely thrilling; in which, after seventeen years, his being recognized again the special tone and familiarity of kindred flesh; the physical warmth, mutuality of *family*, of an intimacy that is amorphous and without frontiers. It was, in that moment, as if he had never been away: as if all his subsequent life since walking out of that door seventeen years ago had been a fantasy, a dream, and this the sole reality. . . .

Violet released him: she stood back to gaze at him; looking him all over; exclaiming, talking, laughing; tears of sheer excitement shining in her eyes. She kept saying, 'I can't believe it. . . . I just can't believe it! . . .' The light of the hall, a single naked bulb, beat down on her, harshly revealing. Alec stared. So this, now, was Violet. A middle-aged woman, stout, waistless, flabby; her hands work-roughened; her black hair ill-kempt and everywhere stranded with silver. Different, and yet, as he saw immediately on looking into her face, peculiarly the same: her own personality, like something unique, indelible, persisting through all that sought to blot out, disguise it: triumphantly withstanding the siege of the years, the accumulating ill-will of Time. Alec felt thrilled, almost exalted to recognize this: he felt as if he would like to acclaim her, congratulate her on having, against tremendous odds, broken through the enemy's line unscathed. . . .

'Well?' Sydney said, affecting to lean one elbow in space, 'do we go on standing here – or do we just go on standing here?'

'Why, of course,' Violet cried: 'Alec – you must be dead beat, poor boy! What am I thinking of?' (What indeed? Alec thought, faintly smiling. . . .) 'Come in and sit down,' she said. 'You know the way, I suppose? . . .' She went before him; and he followed, noticing that he had to walk carefully, now, past angles where he used to dash by as a boy, with a sense of spaciousness: that his fingers fumbled, at a loss, for the handle of the door, finding the knob (what a funny shape) lower, altogether smaller than he had expected. . . .

'There you are, Alec,' Violet said. 'Same old room. Hasn't changed much, has it?'

'No,' Alec said slowly. 'It hasn't changed much': standing rooted, looking about him: his skin almost creeping on his spine as he smelt out here the very ghost and essence of the past. . . . The clock ticked on the mantelpiece as it had done the morning he left the house seventeen years ago: there was the big square table where they all did their home-lessons: there was the gilt-framed picture of a lady holding aloft grapes of an almost surrealist purple: there the tall hearse-like sideboard with its bowl of fruit; the lace curtains heavily starched and darned in places, the linoleum surround about the worn red Turkey carpet, the shaggy pile of newspapers on a shelf under the wireless table. . . .

'Of course,' Sydney said, following his brother's gaze, 'we've made improvements. . . . You'll see. We had power drawn up, for instance: we've got electric fires in all the rooms, now. . . . Yes, those chairs: they're new. Only got them last month. I chose them.' He surveyed the mass-produced 'antique-styled' objects that he spoke of with pride. 'No sale-room junk,' he said. 'The genuine thing: direct from the makers. . . . Nice, aren't they?'

Violet summarily took Alec by the elbow and forced him over to the low chintz-aproned arm-chair. 'Never mind the chairs,' she said. 'You look as if you could sleep on your feet. . . . Sit down – relax.'

Alec obeyed. As soon as he had dropped into the chair, he had the sensation that his forces disbanded; that his joints would never lock together to permit him, of his own accord, to rise again. He lay back. He listened to the ticking of the clock: looked at the room.

'Well – ' Sydney said. He picked up his hat from the sideboard. 'If there's nothing more I can do at the moment – ' He looked at his watch. 'I shall have to be off,' he said.

Alec looked up: surprised. He could not accustom himself to the fact that Sydney no longer lived here: that he had a separate, different life, recognized by his family, sanctioned. . . . 'Where do you hang out these days?' he asked.

'Not far. Jamaica Crescent. About half a minute from here. You must come over, to-morrow. I know Florrie's dying to see you: the kids, too.' He stood fondling his hat between his hands. 'Well, must be getting along now,' he repeated. But still he hesitated. He looked as if there was something he wanted to say: he stood frowning and maltreating his hat. . . . At last – 'Well – glad to see you again, and all that,' he brought out abruptly: and, equally abruptly, he turned on his heel and left the room. A moment later they heard the front door slam behind him as he went off.

'Syd's a good sort,' Violet said quietly. 'It's not easy for him: every one puts the dirty work on his shoulders. He has to bear all the responsibilities about the business – about

Mother, about his own family – not to mention his in-laws. And what a lot *they* are! . . . But you never hear him complain.'

'What's his wife like?' Alec asked, curiously.

Violet made a coarse wry face which enlightened Alec instantly, at least as to the nature of the relationship that existed between the two sisters-in-law. 'Not what *I'd* call a wife,' Violet said. 'A woman who takes not the slightest interest in her home. . . . She thinks of nothing but her face and her clothes. At her age! The place looks like a pigsty whenever you go in there, and as for those children of hers, she never bothers with them, they're dragged up anyhow. It's Sydney who spends his time looking after them, not her. She's too busy manicuring her nails (you should see the length of them!) or running to the hairdresser every half-hour to have her hair set in a new way.'

The peculiar vindictiveness of the virtuous and humdrum woman stood expressed in her face as she spoke. Alec did not like to see it: he interrupted her with a question: 'Is he happy with her?' he asked. 'Goodness knows.' She paused; reluctantly honest. 'Oh, yes, I believe he thinks he is happy. . . . At least, he won't have a word said against her. He just doesn't want to bother to see her faults.'

'How wise,' Alec said. There was a pause. Suddenly, he put his hand to his forehead briefly; and then dropped it again, letting it lie listless on the arm of his chair. 'God, I'm tired,' he said. He looked it: all of a sudden, he was as white as a sheet, the bristle showing up dark around his lips. . . .

Violet gave him a quick penetrating glance. Then – 'Why, what am I thinking of?' she exclaimed. 'You must be starved.

I've got some lovely hot soup heating for you downstairs and a plateful of those big salt-beef sandwiches you used to like – remember? – with mustard. . . . You stay here – take it easy. I won't be a minute.'

She stood up. Alec lifted his head sharply. 'When do I see Mother?' he asked as she went towards the door.

'Not now,' she said. 'When the nurse calls you. . . .'

She went out, closing the door behind her. He was alone in the room. He sat in the big arm-chair, motionless, as she had left him. He listened to the steady ticking of the clock. He thought of nothing at all; incapable even of thought. In a moment, very gently, his eyelids began to close. . . . Vagueness flowed through and about him: the delicious drug-like vagueness, lack of definition, that precedes sleep: sensuously, he felt every atom in his composition begin to disunite, to disperse, to swim away into a darkness beyond control and beyond consciousness. . . . A sharp jerk. Something heavy had toppled over. It was his head. . . . Startled, he roused up, his eyelids rolled back, admitting the light of the actual. He saw the dining-room; the ticking of the mantelpiece clock came through again. The atoms of his being which, a second before, had been mysteriously dispersed, stepped into orderly formation: re-united: instant mobilization of his personality, to meet the demands of the waking world. . . . He looked about him.

'Oh, I *hope* I didn't wake you?'

He turned quickly. On the opposite side of the dining-room table a young girl was standing. She wore a white blouse and she was quite openly staring at him: with interest, with a slight, visible apprehension. He stared back. She was, perhaps, fifteen. A ripe fifteen. With a characteristic round bosom and curly black hair fastened in a slide. 'I came in very quietly because I saw you were asleep,' she said hastily.

'That was considerate of you.'

'You don't know who I am,' she said then, smiling. She had a sudden, wholly charming, smile. 'I'm Phyllis. . . .'

'Phyllis,' he repeated: at a loss. 'I see.' She smiled again: he saw suddenly that she had Violet's eyes: astonishing plagiarism in a person he had never before seen. 'Mummy sent me in to lay the table,' she said: 'I'd better do it.' (Violet's *daughter* – was it possible!) She opened a drawer in the sideboard and took out a white cloth, which she spread over half the table: then rattled in the green baize compartment for cutlery. 'Soup-spoon,' he heard her murmur, 'knife-and-fork . . . bread-knife. . . .' She sorted out these things and laid them in a careful pattern on the white cloth. That done, with a rapid gesture, she tucked her handkerchief under the elastic of her knickers and came over and stood by his chair. She was wearing what was obviously a school uniform: black woollen stockings, a short skirt and a white blouse with a striped tie pinned with a boy's tie-pin on to her soft young bosom. The cheap imitation-tortoiseshell slide confined her abundant hair that, in its glowing coal-darkness, seemed to illumine her round vivid face. She stood gazing at him, a little uncertainly. . . . 'Uncle Alec,' she said at last. (So he was Uncle Alec. He tried to adjust himself to the new relationship.) 'Yes?' he said. He smiled at her. But she hesitated: a little confused. He could see that there was something on her mind: that she had screwed herself up to ask him some question or other. . . . 'Well?' he said encouragingly. Abruptly, she sat down in the chair that Violet had vacated: she clasped her hands together: 'Uncle . . .' her lips parted; into her dark eyes there came a new look, unguarded, almost moving; an expression of shy and yet ardent idealism. . . . 'Uncle Alec,' she said. *'Have you ever met Gary Cooper?'*

He came out of the dining-room into the hall and paused, for a moment, at the foot of the stairs. Now, despite the lingering coldness somewhere between his shoulder blades that nothing seemed to ease, he was warm, feverishly warm: his collar clung about his neck: the palms of his hands were sultry: they left a white damp outline on the polished rail of the banister as he grasped it to ascend. There was a curious weakness in the hollow behind his knees: an incipient tremble in all his limbs. Like 'flu, he thought. But it was not 'flu. He went up the stairs, the dark mahogany rail, the high encrusted dado, mounting with him on either side. The stairs felt awkward to his tread: too high, too narrow, to feet accustomed to the low sweep of the staircase at Addison Road: he mounted with difficulty, as if against a resistance. The nurse preceded him, neatly, quickly: he heard the rustle of starch as she moved. Her small waist was confined in a glossy white belt: her white nun's coif spread in a triangle over her nape. On the first floor landing, beside the sick-room door, she turned, waiting for him: and he came face to face with her. He saw her candid forehead sealed in its white coif: the fountain pen and thermometer case clipped on to the edge of her apron. She

smelled, not unpleasantly, of Dettol: of the atmosphere of another, a closed world. She observed him narrowly for a moment. 'I shouldn't stay too long,' she said as she laid her hand upon the knob of the door. He stood still. 'Does she know I'm here?' he said in a low voice: 'has she been told?' Her level eyes rested upon him. 'She seems to know,' was all she said. He nodded; and she opened the door for him, standing aside to let him pass in before her striped neatly-cuffed arm. . . .

In a moment between passing through the door and coming into the room, the years swung steeply back for him: he remembered a moment in his very early childhood. Then, too, his mother had been ill: mysteriously confined to this room, which he and Violet and Sydney had to pass on tip-toe, voices lowered. He learned later that she had borne a child that had not lived. A woman, it must have been the mid-wife, had opened the door just like this, for him: and he had been allowed in, in his stockinged feet, to see his mother for a few moments. She had lain in the same bed, her face turned away. . . . He did not at once come forward, he remembered: he was afraid; he did not want to see the illness expressed in her face. He hesitated. Behind him stood the woman whose name he could not remember, who had been summoned to assist a birth: just as, Alec thought, this impersonal young woman in her white coif was here, now, to assist a more difficult and mysterious birth: that of a soul out of its own encumbering body. . . .

The door shut behind him. A small heavily-shaded lamp was burning. He came forward, moving ghost-like: recognizing it all: the sloping brass rail of the bed; the dressing-table up against the window with her battered silver hairbrushes, the hair-tidy with its little rings into which she always wound her loose hair; in a corner, the mysterious camphor-smelling wardrobe. . . . The room was ugly, relentlessly austere: even as a child, repelled and yet, in spite of himself, strangely fascinated by this sanctum of his parents' private lives, he used to smell in here a type of coldness and strangeness absent in any other room of the house. That smell of coldness, of concealment, was gone now. He felt its absence instantly and it changed the room for him. A small electric fire was burning, casting its glow across the worn carpet. On the dressing-table, there were two or three small vases of flowers, a bottle of sweets, a plate of grapes, dusty, untouched. . . . A small table stood by the fire and a chair next to it with a book lying on it face downwards: on the table was an array of bottles, round and kidney-shaped enamel basins, objects covered over with medical gauze. . . .

There was silence in the room. She was lying in the bed: so slight, that her outline scarcely raised the bedclothes, as if she were already effacing herself from the visible world. Like a child's, her hair, two pitifully small grey plaits, was laid alongside a face become shrunken; and strangely, exquisitely delicate; refined already of the flesh of the years; ageless. He saw now what he had never yet seen in any human being: the mere essence: all the accidents of personality, the dross of flesh gone. He had a sudden altogether new feeling: he had never been so close to reality, seen the veil so thin, so almost revealing. . . . He forgot even, as she must have forgotten, that

she was his mother: he stood there, deeply moved: in a sort of silent and impersonal awe.

The moments passed. Suddenly he shivered. He became aware of an overwhelming loneliness: something almost physical, so that he felt acutely, like an unendurable affliction, the isolation of his being in space. That torture (of his own solitude) upon him, even the walls of the room in which he was standing seemed agonizingly remote; he looked at them as if he would like to crouch up, to draw them closely about him, to cover, efface this ache of selfness. . . . He said – and it was like a moan of pain – 'Mother. . . .' She did not stir. For the first time, then, the thought came to him that she might never again, in this world or in any other, be able to say even a trivial word to him. . . . He stared at her: unbelieving: like a man appalled before lost opportunity. Why, he thought, in an agony of regret, why then, while that miraculous thing, *communication*, was still possible, did one not seize every occasion to effect the maximum of understanding, of interchange; did one not eagerly, deliberately, knowing what was to come, speak for the future, forestall, invest against, bereavement; gather up each word; save up, in the years of plenty, for the years of famine? . . .

Something of what he was feeling seemed, in some wholly indefinable way, to reach her. She did not lift her lids, which, withered, tenuous, were as if sealed on to the domes of her eyes: but her lips moved, almost imperceptibly. She murmured something. Instantly, with passionate eagerness, he was beside her: bending down. He heard nothing: he came still closer. Her faint ill breath touched his ear. 'Is it . . . Alec?' She spoke, her lips scarcely moving. 'Yes,' he said ardently: 'yes, yes. . . .' She gave a slight faint sigh. And still faintly, as if she were speaking with difficulty through a machine that had broken down, become faulty, she said something else. He pressed forward to hear. '. . . It's . . . been . . . raining,' he heard her say: slowly: faintly: stopping between every word. 'Tell . . . Alec . . . change . . . his . . . shoes. . . .'

The house looked different the next morning: filled with sunlight to the very brim: motes of dust idly promenading in the rays of brightness: the ceiling bathed in reflected radiance. In the dining-room, at this advanced hour, the breakfast table had not yet been cleared. It was still draped in its white cloth: sunlight scattered about it like confetti: glittering motley, broken-up, among the glossy tea-stained cups, the thin shafts of cutlery, the cut-glass jar of marmalade: resting with dazzling effect upon the low matronly bosom of the teapot. Alec sat with a serviette over his knees, chair pulled up to the table, buttering his third round of toast: he scooped with the spoon and dropped a radiant sun-warm dollop of marmalade on to his plate. Opposite him, in the big arm-chair, his father, who had breakfasted an hour ago while Alec was still sleeping, manipulated his little cutter and, with an air of deliberate satisfaction, lit up his first cigar of the day. Of them all, Mr Berman seemed to have changed least: his characteristic and enormous stubbornness seemed capable even of resisting the effects of Time. He had always categorically refused to adapt himself in any way: he refused now, it seemed, and with equal success, all physical modification. . . . When the time came, no lingering, debilitating disease, but some sudden stroke would set its finality upon him: suddenly, clearly, his energy unimpaired, all faculties triumphantly intact. . . . Alec marvelled to see him, as spruce, as active, as ever: the whiteness of his hair merely enhancing the high tenacious rosiness of his face, the sparkle in his grim little eyes. Only when he smiled, there was a certain intimation of defeat: a gap, a look of sudden ineffectiveness: he had lost his teeth: smiling, he was like an old lion, still dangerous, with its fangs drawn. . . .

Mr Berman held his cigar carefully between his stubnailed, nicotine-dyed fingers. Carefully and with the adeptitude of long habit, he nursed the emerging chrysalis of ash; his hand hovering over the ash-tray. There was silence for a moment while he raised the cigar to his lips, sucking the fragrance out of it into his lungs. Then: 'What did you want to marry a *shicksa* for?' he asked suddenly. 'Aren't there plenty of nice Jewish girls?'

Alec reached across for the tea-pot: he lifted it off its cork mat: 'Certainly,' he said: 'there are.' With care, he poured himself a second cup of tea.

Mr Berman paused. 'So you've got a son they tell me,' he said.

'Yes.'

'And what does he call himself?'

'David.'

'David. . . . Hum – that's not so bad. Is he circumcised?'

'Yes.'

A new light came into Mr Berman's eyes. 'Are you bringing him up to be a Jew, then?'

Alec paused. 'No,' he said. 'I doubt if he'll ever feel he wants to be a Jew.'

'What then? A Protestant? A Catholic? Come on – let's hear it. I might as well know what sort of a grandson you've presented me with.'

'He isn't anything at the moment,' Alec said.

'An atheist!' Old Berman's eyes sparkled with delight. 'So this is what it's come to. . . . I've got a grandson who's being brought up as an atheist!' There was more in this line. Alec finished his tea. He fished inside his breast-pocket and brought out a flat monogrammed case: opening it, he selected a cigarette. Mr Berman's interest was diverted. 'That's a nice case you have there,' he said: 'Is it gold?' Alec handed it over. His father weighed it; turned it round and about looking for the gold mark, 'Too flimsy for my liking,' he remarked and passed it back. Without transition: 'Of course, they're all mad about the *fillums* these days. . . . It's a mad world, what can you expect. . . .' He paused: his small shrewd eyes rested upon the figure of his son, smoking at the breakfast table. 'You're doing well, they tell me. . . . Is that so?'

Alec knew what it was that his father wanted to know. Slipping his cigarette case back into his pocket, he mentioned casually a figure: the current amount of his value as a director to British-Alliance Films. He had a faint, delicious moment of triumph as he saw his father's jaw drop. . . .

There was a tap on the door. 'All right, all right, come in!' Mr Berman cried testily, impatient of ceremonial in his own household. The door opened: the nurse appeared; her apron and coif very white in the sunlight. Alec got to his feet. But

Mr Berman regarded her suspiciously. 'Yes?' he said, abruptly. (He had previously told Alec that he thought she and the doctor were 'in league'. In league to what purpose he did not elucidate.) The nurse was unabashed; her grey eyes travelled with a certain coolness over the seated figure of Mr Berman and came to rest upon Alec. 'Good morning,' she said. She appeared to consider something in his countenance. 'If I may say so, you look considerably more wholesome than you did last night,' she remarked.

'I've had a sleep,' he said. He hesitated; looking at her. Then 'How is she?' he said in a low voice.

'Look!' He saw for the first time that she had an empty glass and plate in her hand. 'That's what I came in to tell you. . . . She's had this – nearly a whole glass of milk – and kept it down. She's sleeping now.' Ignoring Mr Berman, whose humours seemed to leave her serenely indifferent, she smiled at Alec: as if he had had some part in effecting this change in her patient. Alec stared back. . . . He had a sudden queer intuition. Something became clear to him: something he would not have dared put into words. His mother had had her way, after all, he thought obscurely: she had managed to bring her son back . . . and now that that son was here, she was not going to miss her opportunity, forgo the pleasure of his company. . . . She was going to get better. . . . He stared at the nurse and saw, quite clearly, an answering thought in her eyes. 'I thought you'd like to know,' she murmured. She smiled faintly: then quickly, noiselessly withdrew, shutting the door after her.

Alec sat down. He said nothing. His cigarette burned

unheeded between his fingers, the veins of smoke pulsing up slowly into the sunny air. . . . Momentarily, there was silence in the room.

The sound of the telephone broke out suddenly in the quiet house. It blared noisily, persistently: then, as suddenly dislocated by an unseen hand, stopped: and silence returned. Mr Berman raised his head, as if scenting out in that treacherous silence the nature of the communications taking place. 'Morning, noon and night they're at that telephone,' he muttered. 'That's the only time you get anyone to move in this house – when the 'phone rings.' He stopped: there were heavy incautious footsteps on the stairs outside. Phyllis burst into the room: a lock of dark hair over her dark eyes: one hand, as usual, either seeking for, or tucking in a handkerchief under the elastic rim of her knickers. 'Uncle Alec,' she said without preamble, 'Auntie Florrie wants to know will you go there for lunch to-day? Half-past one, she says. . . . Will you? . . . She's hanging on – she wants to know, because she's got to do the ordering.'

Alec managed to remember who Auntie Florrie was. 'Tell her I'd be delighted,' he said.

'O.K. Baby.' Phyllis turned. Unceremoniously, she slammed the door behind her. They heard her thunderous footsteps on the stairs outside. Mr Berman looked after his grand-daughter with an incalculable expression in his eyes. 'Like a bear from the woods,' he murmured. . . .

* * *

A very slight wind was blowing, gentle on the cheek; warm with all the sunshine it had winnowed during the golden hours of the day. As he walked along, Alec felt it about him like a caress: gratuitous, impermanent. The air had a clarity and delicacy more of spring than early summer. He made his way down to the front. The apathy brought on by Florrie's copious and well-cooked lunch began to wear off: and with it the atmosphere of Sydney's home life in which he had been temporarily immersed: (the living-room with its shoddy furniture, its smell of meals to come and meals departed: the children shy at first, then clamorous, unrestrainedly showing-off: Florrie, a brilliant blonde, a little 'past it', dressed up to the nines, openly ogling him, full of arch provocation: Sydney himself naïvely delighted, proud of his beautiful wife and celebrated brother, beaming at every sally that passed between them; hushing the children when they tried to interrupt. . . .) Alec subtracted himself from them at last, not altogether unwarmed by their warmth: he shut the frosted-glass door of the flat, with its dusty bib of curtain attached, and descended an obscure flight of stairs to the street. Leaving behind him the fine sweep of Jamaica Crescent (outwardly intact: inwardly degenerated, riddled with flats and flatlets) he crossed over to the front. He walked briskly along: his eye and his step growing more alert as he regained isolation.

The tide lay full in: from the shore to the brim of the horizon: faintly, lazily, rocking. On the left of him, he saw the houses as they had been when last he walked here: tall and cream-painted, with graceful fluted balconies: only most of them, now, bore a gilt garland of letters proclaiming their

conversion into private hotels or boarding houses (Lift to All Floors). Here and there, something altogether new, great bleak-looking blocks of flats, squatted upon the skyline. They looked more like factories than dwelling-places, he thought, staring up as he went past: which, in a sense, of course, they were: factories for the production of standardized living. A design for living which impartially reduced its devotees to a certain scheme of dimensions: to the same proportions, the same angles: induced the same responses to the same gadgets and conveniences: the same flow of constant hot water in all the bath taps, the same constant flow of ideas from the wireless plugged in the wall. It was not inconceivable, he thought (deliberately allowing these speculations to absorb him; prevent him from considering the direction he was all the while taking), that in time, after such intensive subjection to a similar environment and conditions, the inhabitants of any single block of flats must all come indistinguishably to resemble each other. . . .

Not much more than an hour later, he was at Rottingdean. He knew that it was Rottingdean only because he asked the deck-chair attendant to confirm his impression that it might be so. . . . He stood on the front there and stared about him: confounded. Not a vestige of what he remembered remained. It had all been built over, transformed, altered out of all recognition: the small white-washed houses gone: in their place, cafés, a huge licensed hotel, a big modernistic group of flats. He stood stock-still, his back to the sea: staring about him, unbelieving: almost indignantly: it was as if someone had been tampering with his possessions, unlawfully moving about the furniture of memory, confounding him. . . .

He went up the concrete steps, past raw-looking red-brick shops, into the High Street. Here he looked about him: slightly reassured. This, at least, was more or less as he remembered it. . . . There were the small shops, the narrow not altogether straight road: with, at the end, the tall beautiful trees embowered against the sky. He came out on to the Green. His heart leapt. It was unchanged. There was the ancient tree under which he had sat: there the church: there the file of ducks upon the slothful pond. . . . He turned. And there, unchanged, was Oldwood Lodge. There was the house he had come to look upon once again: white, green-shuttered and charming. . . .

A board hanging over the gate caught his notice. He went over to see what it might be. He saw a shield-shaped ensign and on it a painting of the house, shiny, poorly executed. Underneath was written in bold lettering *'Oldwood Lodge. Guest House. Tea Room Open to Non-Residents.'*

He got off the bus at the Aquarium: dropping his ticket and extracting himself from the Saturday crowd milling about the entrance to the Pier. The sun was lower, now. Radiance was still afloat in the clear air, but warmth, perceptibly, had ebbed from it: it lacked body. Over the Pier, the electric sign '*Brighton Greets You*' wanly radiated its message. The strings of coloured lights in Castle Square had not yet been lit.

Alec looked at his watch. It was getting late: they would be waiting for him. He hesitated. He was tired: he did not feel, just then, like facing the dining-room at Lansdowne Road. . . . He crossed over from the front and walked along until he found what looked like a combined Ice-Cream

Parlour and Milk Bar. Through the sheet of plate-glass windows, it appeared to be more than half empty. He went in and sat down in a corner: upon a red-wicker chair, a glass-topped table drawn up before him. Behind a shining white counter, young women, dressed as if for a pantomime, were dispensing and concocting mysterious fairy-like substances out of various machines and taps. He picked up the menu folder and ran his eyes down a list of these nectar-like offerings: peaches and melted caramel and ice-cream soda: orgy of the ambrosial and the infantile. He discovered, with relief, that he could also obtain an ordinary pot of tea: and this he finally ordered ('Indian, please') along with a packet of cigarettes from the cash-desk. He poured himself a strong cup from the small metal teapot with its unpractical scalding handle; put in several lumps of sugar and fumbled in his pocket for matches. He lit a cigarette and sat smoking; watching, through the big plate-glass window, people outside passing and re-passing; soundlessly talking as they went by. . . .

When, at length, he emerged, the electric sign over the pier had visibly gained in strength. The welcome it purveyed, in consequence, appeared at least several degrees warmer. He crossed the road. The last of the sun had gone: dusk was gaining on the town. As he had so often done in his remote boyhood (and yet not so remote, since he re-discovered the attitude as if from yesterday) he leaned his elbows upon the sea-rail. Feeling himself surrounded by, and yet distinct from, the crowds about him. He leaned there, gazing ahead, quietly smoking. The tide was going out, now: slipping stealthily away from the shore: drawn to some new destination. He saw the naked shingle, alive-gleaming, still, from that visitation. He stood without moving, staring at the innumerable unimportant pebbles. Extracting, not pain, but comfort (pleasure, almost) from the act of identifying himself with the things he looked at: objects altogether trivial and unimportant. . . . How he had loved, in his youth, with a sort of sacred passion, every aspect of the physical world! Nowadays, he realised, he scarcely saw anything: a sense-blindness gone too deep even for regret. How easy life had been, then, when all values could be apprehended, simply and passionately, by the eye. . . . A slight breeze came up from the darkening sea: momentarily brightened the tip of his cigarette. It was gone. He found himself, without obvious transition, thinking of his marriage. Without emotion, with a new, impersonal soberness. . . . There were, of course, various sorts of explanations he would still have to offer: here, to his own people; elsewhere, to friends: to acquaintances. But none to himself. . . . That was the important thing. He still believed he had been right. The personal failure of himself and Catherine to live up to an ideal in no way invalidated that ideal. He drew upon his cigarette, watching the returning and receding waters. . . . The ideal world, he thought (in which such marriages were as valid and desirable as any other) did not, of course, exist; if, indeed, it ever would: but it was incumbent upon certain people to behave as if it did. . . . That, in the end, he thought, was the practical viewpoint. Meanwhile, the world would say, 'I Told You So': but the world was wrong. . . .

There were more lights along the pier, now. They shed a

trembling reflection upon the surface of the water. The pier looked like an illumined bridge to another, invisible world. He threw away the stub of his cigarette: then watched it, lying like a glow-worm, on the stones beneath. He wondered what Catherine was doing at that precise moment. . . . Her presence, even knowledge of her actions and habits, now no longer belonged to him. All the emotional content he had vested in her was inaccessible to him: he was left bankrupt: his inner and his outer life equally disorganized. For she would not return to him. That he knew quite clearly. The present arrangement, ostensibly temporary, would become permanent: in time, legal. . . . David mattered more than he did. He had been supplanted by his own son. . . . David, after all, was partly, it seemed, at times, even wholly, a Nicolls. He belonged with Catherine; with Basil: with the Nicolls side. He would be happy there – in childhood at least. . . . Catherine, who would never have chosen thus for herself, had chosen for him the way of least resistance. That she was not proud of having made such a choice, Alec, who knew her well, was even at that moment fully aware. . . .

He roused himself abruptly. It was getting late. He detached himself from the sea-rail and began to walk along in the direction of Lansdowne Road. Lights were lit all along the front, now: the pale electricity of summer illumined the faces of people passing in various directions and with differing purposes along the broad pavement. He walked along amongst them. He was aware after a moment, of something new: a strange lightheartedness. . . . The worst had happened – and now he was free. . . . He was no longer afraid, because

he no longer had anything to lose. He was free from his own desires: from his own apprehensions. Whatever happened now, spiritual or physical exile, he was ready for it. He had lost what most passionately he had wanted; and, losing it, discovered unimaginable compensation. Nothing, now, could touch him. He was free: he was invulnerable, he was strong. . . .

The table was white-clothed, brightly illumined. They were all there: Mr Berman, Alec, Sydney and his wife, Arthur and Cynthia, Ruth, Violet and Phyllis. They sat round the solid family table, as if guarding it: chair touching chair, elbow brushing elbow as they reached out for the dishes, manipulated spoons and forks. Violet had been busy all the morning in the big basement kitchen: she had, now, the triumphant and watchful air of the good cook presiding over her own wares. There was grapefruit, of course: that had become a commonplace, even in the Berman household; chopped herring in a big glass dish, pickled cucumber, big rosy shreds of smoked salmon, fried fish neatly tucked up in its blanket of bread-crumbs, fish-balls in a lemon mayonnaise, potato salad, Russian salad: then cheesecake, beautifully rich and crumbly, fruit salad with meringues; and, with the coffee, Violet's *pièce de résistance*: a fluffy tiered cream-cake tied with a ribbon. The meal was something in the nature of a celebration. The doctor had been and pronounced a marked improvement in his patient's condition. . . . Mr Berman sat in his usual place at the head of the table, his serviette tucked through a button-hole of his waistcoat: the light from the hanging lamp above illumining his brilliant white hair. His little grim, bright eyes darted about the table; following, intercepting every word and gesture: but, Alec saw after a moment, the young people were too quick for him: they had evolved a fashion of communicating with each other, a certain pitch of speech, a manner, rapid, slurred, which he seemed not to understand, not even to hear, and in which they amused themselves in his presence, by passing quite outrageous and inconsequential remarks. . . . It was a game, apparently, which they had brought to a fine art: even Alec could not always detect what it was that set them off, in the first instance, into fits of abandoned giggling and drew down upon them Mr Berman's sharp punctual rebuke. . . . He had Florrie on one side of him. She had put on a different dress, some sort of vivid amethyst affair: her nails were scarlet: a great flashing brooch of synthetic jewels was pinned to her unrestrained bosom: she talked and laughed continuously, raising her voice above the children's. Generously, she praised Violet's cooking and was undismayed by Violet's coolness, her unyielding reception of such overtures. . . .

Silence fell, at last, when Mr Berman, pushing away his empty plate, sent Arthur out into the hall to collect the hats; preparatory to saying grace. They made themselves ready, then: Mr Berman presiding: the children with faces of self-conscious sobriety: the elders quiet, attentive. Mr Berman turned over the yellow pages of his own especial prayer-book, his pince-nez tremblingly astride on his nose. As he did so, Sydney got up quietly and put the door ajar, so that the woman lying on her sick-bed upstairs might hear the harmonious unison of voices. . . . They were ready now. . . . Mr Berman gave the signal. The familiar, long unheard words smote sharply upon Alec's awareness. . . .

'When that the Lord turned again the captivity of Zion, we were like unto them that dream. Then was our mouth filled with laughter, and our tongue with exaltation: then said they among the nations, the Lord hath done great things for them. Bring back our captivity, O Lord, as the streams in the south. They that sow in tears shall reap in joy. Though he goeth on his way weeping, bearing the store of seed, he shall come back with joy, bearing his sheaves.'

Persephone Books publishes forgotten fiction and non-fiction by unjustly neglected authors. The following titles are available:

No. 28 *Little Boy Lost* (1949) by Marghanita Laski
No. 29 *The Making of a Marchioness* (1901) by Frances Hodgson Burnett
No. 30 *Kitchen Essays* (1922) by Agnes Jekyll
No. 31 *A House in the Country* (1944) by Jocelyn Playfair
No. 32 *The Carlyles at Home* (1965) by Thea Holme
No. 33 *The Far Cry* (1949) by Emma Smith
No. 34 *Minnie's Room: the Peacetime Stories of Mollie Panter-Downes 1947–65*
No. 35 *Greenery Street* (1925) by Denis Mackail
No. 36 *Lettice Delmer* (1958) by Susan Miles
No. 37 *The Runaway* (1872) by Elizabeth Anna Hart
No. 38 *Cheerful Weather for the Wedding* (1932) by Julia Strachey
No. 39 *Manja* (1939) by Anna Gmeyner
No. 40 *The Priory* (1939) by Dorothy Whipple
No. 41 *Hostages to Fortune* (1933) by Elizabeth Cambridge
No. 42 *The Blank Wall* (1947) by Elisabeth Sanxay Holding
No. 43 *The Wise Virgins* (1914) by Leonard Woolf
No. 44 *Tea with Mr Rochester* (1949) by Frances Towers
No. 45 *Good Food on the Aga* (1933) by Ambrose Heath
No. 46 *Miss Ranskill Comes Home* (1946) by Barbara Euphan Todd
No. 47 *The New House* (1936) by Lettice Cooper
No. 48 *The Casino* (1948) by Margaret Bonham
No. 49 *Bricks and Mortar* (1932) by Helen Ashton
No. 50 *The World that was Ours* (1967) by Hilda Bernstein
No. 51 *Operation Heartbreak* (1950) by Duff Cooper
No. 52 *The Village* (1952) by Marghanita Laski
No. 53 *Lady Rose and Mrs Memmary* (1937) by Ruby Ferguson
No. 54 *They Can't Ration These* (1940) by Vicomte de Mauduit
No. 55 *Flush* (1933) by Virginia Woolf
No. 56 *They Were Sisters* (1943) by Dorothy Whipple
No. 57 *The Hopkins Manuscript* (1939) by R C Sherriff
No. 58 *Hetty Dorval* (1947) by Ethel Wilson
No. 59 *There Were No Windows* (1944) by Norah Hoult
No. 60 *Doreen* (1946) by Barbara Noble
No. 61 *A London Child of the 1870s* (1934) by Molly Hughes

No. 62 *How to Run your Home without Help* (1949) by Kay Smallshaw
No. 63 *Princes in the Land* (1938) by Joanna Cannan
No. 64 *The Woman Novelist and Other Stories* (1946) by Diana Gardner
No. 65 *Alas, Poor Lady* (1937) by Rachel Ferguson
No. 66 *Gardener's Nightcap* (1938) by Muriel Stuart
No. 67 *The Fortnight in September* (1931) by RC Sherriff
No. 68 *The Expendable Man* (1963) by Dorothy B Hughes
No. 69 *Journal of Katherine Mansfield* (1927)
No. 70 *Plats du Jour* (1957) by Patience Gray and Primrose Boyd
No. 71 *The Shuttle* (1907) by Frances Hodgson Burnett
No. 72 *House-Bound* (1942) by Winifred Peck
No. 73 *The Young Pretenders* (1895) by Edith Henrietta Fowler
No. 74 *The Closed Door and Other Stories* by Dorothy Whipple
No. 75 *On the Other Side: Letters to my Children from Germany 1940–46* by Mathilde Wolff-Mönckeberg
No. 76 *The Crowded Street* (1924) by Winifred Holtby
No. 77 *Daddy's Gone A-Hunting* (1958) by Penelope Mortimer
No. 78 *A Very Great Profession: The Woman's Novel 1914–39* (1983) by Nicola Beauman
No. 79 *Round about a Pound a Week* (1913) by Maud Pember Reeves
No. 80 *The Country Housewife's Book* (1934) by Lucy H Yates
No. 81 *Miss Buncle's Book* (1934) by DE Stevenson
No. 82 *Amours de Voyage* (1849) by Arthur Hugh Clough
No. 83 *Making Conversation* (1931) by Christine Longford
No. 84 *A New System of Domestic Cookery* (1806) by Mrs Rundell
No. 85 *High Wages* (1930) by Dorothy Whipple
No. 86 *To Bed with Grand Music* (1946) by 'Sarah Russell' (Marghanita Laski)
No. 87 *Dimanche and Other Stories* (1934–41) by Irène Némirovsky
No. 88 *Still Missing* (1981) by Beth Gutcheon

If you have enjoyed this Persephone book why not telephone or write to us for a free copy of the Persephone Catalogue and the current Persephone Biannually? All Persephone books ordered from us cost £10 or three for £27 plus £2 postage per book.

PERSEPHONE BOOKS LTD
59 Lamb's Conduit Street
London WC1N 3NB

Telephone: 020 7242 9292
Fax: 020 7242 9272
sales@persephonebooks.co.uk
www.persephonebooks.co.uk